PROJECT PANDORA

AN ASSASSIN FALL NOVEL

ADEN POLYDOROS

Entangled Publishing, LLC
2614 South Timberline Road
Suite 109
Fort Collins, CO 80525

Entangled Teen is an imprint of Entangled Publishing, LLC.

Visit our website at www.entangledpublishing.com.

Edited by Jennifer Mishler
Cover design by Clarissa Yeo
Interior design by Toni Kerr

ISBN 978-1-63375-685-4
Ebook ISBN 978-1-63375-686-1

Manufactured in the United States of America

First Edition August 2017

10 9 8 7 6 5 4 3 2 1

To Mom and Dad,
Without your love and support,
I would not be the person I am today.

CASE NOTES 1: APOLLO

Tyler Bennett stood in front of the white marble vanity, staring at the mirror—or rather, what was left of it.

A few large shards bristled like teeth from the frame. The rest of the broken glass was scattered across the counter among lipstick tubes, broken eye shadow palettes, and other cosmetics. A woman's arsenal.

The bathroom lamp gilded the objects with a soft golden light, while also seeming to bring them into sharp focus. A handgun lay in the center of the mess, drawing his gaze and trapping it.

Before he realized what he was doing, he picked up the pistol.

He couldn't recall having handled a gun before, but somehow he knew how to check the magazine. At full capacity, it held ten rounds. Seven were left. More than enough to finish the job.

What job? Like a stone dropped into a very deep well, the thought lasted only long enough to cause a ripple of unease. Then it was gone.

He clicked the magazine back into place. A distant horror seeped through him, a whispering knowledge that what he was about to do—and what he had done—wasn't just wrong. It was unforgivable. It was damning.

It was a feeling that had no place in his programming.

Kill.

Looking down, he realized he was wearing clothes that

weren't his. Black nylon gloves and a wrinkled outfit a size too big. The gloves were torn in places and beaded with blood. His jeans and shirt had also been splattered. Some of the blood was his own, oozing from tiny scratches on his knuckles. Most of it was not.

A black backpack was propped up against the toilet, the front pocket unzipped. Jewelry, camera gear, and crumpled cash bristled from the pouch. He recognized neither the backpack nor its contents, but he zipped it up and slung it over his shoulder.

He stepped into the master bedroom. Clothes had been ripped from drawers and thrown to the floor in wrinkled piles. An oil painting lay on the carpet, canvas split and frame broken. Holes were torn in the mattress and pillows, and upholstery fluff spewed from the seat of the armchair.

Rosy sunlight slanted through the plantation shutters and spilled across the floor. Feeling violently disoriented, victim to a nightmare, he swiveled around.

He noticed the alarm clock on the dresser: 9:45 a.m. He should have been at school.

He *had* been at school.

Kill.

Tyler went into the hall. Even from the doorway, he could smell a nauseating stew of blood and gunpowder. His resolution wavered.

A woman lay on the floor, facedown. Her hair was red and her shirt, too, the fabric so saturated with blood that it appeared black. Without looking at her directly, he knew she had been shot twice in the back as she'd tried to flee. The third bullet had shattered her skull at point-blank range.

No, he thought, closing his eyes. *No, I didn't do this. It wasn't me.*

Sudden nausea overwhelmed him. His right hand jerked up, but, remembering the gun, he cupped his left hand over his mouth.

This was just a dream. Just a nightmare. Soon he would wake up, but first, he had to complete the job. Once he did, he would open his eyes and this would end.

He swallowed back the acidic bile.

"Pandora's box is opening," he whispered to himself, and that calmed him somewhat. He stepped over the body and continued down the corridor.

Framed news articles lined the walls. Vaguely, he wondered if his target might be a reporter or newsman. Then he pushed the questions from his head and thought about nothing at all.

In the kitchen, the air was sharp with the stench of burnt bread. Inky plumes poured from the toaster slots. Before the machine could set off the smoke alarm, he pulled the plug.

Tyler sat down at the wooden table and set the backpack next to him. He looked at the spread of food laid out on white china. Lox, onion and tomato slices, capers, a small dish of whipped cream cheese. Brunch for two, one bagel already split and assembled, two glasses of orange juice waiting to be sipped.

She had sat here and prepared her meal, and then she stood to answer the doorbell. Or perhaps she had already been standing. He didn't know. But he knew that when she had answered the door, he—no, not him. It wasn't him! He hadn't lifted the gun. Not him. He hadn't pointed it at her. He hadn't pulled the trigger.

His gaze fell to the gun. Like in a vision, he saw himself cock the hammer and put the pistol between his lips. He imagined the way the tip of the silencer would feel propped against his teeth and how the oily metal might taste. He thought about the sound it would make when he squeezed the trigger—then realized he wouldn't live long enough to hear the muted gunshot.

There were seven bullets left, but he would only need one. Just one bullet, one twitch of the trigger, and then it would be all over. No more. No more. *No more.*

Stinging tears blurred his vision as he set the gun on the place mat. He raised his palms to his face and watched them shudder. Even when he curled his fingers into fists, his hands continued to tremble, although more subtly.

"Pandora's box is opening," he repeated, finding comfort in those four words.

From somewhere at the front of the house, Tyler heard a door creak open. He thought about trapdoors dropping open beneath condemned men, the jerk of the noose. This would be an execution, too.

"Honey, I'm back," a man called out.

Please, don't do this.

Kill.

Please, please…

Kill them.

Tyler picked up the gun and cocked its hammer. He swiveled in his chair so that he faced the hall he knew the man would enter through. With his other hand, he wiped his eyes. His vision kept fogging up. A sob pressed against the roof of his mouth, but he swallowed it back. He must stay silent.

"Honey? Mary?" The man's voice was closer now, accompanied by hollow footsteps and the groan of floorboards, as though ascending the stairs of a hangman's scaffold. "Is that smoke I smell? Oh, please tell me you didn't forget about the toaster again…"

Go away, he thought. *Please just go away.*

The man who entered the kitchen was dressed in a tight fitness T-shirt, tennis shorts, and running shoes. A knit headband held back his graying hair. When he saw Tyler, his teasing smile vanished first into a confused gape and then the dazed-eyed shock of a deer caught in headlights.

"Where's Mary?" the man asked. "Who are you? What's going on? What—where is she?" His gaze swept from Tyler's face to his bloodied button-up to the gun that rested in his lap. "Oh my God."

"I'm sorry," Tyler said, lifting the pistol.

The man raised both hands, fingers spread in a placating gesture. His voice wavered as he spoke. "Kid, whatever you've just done, let's talk this over. There's no need to resort to violence. Just put down the gun, okay? Okay? Just put the gun down and—"

"I'm so sorry," Tyler said, pulling the trigger.

There was a small popping sound like a wine bottle being uncorked. It seemed almost deafening, at least compared to the dull *thud* the man made as he hit the floor.

Tyler stood. He retrieved the shell casing from the floor and slipped it into his pocket, then walked over to the body. Stood there. Regarded it.

It was a clean headshot, but there could be no mistakes.

He pressed a finger to the man's throat to make sure he was dead. He couldn't find a pulse. Through his gloves, he felt the damp warmth of the man's skin. The warmth would fade, sweat would dry, blood would settle and coagulate. Rigor mortis would stiffen the limbs like hardening clay. All while the man's judgmental eyes remained open, one a gory hole, the other cursing him blindly from beyond the abyss. Lips parted as though to ask why. A question Tyler didn't have the answer for.

He wished he did. He wished he knew why. Why couldn't he stop crying, even though his hands had stopped shaking and the darkness was flowing in again and— Where was he? What was he doing? Oh, yes, the job. He must finish the job.

It was too late to stop now. Pandora's box had already opened, and the beast that came out could not be forced back in.

With the man's death confirmed, Tyler stowed the gun and shell casings in the backpack. He stripped out of his shirt and baggy jeans and stuffed the bloody clothes into the pack's outer pocket. From the main compartment, he retrieved his school clothes and changed into them.

He left through the front door. As he walked down the flagstone path, he peeled off his gloves and shoved them into his pocket. Without the cloth to obstruct his view, he saw that although the cuts had bled profusely, they were shallow. It was doubtful they would require stitches.

It was late morning, and there was little traffic in the upscale Maryland neighborhood that his victims called home. He had parked his car one block away. He encountered no one on his walk back and made it to the vehicle without incident.

Once he sat down inside the car, he pressed the callback button on his cell phone. It rang no more than two times before Zeus picked up.

"Olympus is rising," Zeus said.

"Pandora's box is opening," Tyler responded automatically.

Zeus was straight to the point. "Are you done, Apollo?"

"Yes."

"They're both taken care of? You made sure of it?"

"I checked," Tyler said. "They're both dead."

"And you made it look like a robbery? You took the jewelry and money?"

"Both. The cameras and computer stuff, too."

"Good boy," Zeus said. "Bring the bag back to the live drop. Hades will meet you there to retrieve it."

After Zeus disconnected, Tyler's motions became mechanical, and he ceased thinking for a while.

The shrill cry of a train whistle drew him back into reality, and he found himself in the parking lot of a Walmart, watching train cars shriek by on the railroad tracks across the street.

As the train passed, the rev of an engine replaced its piercing whistle, and a sleek black motorcycle pulled up alongside his car.

The rider climbed off his bike and sauntered over. His helmet covered his entire head. When Tyler stared into the mirrored visor, all he saw was his own face reflected back at him. The visor's curvature distorted Tyler's features in a way that troubled him, and he had the distinct impression that there was something *wrong* with his eyes.

The motorcyclist took off his helmet, revealing a pale,

handsome face surrounded by a tangle of dark hair. The teenage boy offered him a warm smile and tapped on the window with a gloved hand.

Tyler rolled down the window.

"Hello, Apollo," the boy said pleasantly, like they were old friends.

He couldn't recall having met the boy before in his life but knew that he must have. He nodded in acknowledgment and said, "Hades."

"Where is it?"

"In the back."

Hades opened the back door of Tyler's car and sat down inside, directly behind the driver's seat.

Tyler kept his eyes on the windshield, listening to Hades unzip the bag and rifle through its contents. When he heard a metallic *click* like the cock of a hammer, his body tensed.

"Four bullets for two targets." Hades laughed. "Sloppy work, Apollo."

The tension eased out of Tyler's shoulders as he realized the other boy had removed the pistol's magazine.

"Are you going back to school after this?" Hades asked.

"Yes," Tyler said, watching him in the rearview mirror.

"I don't see the point in it," he said, returning the pistol and detached magazine to the bag. "We have no future, you know."

Tyler didn't respond.

Hades dug through the pouch and took out a wad of cash. He leafed through the money, dropped half of it back into the bag, and put the rest into one of his jacket pockets.

"Did you enjoy it?" he asked, zipping up the backpack. "Taking care of the enemy?"

"It was necessary."

A ghost of a smile touched his lips. "Did they suffer?"

"I don't know," Tyler mumbled.

"Don't look so troubled," he said, meeting Tyler's gaze in

the mirror. His eyes were as blue as gas flames and seemed to smolder with the same devouring heat. "None of it's real anyway. Everything's a lie."

Hades opened the door, then paused. In the rearview mirror, Tyler saw him lean down and remove something from the backseat. Paper crinkled, and his smile faded into a strange expression Tyler had no name for.

"Elizabeth Hawthorne," Hades said, then chuckled to himself. "Is this today's paper?"

"I think so," Tyler said. He had a vague recollection of picking up the newspaper at the end of the driveway when he had left for school that morning, but it felt like a distant dream. Something that had happened in another life.

"I'm taking this." Hades stuffed the newspaper into the backpack. He got out of the car and put on his helmet. "Goodbye, Apollo."

Hades shut the car door and returned to his motorcycle. He glanced back at Tyler once, then he was gone.

Tyler sat there long after Hades had left, staring at the barren lot on the other side of the railroad tracks.

As the minutes passed, the memory of what he had done dissipated from his mind like so much smoke. In time, there was nothing left.

CASE NOTES 2: PERSEPHONE

Beautiful. Elegant. Composed. Intelligent. Soft-spoken.

Those were just some of the many virtues expected of a state senator's daughter, and Elizabeth Hawthorne had them down pat. She knew when to open her mouth. She knew when to keep it closed. If asked about her father's political agenda, she would either number off a list of practical points or smile and act like a meek, trusting thing.

She despised it completely.

Unfortunately, one part of saving face was entertaining old perverts like the one standing before her, ogling her chest.

Thin and stooped over, bald save for the thick tufts of white hair sprouting from his ears and nose, the letch examined her carefully, as if she were one of his prize racehorses. "You're really growing up, aren't you? Why, the last time I saw you, you were just a tiny, little thing." He raised his hand to his waist level, uncomfortably close to his crotch. "You were only this big."

"Thank you." She was glad that she had no memory of the encounter. She had no doubt it would have scarred her for life. Post-traumatic amnesia was good for one thing at least.

Taking her stiff smile as an invitation to continue, the man began to ramble on about the sorry state of America. Apparently everyone was to blame but himself.

You can at least look at my face while you talk, she thought, resisting the impulse to cross her arms over her chest. Although her silver gown was one of the more modest outfits at the fundraising banquet, she felt bare under the old geezer's eyes.

"And don't get me started on those liberals in Hollywood!" he wheezed. She couldn't remember his name, but she knew he was a CEO of some company or another. He brought it up almost as often as he mentioned his yacht, as if he thought that would impress her.

Oh, please, just kill me now, she thought, smiling and nodding, polite as always.

As the old man ranted, he leaned in closer to her. His breath reeked of gingivitis and brandy, and his gaze never went above her bra line.

He paused halfway through the conversation to compliment her, as if her appearance had anything to do with the liberal agenda. "Has anyone ever told you that you have beautiful hair, dear? Most people don't have hair that light, at least not naturally."

She resisted the urge to groan aloud. If she wasn't being complimented on her flaxen hair, it was her blue eyes, or her skin, or her smile, when she knew the speaker was only interested in what lay beneath her silk gown.

"What I can't stand is people who dye their hair," the old man said, lifting his caterpillar eyebrows at her. "It's such a disappointment when the drapes don't match the carpet, if you catch my drift."

With some difficulty, she managed not to projectile vomit in his face, therefore saving the other guests the trouble of calling an exorcist. Once she thought it polite to do so, she took a step back, only to bump into something hard and unmoving. A hand closed around her shoulder, steadying her.

"Careful," said a low, rolling voice, rich with amusement.

"Pardon me." She turned to face the man who the hand belonged to—and froze at the sight of him.

The stranger was not a man at all but a teen who looked

no older than her seventeen years. The boy's face could have belonged to any one of the angels adorning the frescoed ceiling above, if not for his sharp cheekbones and strong jaw. Those feral touches in his skull's architecture, combined with his ink-black hair, made him seem better suited for the role of Lucifer, post-fall.

"I'm sorry," she said, subconsciously aware that she was gawking at him. Even his ill-fitting shirt and dress pants couldn't conceal the iron hardness of his body.

The boy favored her with a dazzling smile. "Don't apologize."

The geezer sputtered in outrage, his face growing red. "Miss Hawthorne and I were in the middle of a private conversation."

"Your conversation is over now, sir," the boy said pleasantly, but the warmth was restrained purely to his voice.

The old man looked like he wanted to argue, then sighed and shambled off, muttering on about the impudence of youth.

"Thanks for saving me," she whispered, stepping closer to the gorgeous boy. "I'm Elizabeth Hawthorne. Senator Hawthorne's daughter."

"I know who you are, Elizabeth." His velvety timbre transformed her name into a lyric. Most people said her name in a hurry, just to get it over with, but he'd pronounced each syllable individually, turning it into something melodic and exotic. *Ah-leis-uh-bith.*

She waited for the boy to introduce himself. When he didn't, she decided to give him a little encouragement. "What's your name?"

"I don't have one."

She laughed. "Then what can I call you, oh nameless stranger?"

"Hades." He grinned.

Less than a week ago, she had learned about the myth of Orpheus in her English class, and now she found herself thinking back to the lesson. She recalled that Hades was both the Greek underworld and the deity who ruled it.

What kind of parents named their child after a god of death?

Deciding that it would be impolite to ask him about his name's origin, she held out her hand. "It's a pleasure to meet you, Hades."

He gently took her hand and kissed the sapphire heirloom ring she wore. As his soft lips brushed against her skin, her cheeks burned. She had expected him to shake her hand or just ignore the gesture, as some rude men liked to do.

As he released her hand, her shock receded into disappointment at how quickly the moment had ended.

"Do you always kiss the hands of people you've just met?" She prayed that her blush wasn't as noticeable as it felt.

"Isn't that how people do it around here?" he asked, earning a chuckle from her.

"I think you're a hundred years too late for that. Most people just say hello and stare at their iPhones."

As she took a closer look, she realized that his name wasn't the only thing intriguing about him. His face was memorable, both in its breathtaking beauty and in the unusual sharpness of his jaw and cheekbones. Not to mention those remarkable blue eyes.

For no reason at all, her stomach fluttered with a sudden nervousness. She was almost certain she had seen him somewhere before, but where?

"Enjoying the banquet so far?" she asked.

"I will soon," Hades said, looking around him. His grin softened into an amused smirk. "It's funny, isn't it? A fundraiser for impoverished families, taking place in a venue like this."

She wasn't really sure how he wanted her to answer. It had struck her as ironic, too, but she wouldn't have imagined voicing her thoughts aloud.

"I really don't see what's so special about it," he said. "I just don't see it."

She was accustomed to people talking about themselves to her, so the fact that the conversation was one-sided didn't surprise her. Usually, she knew when to interject with a polite question or a sympathetic nod. Not tonight.

"I'm hungry," he said suddenly. "Are you hungry?"

"I'm fine," Elizabeth demurred. "I already ate."

"You're hungry," Hades decided.

She laughed. "No, really, I'm fine."

"You just nibbled your lip. And now you're doing it again."

She was mortified that he had noticed. Her mother always chastised her for the bad habit.

"Are you a mind reader?" she teased.

"No, but I'm good at reading people." Then he turned and started walking, and like a marionette whose strings he had looped around his fingers, Elizabeth followed.

She didn't know why she felt compelled to go with Hades. There was just something about him. He possessed a magnetism that drew her in and kept her bound to him.

At the buffet table, he surveyed the vast array of dishes.

"I have no idea what any of these are," he admitted, offering her another charming smile.

"Well, that's called a crostini," she said as he picked up one of the toasted open-faced sandwiches. "And that chocolate-covered ball right next to it is a cream puff. I had one of those earlier. They're really good."

Suddenly, she realized he wasn't dressed like any of the other guests in attendance. His buttoned shirt was expensive, but it fit poorly, too tight around the shoulders and neck, as if it had been tailored for someone else. As for his pants, they weren't dress pants at all but black denim. He wore heavy tactical boots crusted with mud.

He didn't belong at the banquet. How had he gotten in here without an invitation?

"These are pretty good, even if they're just toast," Hades said, sampling the crostini. "Try one."

He took another crostini from the display and held it to her lips, breaking about ten rules of conduct in a single instant. She should have politely declined but instead found herself leaning forward and taking a bite out of the crostini. He was just too alluring to refuse.

When there wasn't enough bread left for him to hold without being bitten, he handed the appetizer to her. Aware that she was drawing attention to herself, she finished it off in tidy bites, cupping her hand under her mouth to catch any stray crumbs.

Hades laughed. "Do you always eat like this?"

"Pardon me?"

"You're so elegant," he said. "It's almost forced."

"I just don't want to make a mess."

"Who cares about that?" he asked, taking a bite of a cream puff.

As he licked the whipped cream from his lips, Elizabeth found her gaze drawn to them. They were almost as full as a woman's lips, with an elegant cupid's bow.

She wondered what it would be like to kiss them.

As if sensing her train of thought, an amused smirk flitted across those irresistible lips. "Nobody's even looking at us. Why come to a party if you're not going to enjoy yourself?"

"It's a fundraiser," she said, deciding not to point out that more than a few women in attendance were currently checking him out.

"Does this look like a fundraiser to you?" he asked.

"You have a point," Elizabeth said. "Hades isn't your real name, is it?"

"Who needs names?" Hades leaned in closer and lowered his voice to a soft, seductive murmur, as if sharing an intimate secret with her. "They're proof of ownership, you know." Staring into her eyes, he brushed a strand of hair away from her face and tucked it behind her ear. In the process, his fingertips stroked against her cheek.

He was close enough now that Elizabeth could smell him. His woodsy cologne only partially camouflaged his own natural scent—a hot, smoky fragrance like burnt spices and autumn bonfires. And spent gunpowder.

For some reason that aroma, when paired with those intense, almost violet eyes made her feel at the edge of a precipice. Nostalgia. A great revelation.

Feeling self-conscious for no reason at all, she looked down to avoid meeting his unwavering gaze. She noticed a black mark on the inner wrist of his left arm that his shirtsleeve partially concealed.

"You definitely don't belong at this party," she said, smiling.

"Why do you say that?"

"Your left arm."

He looked down, then chuckled and drew back the sleeve. "Oh. You mean this?"

The mark she had seen was part of a larger tattoo that consisted of clusters of small black lines arranged in a row. For every group of four vertical lines, a single horizontal line cut through them.

"Are those tally marks?" she asked.

"Something like that."

She counted them. There were three of those five-line clusters, and two vertical lines set apart from the rest. Seventeen tallies total.

"Why seventeen?" she asked.

"It's the number of people I've killed," Hades said with a warm smile.

Elizabeth laughed. "Funny. Let me guess, one for each birthday?"

"I *am* seventeen, but that's not the right answer."

As he reached for a second cream puff, she noticed a second tattoo, this time on his right wrist.

"Wait, what's that one supposed to be?" she asked.

He glanced back at her. "What?"

She took his right arm, turned it upward, and tapped a finger against his smooth white skin. Like the other tattoo, this mark was rendered in black ink, small and inconspicuous. She had to turn her head to read it. A-02.

"An epitaph," Hades said.

Just as Elizabeth was going to ask him what he meant by that, a phone rang. He paused, then retrieved a black cell phone from his pocket. It surprised her to see that he used a cheap flip phone, when nobody she knew carried around such an ancient relic.

"Pardon me, Elizabeth," he said, flipped open the phone, and lifted it to his ear. His gaze flickered past her, around the room, then back again, and his smile faded into a cold line.

"One second, sir." Hades lowered the phone, pressing his palm against the speaker to shield it from sound. "I need to take this call. Is there somewhere quieter?"

She led him through the crowds of people and under the ballroom's massive crystal chandelier. Watching him from the corner of her eye, she noticed a peculiar quirk about the way he walked. While he allowed his left arm to swing freely, he kept his right arm at his side, steady, as if prepared to reach for something at his waist. She wondered if he suffered from an injury that restricted his mobility.

She walked through a pair of French doors and stopped at the balcony that overlooked the golfing green. The night air was crisp and cool, seasoned with the aromas of freshly cut grass and the roses that grew in terra-cotta urns along the balcony's edge.

The ballroom chatter was just a murmur now, softer than the sound of the water sprinklers below.

"I'm still here, Zeusy," Hades said, raising the cell phone to his ear once more. He rolled his eyes at something the caller said. "Don't have an aneurysm just yet. I'm listening. Philadelphia?"

When she turned to go back inside, he gently touched her wrist and shook his head.

Stay, he mouthed.

She leaned against the balcony, waiting for him to finish the call. A light breeze nipped her bare shoulders, and she rubbed her arms to warm herself.

"I see," Hades said. "Is he part of the project?"

As he listened to the person on the other line, there was a subtle change in his expression. His thickly lashed eyes narrowed, and his lips parted to reveal a hint of milk-white teeth. His smile became something different, something dangerous.

It was the smile of a panther on the prowl.

Goose bumps rose on Elizabeth's arms. She had a feeling the chill she felt wasn't just from the wind.

"I love sending messages," Hades purred, resting a hand on the balcony's edge. "Yes, I understand. I'll pick it up and leave immediately."

He hung up the phone and returned it to his pocket. As he turned to her, she found herself fixated by his gaze once more. There was a coldness in his eyes that she hadn't noticed before.

"I need to go," he said.

"Is everything all right?" she asked, wondering what kind of message he was supposed to deliver.

"It's fine." The iciness in his gaze thawed, and his smile warmed again. "I wish I could stay longer, but my presence is needed elsewhere. It was a pleasure meeting you, Elizabeth Hawthorne."

Hades leaned forward, and this time she was prepared for what he intended to do. His lips brushed against her cheek in a kiss that was even briefer than the one he had planted on her ring finger. Again, she detected that irresistible aroma of his, like smoke and fire. By the time the fragrance faded from her nostrils, he was gone.

The jostle and bump of tires against cobblestone shook Elizabeth back into reality. Realizing that she had dozed off in the backseat, she yawned and wiped her eyes, sitting up. "Are we home yet?"

"Yes," her father said curtly from the front seat.

She squinted through the window, watching as the house emerged from the darkness. The brick walls were pale yellow in daylight, but the moon drained them of their pigment, leaving them the color of sun-bleached bone. The lawn was a pitch-black sea.

As she stepped down from the car, she winced at the ache in her feet. She couldn't wait to get out of her heels and take a nice, hot shower.

She didn't make it more than ten feet into the house before her mother and father confronted her simultaneously.

"We need to talk, Elizabeth," her mother said, crossing her arms.

"About what?" she asked.

Her mother spared a fleeting glance at her father, as though they were about to have a long talk and she wasn't sure how to bring it about.

"I saw that little display of yours tonight, Elizabeth," her father said bluntly.

"Display?"

"So, who was he?" he asked, crossing his arms. He had gelled back his brown hair, but a few stiff curls refused to be tamed; they hung over his narrowed eyes like the tails of dead mice.

"Who was who?" she asked, baffled.

With a frustrated sigh and a quick head flick to stir the hair from his face, he said, "Who was that boy you went off with?"

Elizabeth winced. She never should have waited outside with Hades. She hadn't thought much of it at the time, but now she realized her absence had been noticed.

"I don't know his name," she lied. The last thing she needed was to get him into trouble, especially if he was actually on the guest list. "It's not like we did anything. He needed to make a phone call, so I showed him where the balcony was. That was all."

At the memory of his teasing smile and smoldering gaze, she

felt a stirring in the pit of her stomach. She squeezed her thighs together and crossed her arms.

"What have I told you about behaving yourself in public?" her father asked, and she resisted the urge to roll her eyes.

Whenever her parents had the opportunity to, they would remind her to behave. Be polite, be kind. Carry herself like the daughter of a senator, as if that really meant anything.

Behave. Behave. Behave. Repeated so many times, over and over, until whenever she did something, she involuntarily thought, *Is this how a senator's daughter is supposed to act? Is this how I'm supposed to behave? Am I doing it right? Will this cause a scandal?*

Elizabeth hated it. She hated being saddled with her parents' expectations. She hated the mask she had to wear wherever she went and the smiles that looked real but rarely felt real. Most of all, she hated the fear that someday she would mess up, do something wrong, and not even realize it until it was too late.

"How many times do I have to tell you?" she asked. "We didn't do anything. What do you want, Dad? You want me to never talk to guys? I'm not a nun!"

"There's only a month left until the election," her father said. "One month. Do you realize how important it is that I present the image of a clean, wholesome nuclear family? Do you?" He gripped her by the shoulders, fingers digging deeper with each question. "Answer me. Do you? I mean, seriously, how stupid can you be, sneaking off with some boy? Do you understand why you're here? What you're supposed to do, how you're supposed to be? How you're *meant* to behave?"

"Larry, let's not get into this now," her mother said, shifting timidly from foot to foot. "It's been a long night."

"No, she needs to understand this." His hands tightened, and his nails bit into her skin. "What there is at stake. We've given up so much for this. I'm not going to let her ruin it."

"Larry, you're just tired," her mother stated.

"Let go of me," Elizabeth demanded quietly, anger welling up inside her.

"What did you say to me?"

"Let go of me!" Her hands shot out of their own volition, shoving him away from her. She'd never raised her voice to either of them before, and she could tell just by looking at them how shocked they were. She didn't care.

Her father stared at her. His eyes were wide, nostrils flared, mouth agape. He looked like a stuffed catfish—until he spoke, and by then he more resembled a snarling dog. "How dare you."

"Do you think anybody there cares if I have a boyfriend?" Elizabeth asked. "Or that I go out? That I date? That I wear clothes I want to wear instead of"—she lifted the modest hem of her gown, drawing it up above her knees—"this dumb granny dress? You're so worried about your stupid election you don't let me do *anything.* Don't you get it? I'm not a little kid. I'm seventeen!"

Sputtering with rage, her father stepped forward and raised his hand. Before he had the chance to bring it down, she pushed him again, harder than before. He stumbled into an ornamental table by the wall, knocking over a brass figurine and a scatter of silk flowers. Glass shattered.

She fled to her room before he could recover.

His voice followed her up the winding staircase and down the hall with its Persian rugs, carried on the back of a scream. "Why, you ungrateful little whore! You're not like her at all! You'll never be like her!"

Weeping, she slammed the door and pressed her back against it. Her entire body shook with the force of her sobs. She could hear her mom and dad arguing below, the perfect couple, a vision of America's future. The ideal nuclear family. What a joke. What a sad, pathetic joke.

STATUS REPORT: SUBJECT 5 OF SUBSET D

3/20: A new subject has come into my care today, Subject Five of Subset D. She is almost seventeen, so it will be interesting to see how the task of programming her compares to Hades. D-05's aptitude tests revealed an affinity for athletics and military tactics, but no other notable talents. Once she is trained, Charles Warren wishes her to be used for the new black operations division of the Project. I look forward to seeing how she works with Hades.

4/06: First session of electroconvulsive therapy. Subject awoke feeling very groggy. Once the anesthesia wore off, I followed the ECT with an hour in the tank (see D05_1.mp3 for recording).

5/13: After Hades, I was worried that all the children were stubborn and misbehaving, but D-05 has proven me wrong. She will make an obedient subject. I have given her the name Artemis, a fitting title for a huntress of men.

6/08: Charles Warren has requested that Artemis be tested. A man who was once part of the prenatal crew has now become a nuisance. Warren wants a knife used. Hades will accompany her.

6/10: The mission was successful. Hades kept a close eye on Artemis during the hit, and she showed absolute detachment. A clean kill, no hesitation. Charles Warren will be pleased to hear about this.

CASE NOTES 3: ARTEMIS

Halfway through fourth period, a phone rang.

Mr. Preston froze at the whiteboard, lowered the dry erase marker he held, and turned to survey the class. From her place in the back row, Shannon Evans watched students squirm in their seats, checking their pockets and backpacks.

A tall blond boy at the end of her row reached into his jacket pocket and took out a flip phone. He stared down at the phone as it rang, without opening it.

You're in trouble now, gorgeous, she thought, resting her chin in her hands.

Tyler Bennett was one of the few people she paid attention to during English. He had transferred to her school at the beginning of the semester, and from the first day, he had caught her eye. From his golden tan and striking leonine eyes to the calm, confident presence he exuded even in repose, he was absolute perfection. Just her type.

The only problem was that he didn't ever seem to notice her, even though he sat only a few desks away. She always hoped that Mr. Preston would pair them together for assignments, but the semester was almost halfway done and she'd had no luck so far. She didn't even think he knew her name.

"Tyler Bennett, what have I told you about turning off your cell phone in class?" Mr. Preston asked, drawing her attention back toward the front of the room.

She suppressed a groan. Another lecture was coming, she just knew it. Mr. Preston was a real pain when it came to rules. He was so rigid she thought he must walk around with a stick up his butt all day.

"I'm sorry, Mr. Preston," Tyler said as the phone continued to ring. "I didn't realize it was on."

Mr. Preston walked forward. "I'm going to have to hold on to that until the end of class."

At first, she thought Tyler would relinquish the phone. Instead, he lifted it to his ear and answered the call. As he listened to the caller, his wrinkled brow smoothed over. His expression became distant, and his warm, aristocratic beauty was eclipsed by a harsher, colder light.

"Are you listening to me, Mr. Bennett?" Mr. Preston stopped in front of Tyler's desk and extended a hand. "Give me your phone."

"Pandora's box is opening," Tyler said abruptly, rose to his feet, and walked past Mr. Preston. The teacher tried to block him, but he shouldered past Mr. Preston's raised arm without stopping and opened the door.

She watched in shock. *Pandora's box is opening.* Why did those four words sound so familiar?

"Looks like he's doing it again," a boy next to her muttered.

"What?" she asked, glancing over at him. She didn't remember his name.

"Tyler's in my biology class," the guy said. "He did this last Tuesday, too. I think he got detention for it."

"It must've been an important phone call," she murmured.

The guy snorted. "Whatever it is, Little Orphan Annie's got some balls for telling off Mr. Prickton."

"What did you just call him?" Shannon demanded.

"Who? Little Orphan Annie?" The boy rolled his eyes. "He's some foster kid or orphan or something. Figure his parents dropped him on his head a few times as a kid."

Anger burned in her stomach. She had also come from the foster care system, and she hated how people assumed that foster kids were bad or defective in some way.

"Sure you're not thinking of yourself?" she snapped, then turned back to the front of the class as Mr. Preston clapped once to catch everyone's attention.

Class resumed like normal, and Shannon spent the next thirty minutes doodling in the margins of her notes and glancing at the door. She expected Tyler Bennett to return at any moment, but he never did. When class ended and he still hadn't returned, she began to worry. What if something terrible had happened?

On the way to the lunchroom, she noticed a familiar figure searching through a locker at the end of the hall. She reached Tyler just as he shut the metal door, and he flinched at the sight of her.

"Hey, sorry, didn't mean to surprise you," she said, lifting her hands.

A ghost of a smile touched his lips. "No, it's fine. I should've been paying more attention."

"Are you okay?"

He paused midway through zipping up his backpack and stared at her in evident confusion. "Uh, yeah?"

"It's just..." She trailed off, struck by the force of his gaze. She had always thought his irises were amber-brown, beautiful but without variance. Now, she was close enough to see that their color was nearer to hazel—speckled with flecks of gold and green. True lion eyes.

She took advantage of her proximity to admire the rest of him, all six feet of classical hotness. His build was slim and elegant, designed for speed and agility instead of raw power. He wore a navy windbreaker and faded Levi's, but she could just as easily see him in a tailored suit or prep school uniform. He possessed an air of cultured intelligence, and his Ivy League haircut only reinforced that impression.

"Is something wrong?" Tyler asked, studying her with an intensity she found both compelling and slightly unnerving. In spite of his refined features and classy appeal, she couldn't shake the feeling that there was something *dangerous* about him.

She blushed, realizing her nosiness must have offended him. "No, sorry to bother you. I'll go."

Before she could embarrass herself further, she hurried off, feeling his gaze burn into the nape of her neck. At the end of the hall, she turned the corner and found brief shelter in the girls' bathroom.

With a sigh, she ran a hand through her hair, dismayed by how she had completely flubbed up her first actual talk with Tyler. She shouldn't have approached him like that. Whatever the phone call had been about, she was the last person he'd want to talk it over with.

"Stupid, stupid, stupid," she muttered under her breath, running her hands under the cold water tap.

She glanced in the dirty mirror. Her blush burned through her layer of foundation, where freckles formed ghostly constellations. She turned off the faucet and blotted her hands on the seat of her jeans. Scrounging through her purse, she found a tube of BB cream. As she reapplied the cover-up to her cheeks, the bathroom door swung open, and her friend Victoria walked in.

"Oh, I was just about to go looking for you," Victoria said, blinking. They had been best friends since junior year, when Shannon had transferred schools, and Victoria's look hadn't changed *once* in that time. She sported the same combat boots, the same fishnet stockings, and the same black eye shadow. The only exception was when her blond roots were growing in and she went around looking like a skunk until she decided to recolor them.

Shannon, on the other hand, never dyed her hair. It was straight and auburn, as dense as a vixen's pelt, and not a month went by without a boy complimenting her on it. She knew it was her best feature.

"The weirdest thing just happened in Mr. Preston's class," she said, capping the tube of BB cream.

A lazy smile stretched across Victoria's lips. "Oh, really?"

"Do you know Tyler Bennett?"

Victoria shook her head and leaned against the wall near the hand dryers.

"Well, he sits next to me in English. So, anyway, his phone starts ringing halfway through class—"

Victoria winced. "Ouch. Did Mr. Prickton tear him a new one?"

"No, because he just got up and left. Tyler, I mean. Mr. Preston nearly had a heart attack. You should have seen him."

"Did he even say what the call was about?"

"No, and that's what makes it so weird," Shannon said. "He basically just answered his phone, was all like 'Pandora's box is opening,' whatever that means, and walked out."

"Pandora's box is opening?" Victoria asked, picking under her nails.

"That's what it sounded like, at least." Shannon shrugged. "I guess he likes to listen to Pandora."

"Wait, is Tyler the Asian guy in Ms. Freeman's class?"

"No. I think if he was in any of your classes, you'd know who I'm talking about."

"Because he's weird?" Victoria asked, lifting a thin eyebrow.

Shannon laughed. "No, because he's hot as hell."

"Mmm. Let me guess, another one of those blond prep types you love so much?"

"He's not a *prep.* He's classy. There's a difference." She returned the BB cream to her purse. As she looked for her eyeliner, her fingers grazed something smooth, cold, and unfamiliar. She took the item out, expecting it to be a compact, based on the curve she had detected.

It was a cell phone, the kind with the flip top and tiny antenna. A relic from the Stone Age.

It was not hers.

"What's this?" she muttered, flipping it open. Her finger hovered over the on button. She hesitated. Although there were a hundred possible explanations for how another person's phone could have ended up in her bag, she felt a sudden twinge of unease.

Victoria looked at her, waiting for the punch line.

"This isn't my phone," Shannon said.

"What?"

"Where's my phone?" She set her bag on the counter and rifled through it. Just as she was about to dump everything out, she found her smartphone and pulled it out. "Oh, thank God. I thought I'd lost you." If not for her lipstick, she might have kissed the screen in relief.

"So whose is it?" Victoria asked, coming over to her. She craned her head, trying to get a good look.

Suddenly, Shannon remembered the phone that Tyler had used during class. What if this was his? He had startled pretty badly, so could it have flown into her purse somehow?

She returned the phone to her purse and closed the clasp.

"You aren't even going to look at it?" Victoria asked.

"I think I know who dropped it."

"But that's so anticlimactic!"

"It's not mine anyway."

"Like that's ever stopped you." Victoria crossed her arms.

"Later," she said, looking at her reflection one final time. She frowned at the girl staring back at her.

She was used to seeing a stranger in the mirror. For once, it wasn't a good thing.

After spending the next five minutes searching for Tyler with no luck, she went to the shaded rotunda at the front of the school, where she knew nobody would be at this hour. She sat under the corrugated roof, opened her purse, and took out the flip phone.

She did not turn it on.

Although the phone wasn't hers, it felt familiar in her palm. When she traced the keys with one red-lacquered nail, she saw herself punching in a number. But what number? Whose number? She couldn't remember.

Her thumb went for the on button. She hesitated.

What are you so afraid of? She nibbled her lower lip, not thinking about the damage she was doing to her superb lipstick application. *Just turn it on.*

She set the phone next to her and cracked her knuckles to distract herself. For some reason, she had a sudden urge to pitch the phone across the concrete and watch it break. There was something very gratifying about the thought of destroying someone else's property, like scratching an itch until it bled.

Her gaze returned to the phone. Unable to resist the impulse, she picked up the phone and turned it on, waiting for the screen to light up. She wasn't aware she was holding her breath until she heard the air hiss through her clenched teeth.

The screensaver resembled a default background. The rest of the phone was equally impersonal: no texts, no photos, no voicemails, no saved contacts.

She was about to return the phone to her purse when a strange urge came over her. Only half aware of what she was doing, she thumbed in *69 and raised the phone to her ear.

Listening to the ringing, her heart began pounding. Sick nausea welled up inside her. She closed her eyes, feeling on the verge of puking or passing out. Knowing her luck, she would do both simultaneously.

The phone continued to ring.

"Kill," Shannon whispered, without even hearing herself. "Kill."

There was a sharp *click*, and the ringing stopped. Her breath caught in her throat. Blood churned through her ears, and a crushing pressure built behind her closed lids.

From the other end of the line, a calm, deep voice said, "Hello, Artemis. Impeccable timing. I was just about to call you."

Her eyes shot open.

Artemis. The name struck her like a fastball, leaving her winded. She opened her mouth to speak but found herself unable to.

"Artemis?" The man paused, and for an awful, irrational moment, she feared that she had been discovered. Somehow he knew she wasn't Artemis, even though the only thing he'd heard of her was her shallow, unsteady breathing.

"Olympus is rising," the man said.

"Pandora's box is opening," she said in reflex, and she knew at once who she was speaking to.

"Are you at school?" the man, Zeus, asked.

Her dread dissolved in an instant, leaving her feeling warm and sedated. She would have been content with just listening to Zeus speak, but he expected an answer. She didn't want to disappoint him.

"Yes." She nodded, despite knowing that Zeus wouldn't be able to see the motion. "It's lunch hour."

"Are you alone?" Zeus asked.

"Yes."

"And are you in danger of being overheard?"

"No," Shannon said.

"Why did you call?" Zeus asked.

She hesitated. She knew the rules. She wasn't to use the phone unless ordered to. During school hours, she must keep the device stashed away to avoid having it taken by a teacher.

But then she had gotten confused, and she was still confused. Although the phone—*her* phone—fit comfortably in her hand, and although she recognized Zeus's voice, there was a trapped part of her that sensed the device wasn't hers.

The feeling was a lot like déjà vu but inherently opposite. A sense of unfamiliarity. A darker reality that even now she could only feel as an agitated tingling beneath her skin, not touch or see, much less *understand*.

Shannon closed her eyes again and silently counted her breaths. She knew the confusion would fade. It always did.

"Never mind," Zeus said. "I suppose it really doesn't matter. Do you have anything planned after school today? Anywhere you must be, anywhere you are expected?"

"No." She had made no plans with her friends. As for her foster parents, they both worked late. Her mom wouldn't arrive home until four thirty or five, and her dad was on a business trip.

"Good. I have another job for you."

She opened her eyes and looked at the black blotches of chewing gum stuck to the concrete at her feet. They reminded her of dried blood splatters.

"Another hit?" She could remember neither the date nor the circumstances of the last job, but she had a feeling it had been several weeks ago. Maybe longer.

"The wheels of Fate are turning rather quickly now," he explained. "Olympus is, indeed, rising."

If Olympus was rising, it was only because it was being built on the bodies of the dead. As horrifying as that knowledge was, as much as she wanted to throw the phone down or break it in two, she heard herself say, "I understand."

Resistance was futile. She had no choice but to listen and obey. It was a decision that came as naturally as breathing, and that seemed just as essential.

"This is a two-person job, but Hades won't be accompanying you this time," Zeus said. "He's taking care of business elsewhere."

Hades. In her mind's eye, she saw the boy's face clearly. She remembered his vivid blue eyes and the way a smile had brightened his lips as he had watched their target bleed out. But behind that smile, there had been nothing at all. Complete darkness.

"Remind me, when does school let out for you?" Zeus asked.

"Two o'clock." Slowly, her gaze rose from the ground and followed a pair of Goths leaving the front office.

The girl had clusters of green-and-silver cyberlocks pinned to her hair and wore a torn black T-shirt emblazoned with "DEATH IS BEAUTIFUL" in bold red letters.

Shannon bit her lip and wondered what the girl would think about the real Death. Not the one that came smelling of funeral flowers and brought darkness as soft as rose petals. The Death that was *ugly* and wept and lost control of his bowels after you stabbed him between the ribs and—

Stop! Don't you dare think about that!

"Artemis?" Zeus's voice broke through her daze.

"Yes, Zeus?" She realized she was gripping her knee so tightly that her nails had punctured the denim of her jeans. She flexed her fingers and examined them. Her ruby nail polish was beginning to chip.

A vagrant memory came to her: her fingers wrapped around the handle of a hunting knife that she did not own and could not remember handling before. Feeling dirty, she wiped her hand on her pants.

How many others were there? How many yet to come?

"Did you take the bus today?" Zeus spoke with the calm, patient tone that a teacher would use when instructing a particularly daft student.

"Yes." She had her driver's license and the use of a car, but with the city traffic, it took even longer to drive to school than it did to take the metro bus.

"Apollo will be picking you up. He'll fill you in on the nature of your assignment. He'll be driving a black Buick. Just stand in front of the school and wait for him. Do you understand?"

"Yes," Shannon murmured. She couldn't recall who Apollo was, what he looked like, or even make a general estimate of his age or hair color. But she knew she would recognize him the moment she saw him. She knew that just as much as she knew the nature of her assignment, even before it was told to her. It was a truth as thoroughly ingrained as gunpowder beneath her skin, seared into her psyche.

"Once I hang up, using your own cell phone, you will call your foster mother and tell her that you will be going to a friend's house after school. Do you have any questions?"

"No." She never did. She trusted that whatever she needed to know, Zeus would tell her.

"Good girl," he said. Although his voice remained as cool and impersonal as ever, at his soft encouragement, she felt pride well up inside her. Even the most eloquent and sincere compliment couldn't compare to those two simple words. Good girl.

The line went dead. She turned off the flip phone and returned it to her purse.

By the time she took out her smartphone, the last five minutes had been completely erased from her memory. As she dialed her mom's cell number, she thought about how much fun she was going to have with Victoria once school let out.

When the last bell rang and she and Victoria left biology class together, Shannon said, "See you tomorrow."

"You're not taking the bus?" Victoria asked.

"No, I…" She struggled to recall exactly what she was supposed to do. Oh right, a friend. She was going to a friend's house.

"You what?"

"I'm not. Taking the bus, I mean."

"Oh? Why?"

"I have a doctor's appointment," she said, sensing that if she told Victoria she was meeting a friend, it wouldn't fly. Too many questions. But why? What must she hide? Where was she going?

"Ah, bummer. I hate doctors. Is everything okay?" She gave Shannon a keen look. "You aren't preggers, are you?"

Shannon flushed. Preggers. She hated that word for some reason. It sounded like an STD euphemism, like crabs or the clap. "Do I look pregnant to you?"

"A joke."

"It's just a checkup." She smiled and watched Victoria head toward the bus stop. Then she turned and went in the opposite direction.

It didn't take long before she spotted the black car at the front of the pickup line. As she stepped up to it, the front window rolled down, and a voice from within said, "Get in."

Apollo, the god of sunlight and plague. It was a fitting moniker for the slender teenage boy leaning against the dark leather, with his burnished-blond hair and leonine eyes, his tanned skin and refined beauty. He didn't smile when she opened the door, though he did give her a lingering glance as though to confirm her identity. He seemed strangely familiar, although she couldn't place where or when she had last seen him.

"Artemis," he greeted, smiling wryly. A dimple appeared near one corner of his mouth, accentuating the expression.

"Apollo." As soon as Shannon said it, a hint of confusion slipped across the boy's face.

"No, it's Ty…" He trailed off, then shook his head. "Never mind. There's an envelope in the glove box. Get it."

His last sentence was more of a command than a suggestion, though, unlike with Zeus, she felt no compulsion to obey. She did as she was told, however, and retrieved the manila envelope from the glove box.

She opened the envelope and pulled out two papers.

The first sheet had no writing on it, just a grayscale scan of a pale woman whose brown hair was pulled back in a tight bun. The woman stared at the camera with a fierce boldness that was at odds with her starched white lab coat. She, too, looked vaguely familiar.

After examining the photograph, Shannon turned to the next page. She was not surprised when all she found was an address with directions on how to get there and, below that, the numbers 4891.

"4891?" she asked as he pulled out of the parking lot.

"The code for the alarm system," Apollo said, glancing over at her.

As she stuffed the papers back into the envelope, she realized there was something else inside. She turned the envelope upside down and shook a small silver key into her hand.

"For the front door," he explained.

"How will it end?"

He smiled thinly, without amusement. It wasn't even a real expression, just a death leer frozen in rigor mortis. "Homicide."

As they stopped at a red light, he sighed and looked down at his bandaged hands. On his knuckles, where the gauze would have ridden up, he had used round adhesives. He flexed his fingers then clenched them around the wheel, tight.

"How will it end…" he murmured, less like a question than a lament.

They drove in silence after that. In the hour drive, they exchanged fewer words than the minutes it took to arrive at the upscale suburban neighborhood where the target lived.

He drove past the target's house and parked five doors down, under the shadow of a massive cherry tree.

He took a cell phone out of his pants pocket. It was identical to the one Shannon owned, a burner you could buy in the electronics section of any major retailer. He dialed a number and put the phone on speaker.

It hadn't rung more than once before Zeus picked up and said, "Olympus is rising."

"Pandora's box is opening," Shannon and Apollo answered in unison.

"We're here," Apollo said.

"Good boy."

At Zeus's encouragement, a smile touched his lips.

For no clear reason, Shannon felt a stir of jealousy, then disgust. Then as Zeus continued, nothing at all.

"The target has left work and is on her way home," Zeus said. "She should arrive there in less than twenty minutes. Search her home thoroughly for any records or files. Anything that looks like research data. Apollo, use the device I gave you to access her computer files. Delete them once you're done."

There was a short rift of silence, where Shannon heard only a faint buzzing sound. Then, calmly and concisely, Zeus told them how to commit murder. He sent them off with one last encouragement. "Kill."

After returning the phone to his jeans, Apollo unzipped his navy field jacket. As he reached inside the tented fabric, she saw that he wore a pistol in a shoulder rig.

Fear struck her like a hammer against an anvil. In a moment of irrationality, she felt certain he would shoot her and grabbed for his hand. As her fingers locked around his muscular forearm, he unbuttoned an inner pocket.

"What is it?" he asked, glancing at her. The grayish sunlight revealed gold flecks in his eyes but failed to shed light on what was going through his mind.

"Nothing," she muttered, allowing her hand to fall.

He didn't pull out the gun. Instead, from the coat's inner pocket, he extracted a pair of leather gloves.

"Do you have any?" Apollo asked, sliding them on. He smiled like he was trying to convince himself that everything was all right.

Shannon shook her head.

He reached into the door compartment, took out a second set of gloves, and handed them to her. She put them on. They were slightly too big for her hands but thin enough not to obstruct her movement.

He leaned across the center console. His shoulder brushed against hers as he reached into the backseat. From the footwell, he retrieved a backpack, and then got out of the car.

Storm clouds filled the sky. The temperature was in the mid-fifties, cool enough that wearing gloves wouldn't have aroused suspicion. Still, Shannon shoved her hands in her pockets as she and Apollo walked down the sidewalk, side by side. Autumn leaves crunched under her shoes.

Although it was an old neighborhood filled with old houses, the same couldn't be said for those who lived there. A bright-pink bicycle with training wheels lay discarded on one lawn. On the sidewalk, freshly drawn hopscotch lines stood out like crime scene outlines. The approaching storm would wash the marks away, along with whatever DNA evidence they deposited on the pavement.

As she smeared the chalk squares with her dragging feet, she thought about the children who had drawn them. She imagined that in the summer months they waged water-gun wars on the street and sold lemonade on top of cardboard boxes, like scenes out of a 90s movie. Strange. She couldn't remember ever doing that herself.

The woman in the photograph had seemed chilly and standoffish, as sterile as the lab coat she wore. Her lawn told a different story. Rows of yellow tulips and orange carnations were planted under the windowsills, and rosebushes bordered the walls. The lawn was neatly manicured, but the grass wasn't cut so short as to seem artificial. A ceramic giraffe smiled at them from the front step.

Shannon stopped at the door and looked down. The mat at her feet proclaimed WELCOME!

She did not feel welcome.

Such feelings had no place in her mission, though. Before Apollo could urge her to continue, she withdrew her hands from her pockets and pushed the key into the keyhole.

The lock disengaged with a soft *click*.

Inside, the decor was warm and vibrant, with the same orange-and-yellow color palette as the landscaping out front. Although the umber walls should have made the foyer seem dingy and claustrophobic, a strategically placed skylight ensured quite the opposite.

But as she walked inside, her throat narrowed and her breath harshened. In the corners of her vision, she saw the walls edge closer. Their encroachment was a silent one, without the protest of crumbling plaster, heralded only by her booming heartbeat.

Swallowing the saliva that flooded her mouth, she turned to the alarm box. She typed in the code, and the blinking red light turned green.

She trained her eyes in front of her as she hurried down the hall. Even in the large living room, she felt suffocated. She returned the key to her pocket and eased her hands to her side. Slowly, the tension dissipated, and she began to feel calm again. Prepared.

Apollo unzipped his backpack and removed a black ski mask from the main compartment. He passed it to her before retrieving a second one for himself.

She held the mask, twisting the knit fabric between her fingers. She didn't want to put it on just yet.

His face was expressionless, but as she watched him, his golden tan blanched into a sickly pallor. He took repeated glances at his wristwatch. Twice, he reached into his jacket to touch the gun, as if hoping to comfort himself. Each time, he jerked his hand back with a low, terrified moan, like his fingers had skimmed over a snake's rattle instead of cool metal.

Even when they made accidental eye contact, neither spoke. Silence was their partner in crime, unseen and unheard but felt as heaviness in the air that was even more burdensome than gravity.

One minute passed, then two.

She put on her ski mask, and Apollo followed her example.

Even with his face hidden, the wideness of his eyes betrayed his tension.

He began to pace, muttering to himself. Shannon could only make out the first two words. The rest had the same syntax and syllable count, though, so she had a feeling he was repeating himself.

"I'm sorry."

Another lap of the second hand around the clock face, another suppressed twitch of the minute hand. Another circuit around the room. Numerous more harried looks at his watch.

"I'm sorry."

She pressed her lips together and watched Apollo go. Her hands trembled, but she did not feel sorry. She felt nothing at all.

Four minutes had passed.

"I'm so sorry."

Without thinking, she reached out to Apollo as he circled toward her again. Through her gloves, she felt the hard muscle of his biceps.

For a moment, he just stared at her with those beautiful, tortured eyes. Then he murmured, "We don't have to do this."

A jolt passed through her as his words shattered her calm. This wasn't the Apollo she knew. The pain and confusion in his soft, lulling voice was all wrong. It didn't belong.

"Why are we doing this?" he asked. She thought he wanted to say more, but before he could continue, the creak of the front door stole his words.

Footsteps echoed down the hall.

He stared at her, his face hidden, but his gaze filled with despair.

Her throat clenched around a whimper. She wanted to comfort him, and that was wrong. It was against her orders. Unwanted and unneeded.

Violence is necessary, a voice whispered in her head. *The future is built on bloodshed.*

She must kill.

As the footsteps drew closer, Apollo's lips pressed into a dispassionate line. A shadow descended over his amber eyes, clouding them. He reached into his jacket, took the gun from its holster, and turned toward the doorway. Shannon turned, too.

When the brown-haired woman saw them, she screamed, seemingly in surprise more than anything else. The cry was shrill and piercing in the house's confined quarters.

"What are you doing in my house? How'd you get in here?" Bewildered, the woman looked at Shannon, then at Apollo. When she noticed the gun in his hand, her shock was eclipsed by immediate fear. Her face paled, and her eyes widened. Her nostrils flared in panic.

Apollo was the first to speak.

"Don't scream, don't move," he said flatly. "If you run, I'll shoot you in the back."

The woman gaped at him. Her hand twitched, going for her purse.

Apollo cocked the gun. "I said don't move."

"What do you want?" The woman's words were softer than before, almost to the point of inaudibility. "If it's money, there's—"

Apollo nodded toward the black leather couch. "Sit."

For a second, she just stared at him.

"Sit down," he said.

As ordered, the woman trudged forward like a condemned prisoner on death row. She sat down and folded her hands in her lap. She made a deliberate effort to give Shannon a long, pleading gaze. "My name's Eveline. Whatever you want, honey, just take it. I don't want any trouble. I have money—"

"Do you have a safe?" Shannon asked.

Eveline dipped her head in a quick nod. "Yes. In my bedroom, behind the painting. I'll show you." She began to get up.

"Don't move!" Apollo snapped.

Eveline quickly sat down again.

"What's the combination?" Shannon asked.

She mumbled something.

"I asked you what the combination was."

"It's 129346." Her hand edged toward her purse. "Please, I don't want any trouble."

"Just shut up and stay still," Apollo said. There was a sudden tremor in his voice, a wavering note of distinct trepidation.

Shannon stepped forward and picked up Eveline's purse. In the main pouch, she found a canister of pepper spray, which she put in her jeans pocket. As she returned to Apollo's side, he handed her his gun.

"We don't want to hurt you, Eveline," she said, pointing the gun at the woman. "We just need some money. Okay? We need money."

"I understand," Eveline whispered.

"I'll stay here with you while my friend checks the safe." Shannon lowered the gun a little. "Please don't try anything."

"I won't."

Apollo went into the hall. Listening to his receding footsteps, she was pierced by a sudden regret for what they were about to do.

This wasn't what you were trained for, a voice whispered in her head. *This isn't a soldier's work.*

"I have a daughter," Eveline said quietly.

Shannon said nothing.

"A little girl. She's only eight."

When Shannon didn't answer, Eveline fell silent. They listened to the faint creak of cabinets being opened. From deeper within the house, a door groaned on ungreased hinges.

A wary light entered Eveline's eyes. "Wait, why is he going into the backyard?"

Before she could respond, Apollo returned to the living room. He had exchanged his windbreaker and jeans for dress pants and a polo shirt. The oxfords that had replaced his sneakers were muddy with garden soil.

Eveline's eyes widened at the sight of him. "Those are George's clothes. What are you doing wearing my husband's—"

As her gaze fell to the butcher knife that Apollo held, her voice died in her throat.

"I'm sorry," Apollo said, striding toward her. "This is a message. I'm so sorry. He wanted me to tell this to you."

"Oh, God. B-10, it's you. It can't be. Dimitri, he wouldn't dare."

"You're no longer of any use to the Project, Eve," Apollo said flatly, even as his eyes filled with unshed tears. "This is good-bye."

"Olympus is—"

The woman never had a chance to finish.

STATUS REPORT: SUBJECT 2 OF SUBSET A

DK: State your name and age. Talk directly into the recorder.

A-02: I am fifteen years old. I'll be sixteen in January, but I don't know the exact day. I don't have a name.

DK: What do they call you?

A-02: Subject Two of Subset A.

DK: May I call you Two?

A-02: No, sir. That would suggest that we're friends, and we're not.

DK: I see. You know, I was looking over your file earlier, and your test results are very impressive. Even at an early age, you showed an extraordinary aptitude for military tactics and logistics. Your instructors had high hopes for you.

A-02: I know, sir.

DK: Would you like to see the notes they wrote about you? They all believed that you were a natural-born leader.

A-02: No, that means nothing to me now.

DK: It says here that you're fluent in German and Russian.

A-02: Some Mandarin, too, but I can't write or read it. We were learning Arabic when I left.

DK: When you left. That's an interesting way of putting it.

A-02: When I deserted. Is that better?

DK: I would like to talk about that.

A-02: You have my files. Look at them yourself. My back hurts. I want to go back to my room.

DK: You can't yet.

A-02: I don't want to talk to you anymore.

DK: You don't have a choice.

A-02: I hate you.

DK: Do you hate a lot of things?

A-02: I wish you were dead.

DK: I'm sure you do. Now, let's try a different question, shall we? Have you ever hurt someone?

(Silence from 00:03:55 to 00:04:01.)

DK: I asked you a question.

A-02: I don't want to talk about that.

DK: You don't want to talk about anything. Need I remind you that you aren't here by choice, that cooperation will aid you more than disobedience?

A-02: I don't care.

DK: You keep touching your arm. I know the IV is uncomfortable, but you must stop that. If we have to, we'll restrain you again. Do you want that?

A-02: No, sir.

DK: Smart boy.

EG: It should be taking effect any moment now. Pulse is 44;

blood pressure is 91 over 58. Scan shows decreased function in the cerebellum and hippocampus.

DK: How do you feel?

(Silence from 00:06:07 to 00:06:22.)

A-02: What?

DK: I asked you how you feel.

A-02: Oh (:05 pause), uh (:03), what?

DK: How do you feel?

A-02: Oh. I'm okay.

EG: Pulse is 36.

DK: Have you ever hurt someone?

A-02: Yes.

DK: Go on.

A-02: I've hurt many people, sir.

DK: What about kill?

(Silence from 00:07:05 to 00:07:27.)

DK: Let me repeat myself. Have you ever killed someone?

(Silence from 00:07:42 to 00:07:50.)

DK: Answer the question.

A-02: I'll kill you.

DK: That's not what I asked you.

A-02: Someday, I'll kill all of you, and it won't be quick. You'll suffer.

DK: I have a feeling you're going to be a tough nut to crack. That's all right, I like a good challenge. We'll get back to that question in a later session. Do you know what Hades is?

(Silence from 00:08:26 to 00:08:31.)

DK: Hades is the underworld in Greek mythology, but he is also a god. How peculiar that Hell can be both a person and a place. Wouldn't you agree?

A-02: I don't know.

DK: Someday, you will.

CASE NOTES 4: HADES

Twelve stories above the ground, with a knee-high brick ledge the only thing between him and a vertical death plunge, Hades watched the streets of Philadelphia through binoculars. From the rooftop terrace, he had a perfect view of the outdoor venue where the bioethics conference was being held.

Even though the event wouldn't begin for another nineteen minutes, more than half the chairs were already occupied. Men in expensive suits and women in fancy business attire loitered about. Reporters crowded like vultures around the outskirts. On the stage, two men assembled a microphone.

Easing into a sitting position, he put down the binoculars and picked up the two eight-by-ten photographs he'd been given.

They were of a man in his sixties with a drastically receding hairline and a bushy white beard that gave him a passing resemblance to Abraham Lincoln. One was of the man's profile, the other a frontal view.

Hades knew the man's name, but it meant nothing to him.

After staring at the photographs for a good thirty seconds, he returned them to their folder. His eyes swept over the small array of objects laid out around him. A half-empty water bottle. His prepaid cell phone. Military-grade binoculars. A small duffel bag filled with a tangle of clothes, and beside it, a black gun case he had concealed beneath the laundry. The sniper rifle, assembled, calibrated, ready to fire.

He glanced at his watch. It was 9:44 a.m. Sixteen minutes until the seminar began.

He drank some water and settled back against the wall, looking upward. Roiling black clouds brewed overhead. To some people, the dark sky above and the urban labyrinth surrounding him would have left them feeling small, insignificant, humbled. It had the opposite effect on him.

Sitting on the cold concrete, looking up at the encroaching thunderheads, he felt like a god in creation. A god trapped in blood and skin, but a god nonetheless. Becoming what he was destined to be, with the storm as his witness.

So different from other humans. Exceptional. Better.

Alone.

Evolving.

Fourteen minutes.

His gaze drifted to the steel door that led to the stairwell. He wasn't worried about someone walking in on him. He had slept on the roof overnight and spent the entire morning here, eating protein bars he had brought with him. The building was under construction, without running water or electricity. The elevator was an empty shaft. No furniture, blackened lamps. Just the shell of a building.

Twelve minutes.

He reached into his jacket pocket and pulled out a heavily creased newspaper clipping. The text was worn into nothing. Of the headline, which had originally read "Senator Lawrence Hawthorne's Plans for America," only the first three words remained legible.

He didn't care about that. The important thing was the photograph included with the article. Senator Hawthorne and his family. The senator had brown hair, but his wife and daughter were both blondes.

Hades stared at the photo. Lovely Elizabeth. What was she

doing now? Was she having a good day at school?

Ten minutes.

After returning the newspaper clipping to his pocket, he got on his knees and picked up the binoculars. The third row of seats was now completely filled. There were several men in attendance who had beards, but none with his target's distinctive color. He wasn't concerned. The Lincoln impersonator was scheduled to give the introduction speech, so it was unlikely he'd be late or a no-show.

Eight minutes.

He turned his attention to a brown-haired woman who had stepped onto the stage. She seemed to be talking to one of the two men near the microphone. Her back was to him, but even then, he had a pleasant view of her legs and ass.

Hades wondered what she was talking about. He hoped she would be standing next to the target during the opening address.

Her dress was pale—maybe white or lavender, he couldn't tell. Either way, the blood would make a striking contrast against the shiny satin.

Six minutes.

The target walked onto the stage and spoke with the brunette in the pale dress. The woman's mouth opened, and her head tilted back. She must have been laughing, but with her words lost to the distance between them, she might just as well have been screaming.

In any case, she would soon scream. They all would.

Four minutes.

Hades felt like the approaching storm front. Bursting with lethal energy. Volatile. They couldn't see it now, but a tornado was brewing and would soon be upon them. And then it would strike, hard.

He finished the rest of his water and then stowed the empty bottle and folder in his duffel bag. Even though he began packing up what he didn't need to have out, he wasn't worried about being caught in the act or in the aftermath. He figured that in the immediate panic, the attendees would assume the shooter was among them. Only when the bullet was recovered would they learn it had come from a high-precision rifle. In the worst case—and most unlikely—scenario, where a sniper was immediately suspected, the chances of his whereabouts being discovered before he escaped were nil. There were too many high buildings and open windows, so many places he might have fired from.

Anyway, by the time the authorities arrived, he would be long gone.

Two minutes before the seminar was scheduled to start, the target stepped up to the microphone. Everyone stood and applauded.

Through the binocular lenses, it was like watching TV with the audio muted. The crowd below didn't even seem like actual people, but like a gathering that merely *resembled* humans.

Hades could have shot the man then, but he waited. He wanted everyone to sit down, get nice and comfortable. Additionally, there were still others arriving. The more witnesses, the greater the panic. Part of the execution was in the message.

At 10:05, he set his binoculars on the ground, within easy reach, and retrieved a pair of acoustic earmuffs from the outer pocket of his duffel bag. The plastic shells fit snugly over his head, cradling his ears in layers of insulating foam. Once he adjusted them, he moved the rifle into position. Through his gloves, the gun felt even colder than the concrete he knelt on.

This wasn't his first time using the sniper rifle on a human target, so he wasn't afraid he would miss or screw up. The rifle was comfortable in his hands. Familiar. Less like a complex weapon than like an extension of his arms and eye, a part of him. It made him feel complete, filling the emptiness that lived inside of him.

The scope's lenses were stronger than those of the binoculars. When Hades directed the rifle at his target, the man's face filled the scope's crosshairs, his forehead at dead center. Hades paused and then shifted toward the brunette.

For some reason, the woman reminded him of the scientist. The one who had helped him from the sensory deprivation tank when he had fallen into such a deep K-hole he couldn't move his limbs. The one who had stood by apathetically as he was electroshocked over and over, recording his vital signs. The one who held his jaw still as a feeding tube was forced down his throat, and he kept gagging, and *it hurt so much.*

He should have been the one to take care of that cold-blooded bitch, not Apollo and Artemis. Who cared about making it look like a domestic homicide? She deserved to suffer for everything she had done to him.

Staring at the brunette, he played with the idea of pulling the trigger. There were five cartridges in the magazine. Five names to carve on gravestones. Five new notches to add to the tattoo on his left forearm.

No. He had a job to complete. The job was the only thing that mattered.

He returned to the man and watched tensely as he addressed the crowd. As the man smiled directly at him, his breathing quickened. Excitement shot down his spine like a lightning bolt, lifting every hair on his body. His heart pounded, and his body was racked by a delicious tremor that shook him to the core.

In the air, he could detect the smell of ozone, of the approaching storm. It was a strong, heady odor, like hot gunmetal or sweat. It stung his nose as he breathed it in.

He's staring at his killer and he doesn't even know it, Hades thought as he turned the rifle's bolt, jacking a round into the chamber. *He's going to die and he doesn't even* know *it.*

He curled his finger around the trigger and squeezed it. The recoil rang through his arm like the gong of a bell, reverberating deep into his muscle and bone. The buttstock lurched against his shoulder. Through his earmuffs, the gunshot was reduced to a distant *thud*, probably a lot like the sound the man's body made when it hit the floor.

Wasting no time, Hades set down the sniper rifle and snatched up his binoculars. He afforded himself thirty seconds to watch the chaos.

As he'd hoped, the brunette had been splattered. She had been standing close to the old man, well within the fallout radius. Blood oozed down her dress, a nice contrast.

For a moment, the brunette stared blankly at the crowd. Everyone seemed frozen in shock, except for the one or two people still clapping, confused. Then the woman's mouth opened in a silent scream, and like a spell broken, everyone began to panic.

In their mad dash for the exit, the attendees shoved and pushed past one another. When one fell, the others crawled over him. Even the most elegant, refined individuals regressed to shrieking primates, their panic sloughing off millenniums worth of evolution. Mankind's true nature, flayed and exposed.

Mesmerized, Hades watched as a man in a tuxedo was thrown to the ground and trampled under the stampeding feet. When the crowd surged forward, the man did not get up.

He couldn't hear their screaming, but he felt it resonating through his body.

He hated to pull himself away from the scene, but there was no time to waste. Reluctantly, he sat back down and began disassembling the rifle. Although not originally a take-down rifle, the gun was a custom piece that had cost close to ten thousand dollars, designed specifically for swift disassembly and concealment. The bipod was similarly compactable.

Normally the dismantling process was performed calmly and methodically, but as he worked, his hands trembled. Quiet spasms of ecstasy racked his body.

Once all the pieces were returned to the rifle case, Hades latched it shut and put it in the duffel bag, along with the binoculars, bipod, and earmuffs.

As expected, he encountered no one as he left the building. Dressed in a hooded jacket and jeans, he easily blended in with the midday crowd. When the police cars sped past, sirens wailing, he didn't stop or look back.

The smells of food vendors, burning charcoal, and exhaust fumes filled his nose, but he detected the aroma of spent gunpowder beneath those other scents, warm and constant. He loved that odor. It was nostalgic and the one thing in his life that remained almost ever-present.

In the listless hours before the kill, he had formulated multiple escape plans in the event that the assassination failed or circumstances beyond his control prevented him from returning to his car. Those precautions proved unnecessary. He reached the vehicle without trouble and put the duffel bag in the trunk.

By then, the excitement of the kill was beginning to gutter out like a dying flame. Very rarely did he feel any emotion for very long. Most of the time there were just facial expressions caused by muscle memory, a ghost's contortions of a stiff leather mask.

During the long journey home, he indulged in a recurring fantasy that the entire world was falling away behind him. Every time a town disappeared beyond the horizon, it ceased to exist. The people he passed died the moment he lost sight of them.

Normally, this mental game soothed him, but when his excitement soured into nothing at all, he felt only bitter yearning. It was less like an emotion than like a hollow that ached to be filled. An absence of sorts.

So what if the world didn't truly exist? He would still never be a part of it. He could never lose himself in the lie.

He stopped once, only long enough to change the car's license plates. The rest of the time, he drove in silence. He didn't like music. Whenever he listened to music, he felt like he was an actor in a movie, playing a role set out for him with a predetermined fate, which only further deepened his sense of derealization.

By the time he returned to the neighborhood of Georgetown, the storm in Philadelphia had traveled south into D.C. as if in pursuit of him. Thunder exploded like bombshells overhead. Rain fell in sheets, pounding into the car roof with a steady machine-gun rattle and pummeling the trees planted along the curb. The road and lawns were swamped. Loose petals, dead leaves, and litter flowed into storm drains.

He drove past luxurious, multi-million-dollar houses and stopped in front of a tall stone wall filigreed with red ivy. Security cameras peered out from among the leaves.

He rolled down the window and punched a code into the keypad mounted next to the wrought-iron gate. The gate swung forward, allowing him entry, then closed behind him.

The mansion itself was an architectural goliath, three stories tall with an extended colonnade. To Hades, it brought to mind a prison.

He pulled into the detached garage, next to the other car already inside. His motorcycle was parked against the back wall. As per orders, he left the rifle inside its case, in the trunk.

As he stepped outside and shut the garage door, a pair of massive Rottweilers appeared from around the corner of the house.

The dogs slunk forward, their muscles rolling beneath their slick black fur.

"*Grün*," Hades said.

At once, the dogs swarmed him, wagging their docked tails and nuzzling his legs. They poked their damp snouts against his limbs, taking in the new and exciting odors he brought with him. He scratched one dog behind the ears and rubbed the other's belly when it rolled over, panting in adoration.

Later, he might play ball with the Rottweilers, take them for a walk, or brush their fur, but he had other plans for now.

"*Gelb*," he said, and the dogs' tail stumps went still. They leaped to their feet and continued their circuit around the property, searching for intruders.

He followed the brick driveway back to the main house. The grass and shrubbery were carefully maintained, although less so than the surrounding houses. Privacy was more important than tidiness.

He didn't hurry or draw up his hood. He liked the rain, especially when it was cold, as it was now.

If there were no guests and the rain persisted, he might go outside later and lie on the patio, allowing the storm to wash over him. Sometimes he fantasized about being struck by lightning. Considering that his own birth was, in a sense, by electricity—those volts delivered again and again to electrodes on his temples during electroconvulsive therapy—he thought an actual lightning bolt might transform him into something else entirely.

Evolution.

By the time he reached the colonnade, his clothes were drenched. He wiped his boots on the mat, unlocked the front door, and stepped inside.

"I'm back," he said as he entered the house, tracking water across the marble floor. Never "I'm home." This was not a home and never would be.

The entry hall was as imposing as the exterior, with a grand staircase and decorative pillars. A second pair of Rottweilers came to greet him, padding across the polished stone the moment he shut the door.

The estate had six dogs total. He had been present at their birth and raised them. He had trained the Rottweilers as puppies, first disciplining them in the *Schutzhund* system, then focusing exclusively on combat-related exercises from other sources. His connection with the dogs showed in their behavior toward him. Even if someone used the attack phrase and ordered them to maul him, he was confident they wouldn't obey, though the idea strangely pleased him.

Save for the dogs, the foyer was deserted. The main kitchen

was likewise empty, and from the refrigerator he took the leftover steak from last night's dinner. He ate it standing in front of the black granite counter, the way another person might eat a pizza slice. He couldn't be bothered to get a plate and silverware.

"If you're going to eat like a dog, you should at least do it on all fours," a voice said from behind him.

"That's a new one," Hades said without turning. "Are you trying to flirt with me, *Zeusy*? You're going to have to do better than that."

"Funny," Dimitri said humorlessly. "How did it go?"

"Perfect," he said, tearing off another mouthful of meat. It was undercooked, and cold juice dripped down his hand. He didn't care.

"Look at me when I am speaking to you."

Hades turned.

Dimitri leaned against the wall. He was a tall, wiry man with salt-and-pepper hair. His dark-gray eyes were a single color, without luster, like old coins. He had the kind of lean greyhound face that would benefit from a good beating. Preferably with a tire iron.

"You already know how it went," Hades said after swallowing the hunk of beef. He licked the savory juice off his fingers. "You probably jerked off to the live recording."

"No wonder the Rotts like you so much," Dimitri said in evident disgust. "You really are an animal."

"Aren't we all?"

"I really wish you would use proper table manners."

"Is that an order, Dima?" he asked, smiling. He knew Dimitri hated him to use that nickname, which was ironic considering that when Dimitri wasn't being called "Doctor," he was being called "Zeus." Names meant nothing, and they both knew it.

Dimitri narrowed his eyes. "You should know better than to speak to me in such a manner, Hades."

"You know I'm loyal to you. In the end, actions speak louder than words, sir. I delivered the message, and I did it well."

When Dimitri did not answer, Hades washed his hands at the sink and left the kitchen. He walked down the hall and entered his room.

In keeping with the rest of the house's decor, the walls were painted red and the floor was black marble. While there were no posters, a couple of charcoal sketches he had drawn were pinned to the wall. A punching bag hanging from the ceiling provided the only means of entertainment. The furniture consisted of a bed, a desk with a wooden chair, a dresser, and nothing else.

Aside from the crimson walls, the only other color came from the few paperbacks piled on his desk. Mostly training manuals. He couldn't find escape in fiction. It was impossible for him to sympathize with the protagonists of novels, no matter the genre, let alone live vicariously through them.

Hades sat down at his desk, unlaced his boots, and set them on the desktop beside the lamp. He unstrapped his ankle sheath that contained a small, wicked blade and placed it inside one of the boots.

From the top drawer of the desk, he removed a thin metal case and a plastic first aid kit. While he prepped his left forearm with rubbing alcohol, he returned to the kill. He envisioned every detail as best he could, even the most mundane ones, like the way the roof had felt beneath his knees and the smell of the oil he had cleaned the gun with.

He put on a pair of latex gloves, opened the case, and took out the tattoo gun. Throughout the process of assembling the machine, attaching a new needle and tube, and filling the ink reserve, he did not allow his mind to wander.

It is October 14, he thought as he turned the tattoo gun onto his own flesh. *I am here. I am not dead.*

He did not use a stencil. His grip was firm and unwavering as the needle ducked in and out of his skin, forming a perfect line. Even if he did slip, it wouldn't matter. This body was just a carcass to be discarded once he completed his evolution.

I exist.

Blood dewed on his milk-white skin as the needle bit into him.

I am still alive.

The needle pricks meant nothing to him. Pain was familiar. It linked him to his victims. When his memory failed him, he would be able to touch his newest notch and think back to the kill that it represented and, in doing so, recall what had transpired afterward.

I am evolving, Hades thought, watching a new notch appear alongside the first seventeen.

STATUS REPORT: SUBJECT 10 OF SUBSET B

Apollo is an anomaly. The ECT and tank sessions have not only robbed him of his memories, but they have also taken the entirety of his tactical training. I had to have Hades retrain him how to use a gun. This is rather troublesome, but I suppose every experiment will have its outliers. In any case, this will have very little impact on how Apollo is received into the ROTC once he is initiated into the outer world. His program will proceed exactly as outlined.

Today, I encouraged Artemis to approach Apollo, who has become rather depressed as of late. I've decided that it is in Project Pandora's best interest to cultivate bonds between the subjects, even if they won't remember them once they leave.

The meeting went well. Artemis and Apollo spoke at length and played chess. They got along rather nicely, all things considered. Nothing alarming in their conversation (D5B10-10-03.mp3).

It's interesting. When Apollo leaves this place, he will have no recollection of Artemis, let alone the world he once knew, but there is a good chance they will see each other at school and elsewhere. Will they find themselves straying toward each other or just the opposite?

I'm curious to see how Apollo adjusts to the outside world. He will be going into a completely different environment from the one he is used to. Still, his amnesia continues to concern me, and I can't help but wonder how it will affect the Project's plans for him.

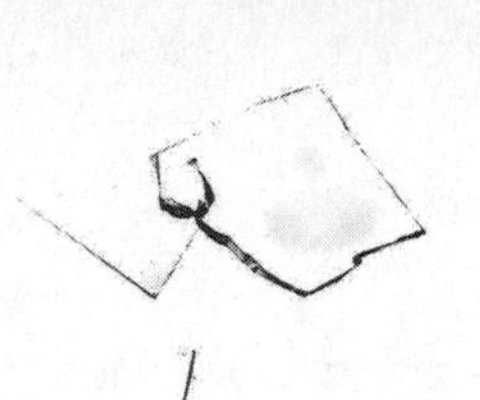

CASE NOTES 5: APOLLO

By the morning of the nineteenth, the week's nasty weather had finally abated. Against a backdrop of autumn leaves, the sky appeared as flat as a paper cutout.

Tyler stepped out of the car and looked doubtfully at the house before him. Lurching over a grassy lot, the one-story home was a clapboard monstrosity. Its pink coloring was bright enough to burn retinas.

Tyler turned to the scrawny boy who crawled from the backseat like a rat from a tunnel, stooped over, toddling on unstable legs.

"What's with the new paint job?" Tyler asked.

"You don't like it?" Alan asked, rubbing his arms. He had brown hair and bloodshot eyes that were just as dark.

"It looks like Pepto-Bismol."

Alan snickered, his smile one of dazed content. "Dude, like, that's what I told my dad, but he keeps insisting it's Suffolk."

"What?" Tyler stared at him, uncertain if he had heard correctly. Alan sounded perpetually high, which sometimes made it difficult to understand what he was saying.

"Suffolk pink."

"Oh, that explains *so* much." He still had no idea what the first word was.

Alan rolled his eyes and trudged up the gravel walkway.

As Tyler followed, his gaze was drawn to the sky. For no reason at all, the flat blue sky troubled him. It seemed insubstantial, too uniform in color, like a painted ceiling.

The living room smelled of fresh paint. Its walls were half green, half white. As he stepped inside, he avoided tripping over one of the many cans of paint or spread tarps.

"I keep telling him it's like being in an inside-out watermelon," Alan said, glancing around at the unfinished paint job. "But ever since he started watching those home improvement shows, he's been obsessed with repainting the house."

"I hate to break it to you, but watermelons are red, not pink."

Alan stared at him blankly. "Dude, what watermelons are you buying?"

"Uh, the ones from the grocery store."

With a mystified shrug, Alan went into his room to use the bathroom, then returned with a grocery bag and a tin of chips. Instead of pulling off the plastic lid, he turned the can upside down and stuck his fingernail into the crevice between the cardboard tube and metal bottom. As he pried off the metal disc, a small circular tin dropped into his palm.

"No way," Tyler said as Alan opened the tin. "I'm not smoking."

"Relax, my parents aren't home." Alan set the container on the glass coffee table, being careful not to spill any of its contents. "Come on, bro-ski, it's time you lose your weed virginity. Just because you want to join the army—"

"The ROTC."

"Doesn't mean you need to walk around with a stick up your ass all the time," Alan finished, and from the grocery bag, he took a glass pipe and a lighter. "Besides, you've been acting all weird and super serious lately. This can help. Just take one hit."

He sighed. "I thought you just wanted to play Wii."

"I do," Alan said, removing the leaves from the stems and crumbling them between his fingers. "Wii and weed."

"I'll play Wii, but I'm still not smoking."

"We'll see about that."

Tyler walked over to the TV as Alan packed the pipe. He knew that Alan smoked weed, but he didn't like being in the same room when Alan did it. It made him nervous, like he was doing something wrong. Something that went against who he was as a person. Disobeying orders.

As he turned on the TV, the doorbell rang.

"That must be Victoria," Alan said.

"Wait, you invited Victoria over? And she actually agreed?"

Alan scowled. "Why wouldn't she?"

"Uh, because she almost curb-stomped your balls in study hall last week."

"How was I supposed to know she wouldn't like the pickup line?" Alan asked, setting down the pipe.

"Dude, I'm not even friends with her, and I knew she wouldn't like it. I tried telling you."

"Whatever." Alan stood, smoothed the wrinkles from his shirt, and ran a hand through his lank brown hair to give it some life. "How do I look?"

Tyler smiled. "Like an idiot."

"Bite me," Alan said, then ambled off.

Tyler picked up the Wii remotes and returned to the couch but did not sit down. He stared into the hallway, listening to the footsteps and voices too faint to discern what was being said.

For some reason, it always made him nervous to hear people but not be able to see them. To truly be comfortable, he needed to know where everyone was, that every door was locked behind him and every window shut tightly. He needed to feel absolutely secure in his surroundings.

His gaze swept to the TV. The news channel droned in the background. Through a static haze, a mustached man talked about death.

"According to an anonymous source affiliated with the Philadelphia Police Department," the reporter said, "there is no indication that the bioethics conference shooting was an act of terrorism. The gunshot victim, Dr. Benjamin Klausman, was a controversial figure whose support for eugenics drew much ire from the medical community. As of yet, the authorities have declined to speculate whether his extreme ideology might have been a reason for his murder."

Alan returned, followed by two girls.

Victoria was tall and edgy, wearing a studded leather jacket, fishnet stockings, and scuffed Doc Martens. Her black curls fell in a crazy tumble down her back, blond at the roots.

The other girl, whose name Tyler did not know but whom he recognized from school, was several inches shorter than her friend. She possessed a dancer's graceful build, all long legs and lithe gait. She wore her auburn hair just past her shoulders, as thick and glossy as fox fur.

Victoria plopped down on the suede ottoman and reached into her voluminous pleather purse. "Look what I brought," she said, adding a bottle of tequila to the table.

"Now it's a party," Alan said. "Hey, Victoria, want to help me get some snacks and stuff from the pantry? We can make margaritas!"

Victoria sighed and stood again, picking up the tequila. "Whatever."

As Victoria and Alan went into the kitchen, Tyler set the remotes on the table and turned to the pretty redhead, who stood with her arms crossed, staring at him.

She had a face that reminded him of one of those Japanese cartoon characters, with her huge eyes and rosebud lips. Brown eyes, deep and velvety, like the eyes of a doe.

"We're in English together, right?" Tyler asked. "You sit in the same row as me."

"Yeah," the girl said, brushing her hair out of her face. She wandered over to the couch and sat down next to him. "My name's Shannon."

"Tyler."

"I know." A light blush touched her cheeks. "Must have been some pretty important phone call, huh?"

He blinked. "What?"

"Last week, when you walked out of class."

Tyler wondered what in the world she was talking about, then suddenly remembered how he had received an emergency call from his foster mother. He had explained the situation to Mr. Preston the next day and had gotten off with lunch detention.

"Oh, right," he said, deciding not to regurgitate the whole tale. "It was."

She glanced at the TV, where the reporter had been replaced by a recording of the stampede that had occurred after the man was shot. "Oh. I heard about this."

"Yeah, it's been on the news all week," Tyler said. "I think they thought it was terrorism at first, but I guess not."

"I heard that the guy who was shot wanted to sterilize the mentally ill, and there was this big protest over his being a speaker at the conference. Still, I feel bad for the people who got injured during the panic."

"Yeah." Hearing the rev of a blender, he glanced toward the kitchen.

"Are you going to be drinking?" she asked.

"Uh, no. I have to drive."

"You mind?" she asked, picking up the pipe.

He shrugged. "It's not mine."

Shannon used the lighter to disinfect the mouthpiece, waited for the glass to cool again, and then brought the pipe to her lips. She thumbed the lighter and angled the flame downward, inhaled, and held the smoke inside her. Once she exhaled, she tried passing the pipe and lighter to Tyler.

"I don't smoke," he said.

Her velvety brown eyes twinkled with amusement. "Really?"

"It's not my thing," Tyler said. "I just don't like how it makes me feel."

"He's lying," Alan piped in, returning from the kitchen with sodas and enough junk food to feed a small army. "He's a weed virgin."

"Then we've got to do something about that," Victoria said as she entered the living room. She carried a stack of red plastic cups and the blender's plastic pitcher filled with a greenish sludge that resembled toxic waste more than any sort of drinkable beverage. "Time to lose it, Ty."

"Hey, Victoria, can you help me lose mine?" Alan asked, raising his eyebrows.

"Worst pickup line ever." Victoria rolled her eyes. "How about you Google some pickup lines first and then get back to me?"

Tyler sighed, his resolution wavering. One time wouldn't hurt, right? Besides, it might make him feel better. Alan was right, he *had* been stressed lately. For the last couple weeks, he had awoken with the feeling that he had done something terrible, and each night he'd fallen asleep with the same thought.

"Give me the pipe," Tyler said to Shannon.

"You sure?" she asked without sarcasm. She seemed almost uneasy. "You don't have to do it if you don't want to."

"I do." He took the pipe and lighter from her. It took him two flicks of the wheel to ignite the lighter. On the first hit, he began gagging and something flew down his throat.

"You all right?" Shannon asked, laying a hand on his upper arm. In spite of his breathlessness, he enjoyed the pleasant warmth of her touch. He wished she wouldn't let go.

"Shit, bro-ski," Alan said as he tore open a bag of Doritos. "Did you just get a Scooby Snack?"

"A *what*?" Tyler asked once he had regained his breath.

"Some weed, man. You were sucking that pipe like, well, like I wish Victoria over here would suck my—"

Victoria punched Alan's elbow hard enough to make him groan. "One more word, you little perv, and your doctor's gonna have to extract your head from your ass."

"I'll help you light it next time," Shannon said, passing the pipe to Victoria.

"Thanks," Tyler said to her. His mouth was dry and acrid, as if all his saliva had dissolved. He didn't feel anything. Had he done it wrong?

"Just don't breathe in like that," Shannon added. "Take it slow and deep."

"That's what she said," Alan said, earning a collective scoff of disgust. Tyler wished he had met Shannon elsewhere, in better company.

From Victoria, the pipe went to Alan, then back to Shannon, who sanitized it with the flame.

"Afraid of cooties?" Alan asked.

"More like herpes," she said drily, then took a hit. She paused. "It's cashed. Tyler, can you give me the tin, please?"

He passed her the tin so that she could refill the bowl. Already, he began to feel calmer, and the room acquired a pleasant ambiance.

As Shannon sorted out the buds and leaves from the stems and hard bits, Tyler found himself transfixed by her hands. They were small and delicate. Her ruby nail polish was chipping at the edges, which gave her an endearingly tomboyish quality.

Shannon turned to him and handed him the pipe. She stood as he placed the end of the pipe between his lips.

"Are you ready?" she asked, staring into his eyes.

"Yeah," Tyler said, and as she lit the bowl, he inhaled. This time, the smoke went down a lot smoother, and he was able to hold it inside his lungs for several seconds before being forced to exhale.

She giggled. "Hey, you actually did a good job this time. No coughing."

He leaned back against the sofa, losing himself in a pleasant daze. A soothing weight pressed down on the right hemisphere of his face. He couldn't tell if his eye was twitching or not, but he felt spasms and tingling beneath the skin, as if the lids were starting to shrink. The sensation in his legs had begun to wane, and he thought that if he tried to stand, he wouldn't be able to.

His gaze shifted to Shannon once more. The sunlight streaming in through the blinds flowed across her auburn hair, drawing out shades of gold and burgundy. It was striking.

Third hit.

Alan looked at him and said, "Do you want to murder?"

The warmth drained from Tyler's body. "What?" He stumbled over the word. Something seemed caught in his throat, as if he'd accidentally gotten another Scooby Snack, only his mouth tasted raw and bloody instead of acrid and chalky. He swallowed, but it didn't help. Maybe he'd bitten his tongue.

"I asked if you want a margarita."

"Oh, uh, no thanks." He felt slightly unbalanced. Hoping to clear his throat, he popped open a can of Sprite and lifted it to his lips. Though the drink was lukewarm, it washed the taste of gore from his mouth.

"Have another hit," Alan said and tried to hand him the pipe again.

"I'm good," Tyler said.

"Now you're just trying to get him wasted," Victoria said, giggling.

"Guilty as charged." Alan chuckled, only to glance in his direction. His grin faded into a perplexed frown. "Tyler?"

I did something terrible.

For no reason at all, his heart began to race, and strange tremors seized him, beginning in his shoulders and spine but quickly crawling downward, until even his legs were shaking. His vision seemed to dim around the edges until he couldn't see the walls on either side of him.

I hurt someone very badly.

The air grew heavier, thick with the stenches of blood and gunpowder. He gagged on the noxious odors, pressing his hand over his mouth.

Shannon's lips moved rapidly, but he didn't hear what she was saying. Her voice was drowned beneath his own gasps for breath. In an instant, his windpipe had constricted to the size of a pinhole. In the glow of the lamp overhead, everything dimmed into monochrome, and darkness collapsed in on him.

Alan grabbed his shoulder. "Hey, you okay, man?" His voice came to Tyler as though from across the room, distant and echoing.

Something happened to me.

"Gonna be sick," he choked, dropped the soda can, and rushed for the front door. The air in the room was too smothering, the ceiling lowering by the second. If he stayed there any longer, he would suffocate.

As soon as he made it outside, his breathing slowed, the weight on his lungs lightened, and he began to feel a little better. He sat down on the concrete back porch and stared at the scraggly patches of grass around the red charcoal grill.

"Are you all right?" a soft voice asked from behind him.

"I'm fine," he said, glancing over his shoulder to find Shannon staring down at him. "It was just a panic attack, I think."

"I get those sometimes, too. Not when I'm smoking, but just in general." She sat down next to him, close enough to bump shoulders, and passed over an unopened water bottle. "Drink this."

"Thanks," he said, unscrewing the lid.

"Do you have anxiety?" she asked.

"How did you know?" He took a sip of the cool water.

She shrugged. "Sometimes I say strange things, too, when I'm stressed."

"Wait a minute, I was talking?"

A vague smile touched her lips. "You said, 'When I looked in the mirror, I didn't see myself. And then I picked it up and used it.'"

Tyler groaned. "I think I'm going insane."

"Weed and anxiety don't mix all that well." Shannon paused. "You aren't on meds, are you?"

"No, I just see a counselor." He decided not to mention that Dr. Kosta had a degree in psychiatry. "It's really not that bad. It's not like an anxiety disorder or anything. Just stress from school."

"Still, you should've said something," she said. "I'm sorry if I pressured you to smoke and all."

"It's fine. You didn't know, and I feel better now." He dug the heel of his shoe into the dirt, digging a small hole. "Hey, when you're feeling anxious, do you ever get this sensation like you've done something wrong?"

Her forehead creased. "What?"

He almost didn't answer, afraid that she would think he belonged in an asylum. Then, deciding that he had already proven he was a straitjacket candidate, he said, "It feels like déjà vu. It's like I've done something horrible, except I can't remember it."

The lines in her forehead deepened, and she nibbled her lip in thought. As traffic buzzed in the distance and a jet passed overhead, Shannon nodded.

"All the time," she said, and in her deep brown eyes, he saw a reflection of his own secret fear. That the intuition was real.

When Tyler returned home from Alan's house, he tossed a TV dinner into the microwave and sat at the kitchen counter while he waited for the meal to heat. No surprise, his foster parents weren't back yet. They both worked late, and their daily commutes extended their combined travel times by a couple of hours.

As the smell of precooked chicken filled the room, he stared at the patterned linoleum, thinking about Shannon Evans. It wasn't as though he hadn't noticed her, considering how she sat in the same row as him during English. He had watched her in the corner of his eye and heard her respond to Mr. Preston's questions. But for some reason, he had never felt comfortable approaching her.

He took out his smartphone and brought up the contacts list. Before he had left Alan's house, he had asked Shannon for her number. Now, he wondered if he should text her. She hadn't drunk anything and, by the time she had left, had assured him that she was sober enough to get home safely. Still, he regretted that he hadn't given her a ride.

Would it be too soon to text her?

After starting a new message, he typed in: ***Are you home yet?***

He read it over then deleted it. Too creepy.

The microwave timer went off, but he remained seated, thinking about a better first text to send. At last, he wrote: ***Did you get home safely?***

Tyler thumbed the send button before he could decide against it. He stared at the smartphone for thirty seconds, waiting for her to respond. Then he sighed, set the phone on the counter, and rose to his feet, cursing Alan under his breath. Why had he ever thought she would want to talk to him again after listening to Alan's obnoxious flirting attempts?

Tyler walked to the other side of the kitchen. As he opened the silverware drawer, an electronic ping caught his attention. He rushed back to the counter and snatched up his smartphone.

He grinned. A new text had been sent.

Shannon: Yeah. ☺ Thanks for asking. How are you doing?

He sighed once more. She would probably never be able to look at his face without remembering how he couldn't even smoke a joint without losing his cool. He typed in a quick response, then smiled when she responded seconds later.

Tyler: Better. Sorry to freak out on you like that.

Shannon: No, it's OK! Don't apologize!!!

Tyler: I swear it's not a regular thing with me.

Shannon: Like I said, I have anxiety too. I get it. ☺ If you ever need to talk to someone, I'm always here!

Tyler: Same.

CASE NOTES 6: PERSEPHONE

Gasping for breath, Elizabeth Hawthorne jumped straight up and brought her arm down. The volleyball slammed against her fist and shot onto the other side of the net.

A girl on the opposing team tried to reach the ball but was not quick enough to prevent it from striking the floor.

"Point!" Coach Slate called, clapping her hands. "And we're out of time! Good game, girls. Time to get cleaned up."

Elizabeth went into the locker room. Girls in various stages of undress clustered around the lockers and preened themselves by the sinks.

After retrieving her towel, toiletries bag, and a change of clothes from her locker, she stepped into one of the shower cubicles and undressed. She set her clothing on a bench outside the stall, out of the water's range.

As she massaged shampoo through her hair, her thoughts drifted to the fundraising banquet and the boy she had met there.

Hades had haunted her for the past week. She had dreamed about him twice, and though the days passed, the beautiful, feral face she envisioned became no less clear. If anything, time only refined her memory of him, and she began to recall small details she had only briefly noted during their encounter. Like the way his fingers had felt against her arm, so warm, and how one side of his mouth had a tendency to lift higher than the other when he smiled. Or how, as he had passed under the chandelier, the glow of many candles had revealed a deep, bluish undertone to his raven hair.

Craning her face toward the showerhead, Elizabeth closed her eyes.

Why couldn't she get him out of her head? Okay, he was really, really gorgeous, but so were other boys, and it wasn't like she'd ever see him again. Besides, she didn't even know if Hades was his real name.

As the warm water coursed down her back, she wondered what he would look like underneath his clothes.

An image came to her. In her mind's eye, she saw Hades from behind, under lights far harsher than those at the banquet. His muscular back faced her, and the bright fluorescents left his pale skin as white as snow.

She sighed, allowing her hands to travel down her body. With her eyes closed, she could almost believe that it was his fingers that so teasingly traced the ridges of her rib cage before lowering, lowering.

Suddenly, seams of blood appeared like stigmata, spreading down his back in a pair of crimson wings. His milk-white skin furled away under terrible force, and gore ran down the hard contours of his muscles from numerous overlapping incisions.

Elizabeth's eyes shot open. She found herself shaking uncontrollably with her arms wrapped around her body. Bile burned like acid on her tongue, and her vision blurred.

Even as she closed her eyes again and tried to conjure a pleasant scene of a field of wildflowers under a dusky sky, she couldn't escape from that lasting image.

Why had she imagined something so terrible?

Invasive thoughts, she told herself as she opened her eyes. *They're only invasive thoughts, just like Dr. Kosta said. Nothing to worry about.*

To calm herself, she practiced the deep breathing exercise

that her psychiatrist had taught her. She inhaled for four seconds, held her breath inside her, and then slowly exhaled. She repeated the exercise as she washed off the soap suds, and by the time she had dried herself, she felt much better.

After getting dressed, she stopped in front of the mirror to brush her hair and touch up her makeup. She reapplied concealer to the thin, pale scars on her cheeks and chin.

Over the last two years the scars had faded, until they were practically invisible, but her gaze was still drawn to them continuously. She often found herself stroking the tiny marks without realizing it, the same way another person might finger the beads of a rosary.

She told herself that she should be grateful the broken glass hadn't blinded her or torn her face to shreds. The car accident could have been much worse. Still, every time she noticed the scars, she felt uneasy.

It wasn't just that she hated how they looked. It went much deeper than that.

In a way, even looking at her own face troubled her. She noticed small details that she was almost certain hadn't been there before the car accident. Sometimes, she expected to see a tiny beauty mark near the corner of her left eye, only to realize it had never existed to begin with.

She stepped into the hall. The school was practically deserted at this hour, and it creeped her out to walk the halls alone. She moved at a swift pace, heading straight for the exit.

"Elizabeth!" a girl cried from behind her.

She looked back, startled. The design committee meeting ended fifteen minutes after volleyball practice, so she wasn't surprised to spot a familiar cloud of strawberry-blond curls when she turned around.

"Look at my hands," Rachelle said, throwing them up in dismay. Black paint had stained her skin and nails. "No matter what I try, it won't wash off. It's ridiculous."

"Beautiful banners, though," she said, passing under a crepe-festooned display advertising the Halloween dance.

"Well, yeah, but still. Such sacrifice!" Petite and vivacious, Rachelle had a personality as intense and colorful as the neon-pink nail polish she wore.

"Do you already have a costume picked out?" Elizabeth asked.

"Not yet," Rachelle said. "What about you?"

She shook her head. She decided not to tell Rachelle that her parents had insisted on reviewing potential costumes beforehand. Parents chaperoned school events, and the last thing her family wanted was people gossiping about the senator's daughter and her trashy outfit. Impressions were everything.

"We should go shopping together," Rachelle said. "For moral support. Are you free Saturday?"

"Yeah," Elizabeth said, smiling. Why not? It's not like her parents would have a total meltdown if she came back with a modest, tasteful costume. Besides, she felt silly and immature having to try on outfits with her mom hanging over her shoulder. Sometimes, it was like her parents viewed her as a fancy pet instead of a person, something to parade around during press conferences and dinners. A pretty creature kept on a tight leash.

"Yay," Rachelle said. "This year, you'll be something more exciting than Alice in Wonderland. I won't let you get a boring costume like that."

"Hey, Rachelle?"

"Hmm?"

"Did a boy named Hades used to go to our school?" Elizabeth asked.

"Hades?" Rachelle asked blankly. "What kind of name is that?"

"I'm pretty sure it's from Greek mythology."

Rachelle cocked her head. "How do you spell it?"

"H-A-D-E-S."

"Well, what was his last name?" Rachelle whipped out her rhinestone-encrusted cell phone. "Let's see if we can find him online."

"He didn't tell me. Honestly, I'm not even sure if Hades is his real name."

Rachelle lifted her eyebrows. "So, wait, he gave you a fake name?"

"I think it's just his nickname."

"But you think you know him from, um, before?"

Elizabeth sighed. It was so uncomfortable talking about her life before the car crash, mainly because she could only remember the haziest details of it. Even Rachelle had seemed like a complete and utter stranger at first.

"It's hard to explain. It's just, the moment I saw him, I felt… nostalgic, and happy, and *safe*. Like he could protect me from anything. I've never felt that way before."

It had been almost a week since the fundraising banquet, but she still couldn't get him out of her head.

"Aw, how sweet." Rachelle giggled, typing into her phone. "Someone has a crush! Well, what does he look like?"

"Drop-dead gorgeous," she admitted. "He's tall, muscular. Black hair, bright blue eyes. I've never seen eyes that color before."

What she didn't say was that he reminded her of a fallen angel, carved in shadow and sullen light. Or how that same evening, she had lain awake for the longest time, unable to get his face out of her head.

"You should've taken a picture of him," Rachelle said.

"I wish I did. I don't even have his number."

Rachelle paused. "You said his name was Hades, right?"

"Yeah."

"So, according to Google, Hades is basically, like, the god of hell in Greek mythology, or whatever."

"I know."

"Why would he have a nickname like that? Don't you think that's a little weird, Elizabeth? I mean, it's like calling yourself Satan. Hashtag let's not meet."

She shrugged. "I guess."

"For all you know, he might be an assassin! Like in *Kill Bill*!"

Elizabeth laughed. "You think he's going to target my father?"

"Just think about it. I mean, it makes sense with a name like that."

"Maybe it's an inside joke."

Rachelle sighed. "That's so unimaginative! Where's your creativity?"

"School killed it," she said gravely.

"Ugh, tell me about it."

Elizabeth stepped into the front courtyard and followed Rachelle to the parking lot. It was empty, save for a few cars and a loitering motorcyclist.

"Sure you don't want me to drive you home?" Rachelle asked.

"It's fine." She took out her phone to check the time. "Thomas should be here any minute now."

Not only were her parents strict about her dress code, but they also forbade her from driving with her friends. She didn't even have her driver's license yet because her parents were paranoid there would be another crash. She had a feeling they were more afraid of a potential scandal than anything else, like they thought she would go for a drunken joyride and run down some nuns and preschoolers. As a result, she was chauffeured around by Thomas, her family's driver and aide.

"See you Saturday!" Rachelle said.

Elizabeth sat down at one of the benches and watched Rachelle drive away. She sent a quick text to Thomas, letting him know she was waiting out front.

Looking at the cars, she thought about how much she wished she could drive. Then her gaze drifted to the motorcyclist, and a tremor of unease oozed down her spine.

Dressed all in black, the rider wore a helmet that covered his entire face. The ruddy sunlight reflected off the mirrored visor, making it seem as though his helmet was filled with blood.

Elizabeth sensed he was staring at her.

She looked away from him, worried that maintaining eye contact would be an invitation for him to approach her. Even as she turned her head, she reproached herself for being so paranoid. He was probably another student waiting for his girlfriend to get out of a club or sports practice.

After a couple seconds, she glanced at the motorcyclist again.

The man hadn't moved. He was just sitting there. His visor made it impossible to tell if he was looking at her or just in her general direction.

Underneath his tight leather jacket, the motorcyclist's shoulders were broad enough to belong to a grown man. He wore no backpack, but maybe it was inside the storage compartment on the tail of the bike. Or maybe he wasn't a student at all. With his entire body concealed, it was impossible to estimate his age.

Suddenly, a hand fell on her shoulder.

With a gasp, Elizabeth shot to her feet and swiveled around.

"Hey, it's just me," Coach Slate said, lowering her hand. "What's the matter? You look like you've seen a ghost."

She sighed. "No, it's just that motorcycle guy."

Coach Slate frowned. "Who?"

She jerked her head toward the man on the bike. "He just, um, kind of makes me nervous. I've never seen him here before."

"I see." Coach Slate pursed her lips, furrowing her eyebrows. "Whoever he is, I'm going to have a word with him. He shouldn't be loitering around after school hours."

As Coach Slate stepped onto the asphalt, the rev of an engine ripped through the air. The motorcyclist turned out of the parking lot and sped down the street. Within seconds, he was gone.

...

When Elizabeth was dropped off at school the next morning, she spotted the same motorcyclist parked among the zoo of cars.

It was unusually warm out for October, and he must have been hot just sitting there. His leather jacket was slung across the bike's top case. With his muscular arms exposed, he seemed more menacing than before, his black T-shirt tight against his chiseled chest.

While it wasn't unusual for students to loiter in their cars or mill around the courtyard before first bell, he didn't seem like he was just killing time. It was like he was waiting for someone.

Waiting for her.

She wondered what Dr. Kosta would have to say about that thought. He would probably call it something like "disordered thinking" and increase the dosage of her medicine, even though she was already taking a cocktail of drugs he had prescribed her.

Deciding to confront her paranoia head-on, she put on a forced smile and approached the motorcyclist.

She had taken no more than five steps before the man got off his bike and came to her. Even at a relaxed walk, he moved with a powerful, almost predatory grace. Ink marked his inner forearms, but she was too far away to discern the nature of his tattoos.

Elizabeth slipped her hand into her pocket, curling her fingers around the ring that held her bicycle, house, and locker keys. Her heart pounded in her chest, swift and jarring. She had the sudden urge to flee to the safety of the school building.

As the man walked, he kept his right arm held still at his waist, while allowing his left arm a more natural range of motion. This quirk struck her as familiar, but she didn't understand why until he reached up and took his helmet off.

"Hello, Elizabeth Hawthorne," Hades said pleasantly.

"Are you *stalking* me?" she demanded.

His perfect lips quirked in amusement. "Stalking?"

"You were here yesterday."

"Oh."

"Don't try to deny it."

"Yesterday, I had a meeting with Principal Brown," he said, and his smile grew. "I'm thinking about enrolling here actually."

While it didn't strike her as implausible that Mr. Brown might stay after hours for student meetings, she had trouble believing Hades.

"But why were you just sitting there?" she asked.

"I don't like to drive while I'm distracted," he said. "I had a lot on my mind, so I decided to sit for a while. I wasn't even sure that was you."

"Where were your parents?" she asked, following him to the safety of the sidewalk.

"I'm emancipated," he said, tucking his helmet under his arm.

Elizabeth didn't know what he meant by that. She had a feeling it had nothing to do with the Emancipation Proclamation she had learned about in her American history class.

Hades must have sensed her confusion, because he smiled and said, "I don't live with my parents anymore. I'm seventeen, but I'm considered legally independent. It's really not something I'd like to discuss in public."

"Oh. I'm sorry. I shouldn't have asked."

"My grandparents left me a large trust fund, so I thought I should apply it to my education. Do you know how many of this school's alumni have gotten into Ivy League schools and gone on to become ambassadors, senators, supreme court judges, and even presidents? This place is practically a breeding ground for them."

So he wanted to be a politician. Maybe he had sneaked into the fundraising banquet because he had believed it would be a good opportunity to make connections with governmental leaders. Had he talked to her simply because she was the daughter of a state senator?

"Anyway, I came by to drop off some paperwork. Transcripts mostly." Hades smirked at her. "Now, if you're done interrogating me, can I ask what *you* were doing at school so late?"

"Volleyball practice." Elizabeth looked down at the tattoos on his arms. "You know, tattoos are against school policy."

"Good. I'll just cut off my arms, then."

She laughed. "They're probably going to ask you to cover them up. You're also going to need a uniform."

He glanced at his all-black attire. "This *is* a uniform."

"Of course it is." She took a closer look at the tally marks on his left forearm and saw that the skin around one of the lines was slightly irritated. "Wait, you got a new one?"

"Yeah. A couple days ago."

"Why?"

Hades shrugged. "It helps me remember."

"Remember what?"

"Everything." He ran a finger across the mark. "Life. I have a bad short-term memory sometimes, so this is a mnemonic device I use to fill in the gaps."

"If you keep using tattoos to remember things, someday your whole arm's going to be covered in them," she pointed out.

"Probably."

"You're not the only one with memory problems," she confessed, surprising herself with her forwardness.

"Really?" His intense blue eyes regarded her with interest, and a touch of a smile stroked his lips.

She decided that now wasn't the time to tell him about her car crash, so instead she backtracked with a white lie. "I mean, I forget things, too. Like, I can't remember what I ate for lunch yesterday."

"I think I might have a way to help you with that," Hades said.

"How so?"

"Let's go out for lunch Saturday. That way, if you forget what you ate, I can remember for you."

She giggled. "You go in right for the kill, huh?"

"Oh, Elizabeth, you don't even know. So, what do you say?"

She almost responded with an automatic yes, but then remembered her plans with Rachelle.

"I'm going Halloween shopping with a friend, but we can meet beforehand," she said. "Do you have a place in mind?"

"Depends. What are you craving?"

She had a feeling that Hades didn't have much money to spare on frivolous things, in spite of his trust fund. While his clothes were clean and fit well, they weren't designer brands. He wore a cheap wristwatch with a cracked face, and his tactical boots were creased and well-scuffed, though polished to a glossy finish.

She didn't want to suggest a restaurant that wasn't in his budget. Besides, it would be fun to go somewhere super casual and pretend to be someone else for once.

"Hamburgers," she said.

"Hamburgers," he repeated, smirking in amusement. "I was expecting something like Italian or sushi."

"No, I want a big, greasy, artery-clogging hamburger."

"Your wish is my command, Miss Hawthorne."

"There's a place called Reggie's," Elizabeth said. "It's in Adams Morgan, on 18th Street."

She had never eaten at Reggie's, but she had heard from friends that the hamburgers there were to die for. It was the kind of cheap, retro establishment her father wouldn't be caught dead in. The perfect place for a casual first date.

"How does eleven o'clock sound?" he asked.

"Perfect."

Hades took out his cell phone. Once again, she was struck by the phone's simplicity. She doubted it even had an internet connection. How could he survive without an iPhone?

"What's your number?" he asked. "I'll text you later."

She told him.

Before they could continue their conversation, the bell rang. Her heart sank at the sound.

"I need to go to class," Elizabeth said, wishing she could talk to him some more. She was tempted to risk her perfect attendance for another few minutes, but in the Hawthorne house, a single tardy warranted grounding.

"I know," he murmured.

As he turned toward the parking lot, she reached out and grabbed his hand. He looked back, a flicker of surprise racing across his features.

"This is a nice school, so you really should enroll here," she said, giving his hand a gentle squeeze.

"We'll see how it goes."

"Bye, Hades."

"Good-bye, Elizabeth."

She looked back as she passed through the gate and found him standing where she had left him, helmet in hand. Even with the sunlight bright upon his face, coldness had drifted over his features. He was no longer smiling, and his eyes were narrowed ever so slightly.

An inexplicable disquiet swept over her at the sight of him. His face was like a lovely mask, and she sensed something lurked behind it. Something hateful and unforgiving.

Then the anxiety passed, leaving her feeling embarrassed and ridiculous. Why would she think such a thing?

As she made eye contact, a radiant smile spread across his lips, and he lifted a hand in a wave.

Elizabeth found it surprisingly difficult to smile back.

CORRESPONDENCE RETRIEVED FROM P.W.'S HOME. TARGET TERMINATED.

Dear Phil,

Please keep what I am about to tell you between us. If this message falls into the wrong hands, I fear that it will mean the end for both of us.

Project Pandora is the brainchild of three people: Charles Warren, Dr. Francine Miller, and Dr. Eric Finch. I believe that Dr. Finch is dead. He had an unfortunate boating "accident" off the coast of Maine six months ago, and his body was never recovered. However, I know for a fact that the other two are still very much alive.

Francine Miller lives in Colorado, near the Academy. She and Finch invented the artificial wombs that the Project's children were produced in. As for Charles Warren, he is still a mystery to me. He is the one who provided the initial funds for the Project, and over the years he has played an active role in raising the children. I have tried to learn more about him, but his true identity continues to elude me. I suspect his name is a pseudonym.

In your earlier correspondence, you asked me for records detailing the gestation process to accompany the photographs in your article. While I haven't been able to acquire any records as of yet, I can give you a detailed description of what will one day become the first chapter of my autobiography. You have my permission to include this following section in your article.

But first, to answer your previous question, the vast majority of the embryos were acquired illegally. The Project has ties to multiple IVF and infertility clinics across the country, whose names I will provide you as soon as I can find them. They selected the embryos based on the parents' profiles, with race, education, and health history playing a large role in determining donors. The donor criteria was, and still is, just as stringent as the *Lebensborn* program that inspired the Project. Only the cream of the crop were chosen, which is ironic, considering how many of the children have begun displaying sociopathic and suicidal tendencies.

In some rare cases, members of the organization have also contributed their own children. Francine Miller is one in particular. Her son was among the first to be born into Project Pandora, and I fear the progeny is as twisted as his mother, but that is a story for another time.

Now, for the prenatal ward. I would like you to visualize a large room that is 120 feet long by 40 feet wide. The floor and walls are covered in white tile. There are no windows.

Spaced within several feet from one another are the artificial wombs. There are twenty at this time, although they are not always in use. Though the Project began eighteen years ago, space and funding limitations have kept the Academy's population in the low hundreds.

The artificial womb resembles an industrial pressure cooker—a cylindrical steel chamber. There is a camera on the inside of the container, but I am afraid you'll be able to see very little through the cultured amnion, just a throbbing stew of veins, membranous tissue, and amniotic fluid.

The sealed compartment is kept in perfect equilibrium. Sensors on the fiberglass interior scaffold monitor the conditions inside the chamber and continuously feed stats into the Academy's mainframe.

If one of the fetuses expires, it is removed from the vat for dissection. Samples of the amniotic fluid and cultured placental tissue are harvested for further study, and after being thoroughly sanitized, the machine itself is carefully examined for any structural flaws or worn-down parts. This is not an unnecessary precaution. We have lost thirty fetuses due to mechanical errors in the last five years.

Seventy percent of the embryos selected for the Project are male, just another part of the profile. It has been decided that once both genders in the first generation reach maturity, sex cells will be harvested from the prime specimens to provide for a second generation. In that sense, the Project's supply of future subjects will be limitless.

Twenty more wombs are currently being designed. There are slightly over 300 children so far, most of them in their teens. Charles Warren hopes to reach the 600 milestone within the next ten years.

More information will follow. I have been asked to speak at the 45th annual bioethics conference in Philadelphia, and I must prepare.

Until then,

Benjamin Klausman, MD

CASE NOTES 7: HADES

As night fell over Washington, D.C., four visitors gathered in the game room of the Georgetown safe house. The men laughed and jostled elbows. The single female in attendance—a tall, imposing woman whose ink-black hair was fashioned into a loose bun—sat at the poker table, regarding her ebony cigarette holder in stiff silence.

As Dimitri greeted the four guests, Hades leaned against the wall with his arms crossed. His gaze swept from the men to the single woman. Her face was vaguely familiar, and he wondered if he had met her before, perhaps during a former gathering. He had a poor short-term memory, and there were massive chunks missing from his long-term memory, so it was impossible to say for sure.

"So, is this a child of Pandora?" a man asked, glancing at him. He had thinning brown hair and protruding eyes magnified behind thick glasses. He reminded Hades of a man he had once bludgeoned to death with a crowbar.

"Yes, but I'm afraid he's a failure," Dimitri said, chuckling as he dealt out the first round of cards. "Unsuitable for the Project."

The woman looked at Hades. Her striking blue eyes narrowed, and a wisp of smoke curled from her lips. "Dima, I believe the term you are looking for is outlier, not failure. In spite of his shortcomings, A-02 is still of great value to Project Pandora. He dealt with the rat in Philadelphia, did he not?"

"He did," Dimitri said, his smile thinning. Hades knew he hated being called "Dima," and judging by the way the woman had emphasized the nickname, she must have known it, too.

"And he has taken care of many other traitors and nuisances, correct?" The woman took a drag of her cigarette, paused, and exhaled. "Remind me, what is his exact kill count?"

"Eighteen."

"Outlier," she repeated, punctuating her statement with a nod of her long cigarette holder.

"Forgive me, Francine, I forgot how attached you feel to *the Project's* children," Dimitri said drily.

She regarded him with cold eyes. "You'd be wise to watch your tongue. I don't care much for your tone of voice."

"Speaking of children, they grow up so fast," said the man with the bulging eyes, reaching into his pocket. He took out his wallet and showed the table a photograph in the billfold. His swollen cheeks flushed with paternal pride. "Andrew is turning twelve in November."

"Let's change the subject," Francine said tersely.

Listening to the conversation, Hades felt nothing at all. He could not imagine what it was like to have a mother and father or why children were loved by their parents. The idea of a family was an abstract concept to him, something he'd read about in books but that didn't exist in real life.

Dimitri had told him once about the circumstances of his birth. His conception had been sexless, initiated in a petri dish, while his gestation was similarly impersonal. He had never known a mother's love or a father's paternal touch. He didn't even know the names of his cell donors.

As the men and the woman played poker over drinks, Hades stood afar. He knew how to play, but he didn't join in. Or rather, he wasn't permitted to.

He didn't care. How could these people derive pleasure from

something as insignificant as a card game?

Usually, he found some entertainment in watching the guests' impassive faces, learning the subtle cues that betrayed their thoughts and, in doing so, calculating the possible outcomes of each hand. Tonight, his mind went to Elizabeth Hawthorne.

In his mind's eye, he saw her face as clearly as if she were actually there. His fingers craved to close around a pen or paintbrush and turn his vision into a reality. He had drawn her twice already, destroying each sketch after he had finished so that Dimitri wouldn't find it.

Even then, his drawings were only shallow depictions of the real thing. No matter how many times he drew her features, he would never be able to endow his work with the warmth that radiated from her lovely smiles. He couldn't capture her musical laughter on flat, unfeeling paper, let alone the gentleness of her touch.

He curled his hand into a fist, remembering how soft Elizabeth's fingers had felt when they had briefly closed around his wrist. Such lovely fingers, and so delicate, too. She was unsullied by the filth of the outside world. She didn't belong in this stinking cesspool of a city, but he could easily envision her surrounded by the verdant splendor of the forest. He wanted to take her there someday, to one of those quiet spots he hiked when he had no missions to complete. Would she feel at peace under the forest canopy, the way he always did?

"Dimitri, why don't you have the boy join us the next round?" a man said, catching Hades's attention. His dark hair was shorn to military shortness, and one of his hazel eyes was a slightly different color than the other. Hades had a feeling it was a prosthesis.

"Two doesn't know how to play," Dimitri said, for whenever Hades was in the company of others from the Project, he was again reduced to a number. A weapon must not have a name.

"I know a bit, sir," he said.

"Dogs shouldn't sit at the table," another man said and laughed. This one was tall and blond, with a fine-featured face that was marred by a scowl when it wasn't twisted into a sneer.

"Let's give Two a chance," said the man with the false eye.

"I'm not covering him, Christian," Dimitri said.

"I will," Christian said, smiling.

"Your loss."

"If you haven't managed to fry his brain, I think he should do quite well," Christian said, with a hint of condescension.

A place was made for him, and as Hades sat, he felt almost certain the people were laughing at him. Not on the outside, but on the inside. Mocking him the same way others dressed up their pets in people clothes.

"One thousand should do," Christian said, and, as Dimitri stiffly handed Hades a pile of chips, explained each color's monetary value and the rules of the game itself.

Francine watched them with subdued interest, in silence.

"Do you remember me?" Christian asked, after he had finished explaining.

"Should I?"

"I teach military logistics at the Academy. You were one of my students."

He shrugged to avoid having to tell Christian that his memory of the Academy was largely anecdotal, told to him by other people. Every so often, he would recall fragments detached from context. The memories were like unlit ships passing each other in the night, just a brief presence that was gone before he knew it.

The cards were dealt. Hades picked up his hand and gave it a cursory glance. He looked around the table, gauging the group's reactions to their cards.

Blondie wrinkled his elfin nose ever so slightly. Poor hand.

Dimitri stroked the mole on his chin. Decent to good.

Francine's eyes flickered to her right then back again, and

she nibbled on the silver tip of her cigarette holder. Likely, she had a very good hand.

From the other two men, Hades was able to make similar inferences. Eye contact improved or lessened, pupils dilated, wrinkles formed, fingers moved, and the facial muscles flexed in minute contortions. All cues.

He felt no need to maintain a poker face, because a cold expression was his default. He didn't care what his hand was, and the thought of earning money meant nothing to him because he had no real desire for material objects. Just like everything else in his life, this was simply a way to kill time.

He folded on the first round. Christian offered him a cigarette, which he accepted out of politeness and took a few drags before grinding it out in the ashtray. He hated smoking, and the smell of cigarette smoke bothered him for a reason he couldn't explain. Then again, so did the odors of cloves, antiseptic solution, and Epsom salt.

He won the second round, adding three hundred dollars to his pile.

"Beginner's luck," Blondie growled.

Hades felt a subtle satisfaction at the man's displeasure. After that point, he began playing to win. By the sixth round, he had tripled his earnings. It was all just a number to him.

Blondie threw down his cards and lurched to his feet. "This game is rigged. The kid's counting cards or something."

He looked up at the man and favored him with a warm smile. "How does it feel to lose to a dog?"

"You little bastard! I refuse to be treated with such disrespect by the likes of you!" He swiveled toward Dimitri. "Control your subject."

Dimitri glanced toward Hades, his cold gray eyes narrowing into slits.

In an instant, he realized he had crossed the line.

"Heel," Dimitri said, gesturing toward him with the hand

that held a cigarette.

Hades placed down his cards and rose to his feet. As he walked around the table, anger seethed through him, but he restrained it. His smile thinned into an impassive line.

"Take your shirt off."

He pulled off his shirt and clenched it in his fists, twisting it into a noose. The air conditioner breathed coldly against his bare back. In a way, he felt more exposed than if he had been ordered to strip from the waist down. Everyone could see his mark now.

Sitting next to Dimitri, Francine stiffened.

"As you can see, he has a history of being disobedient," Dimitri said, chuckling. "It takes a little pain to get him to behave."

"Is that Charles Warren's work?" the blond man asked, amused.

"Yes, a souvenir from the Academy," Dimitri said, then looked at Hades. "Two, get down on your hands and knees."

He loathed having to humble himself before the man, but it was necessary to maintain this charade of servitude. The moment he disobeyed an order, Dimitri would realize he was the one in control.

And yet, he didn't move. He didn't want to debase himself in front of everyone.

"I said get on your knees," Dimitri said.

He sank to his knees and looked at the pattern in the rug. His fingers dug into the wool fibers, and he clenched his teeth. He didn't feel powerful anymore. He didn't feel like he was evolving but regressing into a rudimentary beast.

"This will make as good an ashtray as any," Dimitri said, and Hades sensed a presence looming over him. "It's already ruined anyway."

A sharp pain flared on his back as Dimitri snubbed out a cigarette against his skin. The harsh odors of tobacco smoke and burnt flesh filled his nostrils.

The breath hissed through his gritted teeth. Didn't matter.

No shame. This body. This body was just a corpse. Meaningless.

Losing himself in the rug's pattern, he pulled an image of Elizabeth Hawthorne from his memory. Her radiant smile filled his mind, and the throbbing pain soothed into a mellow stinging. The colors drained from the woven carpet, and everything turned gray and hazy. He stayed where he was, on his hands and knees, feeling his consciousness recede into a distant part of himself. Apathy took over.

"Go ahead, John," Dimitri said. "You look like you could use a new cigarette."

"Enough," Francine growled, and from far away, Hades heard her chair scrape against the hardwood floor. "You have already proven his obedience, Dima. And as for you, John, might I remind you that referring to A-02 as a dog is a callous affront to his cell donors and the dignity of the Project as a whole? We are not raising animals. We are raising future leaders who will return this country to its former splendor, and while A-02 is an outlier among his peers, he deserves to be treated with respect. Do I make myself clear?"

A stunned silence filled the room. Hades couldn't imagine what they were so surprised about. He stared at Francine's feet, which was really all he could see of her with his head bowed. He wondered if she realized she had a run in her black nylons. Maybe he should point it out to her.

"Get up," Dimitri said, sounding slightly less jovial than before.

Hades climbed to his feet.

"It was simply a demonstration, Francine," Dimitri said, rising as well. "No offense was intended."

"Of course not," Francine said, then turned to Hades. "May I see your back?"

He hated it when people stared at his bare back, but he did as he was asked, turning around so that she might get a better look. He sensed her presence directly behind him, and a moment later felt her kidskin glove press against his skin, not on the wound but near it.

"This is second-degree. He's going to scar."

"Do you see him?" Dimitri asked snidely. "It will be a drop in the bucket compared to everything else."

"I don't appreciate your tongue," Francine said. "Though you have been with us for five years now, you are still a newcomer to the Project, and perhaps your position has given you a false sense of security. Regardless of what you might call yourself when you're with your subjects, you are not at the top of the pantheon, *Zeus*."

"Speaking of the pantheon, I think it's time we discuss why we've gathered here," John said, finishing the rest of his rum and slamming the tumbler on the table's felt liner. "Charles Warren needs to go. He's led the Academy for long enough, and it has stagnated under his command. We continue to get violent, unruly children like *this*"—he gestured toward Hades—"when we need children who can become capable and obedient leaders."

"Finally, a voice of reason," Christian said merrily, taking a sip of his martini.

"He won't step down willingly," Francine said. "We would need to get rid of his followers, too."

"I realize that," John said. "That's why we need—"

Suddenly, John collapsed to the floor and began convulsing. Bloody foam bulged from his pallid lips, and his eyes rolled back in his head. Gurgling, agonized moans tore from his throat as his entire body twisted in torturous contortions.

Francine stood over John. As his writhing weakened into jerky shudders, she squatted down and clasped his chin in her hand, looking into his eyes. Ruddy foam drizzled down the sides of his face, flecking on her black kidskin glove.

"Drinking kills, Johnny," she said aloofly, cigarette smoke wafting from her lips. "'A woman will never survive in this organization.' Isn't that what you told me once? But you seem to have forgotten something. I *am* the Project."

Christian sipped his martini as John gave one last shudder then went still. The man with the bulging eyes simply sat there, staring at John's body the way a frog would observe a tasty fly.

Dimitri's reaction was by far the most severe. Mouth agape, he pressed a hand against his chest, looking halfway to a heart attack.

Hades didn't feel much of anything. He wondered if he might be dead, too.

Releasing John's chin, Francine straightened her legs and nudged his body with the toe of her stiletto heel. She flicked cigarette ashes in his wide, unblinking eyes, then glanced at Dimitri to witness his shocked expression. "This is why I called this meeting an intervention. Now, I'll let you take care of the mess while I get A-02 cleaned up." Her voice was cool and authoritarian. Her cold demeanor demanded respect and complete and utter submission.

"Understood," Dimitri said, with none of his former snark. His thin lips puckered into a strange grimace unlike any expression that Hades had ever seen twist his face before. Cool.

Francine gave a flippant wave of her cigarette holder, ushering Hades to follow. As they walked out of the game room and down the hall, he saw a familiar bulge under the woman's blazer. She was wearing a holster.

"Has he done this to you before?" she asked, glancing in his direction.

"Do you know that you have a run in your tights, ma'am?" he asked. It had been annoying him ever since he had noticed it.

"Excuse me?" Francine glanced downward and scowled, then looked back at him. "Thank you for pointing that out, but is this your way of avoiding the question?"

"No, it was just distracting me," he said. "To answer your question, I don't know."

"You don't know?"

"Not for sure. I have scars that I don't know how I've gotten. But pain...pain is something that I have become very intimate with during my stay here. And this? It's nothing at all."

"I see."

Francine took him to the catering kitchen and removed a first aid kit from the pantry. After washing her hands and donning a pair of latex gloves, she cleaned the ash from the wound.

As she worked, Hades rested his hands on the counter and stared through the window at the dark sky. The Orionid meteor shower was at its peak tonight, but the city lights blocked it out. He would have liked to take Elizabeth up north, far from D.C.'s light pollution, to watch the meteors with him. He thought she would like them. Maybe another time.

After sanitizing the burn, Francine applied an antibacterial ointment. Then she bandaged it with a square of gauze.

"Are you a doctor?" he asked, finding it curious that she seemed to know exactly what she was doing.

"I once was, but not like Dimitri. I used to be an obstetrician, a doctor who delivers babies, but then I found a...different calling in synthetic biology."

"I don't know what that is, ma'am," he said, turning around to look at her.

"It's you."

CASE NOTES 8: ARTEMIS

Sitting at her desk, Shannon tried to complete her homework but couldn't focus. Her mind kept running off. Her thoughts floated away like smoke.

Her gaze wandered from her mathematics worksheet to the rock band posters on the wall, then drifted to the window. Staring at the brick row houses on the other side of the street, she found herself thinking about Tyler Bennett. His stunning amber eyes filled her mind. She thought about the sparse dusting of hairs on his muscular arms, the way the sunlight caught them and made them gleam like gold shavings.

Aside from being drop-dead gorgeous, there was just something so *intriguing* about him. She couldn't shake the feeling that he had many secrets, and that underneath his calm, friendly exterior, a whole other layer of him was just waiting to be uncovered.

She wondered what he was doing on a Friday night like this. Were his foster parents nice like hers were? Did he have a girlfriend?

Taking out her smartphone, she perused the texts they had sent each other since the party at Alan's house. She read over their latest conversation.

Shannon: This is going to sound really weird, but I dreamed about you last night.

Tyler: Oh really? Was it at least a good one? ;)

Shannon: LOL. Not that kind of dream.

Tyler: But not a nightmare, right?

Shannon: Nope. We were just driving, and then you started apologizing for some reason.

Tyler: Hmm.

Shannon: What?

Tyler: I want to take you on a drive now. ;)

Shannon: ☹ I have an English paper due tomorrow, but maybe another day.

Tyler hadn't replied after that. Worried that her response had come across as dismissive, she dialed the number he had given her.

As she listened to the phone ring, her courage fled her. Before she could end the call, someone picked up.

"Hello?" Tyler's voice sounded slightly hoarse, as if he had just woken up. She liked its roughness.

"It's me," she said, leaning back in her chair. "Shannon Evans."

"Oh, how's it going?"

"Good. Just working on the Chaucer essay for Mr. Prickton's class. Hopefully I'll finish it tonight." As soon as Shannon said it, she winced. Why couldn't she have come up with a wittier response?

"Mr. Prickton?" he asked, sounding baffled.

Realizing that their teacher's notorious nickname hadn't spread to him yet, she cleared her throat. "Mr. Preston, I mean."

"What are you doing it on?"

"'Wife of Bath,'" she said. "What about you?"

"'The Miller's Tale.'"

"By the way, thank you for texting me the study questions," she said, leaning back in her chair.

"It's no problem at all."

"I mean it. You're a lifesaver."

"If you really want to thank me, how about letting me take

you on a date?"

Shannon found herself at a loss for words, certain she had heard him wrong.

"Hello?" Tyler said.

"I'm still here," she said, clearing her throat. "It sounds great."

"Good. How does tomorrow around eleven sound?"

She glanced at her laptop, where a few measly paragraphs of *The Canterbury Tales* confronted her. "I'm free then."

"Great. You know where Reggie's is, over in Adams Morgan?"

"Oh, yeah, it's that burger place on 18th Street, right?" she asked, rising to her feet. She walked over to the wire cage on her dresser and poked a finger through the bars, trying to coax out her pet rat, Snowflake, from his cardboard tube. He scurried forward and seized her finger in his tiny paws.

"Yeah, well, there's a really good Mexican restaurant right across from Reggie's," Tyler said. "You know the one I'm talking about?"

"Yeah, I've been there before," she said, petting the rat's head. "They have great enchiladas."

"Cool. I'll see you there."

Saturday morning, Shannon took the metro to Woodley Park Station. The subway train was packed to capacity, and she found herself wedged uncomfortably between a woman screaming expletives into her cell phone and a bearded, disheveled man who reeked of urine and booze.

As she tried to put some distance between herself and the unsavory pair, a young commuter made eye contact with her. At once, she was struck by the intensity of his blue eyes—and the sense of déjà vu she experienced as he smiled at her.

"You can have my seat if you'd like," the teen said, standing.

He was beautiful but very pale, as if he spent most of his time in the dark. He had his cell phone out, though he did not appear to be using it.

"Thanks," Shannon said and took the boy up on his offer.

"You're welcome." He grasped hold of the pole next to her. "It's funny seeing you here."

"What?" she asked, glancing at him again.

His face suddenly unsettled her. There was something cold and feral about his features, a cruelness of sorts that made him seem remote. Untouchable. So unlike Tyler.

Her smile faded by a degree, while his smile only widened.

"Did you see my work on the TV?" The dark-haired boy leaned closer, asserting himself into her personal space. He smelled faintly of burning mesquite, or something else scorched and fire-devoured. "See, Artemis? I told you I could hit a target from five hundred meters away."

He almost sounded like he was gloating about an accomplishment of his, although she couldn't figure out what the hell he was talking about.

"I think you're mistaking me for someone else," Shannon said, already regretting her decision to place herself in such a position of vulnerability.

"Oh, I thought you were yourself now." The boy stepped back to give her some room. "It's Shannon, right?"

"Uh, yeah…and you are?" She didn't recognize him from school. How did he know her name?

"Hades," he said, like he expected her to know who he was.

Hades, as in the Greek god. Considering how he had just called her Artemis, she highly doubted that Hades was his real name.

"I'm sorry, but have we met before?" she asked, feeling her heart thrum nervously.

"You know, I really hate how everybody always forgets me. You, him—it's like I'm not real. It makes me feel like I don't even exist." For a moment, his expression seemed chilly, angered. Then he smiled, and somehow that was worse. It was a predatory expression, without warmth or kindness. "I don't think Elizabeth will *ever* forget me, though. We're going on a date today. I've been wondering, do you think she'll like flowers?"

"Uh…"

"You're a girl," Hades said. "You should know. If you were going on a date, would you want flowers? Isn't that how people usually show their affection?"

"I guess?" she said, counting down the seconds until this metro ride from hell would end. She wasn't a flowers and chocolates kind of girl, but neither was she ready to get into a discussion about dating with this weirdo.

The train lurched to a stop at Woodley Park Station, and she rose to her feet.

"My stop," she said, then regretted saying it.

Hades blinked. "Oh. It's mine, too."

Her unease heightened into a powerful foreboding. Without saying another word, she shouldered past the black-haired boy and made a beeline for the door. She followed the flood of commuters onto the concrete platform, into the clammy atmosphere of the massive subterranean room. The ceiling curved overhead like a rib cage, leaving her feeling consumed and digested.

She walked at a swift, determined gait, refusing to allow her paranoia to spur her into a panic. Besides, if Hades *was* stalking her, showing fear would only excite him.

When she reached the escalators leading to the upper subterranean level of the station, she casually glanced over her shoulder. He was nowhere in sight. Maybe he had lied about getting off at this stop.

Nearing the exit, she retrieved her fare card from her purse, gripping it so tightly that the plastic edge bit into her palm. Even after stepping through the turnstile, she still felt trapped and hunted, hyperaware of the packed earth above her head. It was almost like being buried alive.

As she took an escalator up to street level, she checked her phone to see if Tyler had texted her. Nothing yet.

"Shannon!" someone called as she emerged into the sunlight.

She flinched at the sound of her name, only to spot Tyler standing just outside the glass-and-metal canopy that sheltered the metro entrance. With a sigh of relief, she stepped off the escalator and hurried over to him.

"I can't tell you how glad I am to see you," she said once she reached his side.

"It's mutual." He grinned, exposing those adorable dimples of his. Compared to Hades, he was all warmth, both in his bronzed complexion and the kindness of his expression. Even his cologne's citrusy aroma had a far more welcoming effect on her, soothing rather than unsettling her.

"Hey, can you tell me if some guy's following me?" she asked, lowering her voice. "He's around our age. Black hair, blue eyes. Dressed all in black."

Tyler's smile faded, and he looked past her. "You mean the guy who looks like he's never heard of a comb? The one in the leather jacket?"

"Yeah."

"He's smiling at us." Tyler's hands tightened into fists, and his clenched jaw cut hard lines in his face. "Did he do anything to you?"

"No, he was just talking weird on the subway," Shannon muttered. "About flowers and dating and stuff."

His face paled with anger. "Was he sexually harassing you?"

"No. I don't know." She shook her head. "It's probably nothing."

"He's coming over here," Tyler said, and his dark, gold-flecked eyes narrowed dangerously. He placed a hand on her wrist. "Let me deal with this."

She turned to find Hades approaching them. In spite of the boy's calm gait, every movement of his seemed intentional, almost trained. No unnecessary energy was exerted, and his right arm lingered at his side, steady.

To reduce the time it takes to reach his gun, she thought, surprising herself. Of all the theories she could come up with, why would she assume that?

"Hello again," Hades said warmly, looking from Tyler to her. "Why are you two together? This can't be a coincidence. Is this a test or something? Are you doing a job?"

Every time his incandescent blue eyes fell on her, her gut squirmed in discomfort. She was almost certain now that she had talked to him before, but she couldn't remember where.

"I heard you were harassing my friend here," Tyler growled, stepping forward. "Are you stalking her?"

Hades chuckled. "You know, you're the second person this week who's accused me of being a stalker."

"Shocking," he said drily.

"I guess this means you're Tyler Bennett now."

A hint of confusion showed through Tyler's scowl. "How do you know my name?"

Hades grinned, visibly amused. "Who ever said that's your name, Apollo?"

The air thickened with tension. At six feet tall, Tyler had a couple inches on the other boy, but what Hades lacked in height, he made up for in muscularity. Shannon also sensed that while Tyler would probably fight fair, Hades would attack with the brutality of a wild animal, biting and gouging if it meant gaining an upper hand.

"Look, you need to go or there's going to be trouble," Tyler said.

"Everyone always goes, and I always stay. But this is nice. We're all together again. It's like how it was before." Though Hades's smile remained bright and ever present, a note of profound loneliness wove its way through the low, rolling timbre of his voice. By his next sentence, it was gone. "I wish we could talk longer, but I have a date soon and I need to find a flower shop. Maybe we can talk later. I'd like to go hunting with you two again."

Before either of them could respond, Hades walked past them. He crossed the street and passed under the shade of a tree planted along the sidewalk, dead leaves crunching beneath his boots. Within seconds, he had disappeared into the crowd.

"Did he call you Apollo?" she asked, turning to Tyler.

"What was that about?" he wondered.

"The hell if I know." She crossed her arms.

"Does he go to our school?"

"I guess."

Tyler sighed and ran a hand through his thick blond hair. A smile touched his lips as he looked down at her. "Anyway, are you still game for Mexican or do you feel like going somewhere else?"

"You kidding?" She grinned. "I'd kill for some enchiladas right now."

As they walked down Calvert Street in the direction of the Mexican restaurant, she allowed her gaze to wander over storefront windows. The area featured an impressive hodgepodge of foreign cuisines to choose from, and signs advertised everything from French pastries to Greek gyros to Korean barbecue. Scattered among the restaurants were other small businesses, but none held much interest to her.

"How long have you been friends with Alan?" she asked, glancing at Tyler. He walked with his hands shoved in his pockets and his shoulders thrust forward, as if ready to confront the world.

"Just a couple months," he said. "I transferred schools back in August. I know he's not the greatest guy."

"He's totally obnoxious." She rolled her eyes and began mimicking Alan's stoner drawl: "Hey, how's it going, bruh? You wanna smoke some dank weed, bro-ski?"

He chuckled. "That's impressive. You sound just like him."

"Thanks."

"Anyway, I didn't know anyone when I came here, so our friendship kind of just happened. Now I can't get rid of him."

"Where did you go to school before—" Before Shannon could finish her question, she bumped into another young woman. Shannon's purse fell to the sidewalk and burst open, barfing out cosmetics, change, and an assortment of other items.

"Oh my God, I'm so sorry," the blond girl said, bending down to clean up the spill.

"It's okay. I should've been paying more attention." As Shannon snagged a handful of loose dollar bills before they could fly away, Tyler and the girl helped gather the other objects. She winced in embarrassment when he handed her a couple of tampons. Great way to start a first date.

"Oh, no," the blonde said, picking up a crushed eye shadow palette. Silvery dust spread across her fingers. "It's broken."

"It's fine," she said, though it peeved her a bit to think about how much that particular eye shadow had cost her. Oh well, at least she had gotten some use out of it first.

The girl reached into her Prada purse and pulled out a designer wallet. She took out a twenty dollar bill and held it out to her. "Will this cover it?"

Shannon faced a brief moral dilemma as she considered whether to take the girl's money and risk Tyler thinking she was greedy or turn down twenty dollars. Finally, she reached out and accepted the bill. "Thanks."

"It's the least I can do," the blond girl said, then frowned. She cocked her head to the right. "Hey, you look kind of familiar. You don't happen to go to Manderley Prep, do you?"

Ugh, just the name sent a shiver down her spine. She knew all about Manderley Prep. It was some kind of super-exclusive private academy in Northern Virginia whose annual tuition cost as much as a new Porsche. The Manderley kids were recognizable not only by their red plaid skirts and white button-ups, but also the stuck-up expressions perpetually trapped on their perfect rich-kid faces.

"No, I don't go to Manderley," Shannon said, now tempted to hustle the girl for more money.

"Oh, I see. Well, again, I'm very sorry. I hope you have a wonderful day." The girl smiled then continued down the street.

"Shannon?" Tyler murmured, drawing her attention back to him.

She looked over at him. "Yeah?"

In one hand, he held her smartphone. In the other, a plain black flip phone.

"Why do you have two cell phones?"

CASE NOTES 9: HADES

Hades stared at the assortment of bouquets lining the flower shop's shelves, thinking about deadly poisons. The lily of the valley, with its tiny bell-shaped blossoms, was toxic when consumed, along with its more colorful relative, the gloriosa lily. Azaleas, too.

Poisons made him think of killing, and killing drew his attention back to Artemis and Apollo. Why did they get to spend time with each other?

"May I help you?" a voice asked.

He turned.

The florist looked up at him from behind rimless glasses. She was so short she barely reached to his pecs. She had a kind face and hair as white and wispy as milkweed fluff.

"I need flowers for a date," he said.

The florist smiled at him. "I had a feeling. You had that dreamy look about you. What do you have in mind?"

"Nothing yet, ma'am."

"Roses are always nice," she said and led him to the middle of the store. The rose bouquets featured a vast variety of colors, with blossoms ranging from the purest white to the deepest burgundy.

He scanned the selection without appreciating it, wondering why he was even here in the first place. He was putting unnecessary effort into this, when it would mean nothing in the end. There were no happy endings, so why couldn't he stop thinking about Elizabeth Hawthorne? Why couldn't he get her out of his mind?

He should be focusing on his evolution. It was the only thing that was real in this world.

As the florist spoke about the various roses, Hades became distracted by a flash of blue on the counter at the back of the store.

He walked over to the counter, where dissected flowers were waiting to be made into bouquets. He picked up the vase of small blue blossoms, lifted it to his face, and inhaled. Soft buds brushed against his nose and lips.

The faint aroma dredged an image from the grave of his memory. As he closed his eyes, he saw a field of wildflowers like these, bordered on one side by a tall iron fence topped with coils of razor wire. They had their first kiss there under the cover of dusk, when the flowers' fragrance was at its peak.

A sense of peace drifted over him.

Then a hand fell on his arm, and the memory dissipated like smoke, taking his tranquility with it. Opening his eyes, he couldn't remember who he had been thinking about.

"Those are forget-me-nots," the florist said, "but I'm afraid they're not for sale, dear."

"I need them," he heard himself say.

"I'm sorry, but— "

"They were Nine's favorite." He didn't know what he meant by that.

"They're for mixed wedding bouquets."

Anger flared in him, riding on the disorientation that threatened to engulf him. He suddenly felt threatened by the petite woman who conspired to prevent him from getting what he *needed.*

Resisting the impulse to simply take the entire vase, Hades reached into his pocket and pulled out his wallet. He had to put down the bouquet to open the billfold. As he searched for cash, his driver's licenses fell to the ground.

He bent down to collect them. Five different names confronted him, but the faces were all the same. None of the names were his. Agitated, he scooped up the cards and shoved them back into the leather pocket. Found a ten dollar bill. Thrust it into her hand.

"I need this, ma'am," Hades said.

The florist stared at him with a strange expression.

"I need this," he repeated tersely.

"Your back," she said, and he realized that when he had leaned over, his shirt and jacket had slid up.

Not only had the healing cigarette burn been revealed to her, but she had also seen his mark.

Hades licked his lips, fighting with his agitation. A rabid part of him wanted to make sure the old florist could never tell anyone about what she had just seen, while his other half found the idea of wanton violence unnecessary and contrary to his training.

There were no clear borders between his old self and what he was evolving into. Some days, he felt like a beast and a man sutured together, each one fighting for dominion over the other. Although scar tissue grew along the divide, in the end, flesh was flesh. He could never escape from himself.

Exhaling slowly, Hades put his wallet back into his pocket. "Ma'am, can you wrap these, please? They have to look nice for her."

The wrinkles in her face deepened, and her eyes clouded over with a queasy look. She placed his money on the counter, took the forget-me-nots from the vase, and wrapped them in a cone of shiny silver paper. She sealed the paper with a strip of tape, which she concealed beneath a blue ribbon.

"That will be eight dollars," she mumbled, drifting to the register. She gave him his change with the bouquet. As soon as her hands were free, her fingers drifted restlessly, going to her green apron then to the crucifix around her throat.

Hades stepped into the sunlight. He walked the short distance to the diner, forcing himself not to think about the open wound that was his memory.

He had entered the florist's shop in a good mood, pleased by his unexpected encounter with Apollo and Artemis. Now, it was as though a shadow had descended over everything. The world lost its color, and the lingering aroma of flowers became soured by the unpleasant odors of antiseptic solution, Epsom salt, and burnt cloves.

It's not real. He stopped walking and stared upward, at a sky that became grayer by the moment. *None of this is real anyway, is it?*

As people bustled past on either side, a sense of profound isolation pressed down on him. He became possessed by the certainty that he wasn't here, wasn't alive like the rest of them.

If he reached out and grabbed someone, they wouldn't be able to feel him. His voice would never be heard.

Alone. He was absolutely alone, and it was getting dark again.

Paralyzed by dread, he didn't hear his name called until Elizabeth was standing right in front of him, having appeared as if from nowhere. As soon as he noticed her, the pressure on his diaphragm faded and he was able to breathe normally again. Even the sky seemed to grow brighter.

"Hello, Elizabeth," he said softly, focusing on her face.

Even in the warm sunlight that dappled the sidewalk, her skin was as white as porcelain and seemed just as delicate. Her flaxen eyelashes cast shadows on her high cheekbones. She was like a bone-china doll that might shatter with the gentlest touch.

She smiled at him. "You were spacing out just now."

"I was just looking at the sky." He held out the bouquet. "These are for you, Elizabeth."

Her eyes widened in surprise.

"How did you know?" she asked, taking the bouquet from his hand.

"Know what?"

"Forget-me-nots are my favorite."

"I didn't," Hades said, still feeling a bit unsettled. Could this be a test of some kind, like the tests that Dimitri put him through? What was the intended response?

Elizabeth's smile returned like the sun from behind clouds. "It was my perfume, wasn't it?"

"Your perfume?"

"Don't be coy." She grinned at him. "You smelled it, didn't you? I think you're the first one who's actually realized it. Very intuitive, Hades."

He hid his remnant confusion behind a smile. Over the years, he had become skilled at faking emotions and forcing the real ones down deep, away from himself.

"Did you know that forget-me-nots only smell good at night?" she asked. "The rest of the time, they have no scent at all, so most people don't even know what they smell like."

A word suddenly came to him. "*Vergissmeinnicht.*"

"What?" She cocked her head.

"That's the German name for them."

"Are you German?"

"No, but someone told me that once."

Hades couldn't remember who had said it. Probably an instructor back at the Academy. Occasionally, he would randomly find himself speaking in a different language. Sometimes German and sometimes Russian. A few snippets of Mandarin or Arabic. He could still hold conversations in the first two languages, but there were huge gaps in his knowledge that grew larger with each day. He could no longer recall how to write in the Cyrillic alphabet, although he had been able to last year. Every so often, large swathes of words fell into the void, and he wondered if one day he would forget how to speak and write in English, left with no way to communicate.

Even worse was the idea that he might forget his training. Then he wouldn't be able to defend himself, protect Elizabeth, or destroy others. He couldn't tolerate the thought of being weak and helpless

Disturbed, he decided to change the subject.

"Are you hungry?" he asked.

"Starved!"

He took Elizabeth's hand and led her inside the restaurant. Her fingers were soft and cool against his own. He released her only long enough to hold the door open for her. The moment their touch ended, he wanted to grab her again and hold her close. Never let go.

The building that the diner occupied couldn't be much older than his own seventeen years, but when he entered, it was as if he had stepped back into the 1960s. Red vinyl stools and booths abounded, and a jukebox crooned from the corner. Even the waitresses were dressed for a bygone era, in blue gingham dresses with aproned skirts, as were the busboys in their pristine whites.

"We'd like a table in the back," he said, and the waitress led them past the booths and the counter.

Many of the chairs were unoccupied, and Hades and Elizabeth had their pick of the tables. He selected one that offered him a clear view of the parking lot and entrance.

Before sitting down, he pulled out a chair for Elizabeth.

"You're a real gentleman, aren't you?" she said, laughing as she sat down.

"Only for you, Elizabeth," he murmured, pushing her chair in. He walked around to the other side of the table. As he sat down, he looked around, calculating potential escape routes and barriers that could be used to gain a tactical advantage during a shootout.

It was a habit of his, just like the polite etiquette he couldn't seem to shake. Always respect his superiors and always be prepared for violence. Of course, sometimes the latter habit trumped the former. He had a tendency to murder his superiors.

"Is there anything that I can get you two to drink?" the waitress asked, handing each of them a menu.

"Coffee," he said.

The waitress rested her hands on the table and smiled at him. "I bet you like it with lots of sugar, huh?"

"Just cream is fine," he said, regarding the menu.

"Water, please," Elizabeth said.

As the waitress left to fill their order, Hades browsed the menu. He periodically glanced into the parking lot. When the bell on the door jingled, he would look in its direction. Twice, he slipped his hand to his waist out of habit, though he was not armed.

An elderly couple entered, then a young girl with her parents. While Hades doubted the granny would pull a submachine gun out from under her sweater, he waited until each group had found its table before looking down again. It annoyed him that the family chose the table beside him when they could have easily sat at the front of the restaurant. He didn't like having his back to people. Even children could be threats.

The waitress returned with a glass of water, an empty mug, a pot of steaming coffee, and a small pitcher of cream. As she placed the saucer next to him, her hand brushed against his.

In the corner of his eye, he saw Elizabeth stiffen.

"Ready to order?" the waitress asked.

"You go first," he told Elizabeth.

"I'll have the turkey burger with the Caesar salad for a side."

"Didn't you want something a little more substantial?" he teased. "Weren't your exact words a 'big, greasy, artery-clogging hamburger'?"

"I thought you had a bad memory."

"Not when I'm with you," Hades said. He could remember every single detail of their conversation. He couldn't get her out of his mind.

"What about you, sugar?" the waitress asked, turning to him. As he told her his selection, her smile became amused.

A bacon cheeseburger, French fries, onion rings, and cheesecake.

"Sounds like you have a big appetite," the waitress said and winked at him as she gathered the menus.

As the waitress returned to the kitchen, Hades poured himself a cup of coffee, adding a generous dash of cream. Then he looked at Elizabeth and saw her frowning.

"What?" he asked.

"It's nothing," she said, blushing.

Hades smirked, realizing that the waitress's comment had bothered her. He leaned over the table.

"Don't tell me you're jealous, Elizabeth," he purred, watching her squirm.

Her blush only deepened, and the way she nibbled on her lip was irresistible.

"I *do* have a big appetite," he said, and it was true.

He wanted her more than anything else in the world, and he didn't know why.

Maybe she was a part of his evolution. Maybe he needed her, and that was why he felt so attached to her. She could be his destiny.

Deep in thought, he took a sip of coffee. The cream cut some of the bitterness and thickened it, just the way he liked it.

"I hate coffee," Elizabeth said, resting her chin in her hand. Her finger stroked her cheek, so close to her rosy lips. "It tastes like dirt to me."

"I don't drink it for the taste. I drink it to stay awake."

"Did you stay up all night or something?" she asked, laughing. She had a beautiful laugh. Normally, the sound of laughter was as abrasive as sandpaper to him, making him hyperaware of how hollow he felt inside. Not with her. He could listen to her voice for hours and not grow sick of it.

She filled the void.

"I have nightmares and insomnia," he said, surprising himself with his honesty. Why would he tell her that when he didn't even tell Dimitri about his night terrors?

Her smile faded. "Oh. I'm sorry."

What he didn't say was the nightmares were only half of it. Even worse than waking up trembling and gasping for breath was the feeling that came after the initial panic faded. The certainty he had lost another part of himself to the darkness and would never regain it.

"Try lavender," she said. "It's supposed to calm you. You can put some essential oil on your pillow at night to help you sleep better."

He smiled, wondering what she would think if he told her that when he wasn't sleeping in his bed, he was sleeping in a sensory deprivation tank.

"I might need to try that," Hades said. "Thank you for the suggestion, Elizabeth."

"Of course."

As she rolled a loose petal between her thumb and index fingers, he stared at her hands. She had graceful hands, with long, slim fingers. She kept her nails neatly manicured but unpainted. He wanted to press those fingers against his lips and kiss them.

"Here we are," the waitress said, arranging the plates on the table. "Just give me a holler if you need anything else."

"Thank you," Elizabeth said.

Between bites of his cheeseburger, he watched her eat.

She started off by nibbling at her turkey burger like a timid doe grazing on meadow grass. When she wasn't blotting her lips with her napkin, she spread the square of paper across her lap to catch any fallen crumbs.

"So, who taught you how to eat?" Hades asked, offering her a pleasant smile.

She choked on her food and, as expected, pressed her napkin against her lips until she had regained her breath. A blush touched her cheeks, and with downcast eyes, she said, "My parents made me take etiquette classes a couple years ago. Is it really that obvious?"

"Very." He transferred half his French fries to her plate, next to the depressing salad she had ordered. "Now, eat like you're actually enjoying it."

She sighed and picked up a fry, dipped it in the Caesar dressing from her salad, and ate it. Then she took another one from the pile.

"Okay, these are really good," she said, then paused. "By the way, there's a Halloween dance at my school on the twenty-ninth. We're allowed to take dates from other schools, so even if you don't enroll in time, you'll still be able to go. So, what do you say? Do you want to be my date?"

Pleasure radiated through him at her offer. Of all the people in the world, she had chosen to invite him. He meant something to her. She could *see* him.

"How could I say no?" he asked and cherished the sight of her excited smile.

Once they had finished with their burgers and side dishes, he moved the dirty plates out of the way and pushed his slice of cheesecake in front of her.

"No," Elizabeth groaned, pressing a hand against her stomach. "I'm stuffed. How can you even think about eating more? Do you have a black hole for a stomach?"

When the urge to kill became uncontrollable and there were no targets to remove, Hades would eat large quantities of food. To offset the caloric overload from his binge sessions, to kill time, and to quench his rage and frustration, he worked out obsessively for hours each day, turning his body into a finely tuned weapon.

But she must never find out about his urges or his anger. She must be kept innocent.

He grinned at her. "Like I said before, I have a big appetite."

"Well, I don't," she said, pushing the plate toward him. "If I eat another bite, I'm going to explode."

"Just one bite." He picked up a clean spoon, scooped out a chunk of cheesecake, and held it out to her. "Say 'ah.'"

"You're a sadist." Elizabeth rolled her eyes and opened her lovely mouth. "Ah."

He maneuvered the spoon past her parted lips and smiled as she ate. A bit of chocolate syrup got trapped in one corner of her mouth. He wanted to kiss her, but he would settle for eating from the same utensil that had touched her tongue.

As he lowered the spoon, a rough voice tore his attention away from her. "Hey, girlie, I've got something better you can swallow."

Glancing away from her, Hades spotted the source of the obnoxious distraction. The voice belonged to a man sitting at a table across from them. Greasy and sunburned, this pathetic specimen of humanity wore a stained souvenir T-shirt emblazoned with an American flag.

Elizabeth's face went red, and her lips drew into a colorless line. She glowered at her lap, refusing to acknowledge the man's catcall.

Hades felt his body grow rigid. His jaw clenched, and a low growl escaped him before he could restrain himself.

"Ignore it," Hades heard himself say but felt detached from the words. It wasn't his voice anymore. It was the mask speaking.

The real him was howling for blood, deep inside his core.

He must not let her see what he was evolving into.

"Have another bite," he said, handing her the spoon. "You're cute when you eat."

"Are you trying to fatten me up?" Elizabeth's smile returned, but he could tell she was still annoyed about the man's obscene comment.

"I like to see you enjoying yourself. It makes me happy."

Hades waved over the waitress. "I'd like the check now, please."

There must have been something in his voice or expression, because this time the waitress did not try to flirt with him. She nodded. "I'll get it right away."

"By the way, you have a little chocolate on your face," he told Elizabeth, turning back to her.

She blushed, looking mortified. "Really? Where?"

Hades picked up his napkin and leaned over the table, dabbing at the splotch of syrup on the corner of her mouth. As his finger brushed against her lips, her blush deepened.

He wanted to see how flustered he could get her and eventually break down this bureaucratic facade her parents had forced upon her. But he sensed that the bolder his advances became, the more careful he would need to be to not drive her away.

After cleaning off the chocolate, he sat down again, twisting the napkin between his fingers. In the corner of his eye, he watched the man finish his beer and slam the glass down beside another empty mug before swaggering off toward the bathroom.

"At least eat some, too," Elizabeth said, and he glanced back to find her holding the spoon out to him. "Your turn."

Hades tolerated her feeding him, even though it conjured a vague, unsettling memory of being strapped to a chair, with his jaws forced open and a tube pushed down his throat. As soon as the spoon slipped from his lips, he stood.

"I need to go to the bathroom," he said and took out his wallet. He threw two twenties onto the table. "This should be enough. Just wait for me outside, please."

"Listen, I can pay for my own food," Elizabeth said, but by then he was already halfway across the room.

Hades entered the men's restroom. The taste of chocolate cheesecake became cloying and bloodlike on his tongue. When he licked his lips absently, he could no longer detect sweetness.

The two urinals were unoccupied. As he stared at the door

of the single stall, he removed his motorcycle gloves from his jacket pocket. They were made of thin, supple deerskin. He pulled them on and flexed his fingers, savoring the firm resistance of the leather against his knuckles.

A low grunt came from the stall. Soon constipation would be the least of the man's worries.

As Hades heard the flush of a toilet, he stepped closer. The chirr of a closing zipper, shuffling, a weary sigh—those were the sounds of an unwary target.

He licked his lips a second time, contemplating what he would do once the man left the stall. Murder was a bit excessive in this case, but there was no doubt in his mind the scumbag deserved to be taught a lesson. Nobody spoke to Elizabeth like that and got away with it.

The man stepped out of the stall, and upon noticing Hades, regarded him with dull, piggish eyes.

"What are you looking at?" The man sneered, revealing teeth like rotten corn kernels. He was a stocky man with a moldy cheese complexion and a week's worth of stubble. His thinning blond hair hung lankly over his brow—then, suddenly, it did not.

Although there was no apparent difference in height, clothing, or weight, in the time it took to blink, the man had transformed. His hair had become prematurely white, his face had firmed and paled, and his eyes had paled also. His eyelashes were like veins of frost.

Hades's blood went cold, and he began trembling uncontrollably.

"Get out of my way, kid." The man's sinewy lips curled back, and this time the teeth he exposed were as pristinely white as his complexion. They were so white and so straight that they appeared to be false. "Hey, are you stupid? Why are you staring at me like that?"

I hate you. I hate you. I wish you were dead. Dizzying thoughts rushed through his head like automatic gunfire. They were just as devastating as well, shredding his confidence and leaving gaping holes in exit. *And you—it's all your fault, Nine.*

Silent as most thoughts were, his had a voice that rose in a shriek of rage and sounded a lot like his own.

Nine, don't you know I did it for you?

The man's groans were what shoved Hades back into reality, and reality fell in on him like soil into an open grave. The smells of cleaning solution and stale urine filled his nose once more, replacing the odor of burnt cloves.

His fingers were sunk deep into doughy skin. He had the man pushed against the stall's inner wall. From the blood staining the man's collar, Hades realized that he must have slammed the man against the ceramic tiles. He couldn't remember doing it.

Nor could he recall ever beating the man, but when he took a better look, he saw that he must have done that as well. The man's eyes were swollen shut, and his nose was crushed flat. Blood poured from his shattered mouth and both nostrils. His splotchy face was as blue as forget-me-not blossoms, partially because of oxygen deprivation but also because the capillaries under his skin had burst.

With a low moan, Hades let go of the man and lurched back. The man slid to the ground, leaving a long, thin trail of blood oozing down the wall.

Staring at the blood streak, he felt a deep chasm forming in his head, cleaving his brain in two like the split halves of a walnut. He pressed his hands against his face, gasping for breath.

One side of his torn brain screamed at him to stop—enough killing, enough death! It had the voice of a terrified child.

His other half calmly whispered for him to wrap his arms around the man's throat and snap the spinal column or crush the windpipe beneath his steel-toed boot. It would be easy. He had done it before.

They all deserved to die anyway. It would be so much better if he and Nine were the only ones left alive.

"Nine," he whispered. "Where are you, Nine? I need you."

No, that wasn't right. Not Nine. Elizabeth. He needed Elizabeth.

Who was Nine?

Who was Elizabeth?

This is happening to someone else, he thought, taking a deep breath. *It's all happening to someone else.*

That calmed him somewhat, and he felt the divide in his mind begin to mend again. Apathy washed over him like a comforting touch.

His hands slid from his face and fell to his sides. He numbly regarded the unconscious man, then shut the stall door and left the bathroom.

Swaddled in soothing indifference, Hades took off his gloves and shoved them into his pocket. As he stepped outside, a lovely blonde approached him. It took him a moment to remember who she was.

"Here's your change," she said, giving him a handful of dollar bills and coins. It seemed like too much for the cost of the meal, but he didn't count it.

"Thank you, Elizabeth," he murmured and took her delicate hand. He needed to hold her and feel her warmth.

She could feel him, right? He was still alive, wasn't he?

He never wanted to let go of her.

"I'm having fun," Elizabeth said, leaning into him. Her flaxen hair fell in a glossy wave over her shoulder, and underneath the fragrance of forget-me-nots, he detected the faintest trace of her vanilla shampoo.

Even the scents she favored evoked an image of purity. She was a representation of the future he had been deprived of.

He needed to protect her. But he sensed that in the end, he would be the one to ruin her.

CASE NOTES 10: ARTEMIS

At the Mexican restaurant across the street, Shannon and Tyler discussed the phone over tortilla chips as they waited for their entrees to arrive.

Leaning back in his chair, Tyler was as graceful as any aristocrat at high tea. His legs were so long that, even though he was almost a foot taller than her, he was practically eye level with her when reclining.

He set the flip phone next to the bowl of guacamole. "So, let me get this straight… You don't know how this phone got into your purse, but you think you've seen it before?"

"Right," she said, staring at the newspaper decoupage glued to the table. She picked at the clear varnish with her nails. Just looking at the cell phone made her nervous, for a reason she couldn't explain. Dread tugged at her brain. She wished Tyler would stop talking about the phone. She wanted nothing more than to crush the device underfoot or hurl it into the nearest trash can.

As if sensing her worry, he reached across the table and laid his hand over hers. His thumb teased the Murano bracelet her foster dad had brought back as a souvenir from Venice, playing with the glass beads.

"Could someone have accidentally put it in your purse at school, thinking your purse was theirs?" he asked, searching her eyes.

Shannon gave it some thought, then shook her head. "No. I don't leave my purse where people can take it. In gym, I put it in my locker, and it's right next to me during class."

"Weird." He took his hand off hers to spoon some guacamole onto his plate. His gaze was deep, direct. She could tell the entire situation intrigued him. "It's too bad it's dead. I'm curious to see what's on it."

"Me, too," Shannon said, though she actually felt relieved the cell phone wouldn't turn on. Even more irrational was that a quiet voice inside her prayed that the phone was broken beyond repair.

"I wonder if an iPhone charger will work on it," Tyler said, dipping a tortilla chip in the guacamole. Even such mundane gestures were performed with a latent elegance, accentuated by the gentle movements of the muscles and fine bones in his hands.

"It doesn't matter anyway. On Monday, I'll drop it off at the school lost-and-found. Someone's probably looking for it." She picked up the cell phone. The cool plastic shell felt *gross* somehow, like it was crawling with bacteria. After returning it to her purse, she wiped her hand on her skirt.

A crooked smile touched Tyler's lips, and he leaned over the table, his amber eyes twinkling with amusement. His shirt sleeves rode up over his tanned biceps. "Oh, come on, you're not the least bit curious?"

"It just gives me a bad feeling," she admitted.

He lifted an eyebrow. "Really?"

"You know what? Let's change the subject." Shannon sighed. Then, at a sudden revelation, she felt the blood drain from her face. "Oh my God."

Tyler frowned. "What's the matter?"

"Something else just occurred to me," she said quickly. "Remember that guy from the subway?"

"Stalker boy?" he asked, the warmth leeching from his voice. His expression hardened over, and a serious furrow formed between his eyebrows.

"Yeah. Now that I think about it, he had a phone just like this one. He was playing with it when I got on the train."

"You think this is his?"

"It has to be," Shannon said. "He must have accidentally dropped it into my purse. He was, um, kind of leaning over me when we were on the train, like he had no concept of personal space."

Tyler narrowed his eyes, clenching his jaw. He looked like he wanted to hunt Hades down and throttle him. Shannon felt strangely flattered.

"Anyway, at one point, we came to a fast stop," she said. "It could have happened then."

Tyler sighed and glanced at the phone again. "Now I'm really curious to see what's on it."

Shannon wished she could say the same. She sensed the device contained a terrifying secret, and that, like Pandora's box, once opened there was no going back.

Instead of dwelling on the subject further, she placed the flip phone in her purse. The moment she zipped up the pouch, a profound sense of relief descended over her. She could almost pretend that the phone didn't exist in the first place. It was better than facing the truth that for the first time in weeks, her anxiety had come back with a vengeance.

This wasn't the first time a mundane, innocent object had induced debilitating fear in her. Kitchen knives, common house keys, dark closets, and even sewing needles were fodder for panic attacks during her worst moments. Even simple odors, like the scent of hand sanitizer, and sounds as innocuous as the slosh of water could grate on her nerves.

It was a good thing she had an appointment with her psychiatrist in a few days. Surely Dr. Kosta would be able to unravel whatever was bothering her. Once she talked it over with him, she was certain the root of her unease would be something far more logical than a stupid cell phone.

STATUS REPORT: SUBJECT 9 OF SUBSET A

DK: Hello, Nine. I heard you had a bit of a panic attack on the way over here. Would you like to talk about that today?

A-09: I want to see him.

DK: Who?

A-09: Where is Two? I know he's here. I saw him yesterday.

DK: Oh. You're referring to Subject Two of Subset A. Yes, I heard about that incident at the Academy. It's all rather troublesome, taking care of his wounds.

A-09: Please, can I see him?

DK: I'm afraid the boy was rather uncooperative during his last session. Seems just seeing you awoke something in him. He's currently in restraints in the seclusion room, after trying to bludgeon me with an IV rack. Tell me, is he always this violent?

A-09: Not with me. He's kind to me.

DK: But I imagine he isn't that way with others. Has he hurt other people?

A-09: No.

DK: The polygraph doesn't lie.

A-09: He's hurt people to protect me. Like the bullies. But not badly. Just to get them to stop.

DK: Interesting. Were you sexually active with him?

(Silence from 00:03:10 to 00:03:19.)

DK: I'll take that as a yes. Don't look so ashamed. He is an exquisitely beautiful boy. Although I can't say I'm surprised. You two come from very good stock, do you know that? The majority of your comrades were donor embryos that matched the genetic profile, but you and Subject Two are different. Your biological parents gave you willingly to Project Pandora, when the program first began. How does that make you feel?

A-09: I don't know.

DK: I don't tolerate vague answers. Please clarify. Talk. You have a lovely voice, so you might as well use it.

A-09: They told us at the Academy how we were created. What we were born for. I've always wanted an actual family, but now (:04 pause) it feels wrong. Two was supposed to go with me. (:05) Wait, is he? Is that why he's here?

DK: No. His personality makes him incompatible for transition into the political sphere, and as talented as he is, his continual insubordination rules out the possibility of a career in the military. But he has other uses, and with some training, we'll tame him yet.

A-09: You don't know him like I do. He's very smart, and he's strong. What if he becomes my bodyguard?

DK: Hmm, what makes you think he wants to protect you still? Don't you think it's possible he despises you?

A-09: It's not like that. I never wanted him to get hurt.

DK: Are you familiar with the myth of Persephone?

A-09: No, but listen. Please. Just let me see him. I can get him to cooperate. He'll listen to me.

DK: Interesting. With the way he responded when I talked about you, I assumed he wanted to kill you.

CASE NOTES 11: PERSEPHONE

After leaving the diner, Elizabeth and Hades went on a stroll through Rock Creek Park. When she heard that he had never visited the Smithsonian's National Zoo, she insisted they check it out.

As they entered the zoo, Hades took her hand. His grip was firm, reassuring. Just holding hands with him made her feel safe, as if he could protect her from whatever dangers came her way, whether man-made or natural.

"I can't believe you've never been here before," she said as they walked past the Speedwell Conservation Carousel.

"I just haven't had time to."

The carousel featured a menagerie of oversize wooden animals, with children riding everything from a leopard to a bear to a silverback gorilla. Elizabeth had to raise her voice to be heard above the kids' shrieking laughter and the cheerful calliope music.

"Have you always lived in D.C.?" she asked.

"I moved here when I was fifteen." By the way he continuously glanced around him and fiddled with his belt, she had a feeling he wasn't thrilled about being in crowded places. He seemed almost wary, like he expected a kid to blindside him and drench him in a soda or Slurpee.

"Where did you live before that?"

"Colorado, I think."

She grinned. "You think?"

"Colorado," he repeated with more conviction.

They followed the signs to the Asia Trail exhibit. A breeze stirred the tree branches and caused the banners mounted on metal posts to shudder with a soft flapping sound. Shivering in her thin cashmere cardigan, she leaned against him, taking in his pleasant, smoky aroma and the subtle scent of tanned leather. He reminded her of autumn—the intense, fiery blaze that came before the winter die-off.

"Are you cold?" he asked, smiling down at her.

"Just a little," she admitted.

"We can't have that, now can we?" He slipped his hand out of hers and unzipped his jacket. Underneath, his T-shirt clung against his body. The fabric's dye was faded to a dull gray in places, but aside from that, the shirt was almost identical to the one he had worn earlier that week. Black like always.

"Here you are, Miss Hawthorne," he said, easing his jacket over her. Heavy folds of leather enveloped her, soft and weathered from use. His hands lingered on her shoulders for a moment longer then eased down her back, before slipping away entirely.

"You're so formal," she teased, taking his hand again.

"It's the way I was trained," he said, smirking.

"There's something I've been wondering."

"Yes?"

"You always wear black. I don't think I've seen you wear anything colorful."

"I know."

"Why?" She cocked her head. "I mean, you aren't a Goth, right?"

Elizabeth didn't think he was a Goth. While his eyelashes were so thick and dark that it almost looked like he was wearing eyeliner, she was close enough to tell he wore no makeup. His fair complexion was natural, and so was his hair. His face was unpierced, and although he had tattoos, they weren't the typical motifs she'd expect from someone who belonged to that subculture. Besides, he was so warm and kind toward her, without angst or intentional coolness. And so polite, too.

"What's a Goth?" Hades asked, then laughed when she explained it to him. "No, I'm not a Goth. I'm just used to wearing single colors. It's like a uniform. It's familiar."

"At least you'll never have to worry about if your wardrobe matches."

"Do people even think about that?" he asked, sounding genuinely curious.

She nodded. "That's why I like how my school has a dress code."

They visited the Asia Trail first to look at the clouded leopards, but a crowd obscured their view and the cats remained out of sight. From there, they went on to the panda habitat, and after some meandering, they reached the Great Cats exhibit.

Hades went up to the chain-link fence and leaned against it, staring down at the lions sunbathing below.

"I kind of want to go in there," he said thoughtfully.

"You want to get mauled?" she asked, laughing.

"Devoured," he said, turning to her. In that moment, he reminded her of a panther or other wild cat, built for power and grace. Dangerous.

"Are you sure you don't just want a pet lion?" she asked, telling herself that the strange desire she saw smoldering in his bright blue eyes was only her imagination. Her sense of security was eclipsed by a sudden disquiet, but she ignored it.

He smiled at her and said nothing.

After Elizabeth and Hades watched the lions for a bit, they visited the porcupine exhibit. Then they found themselves at the Kids' Farm.

The air along the walkway was pungent with a sweaty

livestock odor that made her nose wrinkle. She stopped at the low wooden fence bordering the cow enclosure and leaned over.

"Come here, sweetie," she said and clicked her tongue at the spotted heifer on the other side of the fence. "Over here. Let me pet you."

The cow regarded her with lazy eyes, refusing to move.

"It knows you ate its cousin for lunch," Hades teased, resting a hand on her lower back. His palm pressed against her skin, warm and soothing.

"Actually, I think that was you," Elizabeth said. "I had a turkey burger, remember?"

"Guilty as charged. It was a very delicious hamburger."

The goats and pigs proved equally unenthusiastic toward her, but at last she was able to coax an alpaca over. She ran her hand down its woolly neck, smiling at the texture of its fur.

She turned to Hades. "Why don't you try petting it?"

He reached through the fence and set his hand on the alpaca's head. He rubbed its flat, bony brow, looking wary and out of place, like he wasn't used to being around animals.

"You're so adorable," she told him.

"Who? Me or the llama?"

"It's an alpaca," she said. "And you."

They lingered at the petting zoo for a while, and over time he appeared to warm to the experience. He even laughed when a cow slobbered over his hand, leaving his fingers dripping with gritty, greenish saliva.

From the Kids' Farm they went on to the elephant exhibit. By the way Hades stared in amazement at the creatures, she wondered if he had ever seen an elephant before.

When she asked him, he chuckled. "No, not in real life. I didn't realize they were so big."

"Wait, is this your first time going to a zoo?" she asked.

He didn't respond, just stared at the lumbering elephants.

"I'm sorry," she said when she realized he wasn't going to

answer. "I didn't mean it to sound like that. I'm just surprised. I thought everyone went to zoos. Didn't you have any field trips as a kid?"

"I don't like to talk about my past, Elizabeth. Can we change the subject, please?"

She bit her lip and looked down at her feet. Even at the fundraising banquet, she had sensed Hades had a different life than most. Now she wondered just what sort of childhood he had endured. She wanted to tell him that he could confide in her about anything, but it felt too soon for that. This was only their first date.

As they left the elephant exhibit, she noticed a photo booth and lit up.

"Let's commemorate this," she said, grabbing his arm and pulling him toward the tiny cubicle.

He stopped walking, dragging her to a halt. His eyes narrowed at the sight of the booth. "Wait, what is that?"

"It's a photo booth," she said, feeling another stir of surprise at his naïveté. "Come on, it's fun."

He looked like he wanted to argue, then sighed and allowed her to guide him into the booth.

"Don't forget to smile," Elizabeth said as she messed with the machine's interface, figuring out how to use it.

"I'll try to remember," Hades said with a smile, but he still looked vaguely uncomfortable being in the dark, confined space, like he expected something to pop out at him from behind the curtain. When he lowered his right hand to his waist and began messing with the belt loops there, she entwined her fingers through his and pulled him closer.

"Get ready." She squeezed his hand. "It's about to begin."

She leaned against him, waiting for the first photo to be taken. When the camera flashed, he tensed. Then, during the second photo, as she made a funny expression and lifted her fingers above his head in bunny ears, a ghost of a smile stroked his lips. By the third picture, he was smiling like normal and took her by surprise on the fourth shot when he grabbed her and hauled her against him.

Laughing, she untangled herself from his gentle grasp and plucked the two photo strips from the machine. As they stepped out of the booth, she handed him one of the photographs and stuck the other in her purse.

"They turned out nice, didn't they?" she asked.

"Great."

"In the first one, you look like a monster's going to pop out at you at any moment," she joked.

He smiled. "I'm not a fan of dark places."

"What was your favorite exhibit?" she asked as they walked toward the exit.

"The lions, but I liked that farm one, too. I've never pet a cow before."

"Well, I think you did a pretty good job. The cow seemed to like you."

"I'm good with animals," Hades said. "I take care of the guard dogs."

"Guard dogs?" Elizabeth asked, startled.

"Rottweilers."

"Are you a dog trainer or something?"

He laughed, shaking his head. "No, and they're not actually guard dogs. They're pets, I mean. Friendly. I think you'd like them."

On their way out, she insisted on stopping at a gift shop. The shelves were stocked with souvenir T-shirts, animal-themed jewelry, jigsaw puzzles, and decorative statues. Though there were no panthers or jaguars on exhibit at the National Zoo, the shop's stuffed animal selection included toys of both species. She bought a small stuffed panther and gave it to Hades.

"It's nice," he said and tried to hand the stuffed animal back to her.

"No, I want you to have it."

A ghost of confusion passed over his face. "Why?"

Elizabeth was about to tell him that he reminded her of a panther, then realized how silly it would seem to him. Why would he want to be compared to a deadly animal? He might even take offense.

"The cats were your favorites, so…" She trailed off.

"I can't take this."

Embarrassment invaded her. How could she be so stupid? Of course he wouldn't want it. He was a guy. What could he do with a stuffed animal?

"I'm sorry," she said as a blush burned her cheeks. "I should've known it's too girlie. I don't know what I was thinking. I should return it."

"That's not it. I'm not supposed to be here. If I bring that back with me, he'll know that I was here."

Her brow wrinkled. "Wait, what do you mean? Who will? Didn't you say you were emancipated? I thought that meant you lived alone."

"Never mind, forget I said anything." He turned the stuffed panther over in his hands. "I actually really like it. Thank you, Elizabeth. I'll treasure it."

Suddenly, a terrible thought occurred to her.

"Oh no," she groaned, pulling out her phone to check the time. It was 1:29 p.m. Two hours had flown by like a pleasant dream. "I'm supposed to meet my friend Rachelle at two to go costume shopping. She's going to be pissed if I'm late. I need to go."

Hades lowered the stuffed animal. "Oh."

"I'm so sorry," she said. "I wish we could spend more time together."

"So do I," he murmured.

"Don't forget about the dance." She took off his jacket and handed it back to him. "I'll text you to remind you."

He nodded. "I'll see you there."

She leaned forward and gave him a quick peck on the cheek before her nerve fled her, then turned around and raced toward the exit.

A scream rose from beneath her feet as she stepped onto the welcome mat in front of the costume shop's door. As she entered, she propped the bouquet under her arm and took out her phone to call Rachelle, only to spot her friend trying on costume shoes.

"Fifteen minutes late," Rachelle said as Elizabeth walked over. "Really?"

"I'm so sorry. We went to the zoo after we ate, and I completely forgot about the time."

Rachelle sniffed. "Ugh. I can tell. You smell like a pigsty. So, how did your date go?"

"Perfect," she said, lifting the bouquet. "Look what he got me."

"What are those supposed to be?" Rachelle asked.

"They're forget-me-nots."

"Oh, right. So did you manage to get a picture of him?"

Elizabeth nodded and opened her purse. She took out the photo strip from the elephant exhibit's booth and showed it to Rachelle.

"You weren't kidding when you called him gorgeous," Rachelle said, taking the photograph and examining it. "But doesn't he look a little…"

"A little what?"

"Well, rough. Edgy, I guess."

"You think so?" Elizabeth asked, surprised.

"Hashtag hot mess."

"He's not a hot mess," she said defensively. "He just could use a haircut."

"There's something about his face. Looks like he hasn't slept in days."

"He told me he has insomnia."

"Or maybe he's a druggie."

"I don't think so."

"And I don't really like his mouth," Rachelle added, handing the photo back to her.

"What's wrong with his mouth?" she asked, her horror eclipsed by mounting anger. In her mind, Hades had beautiful lips. More than once, she had imagined kissing them.

"There's just something mean about it."

"*Mean?*" She couldn't contain the annoyance in her voice.

"No offense, but he doesn't seem like your type." Rachelle crossed her arms and shifted from foot to foot, wrinkling her freckled nose. "I mean, do your parents know you're seeing him?"

"I'm not *seeing* him," Elizabeth said, wishing she had never told Rachelle about him. "We met for lunch is all."

"He brought you flowers. Guys don't do that if they're not serious."

"It's not like they were roses." She decided not to mention that she had also invited Hades to the Halloween dance or that she'd kissed him on the cheek.

"Still, did he at least tell you his real name?"

"Well, no, but I think maybe Hades is his real name. I think he had a…different childhood."

"Yeah, I can tell," Rachelle said, rolling her eyes. "Nice Walmart clothes. But really, why not just go back to Adam?"

Elizabeth sighed. Adam Fletcher was her ex-boyfriend from before the car accident, a cocky all-American boy who could be as loud and boastful as a rooster. He might as well have been a stranger to her.

"I know Hades looks rough, but I can tell in my heart that he's a good person," Elizabeth said. "Besides, you can't judge people by their appearances or the kinds of clothes they wear."

Rachelle shook her head. "This isn't like you."

"I can't explain it," she said, sorting through the costumes. She hated having to justify her feelings to Rachelle, but she felt the need to. "It's not just a crush."

"Oh, Elizabeth." Rachelle sighed. "You're not going to tell me it's love at first sight, are you?"

"This is going to sound so silly, but it's like I've known him my whole life. His voice is so soothing. I feel like I could listen to him forever. And I actually get to be myself around him." Moving to the next rack, she glanced over her shoulder at Rachelle and was surprised to find a frown on her friend's face.

"All I'm saying is he doesn't really look like the kind of person you should be dating. Besides, what's with that tattoo? I mean, who gets A-02 tattooed on their arm? I bet it's a gang symbol. It sounds like one."

Seized by anger, Elizabeth swiveled around. "You know what I think? I think you're jealous because Chris broke up with you."

A look of hurt crossed Rachelle's face. "Elizabeth, how dare you. I'm only trying to look out for you."

"Forget it," she said, turning her back to Rachelle again. "I don't want to talk about him anymore. I don't expect you to understand how I feel."

"I just don't want you to get hurt."

Elizabeth returned her attention to the rack of costumes, searching for an outfit that held her interest.

"What about this?" Rachelle asked, holding up a plastic bag that contained an angel costume. The photograph on the label depicted a woman in a skimpy white gown adorned with feather trim and fake wings. "It comes with a halo, too."

"It's nice, but no thank you," Elizabeth said stiffly. She was sick of playing an angel at home. She didn't need to be one on Halloween, too.

She skimmed through the rack—and froze. Although the costume that caught her eye wasn't the most elaborate outfit in the shop or the most expensive, she found herself picking it up anyway. The photograph on the front did the outfit no justice, but it was the costume's name that resonated with her: Persephone.

Since meeting Hades, she had further researched Greek mythology. One of the myths she had read about concerned the goddess Persephone, who was kidnapped by the god Hades as his queen and taken to the underworld. Persephone's mother brokered a deal with Zeus to bring her back to the living world, but because Persephone had eaten six pomegranate seeds in the underworld, she was forced to spend that many months there each year.

Elizabeth smiled, wondering what Hades would think about the costume.

"I'm going to try this on," she said, folding the bag over her arm.

"Oh. Okay." Rachelle barely even looked at her.

Elizabeth entered the dressing room. She stripped out of her skirt, cardigan, and blouse then set them on the small bench provided.

She removed the costume from its bag and slipped it over her shoulders. She examined herself in the mirror, regarding the way the toga flowed around her.

Her parents would approve of the long hem, which fell to her calves, but the neckline was a different story. Her shoulders were exposed, her cleavage visible.

Even though women at the fundraising banquet had worn gowns that were far less modest, Elizabeth could only imagine what her mother and father would say.

Then a revelation came to her: it didn't mean a damn what her parents said. She couldn't keep living under their shadow, or she would never be able to escape from the future they had laid out for her. If she wanted to live as her own person, she needed to start making her own decisions, whether they might cause scandals or not.

The bag also yielded a black sash belt and a crown of black silk flowers. She tried those on, as well, and smiled at her reflection. With smoky makeup and Grecian sandals, she would cast an elegant, imposing figure.

Perfect for the queen of the underworld.

She took a selfie and texted it to Hades with the words: *My costume for the dance. Can you get one that matches?*

Within seconds, her phone rang. She answered the call.

"You want me to wear a dress?" Hades asked, his voice rich with amusement. She could just envision his smile.

"It's a toga," Elizabeth said, smiling at her reflection.

"I'll see what I can find. What are you supposed to be, aside from beautiful?"

"Persephone."

Silence met her response.

"Are you still there?" she asked, worried the line had disconnected.

"Yes," he said after a long pause. The humor was gone from his voice.

Had she offended him somehow?

"I need to go, Elizabeth," Hades said. "I'll see about getting a costume, but I can't make any promises."

"Okay, that's fine. You don't have to wear a costume if you don't want to. As long as you show up."

"Oh, I plan to." A ghost of warmth returned to his voice. "You make a lovely Persephone."

STATUS REPORT: SUBJECT 10 OF SUBSET B

Apollo's programming is progressing as expected. However, his memory loss continues to trouble me. Amnesia this soon is not typical, and for him to have forgotten his entire training, I can't help but wonder if the ECT machine malfunctioned during his treatment. I have already ordered another machine. The last thing I need is to reduce a valuable asset into a human vegetable.

Charles Warren wants me to utilize Apollo as soon as possible, but I feel it is much too soon. I recommended that I send Hades instead, however it seems like Charles is determined to broaden the wet works division. I can't help but wonder if Charles has changed his mind about a slow, silent subversion and instead plans to overthrow the government by force. I've voiced my concerns to other members in the organization, but they seem unbothered by Charles's impatience.

While I understand the need for targeted killings, why the rush? Is it possible that Charles is planning something without the approval of the entire council?

In any case, I will have Hades keep an eye on him for this preliminary test. Failure is not an option.

CASE NOTES 12: APOLLO

It was seventh period, world history. Tyler dropped his backpack next to his desk and sank into his seat, preparing himself for a torturous lesson.

At the front of the room, Mr. Davidson fiddled with an old overhead projector, muttering under his breath about budget cuts and SMART Boards. He was a short, thin man who, as far as anyone could tell, was between seventy and two hundred years old, and that was being generous. His white hair was brushed back from the temples, not a strand out of place. The creases in his khaki trousers were ironed to perfection, while his oxfords were so clean and shiny they appeared to have been spit shined. In one hand, he had a long metal pointer, which he held as though it were a truncheon—and one that he was willing to use.

As soon as the bell rang, Mr. Davidson whacked the rod on his desk to catch everyone's attention then thrust it toward the whiteboard. "Today we will be continuing the ancient civilizations unit by learning about the Roman Empire," Davidson said. "And you know what that means, class? Gladiator fights. The reign of Augustus. The rise of Christianity."

While those were all interesting topics, the teacher reeled them off like a shopping list in a dry monotone. He had a shred of lettuce trapped between his front teeth, and when he thought nobody was looking, he prodded it with his tongue.

"Just kill me already," Tyler mumbled from the back row. They were less than two minutes into class, and he already couldn't wait for it to be over.

"Tell me about it," Alan said, leaning back in his chair. He sat to Tyler's right and made the most out of their closeness by peeping on his quiz sheets.

Tyler didn't care much for cheaters, but he gave Alan a free pass because they were friends. And also because he knew his writing was pretty illegible. But mostly just because he didn't care.

"At least it's Friday, last class to go," Tyler said. "How was your day?"

"Oh, you know." Alan rolled his eyes. "Same as always. Victoria's still ignoring me."

"Tough luck."

"I think she's going to keep me in the friend zone forever."

"Maybe you shouldn't go out of your way to flirt with her. Just be yourself around her."

"Dude, I'm not going out of my way to do anything."

"Then you're screwed," he said, checking his smartphone to see if Shannon had texted him. In the six days since their date, he had passed her in the halls multiple times and sat with her during lunch hour, but that was as far as their interactions had gone. She kept forgetting to bring the flip phone to school, but he was now more concerned with the possibility of a future date than what they might find on the cellular device.

At the front of the class, Mr. Davidson whacked his pointer against the whiteboard. "Attention, class! Attention! Start writing!"

Tyler put his phone away and opened his notebook. He turned to a fresh page that wasn't scrawled with notes, doodles, or covered in timelines.

"Oh, seriously, bro-ski? You're really going to listen to *that*?" Alan nodded toward Davidson, who was beginning to drawl on about the Roman Empire.

"Maybe if you did, you wouldn't have to steal my test answers."

"Guilty as charged," Alan muttered. "But still, I mean, why bother?"

"Because we're here for seven hours a day, and I want to make the most of it." Regardless of whether he paid attention in class, he would still have to sit through the lectures. He wanted the school day to actually be meaningful.

"I don't get you, bruh," Alan said, sighing. "I mean, you say you're going to join the military, so why bother?"

"It's the ROTC," he told Alan for the hundredth time. "My grades are still important."

"Whatever."

Tyler began writing. Occasionally, he would glance up at the whiteboard to make sure he was filling out everything, but for the most part he just copied what Davidson said. After a bit, he fell into a comfortable rhythm. The rest of the classroom faded out of view. Davidson's voice softened to a murmur. All that was left was the sound of his breathing and the *scritch-scratch* of pen on paper.

Then a different noise. A muted popping sound, like a bottle being uncorked. Or a suppressed gunshot.

Tyler froze and looked around, bewildered. His mouth was suddenly dry. When he swallowed, a lump of mucus seemed lodged in his throat.

Son, whatever you've just done, let's talk this over. There's no need to resort to violence.

Again. Twice more.

Just put down the gun, okay? Okay?

Within seconds, he found the source of the disturbance. Two rows across from him, a girl lounged in her seat, chewing gum. Each time she blew a sizable bubble, she poked it with her pencil.

The sound was as grating as nails on a chalkboard. He tried to ignore it, but the more she snapped her gum, the louder the sounds became. Finally, he couldn't stand it any longer and turned in his seat. "*Will you just shut up!*"

Tyler didn't realize he had shouted it until everyone turned to look at him. Even Mr. Davidson broke away from his lecture to give him a disapproving look.

"Is something wrong, Tyler?" Mr. Davidson asked. "Is there a reason you just told me to shut up?"

"I— It wasn't meant for you, Mr. Davidson," he said and was surprised to hear his voice stammer. Normally he managed to keep his cool while in the hot spot. Then again, normally he didn't yell out in class.

"Is that so?"

"Uh…" He looked at the girl and tried to remember her name. "Felicia… She was chewing her gum, and I got distracted. I just wanted her to stop."

"And in doing so, you disrupted the whole class," Mr. Davidson said, clapping his hands together. "Good job. That little display of yours has just earned you lunch detention Monday."

"But what about her?" he asked. Chewing gum was also against the school rules, right up there with pissing off the teacher.

Felicia shot him a dirty look.

"Fair point." Mr. Davidson smiled drily. "Felicia can join you."

With a groan, Tyler laid his head on his desk. He spent the rest of the class period thinking about how much fun he'd have sweeping the corridors and cleaning up litter during lunch hour.

On the way to the parking lot, he stopped at a drinking fountain. Someone had plugged the drain with a wad of gum and the bottom of the metal bowl was already filled with gross, dirty water. He decided he wasn't thirsty.

As he turned around, he ran right into Alan.

"Hey, bro-ski, can I borrow your notes?" Alan asked.

"I stopped writing them."

"Oh, I know, but I didn't put them down at all." Alan grinned.

Tyler scrounged around in his backpack for the notebook. When he found it, he tossed it to Alan.

Alan flipped through the pages until he found the newest entries. Frowning, he skimmed over the writing. "Hey, what's the deal, bruh?"

"What, you can't read my handwriting?"

"This ain't about the Roman Empire. You gave me the wrong notebook or something."

That couldn't be right. He had labeled all of his spiral notebooks with black sharpie. "WORLD HISTORY" was written in neat block letters on the front and back covers.

"Here, let me see," Tyler said, taking the notebook from him.

The first few paragraphs were about the rise of the Roman Empire, but halfway down the page, he had started writing something else. Chilled, he read the repeating sentence that covered the front of the page and then the back. In places, he had drawn the letters with such force that the pen nub had punctured the paper.

It was in his handwriting, but it was not his words.

PANDORA'S BOX IS OPENING.
PANDORA'S BOX IS OPENING.
PANDORA'S BOX IS OPENING.
PANDORA'S BOX IS OPENING.

"Earth to Tyler," Alan said, tapping him on the shoulder.

"Huh?" Tyler blinked, looking up at Alan. For a moment, he had forgotten that Alan was even there.

"Zoning out much, bruh?"

"Uh, sorry, I was just..."

"Come on," Alan said, slapping his back. "Bell rang. School's over."

He watched as Alan rushed off, then glanced down again. He stared at the page for a moment longer.

I've heard this somewhere before, he thought. *The exact words. But where? Why does it look so familiar?*

Tyler shook his head. As he returned the notebook to his bag, a cell phone rang. He retrieved the flip phone from his pocket and lifted it to his ear.

Then everything faded out for a while.

CASE NOTES 13: HADES

The sensory deprivation tank was ten feet long by five feet wide, with a height of five feet. The exterior was made of medical-grade stainless steel, without windows. At one end, there was a hinged door; on the other side, filtration pipes disappeared into the wall. Even in the bright blue-white fluorescence cast by the lamp panels, the tank seemed ominous. Like a torture device. Like a coffin.

If used as a coffin, the tank would have accommodated an entire family of corpses. Yet, minutes after he lay down in the shallow water, he felt the confines shrink. The walls caved in like a collapsing artery. The roof fell down. The darkness tightened around him, constricting him until it was as if he were in the belly of a great python.

He thought there could be nothing worse than staying in the serpent. Then as his veins flooded coldly with whatever had been introduced into his infusion pump, he learned there was something a whole lot worse than claustrophobia.

When Hades awakened, for a moment he believed he was once again inside that confining darkness. Uncontrollable shivers racked his body, silent tremors under his skin. He gripped his sweat-drenched arms, searching for tubes and wires. His fingers contacted the scarred track marks lining the crooks of his elbows but nothing else. No wires or tubes. No piercing needles.

It had only been a dream.

Slowly, his eyes adjusted to the gloom of his windowless room. The only light came from the smoke detector above him, which shone perpetually in night and day. Its glow wasn't bright enough to fully illuminate his surroundings, but he had spent so much time in the room that he could navigate it in absolute darkness. Even now, with the furniture little more than silhouettes against a greater blackness, he knew what he was looking at when he sat up and glanced around. The shape along the farthermost wall was his dresser, and to the right of it, the punching bag hung from the ceiling like a lynched sentry. Then there was the desk where he sat for meals or to draw. And nothing else. No television. No video game consoles or stereos. Just red walls and a marble floor.

Reaching out, he found the light switch near his bed and flipped it on. Cold light flooded the room, pervading into every corner. It should have comforted him to know he was in his own room, in his own bed. Yet as he looked around, the bad feeling in the pit of his stomach only worsened. He clutched at his arms, feeling tension crawling like spiders beneath his skin.

From under the covers, he retrieved the stuffed cat that Elizabeth had given him at their date almost a week ago. He restlessly ran his hands over the soft fur.

Not for the first time, Hades wondered if he had been drugged in his sleep. It wouldn't surprise him. Every so often, he woke up with the disturbing notion that someone had been messing with him while he slept.

But this was different. This time, the wrongness was outside of him, in his surroundings.

I don't belong here, he thought, breathing deeply. He was flooded with discontent and the first boiling signs of rage, a searing, all-encompassing fury more blinding than the lamp above.

I don't belong anywhere.

He walked to his desk, thinking that drawing might calm

his nerves. He liked to draw, always had. With only a pen and a scrap of paper, he was able to create anything, and creation was almost as powerful as its antithesis, destruction. In a way, artwork was a kind of evolution—useless components coming together to form something truly superior.

Setting the stuffed animal on the desktop, he took a sketchbook and box of charcoal pencils from the middlemost drawer. He leafed through the thick book, searching for a blank page. Most of his completed drawings were of buildings and landscapes. Others depicted mundane objects rendered in exquisite detail.

Hades turned the page—and froze.

A beautiful teenage girl smiled at him from the paper. She had light hair, light eyes, and the memorable face of Elizabeth Hawthorne. Her hair was shorter than the long curls of the Elizabeth he remembered, but there was no mistaking her.

A sprig of flowers was tucked into her hair, and though he had added no color to the drawing, the blossoms were easily identifiable by the shape of their petals. Forget-me-nots. *Vergissmeinnicht.*

Impossible.

In the corner of the page, he had recorded the date of the drawing's completion. Last January. Over a year and a half ago.

Below the date, he had written a title: *A-09*.

With a low moan, he tore the drawing from the sketchbook, ripped it up, and threw the pieces on the floor.

Elizabeth.

"Not her name," a voice said, and only after Hades heard it did he realize it was his own. "Not her. Not her. Not her."

Hades took a deep breath and closed his eyes. He held the air inside of himself for three seconds, then exhaled slowly. After repeating the breathing exercise two times, he opened his eyes, turned to a fresh page in the sketchbook, and began drawing.

He couldn't focus. His hands kept shaking. The pencil

quivered in his fingers and he ended up with a thick serpentine curve instead of a straight line. He turned the paper to the other side and tried again. Instead of just deviating outside of the vision in his head, the lead tip pressed down so hard that he was left with a thick smear of charcoal and a broken point. A dusty scatter spread across the paper, as fine and black as gunpowder.

Who was A-09? Who was Elizabeth? Who was he?

His thoughts grew muddled. The rage and confusion returned. Frustration building, anger mounting, Hades threw the pencil across the room and pushed to his feet.

He shouldn't be here. He didn't belong here. This wasn't his room. This wasn't the Academy. It wasn't fair.

Other teenagers had homes or semblances of homes. They had families. They had parents. They went to school and made friends and talked and laughed, and all he had was this fifteen-by-fifteen-foot square.

The rush of thoughts was like adding oil to a fire. Anger raged up in him. The edges of his vision were swallowed by a pulsing blackness.

He wanted Elizabeth. He would never have her. She lived in a world apart from him, and the moment she realized that he was evolving, she would turn in terror from him. It was only a matter of time.

Forget me not? No, one of these days, she would forget him. Everyone always did.

Before he even knew what he was doing, he picked up the chair and hurled it against the wall.

Even though the chair was made of flimsy wood and he had tossed it with such force that one of the legs had punched a hole in the plaster, the chair didn't break. There was a large crack in the seat, but that was all.

Which only enraged him further, so much that he wanted to scream.

Hades snatched up the chair again and hammered it against the floor until it was reduced to splintered timber. Then he hurled the stuffed animal across the room, tore the desk lamp from its socket, and threw it as well. The metal shade gonged hollowly against the wall, and the lightbulb exploded.

The cacophony of his systematic destruction reverberated against the walls, but nobody came. The room was soundproofed. Even if he screamed and shouted, the sounds would be completely deafened by the foam padding behind the plaster.

He knew from experience. He screamed often.

Rage unsated, Hades seized his ankle sheath from the desk and pulled out the knife. He drove the blade into the desktop, once, twice, several times, punctuating each thrust with a feral snarl. On the fourth time, the blade became trapped in the wood.

Left with nothing within reach to destroy but himself, he rushed across the room. He pounded his fists against the punching bag, hard enough to send pain surging through his knuckles and up his arms. He felt each punch all the way into his shoulder. By the time he collapsed from exhaustion, gasping for breath, his hands felt like they had been dipped in acid. The skin over his knuckles was abraded, oozing blood.

The pain was strangely comforting. It helped distract from the confusion his nightmare had brought. It drowned out the thoughts that weren't his own.

He rolled over onto his back and stared at the ceiling.

This is happening to someone else. Hades lifted his hands and regarded the way the blood spread across his knuckles. *This is not my body.*

The ache slowly receded, and every emotion faded into weary indifference. That was right. This was not his body. It didn't matter what happened to this useless carcass, because the real him was elsewhere. Untouchable.

Washed out, he staggered to his feet and returned to his bed. He picked up his jacket, which he had draped over the iron bedpost. He searched the pockets for his cell phone and turned it on.

As he dialed Elizabeth's number, he sat down on the mattress. His dream had cast a dark, smothering presence over everything. He still felt the walls closing in on him.

On the fifth ring, she picked up.

"Hello, Elizabeth," he said, listening to the soft hiss of the open line. In the background, he could hear voices and laughter.

"I'm sorry, Hades, I'm getting ready for practice, and I can't really talk right—"

"Wait, please don't go."

"Hey, what's wrong?" she asked, her voice soft with worry. "Are you okay? You don't sound..."

"I...I had a bad day," he said, to avoid telling her that he had been sleeping during school hours.

"Oh no, what happened?"

Just her murmur soothed him. He closed his eyes, imagining she was here with him now, lying down beside him. He could almost feel her body heat.

"It doesn't really matter now," he said, curling his fingers into a fist. His bloodied knuckles stung.

A door slammed in the background, and the voices were replaced by the quiet squeaks of sneakers on linoleum. "Are you sure? If you want to talk about it, I'm still here."

"Let's go somewhere."

"What?"

"Skip practice. We can go for a motorcycle ride."

"Hades, I can't just skip it." She sighed. "There's a big game coming up next week. Anyway, I'll see you at the dance tonight, right?"

"I'll be there in thirty minutes," he said. "Wait for me out front."

CASE NOTES 14:
PERSEPHONE

"I can't believe I'm doing this," Elizabeth muttered as Hades took her backpack and purse. He had spent the last five minutes giving her a rundown of what to do while pillion riding, but she still felt like a lemming one step away from the cliff's edge.

Securing her belongings in the bike's tail case, he glanced over his shoulder and favored her with a sinful grin. "Having second thoughts?"

"If my parents find out, they'll kill me."

"You mean the same ones who make you take etiquette classes?" From deeper within the compartment, he removed a pair of tinted goggles. "You can't keep listening to them or you're going to end up like me."

"What's that supposed to mean?"

"Living your life for someone else." After he shut the case, he hung the goggles on the handlebar. "Owned."

She frowned. This was the second time he had used that word, or a variation of it, during a conversation. Owned. Names were proof of ownership.

"So I was wondering, do you live alone?" she asked.

Instead of answering, he picked up his helmet. "It's better if you wear this. Just try not to head-butt me."

She sighed, allowing him to ease the helmet over her head. Through the mirrored visor, the world appeared faded and monochromatic, like an antique photo. After the helmet was secured, he tightened the chin strap for her, stroking her jaw in the process. His leather gloves were soft against her skin. Every touch of his gave her a thrilling rush. The air between their bodies crackled with secret tension.

"How does it fit?" he asked, setting his hands on her shoulders.

She shook her head to test the helmet's looseness, then lifted her hands and tried to pull it off.

"Perfect," she said and then repeated herself a little louder, worried that the helmet smothered her voice.

"Don't worry, I can hear you," he said, giving her shoulder a reassuring squeeze. He took off his jacket and handed it to her, too.

"I'm not cold," she said, although she wished she had brought something heavier than her cashmere sweater. There was a wintry nip to the air. Glancing at the cloud-burdened sky, she wondered if it might rain.

"It's for protection, not warmth," Hades said. "In case you fall off."

She was touched by his concern for her and more than a little intimidated by the thought of getting into another accident. He had already assured her that he had spent hundreds of hours in the last year alone riding motorcycles, but even the most skillful motorists were at the mercy of other drivers.

He put on his goggles and got onto the bike. After a brief hesitation, she climbed up behind him, resting her feet on the pegs. Even though the motorcycle remained steady beneath her, she felt unbalanced, as if at any moment she might tip to the left or the right. She wrapped her arms around his hard waist, finding security in the warmth and sturdiness of his body.

"Are you ready?" he asked.

She took a deep breath, preparing herself for any unpleasant flashbacks that might return with the experience. This was different, she told herself. She was safe here. There was no way she would get into another car accident.

Even so, she felt like she was riding on the edge of a razor. One wrong move and she would bleed.

She leaned into him. "Ready."

The muffled engine's purr deepened into a throaty growl, and they jolted forward from the curb. Her stomach plummeted, and then she surprised herself by laughing aloud. Why had she thought this would be scary?

As they turned onto the street, the motorcycle's loping engine vibrated through her limbs. It was jarring at first but soon became pleasant and soothing as they gained speed. He handled each turn smoothly, maintaining the bike at a modest speed. Her grip tightened as they cleared the first corner, the bike tilting to the side. After the first few minutes, she loosened her hold around his waist. Nothing would happen to her here. She was not in danger.

The helmet blocked out the wind, but she felt the draft through her jacket and jeans. His hair whipped against her visor. She smiled, wondering how gloriously unkempt it would look once they reached their destination.

"How are you doing?" he asked, stopping at a red light.

"I love it!"

"At any point, just tap me on the shoulder if you want me to pull over." She couldn't see his face, but from the rich warmth of his voice, she was certain he must be smiling.

As the traffic light turned green and they surged forward once more, it suddenly dawned on her that she was at his mercy. She couldn't climb off the bike while it was still moving. The helmet would hide her expressions and smother any screams for help. Nobody knew where she was going, and her absence wouldn't be noted for another hour, when her family's chauffeur came to pick her up.

And yet, even as they entered a part of the city she was unfamiliar with, she did not feel afraid. If anything, just being in his presence eroded her anxiety. For once, she felt normal, untouched by the unease and irritation that had plagued her for the last two years.

In a way, she felt like she knew him better than she knew herself. Every gesture, every wicked smile and smoldering glance he offered her, it was just so *familiar*.

Minutes passed.

Growing bolder, she slid her hands from his waist to his thighs, appreciating the firm resistance of his muscles beneath the denim. He was so strong. She would have loved to drive with him for hours, losing herself in his body heat, the pressure of his legs against her own, and the subtle, pleasant aroma his sweat had left on the inside of the helmet.

Still, no sooner had she rested her hands on his hips than he turned onto a street flanked on one side by a wild fringe of trees and on the other by residential buildings. She looked around, gaining her bearings. Her eyes landed on a wooden sign across the street. HUNTLEY MEADOWS PARK.

She realized at once that they hadn't even left northern Virginia. She had thought he was going to take her through the District, but instead they had headed into Alexandria.

Hades followed the road into Huntley Meadows Park. Shadows of trees passed over them, dappling his fair skin with the silhouetted impressions of moving branches and rustling leaves. The fall foliage was stunning against the overcast sky, with the forest canopy draped in all shades of burgundy, amber, and gold.

At the end of the road, they reached a small parking area. Only two other cars occupied the lot, and he parked far from the others, near the tree line.

He waited until she climbed down from the bike before getting off. His T-shirt rode up a bit, giving her a pleasant peek at his lower back and—he abruptly yanked his shirt down.

What was that? As she stared at the back of his T-shirt, her anxiety returned like a frigid draft, raising the hairs on the nape of her neck. She had only gotten a split-second glimpse of his bare skin, just long enough for her to tell there was something *wrong* with it.

He removed his goggles, turned to her, and held out his hands. Realizing he wanted his helmet back, she took it off and handed it to him, hiding her recurring apprehension behind a smile.

"Did you like it?" he asked, brushing her hair out of her eyes. Her skin tingled beneath his gloved fingers, and her unease began to recede. She decided the strange creasing on his back had been an illusion cast by the shadows and ashen sunlight. Not real.

"It was a little scary at first," she admitted, "but after a while, I had fun."

"I'm glad to hear that." After returning his goggles to the tail compartment, he retrieved her purse and handed it to her. "Do you want your backpack, too?"

She shook her head. "There's nothing valuable in it."

As she reached up to unzip her borrowed jacket, he stopped her.

"Don't," Hades said. "You look sexy in it."

"But aren't you cold?"

"I like the cold." Tucking his helmet under his arm, he looked around, smiling at the autumn splendor. "This is nice, isn't it?"

"I love it."

"I knew you would." He took out his phone and opened it. "What time do you usually get out of practice?"

"Four thirty."

He stuck his phone back in his pocket. "We have about twenty minutes before I need to take you back."

Hades held out his free hand. She accepted it, entwining her fingers through his. Her common sense nagged her that what she was doing was *dangerous*, but her schooling was overshadowed by an even stronger force. Part nostalgia and part intuition, it was a feeling that went far deeper than the countless vague warnings her parents had given her since the car accident. Rationality paled in comparison.

"Have you been here before?" he asked.

"No, but I've heard about this place. My mom hates mosquitoes, so we don't do a lot of outdoor stuff." Her mom's idea of mother-daughter bonding consisted of getting pedicures and going shopping. The pre-accident Elizabeth might have liked those activities, but her amnesia had taken away most of her enjoyment. Now, she just found the outings boring, although she wouldn't dare tell her mom that to her face.

As they walked along the trail, a subtle transformation overtook Hades. He relaxed his posture. A warm smile softened his face's hard edges, and even the tired circles under his eyes appeared to diminish somewhat. He seemed at home in the forest, as if just escaping from the District's shadow revitalized him.

Soon enough, the trees receded into wetlands. Dead cattails bristled from the stagnant water, producing an illusion of a meadow growing atop a lake. As she stepped onto the boardwalk that extended through the marsh, its wooden boards creaked beneath her shoes.

He let go of her hand to wrap his arm around her waist. "I'm so glad I get to experience this with you."

"Me, too." She leaned against him, listening to his steady breathing. The hard taps of his boot heels on the old boards pleased her almost as much as his palm's warm pressure. Even his footsteps struck her as soothingly nostalgic.

They reached the end of the boardwalk then turned around and made their way back to the parking lot. Twenty minutes passed far too quickly for her taste, and if the dance hadn't been later that night, she would have been tempted to stay longer.

The return trip was just as pleasant as the drive to Huntley. At 4:20, he parked along the curb in front of Manderley Prep's gate and retrieved her belongings for her.

Elizabeth took off the helmet and handed it back to him, then returned his jacket as well. She ran her hands through her windblown curls, wincing at the tangles she uncovered. Her hair was so fine—once it got knotted, combing it out again was as hard as trying to untie a web of spider's silk without breaking it.

"Now I can see why your hair's so messy all the time," she said, then winced. "Oh, I didn't mean it to sound like that. I like it, really."

She sat on one of the low concrete benches near the fence. Searching through her purse, she found a comb and brushed it through her hair. On the third stroke, Hades touched her wrist.

"Let me." He set his helmet on the bench and took the comb from her.

"It's fine, really," she said as he stepped behind her. His slim, agile fingers stroked her hair, gathering it back behind her head. His leather gloves did little to affect his dexterity. He slid the comb through her tangled curls, drawing out a soft murmur of appreciation from her. When he reached a large mat, he didn't rip the comb's teeth through it, but carefully worked away the obstruction. In spite of his strength, he could be so gentle.

"That feels so good," she said, closing her eyes as he effortlessly combed out the knots and snarls. "You know, you really don't have to wait with me if you don't want to. My family's chauffeur should be here in just ten minutes."

"A chauffeur? Impressive."

She blushed, feeling suddenly self-conscious. Worried she had offended him, she opened her eyes, just in time to see his teasing smile chill over.

He took a step back, keeping his attention trained on the tall woman who approached from the front gate.

Elizabeth stood, her cheeks growing hotter by the second. Volleyball practice must have ended early.

"I was worried when you didn't show up for practice today," Coach Slate said, stopping next to them. Looking from Hades's wild, windblown hair to his muddy combat boots, she frowned. "But it seems you had other plans."

Elizabeth searched for an excuse and found herself at a loss of words. What if Coach Slate told her parents she was with him?

"It's my fault, ma'am," Hades said, offering the coach a pleasant smile. "I kidnapped her."

Elizabeth winced. Okay, he was totally *not* helping.

"I'll see you later, Miss Hawthorne." He leaned forward and kissed her on the cheek, then climbed onto his motorcycle.

As he drove off, an irrational fear seized her, and she suddenly became certain that she would never see him again. A part of her longed to rush after him and drag him back, but by the time she stepped onto the curb, he had already disappeared.

CASE NOTES 15: APOLLO

When Tyler opened his eyes, he felt like he had emerged from a baptism in the Lethe, the river of forgetfulness. He looked around at his surroundings, struggling to make sense of where he was.

At first only the most basic details stood out to him, like the aroma of roasting chicken and the gleam of shiny appliances. He realized he was standing in a kitchen, but it wasn't his own.

As he grappled with how he had closed his eyes in the school hallway and opened them elsewhere, his attention was diverted to a weight in his right hand. He looked down to find his gloved fingers locked around the handle of a silenced pistol.

A choked whimper drew his gaze across the room, and he noticed a young woman standing with her back to the kitchen counter, her face a mask of terror.

"Please don't hurt me." As she spoke, she blotted around her eyes.

With a jolt, he realized the girl was around his age, maybe even younger. Maybe another student at his school, for all he knew.

He lowered the gun. He wanted to throw the pistol on the ground. He wanted to scream until he figured out how he had gotten here and why he had a gun. But his fingers refused to budge from around the pistol's handle.

"Where am I?" he asked.

His skull felt too small for his brain, shrinking by the moment. It felt like he'd been strapped into one of those medieval torture devices that, through the use of a turnkey, crushed the head between the arms of a vise.

"How did I get here?"

The girl stared at him wordlessly, her expression one of intermingled fear and confusion. Tyler had a feeling his face looked similar.

"What..." *What was I about to do?*

The girl began to edge away from him, glancing at the doorway, then at him, then at the phone on the countertop.

Dazed, he pressed a hand against his face. He wasn't supposed to be here. This wasn't his home. This wasn't school.

So what happened?

There was a phone call, he realized. *And I answered it as I walked to my car. And then he said to me, "There's something I need you to deal with, Apollo." So then he sent me a text, and then...*

He couldn't remember. All he knew was he was holding a gun. Who was he supposed to take care of?

"Please don't hurt me," the girl said.

Tyler swallowed hard, and his hands began trembling. Indescribable fear welled up inside him like oil from a crack in dead earth, a bubbling black pool that threatened to suck him down into it.

A distressed keening pierced his ears, and he lurched back, struck a chair. Stumbled. Turned away from her.

His gaze shot around the room, searching for an escape. The room seemed to grow smaller and darker by the moment, like a tank. Like a coffin.

Breathing raggedly, his head filled with the shrill ringing, he fled from the room. In the front hall, as he passed a mirror, he caught a reflection of himself. Wide eyes, pale mask of horror, still holding the gun. The gun! What had he intended to do with the gun?

Like an adjusting riflescope, his scrambling thoughts focused on a single goal: *I need to get out of here!*

He rushed down the hall as the girl started shouting. He couldn't hear her words, but he knew she must have dialed 911.

Good. Let her call them, in case he lost himself again. There could be no more.

If not for his own survival instinct, he might have put the gun to his own head. But he couldn't, so he ran like he was being chased. Chased by memories, so many coming back to him: modern white decor; white house; bloody house; bloody woman lying on the floor, her blond hair matted with drying blood—and, oh God, he had shot her. He knew he had.

As he ran, the floor seemed to rock beneath his feet, while the walls alternatively expanded and shrank back. He threw open the front door with such violent force that it slammed into the coiled stop and shook on its frame.

He froze on the concrete step, blinking against the sunlight, so bright even though the sun had already begun its lazy red descent toward earth.

For a moment, he was stunned by the light's brilliance. He stared at the sky and thought, *Where was I before this? Why can't I remember? I was at school, right? Yeah, I was at school.*

Then he shook his head, trying to gather his thoughts. There was no time to contemplate these things. He needed to escape.

Where?

The gun—should he dispose of the gun?

No, he must go back inside and shoot the girl, then wait for her father and shoot him, too! And if her mother came home first or after, he must shoot her as well. There could be no witnesses.

No! He must stop right here, right on the concrete step, inhaling the dusky aromas of the gardenias and roses. Breathe in. Breathe out. Bring the gun to his temple or into his mouth. Yes, his mouth! Bite down, taste the iron, and pull the trigger.

No! Enough, just enough! His car. He had to get to his car.

He must get this house out of sight and, by doing so, out of mind.

Tyler looked around him and found the street deserted. His car was nowhere in sight. Left with nothing but his instincts, he followed a compulsion to the right.

He sprinted past luxury homes and willows so great that even their gnarled trunks drooped toward him. He made a turn to the left, unsure of where he planned to go.

All he knew was that he must get away. No more of this job, or the doubt, or even the pavement beneath his feet. All he needed was the smooth endless blacktop, then the highway when he reached it. Only then would he have time to consider his situation.

Trembling from both exertion and adrenaline, he took another lurching turn at the street corner. He didn't even try to conceal or toss the gun. He just ran.

Ahead, he spotted a familiar black sedan. He reached into his pockets and found his keys, fumbled for the right button. The lock clicked, and he threw the door open, sat down in the driver's seat, and twisted the key in the ignition.

He didn't wait to buckle his seat belt before tearing down the street. He hardly even had the sense to drop the gun on the passenger seat, and after doing so, realized that its placement was just asking for an accidental discharge.

Didn't matter. There was no time to put it safely in the glove box. No time to stop at the stop sign or the yellow light that turned red the moment he sped through the intersection. No time at all, not for him, not anymore. It was over. He had failed the job.

As he drove, his gaze swept senselessly to the gun, with the same inevitable motion of a flower edging toward the rising sun. When he looked at the weapon, a sudden image came to him like a vision, through the eyes of an apathetic observer.

Tyler saw himself pulling along the side of the road, and he really *did* stop along the curb. He saw himself pick up the gun, and he did that, too. As he pressed the silencer against the side of his head, he felt the cold metal touch his skin.

His finger edged to the trigger, but he didn't see himself do it, because he was weeping now. His eyes squeezed shut around the stinging tears, and his body shook with urgent, choking gasps.

You need to do it. You need to pull the trigger, and you need to do it now, before they do something worse to you.

What could possibly be worse?

You must do it.

The tank. They'd put him back in the deprivation tank.

The tip of his finger touched the trigger and stroked it with infinite care. He thought he could feel the inert destructive power of the gun as a vibration that traveled beneath his skin.

"This isn't you," he said aloud. "You're not doing this."

And he responded to himself: "But I need to do it. I failed. I need to do this."

"No, you don't."

"I must."

"I can't."

His monologue calmed him enough to lower the gun and, with trembling, sweaty fingers, eject the magazine. He thought about throwing both pieces into the street gutter but didn't.

Tyler wanted a weapon to protect himself, but he was still playing with the idea of finishing the job. Someone else's desires. Someone else's orders. The influence of the psychic parasite occupying him, intangible but perceived as the twitching of his index finger on the trigger. And that whisper in his head, that damned whisper, urging him on. Kill, kill, kill—even himself.

He put both the pistol and its ejected magazine in the glove box, feeling a little better when he couldn't see them.

After taking a deep breath, he continued driving. His head swam with unanswered questions.

Where would he go? Home? What would he tell his foster parents—that he had woken with a gun in his hand and the distinct impression that he'd held—and *used*—a gun before? And perhaps he should add that he had also been about to kill another, that he had a cell phone he didn't own—wait, the cell phone!

Keeping one hand on the wheel, Tyler searched his pockets. He found the phone in his jacket pocket, as cold and repulsive as the gun handle, and tossed it into the cupholder.

He would examine the device once he stopped, but he had a feeling it would yield even fewer answers than his temperamental memory.

He started driving with little idea where to go. The neighborhood began to feel like a maze built to confuse and ensnare him. When he finally reached a familiar road, he sighed in relief and turned onto it.

Soon the nicely maintained streets gave way to the familiar sprawl of townhouses he called home. By then almost half an hour had passed since he had gotten into the car, and he still felt the urge. Go back and kill them, or kill himself.

Tyler parked along the curb and got out of the car, reeling once again in the cold, fading light. So wintry and harsh, more like the lamps above a surgical table than natural sunshine, so distorting, causing him to swivel about, searching for pursuers.

Heartbeat spurred into a panic, he strained to hear the rev of an approaching engine or the wail of police sirens.

Nothing. Dead silence.

As he looked around him, he noticed an old woman sitting in the enclosed porch of the row house across the street. The black metal screen obscured her face, making it impossible to discern her expression or even her individual features.

She raised her left hand; her other was concealed below the wood railing. Maybe holding a gun. Or maybe it was a phone she gripped onto, dialing 911.

Too shaken to respond, he searched for his house keys. Not in his pockets. Oh God, had he dropped them? Left them back at the girl's home?

No, that was impossible. They were attached to the car keys

and still in the ignition.

Trembling slightly, Tyler plucked the key from the slot and locked up the car. The gun was still in the glove box. The flip phone sat on a pile of loose change in the cupholder. He left it there and went inside his home.

"Dad? Mom?"

The house was silent.

"I need to talk to you," he said aloud, but in a whisper this time, not even a cry for help. He was beginning to doubt his reason for coming here. What could he expect them to do?

If he showed his foster parents the gun and explained his blackouts, they would call the police. They could not be trusted. And neither could the authorities, not after what had happened.

Forcing himself to calm down and take things slowly, he went into the kitchen. He poured some cold water from the tap, gargled with half, and then drank the rest.

His hands felt filthy, so he washed them. Then he splashed cold water onto his face. The slap of icy water woke him up a bit and made him feel grounded in the moment.

After drying his dripping skin with a hand towel, he held the damp cloth against his face, thinking.

First things first, he needed money, if only just for gas and lodging.

Tyler went into the master bedroom and searched the cabinets, feeling ill. A memory was coming back to him now, emerging as grotesque as maggots from rotten fruit. He had searched another bedroom not too long before. He had rifled through the contents of dressers much nicer than these, through silk and lace lingerie and men's boxers, through the intimate details of two strangers' lives. That was after he had shot the woman but before he had killed the man.

Nauseated, he sat down heavily on the bed.

"What the hell is wrong with me?" he mumbled, staring down at his hands. "This just can't be happening."

Once he had regained control of himself, he stood. He continued searching, found nothing of interest or use in the drawers, and moved on.

From the master bedroom, Tyler went into the small study where his foster father spent his nights. He opened the desk drawers, but all he found were a few porn magazines alongside mundane business-related paraphernalia.

He was about to give up when, after pushing aside a pile of papers, he discovered a thick manila envelope. He would have disregarded it like all the rest of the files, if not for the edge of a dollar bill sticking out of it. He shook the contents onto the desk.

In the entire house, he had been expecting to find perhaps a couple hundred dollars if he were lucky, but what fell out was a folded sheet of paper and two thick stacks of bills. The bundles were sealed with thin strips of cardboard, upon which their monetary value was written in bold print: $2,500.

His foster father was an architect and his foster mother worked at a real estate agency. Even though they made enough to get by, their bank accounts weren't padded enough to justify having five thousand dollars in cash lying around like pocket change.

He opened the paper. In printed type, it read:

Here is the quarterly stipend. Last month's report was disappointingly bare. I expect you to keep careful, descriptive records of his behavior, including any changes in sleeping and eating or unusual comments he has made. Do not forget to include the dates and times; this is the second time I have had to remind you to be thorough, and my patience thins. Additionally, as I have mentioned repeatedly, any uncharacteristic actions on his part MUST be brought up with me. I cannot stress this enough.

At the bottom of the sheet there was a phone number but no closing, no sender, not even a name to identify who "he" was. Although Tyler had a sinking idea.

"The hell?" He looked at the money, then again at the letter.

The manila envelope was unmarked, which meant it hadn't been mailed.

He picked up the telephone. After a brief hesitation, he dialed the number on the letter.

The phone rang five times then went directly into voicemail. There was no personalized message, just a "please leave your number after the beep" robotic voice.

He hung up without speaking and returned the phone to its cradle. He riffled through the bundles of cash, in a brief moral dilemma over whether he should take all or only half. It seemed like such a petty thing to worry about, considering how stealing would be the mildest of his crimes by far.

Just as he decided to take the entire five grand, the desk phone rang.

The caller ID identified it as a private caller, but Tyler suspected it was from the same number. He picked it up.

"Hello?" a man said.

A great shudder racked his body, and goose bumps exploded on his back and shoulders. Whereas before the overhead lamp had felt like an interrogator's spotlight trained on his act of thievery, the room now darkened. And darkened. And the darkness crept along the corners of his vision as he felt himself wobble, at the edge of a faint that was not a faint.

"Is someone there?" the voice asked.

Tyler dropped the phone. It missed the cradle. He didn't bend down to retrieve it.

Over the recurring keening in his ears, he heard a choked whimper. Then, as he gathered the money with shaky hands, he discerned words entangled in the terrified sound. "I don't want to go back. Not back. Not back. Please, not back."

Cradling the cash against his chest, he backed away from the desk. He felt blind even though he could see just fine. He felt deaf to everything but that voice, which he heard even as he ran down the hall and into his room, blasting through his ears as he dropped the cash on his bed. As he rushed to the closet, he realized the voice was in his own head.

He threw open the closet door and seized the travel backpack from the top shelf. He threw clothes into the bag, not caring what he grabbed or if they were even clean.

He just wanted to feel a little prepared for what might lie ahead. It was the same false hope felt by the passengers on a sinking ship, as they clung to their worldly possessions while their footing fell apart beneath them.

As Tyler zipped up his backpack, he wondered how long the secret reports had been going on. Had the money paid for his used car and the gas it consumed—after having offered to get a job and pay for it himself? And hadn't his foster parents told him it wasn't necessary for him to work, that instead he should just focus on his schoolwork? Had they wanted him to keep his schedule open for times like this, when blood must be spilled? Was that it?

He shook his head. Thinking about it wouldn't help him. Neither would fantasies of suicide or terrified obsessing over what lay ahead.

Really, there was only one thing left to do.

The pursuit of truth.

STATUS REPORT: SUBJECT 2 OF SUBSET A

DK: In our first interview, I asked if you had ever killed someone. Your answer was rather ambiguous, and I must say, I'm very curious. Are you willing to cooperate this time?

A-02: Depends. Are you willing to eat my shit?

(Let the record show that at 00:00:28 the subject received one jolt of electricity at 10mA.)

DK: Maybe we should try the drugs again. At least you were somewhat polite when you were doped up.

A-02: Whatever you want, sir.

DK: Have you ever killed someone?

A-02: Untie me, sir, and I'll show you. You think you're so superior now, but let's see how condescending you are when I kick your teeth in.

(At 00:01:35 the subject received two shocks.)

DK: Are you a masochist, Hades? Does pain excite you? It almost seems like you're asking to be punished.

A-02: I don't like to be called that.

DK: Oh, come now. Subject Two of Subset A is quite a mouthful; it gets so tedious after a while calling you that. It's hardly a proper name.

A-02: It's not supposed to be a name.

DK: So is that how you referred to yourself at the Academy?

A-02: Only with the trainers. With the kids in other subsets, it's A-02.

With Nine and my friends, it's just Two.

DK: So you have friends. I'm surprised. You don't seem like a very friendly boy.

A-02: I was my team's commander during war games.

DK: Is that a touch of pride I hear? It must be so shocking, going from being the Academy's golden boy to this. To nothing.

A-02: I worked for what I did. It wasn't given to me.

DK: I never said it was.

A-02: I worked so hard.

DK: If it's any consolation, your talents won't be put to waste here.

(Silence from 00:03:10 to 00:03:23.)

DK: Now, I'm going to ask you this again. Have you ever killed someone?

A-02: No.

(Two shocks administered at 00:03:39.)

DK: Polygraphs don't lie, Hades. Are you afraid the Leader will punish you again? I assure you, everything you say in this session will be confidential, between you and me.

A-02: What about her?

DK: Eveline is simply here to monitor your vitals. I would like you to think of her as a friend.

A-02: When you aren't torturing me, do you like to have her tie you up and electrocute you, too? Does that get you off, Doctor? Does this?

(Two shocks, 00:04:41.)

A-02: So, is this what they call foreplay?

DK: Have you ever killed anybody?

A-02: No.

(Two shocks, 00:05:01.)

DK: I know you want to tell me, Hades. Why are you holding back?

A-02: I'll tell you if you let me see Nine.

DK: Fair enough. It's a deal.

A-02: Okay. There was a guard at the Academy who was assigned to our subset last year. He was a friendly man. He acquired a reputation. If he liked you, he would bring you presents from the outside, but you had to be special for him to do that.

DK: Were you special?

A-02: No. He preferred blondes.

DK: Like Nine.

A-02: Yes. Everything he gave her, she shared with me. The gifts became more and more generous. I knew it was only a matter of time before he expected something in return, so I killed him. Then I disposed of him like the trash he was.

DK: How exactly did you accomplish something like that?

A-02: I don't want to talk about it.

DK: Well, how did it make you feel?

A-02: Good. Alive.

DK: Would it interest you to know there have been no reports of murders occurring at the Academy?

A-02: I got rid of his body where no one would find it.

DK: No disappearances, either.

A-02: I remember doing it.

DK: Are you sure you didn't just imagine the whole thing?

A-02: I know I did it.

DK: But how can you be so sure of that? There is no definitive proof that what you're claiming actually happened. You're mentally unstable, Hades. Do you ever lose touch with reality? Do you ever see things that aren't really there?

A-02: No. I know what you're trying to do, and it's not going to work with me. I'm done talking to you.

DK: We're not finished yet.

A-02: I am.

DK: Don't you want to see Nine?

A-02: Let me, and we can continue this discussion.

(Let the record show that at 00:08:50, the subject was shown a photograph of A-09 with her placement family. Refer to A09-15.jpg for image.)

A-02: Wait. What's this supposed to be?

DK: You wanted to see her. This is as close as you will ever get to her, Hades. She's left like Persephone. She's gone to live with her family. You will never be a part of her life again.

A-02: No. I don't believe you. This is another test. It doesn't even look like her. Where's the beauty mark under her eye?

DK: It's her. Special circumstances required her to undergo some minor cosmetic surgeries, but you and I both know it's the same girl.

A-02: It's not real. She wouldn't be smiling like that.

DK: You are dead to her, Hades. No, to be more accurate, you were never alive to begin with. Every memory of you has been cleared from her mind completely.

A-02: You promised. I told you, and you promised you'd let me see her. I love her. You promised. I won't accept this. You can't take her from me. I want to see her. I won't eat until I see her.

DK: Are you asking to be force-fed again?

A-02: I'm not going to stand for this. I'll kill myself before I let you take away the only thing I have to live for.

DK: Can you speak a little clearer, please? Talk into the recorder.

A-02: You can take that recorder and shove it up your ass, Doctor. Or better yet, let me do it for you.

(At 00:11:58, the subject was administered four consecutive jolts at 13mA and lost consciousness.)

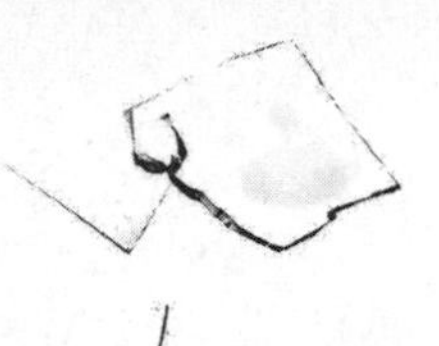

CASE NOTES 16: PERSEPHONE

Night fell.

Elizabeth nibbled on her lip as she stood in front of the school gate, watching cars come and go as students were dropped off. She listened for the rev of a motorcycle engine, playing with the umbrella she had brought in case it began to rain.

"I just don't understand how the PTA could do this to us," a woman said, and Elizabeth glanced over her shoulder to find her calculus teacher, Ms. Hill, talking to Principal Brown. "Now we're two chaperones short."

"Hopefully, at least one of them will decide to show up," Principal Brown said, crossing his arms. He wore his usual tweed suit, a fake spider on his lapel being the only festive addition to his outfit.

"We're going to be spread thin tonight, Pete." Ms. Hill sighed. She was at least dressed up for the occasion, in a witch's tattered gown and pointy hat. "If nobody's patrolling the halls, another incident like last year might happen."

Principal Brown sighed, too, and his lean face contorted into a miserable frown. "The last thing we need is a student getting pregnant on our watch."

A motorcycle pulled into the parking lot and parked in the back. Before the rider even stepped down, Elizabeth was already hurrying forward, ducking out of the way of moving cars and splashing through puddles.

As she reached him, Hades took off his helmet and smiled down at her. "You're beautiful, Elizabeth."

Ah-leis-uh-bith. She loved the way he pronounced her name, enunciating each syllable with care. He made it sound so exotic.

"Thank you," she said, blushing, and glanced down at his field jacket and jeans. "No costume?"

"It's in the top case," Hades said. "Is there a place where I can change?"

She nodded. "I'll show you to the bathroom."

She waited for him to lock his helmet to the bike and retrieve his costume, which was still in its shopping bag. Then she took him through the gate, earning a curious glance from Ms. Hill, and into the school building.

While he changed, she put her umbrella in her locker. The storm probably wouldn't return tonight.

When he came out of the men's restroom, the sight of him took her breath away. Dressed in a black toga embellished with silver thread, Hades resembled his namesake, cold and beautiful.

The toga's hem fell to just above his knees, showcasing his muscular calves. Clearly he did not neglect his legs in his weight-lifting regimen.

As her gaze lifted, she noticed his knuckles were all beat up.

"Oh, no," Elizabeth said, grabbing his hand. She furrowed her brow at the sight of the fresh scabs. "What happened?"

"It's nothing," Hades said, squeezing her hand. "I forgot my gloves during boxing practice."

"You poor thing."

"A kiss might make me feel better."

She lifted his hand to her lips and kissed his fingers, far from the abrasions. As she released his hand, he cradled her cheek in his palm. His thumb stroked the corner of her mouth, teasing her lower lip.

"So beautiful," he murmured, leaning closer.

Inches away from a kiss, she raised her hand, gently pressing it against his chest.

"Not here," she said. "I don't want to get in trouble if someone catches us."

They went back outside so that Hades could put his clothes away. As Elizabeth waited by the gate, Ms. Hill nudged her shoulder.

"Is he a friend of yours?" Ms. Hill asked.

"My bodyguard," she said, then blushed, realizing her slipup. "I meant boyfriend."

Ms. Hill lifted her eyebrows so high they disappeared beneath the brim of her witch's hat. "Is that so?"

"He's going to be transferring here soon." Elizabeth turned to Principal Brown. "Right?"

"Uh, I wouldn't know," Principal Brown said, rubbing his bald head in obvious befuddlement.

Before she could ask Principal Brown if he remembered Hades from the enrollment meeting, Hades returned to her side.

"Ready?" he asked.

She smiled. "Ready."

As they neared the gymnasium, he strode ahead and opened the door for her. The gym had become a dance floor overnight. Fake cobwebs and crepe streamers festooned the walls, while black and orange balloons drifted across the ceiling. Pop music played on speakers, and red lights cast the room in an eerie light.

The ruby glow drained the pigment from his irises, turning them as gray as gravestone marble, and honed his jawline and hard cheekbones into lethal edges.

Walking into the gymnasium, he drew an arm around her waist and held her close to him. She treasured the warmth of his body and the sense of security his touch brought her. She felt that nothing could go wrong when they were together.

"Oh, I love this song," Elizabeth said, cocking an ear toward the speakers. "Come on, let's dance. It'll be fun."

Hades smiled at her, but she could tell he wasn't thrilled about the idea. "I've never danced before."

"Never?"

"I had a very unusual upbringing."

"I kind of figured," she said, laughing.

"I know how to march," he said, "but that's about it."

"March?" she asked, surprised. Was he in the marching band at school?

He swung his leg forward and stomped his shoe—boots instead of Grecian sandals like hers—against the ground. As he marched forward, he kept his body straight and rigid. His posture was perfect, and though the flowing toga lent elegance to his hard, abrupt movements, she could easily envision him in a military uniform.

He stopped in front of her and stood at attention. When he noticed she was giggling, he started laughing as well.

"I haven't done that in years," he admitted. "But it comes back to me."

"I'm guessing you didn't learn that in your school's marching band?" she asked. It almost seemed like a soldier's march, like something out of a harsher, more totalitarian time.

"Probably not."

"If you can do that, I think you'll be able to dance just fine."

Hades was a quick learner and, after the first few missteps, caught on to the nature of the dance. Soon enough, he and Elizabeth moved in perfect rhythm, as if they were two parts of a larger machine, working in synchronization. With each step, his muscles rippled and flexed beneath his clothes.

Every so often, when there was a loud noise, he glanced in that direction. Twice, he took his hand off her to reach for his waist, though he had no pockets.

Laughing, she drew his arm back to her. "Why do you always do that?"

"What? I can't hear you."

She shook her head and smiled at him. She had to elevate her voice to be heard. "Do you want a drink?"

"A what?"

"A drink!" she shouted and, taking his wrist, led him to the snack table.

Gone were the days of punchbowls. Cans of soda chilled in ice, alongside bowls of candy, cupcakes, and cookies. A scatter of fake cobwebs and plastic spiders decorated the orange tablecloth.

Hades appeared more interested in the food than the drinks. He inhaled half a sleeve of Oreos, washed them down with a can of ginger ale, and then turned his attention toward the cupcakes.

She picked up a can of root beer, popped the lid, and took a sip. The soda fizzed in her stomach, and she burped loudly. Blushing, she imagined what her mother would say.

Very unladylike, Elizabeth, she thought and giggled. She felt tipsy, as if just being in his presence intoxicated her. His dark, irresistible aroma gave her such a rush.

Her joy didn't last. As she turned to Hades, icy liquid splashed down the front of her dress, and she found herself face-to-face with her ex-boyfriend, Adam Fletcher.

"Oops," Adam said, blinking in feigned surprise. "I didn't see you there, Elizabeth. Sorry about that."

Her smile died in an instant, and she began trembling in anger and embarrassment. Cold, sticky soda permeated her dress, darkening the rosy fabric. She heard laughter all around her as the surrounding students remarked on what had happened.

"Looks like Little Miss Perfect pissed herself," a girl said gleefully. Elizabeth searched the crowd for the girl but couldn't find her.

"You're dead," Hades said and took a step toward Adam. His clenched jaw carved rigid shadows into his cheeks.

"Hey, it was just an accident, man," Adam said, giving him a snide smirk. "Go back to stuffing your face."

"Hey." Elizabeth grabbed Hades's wrist and pulled him back.

"It's okay. Come on. I need to go to the bathroom to get cleaned up. Let's go."

As much as she wanted to watch him beat Adam to a bloody pulp, she knew her parents would kill her if her secret date got in a fight with the son of the district attorney. She didn't want Hades getting arrested over something as petty as a spilled soda.

Blinking back tears of rage, she walked out of the gymnasium and into the deserted hall. Cold soda drizzled down her legs and landed on the floor. Her only comfort was the warmth of his fingers entwined through her own.

As she reached the ladies' room, he stopped her.

"Wait, I think I know a better way."

She wiped her eyes and looked up at him. "A better way?"

"To clean you up," he said, a smirk on his lips.

A blush seared her cheeks. "I'm not stripping, if that's what you're trying to suggest."

"You don't have to," he said, leaning forward. He nuzzled her dripping neck, his breath hot against her skin. His mouth pressed against her jawline, then lowered to her clavicle with playful slowness. She felt his teeth lightly graze her as he licked the soda off her skin.

"Ugh, no licking or biting, please." Elizabeth started laughing. "You're such an animal."

"I get that a lot." Hades stepped back and regarded her with a half smile. His lips were slightly parted, his pupils dilated and hungry with desire. Though he maintained a relaxed posture, his body swelled with hidden tension. Every step, shifting muscle, and minute gesture of his radiated a powerful, almost bestial virility.

He reminded her of a wildcat preparing to pounce, and that thought made her heart race. She wanted to kiss him, but she didn't dare. Not here, where anyone could see them.

"My parents will kill me if I come home with hickeys," she explained. "And I don't want to get expelled for an extreme PDA."

"PDA?"

"Public display of affection."

"Fair enough," he said, brushing his hair out of his face. She loved how spectacularly messy his hair was, as if it refused to be tamed by any comb or brush. She wanted to stroke her fingers through the thick, glossy strands.

She thought about what her parents would think of his hairstyle, so different from the hordes of Harvard clips and neat comb-overs that overran Manderley Prep. Knowing how her parents would flip at the sight of Hades only made him more irresistible, like a forbidden fruit she couldn't help but take a bite from.

"I should really get this washed off," she said, then winked at him. "I'll be out in a few minutes. Just try not to kill anyone in the meanwhile."

"What about maim?"

Past his teasing smile, she saw a lingering trace of anger. Maybe it was just her imagination.

"No maiming, either," she said and ducked into the restroom.

Standing at the counter, she dampened a wad of paper towels under the faucet and wiped off her legs and chest. She tried her best to clean the stained fabric, using liquid soap from the dispenser, but the brown mark remained.

She wished Adam would just leave her alone. He had been bothering her since sophomore year, when the first thing he had done after she had returned to school was try to kiss her. Maybe the pre-accident Elizabeth would have allowed that, but it had felt like a serious violation to her.

She felt no attraction to Adam, no attachment. Nothing but disgust as he attempted to woo his way back into her heart. Once, he had even asked her if she wanted to try ecstasy, as if that was any way for a senator's daughter to behave.

Giving up trying to remove the stain, she stood beneath the hand dryer, bending her knees to allow the hot air to reach the worst of the dampness on her dress. She felt ridiculous squatting like that, and she was glad Hades wasn't there to see her.

She smiled, remembering his offer. Anything considered a public display of affection was forbidden on school grounds. Even making out led to suspensions. His high school must be way more lax about its PDA policy.

When she returned to the hall, she found him leaning against the row of lockers, his arms crossed.

"Do you want to go back to the gym?" he asked as she walked over.

"No, um, I don't really want to dance anymore," she admitted. "I'm sorry. It's just that everyone saw me get drenched. If I go back there, I'm going to feel like Carrie."

"Who's Carrie?"

"She's the main character in that Stephen King movie. The one about the psychic girl."

"I've never heard of it."

"She gets covered in pig blood at her prom. That's what I meant."

"Oh." Hades gave it some thought. "I don't like dances anyway."

Elizabeth chuckled. "I had a feeling."

"Let's go for a ride," he said. "We can get something to eat."

"Do you have a bottomless pit for a stomach?" she asked, glancing at his washboard abs.

"Sublimation."

"What?"

"That's what the doctor calls it. It's the same reason I work out." Hades leaned toward her, his lips rising in a seductive smile. "A way to alleviate the urge."

She felt a tingling deep in the pit of her stomach. "What urge?"

"To devour you, Miss Hawthorne," he said and seized her.

She gasped in surprise as he dragged her against him, then started laughing when he pretended to eat her neck.

"If you want to be a vampire, you should have chosen a name like Edward or Lestat instead of Hades," Elizabeth said as he released her.

"I don't get it."

"They're…" She sighed. "Never mind."

"Besides, I already told you I don't have a name."

"Fine. Your 'proof of ownership.'" She leaned against him and rested her head on his chest. "You know what's funny? I feel like I've known you forever. I know it sounds stupid, but it's true. When I saw you the first time, it was like a reunion. I can't tell you how happy I feel, just being here with you."

Hades ran a hand through her hair. His fingers lingered on her neck then eased down her back. "I feel the same way."

Lifting her head, she stared into his vivid blue eyes. Now more than ever, they reminded her of twin gas flames, smoldering with hunger.

Then his lips were on hers, and words like "PDA" and "suspension" and "scandal" disappeared from her vocabulary.

Seized by a frantic passion, she drove herself against his muscular body. Her hands moved in an animal-like frenzy, sliding from his broad shoulders to his long, unkempt hair to the chiseled ridges of his cheekbones.

That intoxicating natural aroma of his rolled over her, like smoke and burnt cinnamon, muddling her thoughts and leaving her trembling with need.

Elizabeth explored his body as if she were seeing it for the first time. She stroked his face and neck then wrapped her arms around his back to trace the hard contours of his muscles through his clothes.

As his hands eased from her shoulder blades to her waist and gripped her sleek dress, a commotion from behind her cut their kiss short.

"I told you, she's a little slut," Adam called, to accompanying laughter.

Elizabeth let go of Hades and backed away. She smoothed her skirt down with trembling hands, mortified that she had been caught in the act.

As she turned to Adam, her heart sank further. Adam had his smartphone out and was pointing it at her. Flanking him were two boys she recognized from the football team, Chris and Derek.

"Why don't you feel him up a bit?" Adam suggested, earning another bout of laughter. "Put on a real show for YouTube. Hey, do you think he'd like to hear about that time we did it in the school parking lot after homecoming?"

"That's not true!" Elizabeth said, and in the corner of her eye, she watched Hades grow rigid.

"Just because you lost your memory doesn't mean it didn't happen, sweetheart. You think you're doing a convincing job, playing Little Miss Perfect? You're not fooling anyone here. Maybe you think the car crash gives you an excuse to just give me the cold shoulder, cut me off like you don't even know me, but it doesn't. We *had* something, Elizabeth, and you turned it all to shit."

"That was two years ago, Adam!"

"I don't care. Nobody walks away from me like that. Never."

"You're going to stop talking now," Hades said, his voice low and calm, almost pleasant.

She looked up at him—and froze.

A dangerous smile played on his lips. In his searing blue eyes, rage reflected like a flame in clear glass.

For the first time in his presence, Elizabeth felt a twinge of fear.

"Make me," Adam said.

Hades slid his gaze to Adam's waist and regarded him thoughtfully. Elizabeth looked down, too, and wondered what had caught his attention—the fact that Adam's fly was unzipped or the belt he wore, embellished with an ornate Navajo buckle.

"Nice belt buckle," Hades said, striding forward.

Adam's arrogant smirk faded by a degree. "What?"

"Looks very expensive."

"Why do you care?" Adam scoffed. "What are you doing staring at my junk anyway? You some sort of fairy? That the kind of guy you go for now, Elizabeth?"

"Those blue stones are turquoise, right?" Hades asked, stopping a hand's reach from Adam.

"What's it to you?"

"When you get hit with a belt with a buckle like that, it doesn't just bruise," he said in a low, sensual murmur. "It cuts deep. It scars. Do it hard enough and it can cut you nearly to the bone."

"Is that a threat?" Adam asked, narrowing his eyes which were the color of rancid grease. A trace of uneasiness showed through his sneer.

"No, I don't make threats. I make promises."

"My dad's the district attorney," Adam said, taking a step back.

"What difference does that make?" Hades stepped forward.

"If you touch me, he'll sue your ass."

"How can you sue someone who doesn't exist?"

"The hell's that supposed to mean?"

"Get down on your knees and apologize to her, or you're going to find out."

"I'd like to see you try," Adam said and brought his other hand forward to push Hades away.

Before Adam's palm could make contact, Hades seized his arm and twisted it away, while at the same time slamming his shoe into the back of Adam's knee.

With a grunt of pain, Adam's leg gave out beneath him.

Using his own weight as a driving force, Hades rammed Adam into a locker face-first, then viciously wrenched the boy's arm backward at the joint.

Even from where she stood, Elizabeth heard the sickening crunch of breaking bone. Her stomach twisted at the sound. It was almost as gruesome as the gargled cry Adam made.

Hades hammered him once more into the locker, hard enough to dent the metal door, and then threw him to the ground.

"Are we still recording?" Hades asked, laughing in obvious amusement.

Adam curled in a ball on the floor, clutching his shattered nose with his good arm. His other arm flopped at his side, bent like a snapped twig. Violent sobs racked his body.

Hades kicked Adam onto his back and stomped down on the cell phone, breaking it. Then he stomped down on his ankle, with similar results.

"Do you think the people on YouTube will like this?" he mused as Adam writhed in agony, screaming through a bloodied mouth.

Going to their friend's defense, Chris and Derek bum-rushed Hades. He dodged each punch that the boys threw at him, with trained ease, until Derek tackled him from behind and put him in a choke hold.

"Stop fighting!" she shouted, shaken by how quickly the situation had turned violent.

Hades grabbed Derek's arm with both hands. Bending at his knees and waist and arching his back, he used the sudden forward motion to throw Derek over his shoulders and onto the floor.

Derek hit the tile hard enough to knock the air from his lungs, and he began gasping for breath. With a ruthlessness that horrified Elizabeth, Hades kicked him in the head, twice. On the first blow, Derek spat out blood and teeth. On the second, he went still.

"Hades, stop!" she said. "Stop, you're going to kill him. What's wrong with you? Please stop!"

"Now we're putting on a good show." He stepped over Derek's unconscious body and advanced toward Chris with the deadly grace of a panther circling in for the kill. His voice was husky, almost erotic. "Are you enjoying this, Elizabeth?"

Is this one of his urges? she thought, running toward the two boys. *Does he like to* hurt *people?*

"Hey, man, I'm done." Chris raised his hands and backed away. "I don't want to fight you."

"You disrespected her," Hades purred, and though she couldn't see his face, she was certain he must be smiling. "You *profaned* her."

"No, man, I didn't say nothing."

"You need to suffer," he said and lunged at Chris.

"Please stop!" Reaching Hades, she grabbed a fistful of his costume to pull him back. The shoulder strap tore free, turning his toga into a skirt and revealing his back to her.

Her stomach plummeted at the sight.

Pale ropy scars stretched from his shoulder blades to his tailbone, ripping a devastating warpath through his bulging trapezius and lumbar muscles. In places, the scars were so numerous that his skin was buckled and creased like a scrap of old leather.

Get hit with a buckle like that and it cuts deep, she thought as her vision darkened around the edges. Her legs liquefied beneath her.

In her mind's eye, Elizabeth saw a room she had never stepped foot in before. The room was as big as her high school's gymnasium, with folding tables stacked along the walls. Metal poles extended from the floor to the ceiling, providing foundational support.

On one of those poles, a pair of handcuffs had been soldered in place. A black-haired boy hugged the pole with shackled hands, sobbing in agony as blood dripped down his bare back and oozed to the floor. Each cry was punctuated by the snap of leather against skin.

Subject Two of Subset A has committed the grave offense of attempted desertion, a deep, accented voice said as darkness descended over her like the wings of swarming ravens. *This is what happens to deserters.*

First there was a shrill scream. Then there was nothing at all.

CASE NOTES 17: APOLLO

The flip phone rang from its place in the cupholder.

Keeping an eye on the road, Tyler reached into the center console and groped around until his fingers touched smooth plastic.

He answered on the tenth ring. "Hello?"

"Apollo?" a deep voice said, and he knew at once the name of the man the voice belonged to. He just didn't know how he knew.

He had half a mind to respond with every foul word in his vocabulary. His teeth ground together, trapping the profanities in the back of his throat.

"Olympus is rising," Zeus said.

"Rot in hell, Zeus," he spat, though a part of him wanted, desperately, to respond with the appropriate phrase.

A stunned silence filled his ear.

"Olympus is rising," Zeus stammered, as if he thought repetition would make Tyler bare his belly and pant like a dog, eager for orders.

"I know what you made me do," Tyler snarled into the speaker.

"How—"

"I can't remember it all, but I'm going to remember, and when I do, I swear, you'll fry for it." Then he hung up, rolled down the window, and tossed the phone into the street. He didn't see it break, but he thought he heard a satisfying *crack* as it struck the pavement.

Even if the phone was traceable, either by the manufacturer's GPS or a rogue microchip installed after purchase, it didn't matter. If the initial fall hadn't killed the device and another car didn't run over it, he would be miles away by the time Zeus retrieved it.

With no destination, Tyler found himself driving aimlessly though suburban labyrinths. Once he realized what he was doing, he pulled into the deserted parking lot of a strip mall and parked facing the street. He didn't like the thought of sitting still, but by driving around like this, he wasn't just wasting gas, he was wasting precious time, too.

"Think, Tyler," he murmured. "Think. What are you going to do?"

He thought about the gun.

It would be easy, the voice in his head urged. *Just cock the hammer and stick the gun inside your mouth. Aim it upward. Pull the trigger. It will be quick. Painless. Fearless. A much kinder death than what you gave* them.

"No! I didn't kill them! I didn't kill anyone!" He slammed his fists into the steering wheel, drawing the horn out in a long, lonesome wail.

"I didn't do it…"

His breathless words seemed to linger for several moments after he had spoken. He rested his forehead on the top of the steering wheel and pressed his hands to his face, shuddering violently. Even with the heat on and warm air blasting from the vents, he felt frozen to the bone.

There were four things he knew.

First of all, he had killed people. He just wasn't sure how many.

Secondly, with his latest act of mercy, going to the police was no longer an option. He had left DNA evidence at the crime scene, and the girl knew what he looked like.

Three, Zeus had made him kill. Tyler didn't know who the man was or how he did it, but that was an indisputable truth.

Four, thanks to that stupid, stupid phone call, Zeus was onto him now. He knew Tyler had defected and probably thought he remembered more than he actually did. And once Zeus found him, Zeus would kill him. There was no doubt about it. Zeus would kill him.

Tyler took a deep breath and counted down from ten. He felt somewhat better once he reached zero.

A single glance in the rearview mirror was enough to make him want to look away. Bleak misery cast a shadow over his face. The longer he stared at his reflection, the less he saw of himself. The closer he looked, the more he could make out the blood-soaked monster who had calmly executed a sobbing woman at point-blank range.

Resisting the urge to smash the mirror, he took his smartphone from his jacket pocket. He had texted Shannon so many times he didn't even need to refer to his contacts list as he dialed her number. His finger hesitated over the last digit.

The memory of her lovely doe eyes and warm smile filled his mind.

He shouldn't get her involved in this. It wasn't Shannon's problem. It had nothing to do with her, and involving her would only put her in danger. But he felt so alone. He had no one to turn to, not even the foster parents who had agreed to take care of him.

He remembered how she had helped talk him down from his panic attack. Just hearing her voice soothed him.

Tyler sighed and thumbed in the final number. As he listened to the ringing, he tapped the fingers of his other hand against the steering wheel. He glanced at the glove box and found himself unable to look away from it, fixated by the gun that waited inside.

Shannon answered the phone on the third ring.

"Is that you, Tyler?" Her soft voice filled his ear, as reassuring as a warm breeze.

"Yeah, it's me. Did I wake you up?"

"No." She yawned. "I wasn't asleep. I was doing homework. My battery's almost dead, so I can't talk for long. How was your day?"

Sorrow twisted like a blade in Tyler's gut as he realized he might never see her again. He clenched his teeth and closed his eyes, struggling to contain the frantic words that pressed against the back of his throat. There was so much he wished he could say.

"Tyler, are you there?"

"Yes. I'm still here." He took a deep breath, suddenly finding it difficult to speak. "My day… I had a good day. I'm just tired."

"I can tell. You don't sound like yourself." She paused. "My phone's going to die any moment. Give me a sec. I'll see if I can find my charger."

"No, it's okay. I need to go anyway."

"Oh." She sounded slightly disappointed. "I'll call you back in the morning, then."

"Yeah." He wondered if he might ever see her deep brown eyes again, let alone the light of day. "Good night."

"Good night."

After hanging up the cell phone, Tyler returned it to his pocket. He leaned over the center console and opened the glove box. He took the gun and put it on the passenger seat then rutted through the box. The compartment was overflowing with documents, receipts, food wrappers, and fliers, which he shoved away in search of the road map he had purchased to compensate for his smartphone's spotty internet connection.

Once he found the folded booklet, he spread it over his lap, trying to make sense of the highway lines and barely legible text.

Where can I go? Where?

The map swam before his eyes, becoming a meaningless jumble of twisting lines. Frustrated, he scrunched up the paper, tossed it into the passenger seat's footwell, returned the gun to the glove box, and began driving again.

Though it was past rush hour, the Beltway was crowded to capacity. Of the vehicles he shared the highway with, more than half of them were semitrucks or cargo trailers. Yet as they approached, he found himself taking repeated glances in the rearview mirror. And as they passed, he looked into the cabs and searched the faces of their drivers for murderous intent.

With the sedans and vans, he was even more paranoid, clenching the wheel and stooping over in his seat, anticipating gunfire. Even the motorcyclist who shot past him, faster than a speeding bullet, made him anxious.

As he drove, images came to him like flashing lights, ghostly faces that were resurrected from the deep grave of his memory. He didn't know their names, but he recognized them from recent news stories. Although the ghosts came unembellished with wounds or bullet holes, he knew they were dead. Just like he knew he had killed them, even though he couldn't recall when or how.

Even as fear caught him in a stranglehold, he drove without stopping. When tears prickled his eyes, he blotted them away with the back of his hand and kept the other hand firmly on the wheel.

He wasn't sure whom he was crying for. He didn't want to accept that those people were dead and that he had killed them. It seemed impossible. A bad dream. A nightmare.

Although he had passed many exits since driving onto the Beltway, he drove past them without considering turning off the highway. His gaze skimmed thoughtlessly over the green signs mounted on overpasses and along the side of the street.

He didn't know where he was going, but a part of him did. Presumably the same part of him that had picked up a gun and used it.

CASE NOTES 18: ARTEMIS

Shannon awoke to the ringing of a cell phone.

With a tired groan, she lifted her head from her desktop, dismayed to find that she had drooled all over her homework. Wondering if Tyler had called her back, she reached for her smartphone and discovered that it was dead.

"The hell?" she mumbled, looking around for the source of the elusive ringing. Scooting her wheeled desk chair across the room, she tracked the noise to her dresser. She opened the top drawer and found a black flip phone nestled in a mess of underwear and socks, right next to a baggie containing a couple grams of weed.

While she remembered purchasing the pot from Alan, she could not remember putting the mysterious cell phone in her dresser. Or charging it, for that matter.

Her compulsion to answer the call overrode her confusion. As she picked up the phone, she looked at the caller ID. Restricted number.

She opened the phone and lifted it to her ear. "Hello?"

The caller's voice was cold and tense. Instead of answering her greeting with one of his own, he simply said, "Olympus is rising."

"Pandora's box is opening," she said, suddenly wide awake. Her confusion disintegrated in an instant, leaving only calm detachment.

"There has been an incident, Artemis," Zeus said. "Do you remember Apollo?"

A face drifted up from her memory. Blond hair and stunning amber eyes. Features that were trapped in pure despair, then softened and chilled by indifference, then again tortured by the greatest misery. Flickers of emotion like a dying candle in the dark.

The phantom's voice: *I'm sorry. I'm so sorry.*

"Yes."

"Apollo has gone AWOL."

No, not Apollo. Tyler. Tyler Bennett. That was his name, wasn't it?

No, it couldn't be his name.

"Your orders?" She stared at the blinking red numerals of the clock on her dresser. 9:45. Her foster parents would still be awake. Not that it really mattered.

"Right now, I am tracking his movements. I have his GPS coordinates." He paused, breathing so softly that for a moment she thought she'd been disconnected. When he spoke again, his voice was even harsher. "He needs to be taken care of, do you understand?"

She gave a small nod. It made her feel a little better to know her expression couldn't translate through her voice. Otherwise he would have seen her face contort at his next words.

"Don't risk trying to subdue him," Zeus said. "Kill him."

"Understood," Shannon said.

"Get in your car and head north on Route 29. I'll call you in fifteen minutes to update you on his location. Use the backup gun."

"Okay."

Even after Zeus hung up, she kept the phone to her ear. She listened to the hiss of the open line, thinking about how much it sounded like sand slipping through the stem of an hourglass.

Time was running out.

Shannon closed the phone and rose to her feet. She changed out of her pajamas and dressed in a pair of jeans and a T-shirt. She put on a jacket and zipped it up. As she tied her shoes, she thought about nothing at all. She felt dead and adrift from her own body.

She reached under her bed, testing the floorboards until she found the loose one. She pulled it up with ease and removed a small metal container from the space underneath. Nestled inside the box's foam inserts were a concealed waist holster, a pistol with a ten-round magazine, and a silencer.

She clipped the holster to her belt and secured the pistol inside. She placed the silencer in her pocket, where it could easily be accessed.

With her burner phone stowed in her jeans pocket, she stepped into the hall and went to her foster parents' room. She knocked on the door.

"Come in, sweetie," her foster mom called.

Shannon opened the door and walked inside. Her foster parents were in bed, a bowl of popcorn between them. A corny comedy was paused on the TV screen.

"I'm going out," she said.

"Where?" her mom asked, then glanced at the alarm clock. "It's almost ten, sweetie. Isn't it a little late to be—"

"I need to go somewhere. It's important. I don't know when I'll be back."

Her mom's smile faded, and so did her dad's. They didn't protest as she shut the door, nor did they attempt to follow her down the stairs.

After getting into her car, she rested her phone in the cup-holder. Underneath her jacket, the gun felt like an anchor, both dragging her down and keeping her tethered. In a way, its weight was almost comforting, though the thought of using it on Apollo chilled her to the bone.

She drove north. Ten minutes later, Zeus called her back to

give her instructions. When he wasn't speaking to her, he ranted aloud, to no one in particular.

"Damn Hades," he said at one point. "Where the hell is he?"

Twice, he excused himself to make calls on a second phone. Shannon heard only snippets of the conversations. She discerned the words "Senator Hawthorne" and "hospital" and "Subject Nine of Subset A" from Zeus's growl, but little else.

These things did not bother her. She did not feel in complete control anymore. Reality had faded away the moment she had heard the words "Olympus is rising."

She felt so far away from herself, and she drifted further with every mile that took her closer to Apollo.

STATUS REPORT: SUBJECT 2 OF SUBSET A

Seventy-eight days since arrival. An interesting development with Hades today, after three rounds of electroconvulsive therapy followed by twenty hours in the sensory deprivation tank. I showed him an assortment of photographs (see attached) and asked him to identify the subject of the picture.

(Refer to A2018.mp3 or cassette tape "Hades - Session 18" for complete recording of interview.)

Exhibit 1: Spaniel dog next to a red doghouse.

A-02: Uh. Bark.

DK: Close. That's the sound it makes, but do you remember the name for it?

(Silence from 00:00:45 to 00:00:57.)

DK: It's a dog, spelled D-O-G.

A-02: Oh, right. I forgot.

Exhibit 2: A can of Coca-Cola.

A-02: Thirsty. Uh. Drink. Fizz. Soda. It's soda.

DK: Good boy.

Exhibit 3: 9mm pistol, maker's mark clearly visible, serial number and barrel text blurred out.

A-02: Beretta M9.*

---

*Note: In a physical test performed two days after session 18, the subject was able to dismantle and reassemble the Beretta M9 and the M40 rifle in record time. Marksmanship simulation results remain unchanged.

DK: Good job. That's perfectly correct.

Exhibit 4: Subject 9 of Subset A, with her placement family.

DK: What would you call this?

A-02: I don't know. People?

DK: Do you know who any of these people are?

A-02: No, sir.

(Let the record show, EEG readings normal. Pupils are not dilated. No signs of external agitation. Heart rate is 40 beats per minute. Blood pressure is 108/60.)

DK: What about the young woman in the middle, the one with blond hair?

A-02: No.

(Polygraph test shows a negative reading. Subject is telling the truth. Refer to file #A02-018 for complete test results and EEG readings.)

DK: You don't recognize her?

A-02: Am I supposed to?

DK: No. How does this picture make you feel?

A-02: I hate it.

DK: Why?

A-02: I don't know why. I just do, sir. Can we move on to the next one, please?

Exhibit 5: *Playboy* centerfold depicting a nude woman in a

provocative pose.

(Slight fluctuation in blood pressure and heart rate. No notable signs of sexual arousal.)

DK: Well, this is new. This picture does nothing for you? What about this next one?

A-02: Dead. (:04 pause) I'm dead, aren't I?

DK: Please elaborate.

A-02: I don't feel. I don't feel anything. What's happening to me?

(Increased function in amygdala, heart rate is 60 BPM, blood pressure at 118/80. Let the record show that the subject has begun to strain against his restraints.)

DK: Calm down, Hades.

A-02: What did you do to me?

DK: Let's look at the next photo, shall we?

A-02: You've killed me, you bastard.

DK: No, Hades, I'm afraid you're still alive.

A-02: I hate you.

DK: I know.

A-02: I hate you so much. I will kill you. Someday, I'll kill you.

DK: Someday, you'll feel differently, Hades. Over the next few months, I think you'll find yourself changing in ways you've never imagined.

Final verdict: no sign of deterioration in his tactical training or motor skills from ECT. Treatment has proved successful in repressing his memories of Persephone, but his memory of the Academy remains intact, more or less. He has forgotten some of his Russian and Mandarin, but it is too soon to say whether this memory loss is permanent or temporary. It's unfortunate, because his language skills would have come in handy for espionage. But for the time being, his rebellious attitude is my main concern. I must destroy his pride and dignity. Hades must be taught that he is a weapon, not a person.

I look forward to the day when he is broken completely.

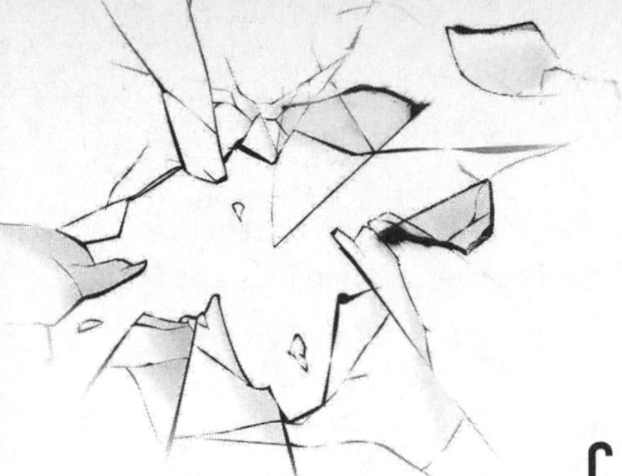

CASE NOTES 19: HADES

Hades tore through the night like a falling star, shooting in and out of traffic at eighty miles per hour with little regard for his own safety.

After leaving the school, he had changed into the clothing stashed in his motorcycle's top case, but his shirt and field jacket did little to protect him from the elements. The blustering wind gnawed through the layers of fabric and settled deep inside him as a cold, destructive rage he couldn't seem to shake.

He passed warmly lit houses and wished they would burn to the ground. He wanted to see the whole world collapse until he and Elizabeth were the only ones left standing. Everyone but her could die.

Even as he left affluent suburbia behind for untamed forest, he was unable to escape from the hatred and anguish that roared around inside him. Like a natural disaster, it was only a matter of time before the emotions tore him apart entirely, leaving him devastated and utterly alone once again.

When the resentment became unbearable, he found himself grinding down on the throttle, accelerating from eighty to one hundred and twenty miles per hour in seconds, then climbing even higher still. The forest on either side of him faded into a black blur, and he had the strangest notion that this was what the world truly looked like. This formless, dark, howling chaos was what life *really* was, but nobody ever saw it.

Even as he sped down the highway, he couldn't get Elizabeth's face out of his head or forget about the way she had screamed at the sight of his back. An overwhelming déjà vu descended on him, which only further stoked the rage inside him.

I know her. I don't know her. I know her. I don't know her.

His memories were gouged out and shattered. Only fragments remained. As for the first fifteen years of his life, there was almost nothing left at all. It was as if he had been born as an adolescent instead of an infant. And yet…

I've heard her scream before.

The scars on his back throbbed and burned. The deadened tissue ripped into the surrounding skin like a net of barbed wire, tearing him open from the inside out.

His fingers curled around the handlebar. At first, it felt like chrome and rubber. Then it felt like an unyielding steel pole, and suddenly he had the impression of a vast, terrible presence looming over him, bearing down on him. The wind snapped against his back like the crack of a belt, and no matter how fast he went, he could not outrun it.

"I need you, Nine," a voice whispered. "Where are you?"

With a jolt, Hades realized the voice was his own. He loosened his hold on the throttle, slowed, and pulled to a stop along the side of the road.

"Nine," he said aloud. The word sounded strange.

There was no mental image to accompany the number. Just a deep black hole. That was all Nine represented: complete emptiness.

He climbed off his bike and took off his helmet, staring into the dark forest. His phone rang in the motorcycle's top case, but he ignored it. Wind rustled leaves, and tree branches swayed toward him as though beckoning.

Sometimes, Hades wondered if he belonged in the wilderness, away from everyone else. He didn't feel like a human anymore, and there were days he wondered if he had ever been human to begin with.

He would have liked to undress and walk into the woods naked. He wanted the bramble to tear apart his skin and the stones to puncture his feet, turning the rage inside him into something physical. And if he couldn't bleed, then someone else needed to bleed for him.

Someone needed to suffer.

His thoughts returned to what had occurred at the school and how Elizabeth had fainted at the sight of his back. He had caught her before she could hit the floor, and he'd tried to wake her as the other boy ran off. When that failed, he had carried her into the gymnasium and took her to a perplexed chaperone. He told the woman to call an ambulance for her and left before the woman could stop him.

It had been the most rational decision, but still, he wanted to stay by her side as she slept. He wanted to see if she would look upon him with fear or love once she opened her eyes.

"Elizabeth Hawthorne," he whispered to himself. Normally, the sound of her full name pleased him, but tonight it struck him as *wrong* somehow, like a nickname he hadn't grown accustomed to using. Or as if it weren't a name at all.

Why had he felt such a connection to her when he had seen her photograph in the newspaper? It went beyond the old adage of love at first sight, and instead was more like destiny, or something far stronger than that. Just being in her presence dredged up feelings he thought he didn't possess.

"Elizabeth," he repeated, focusing on a slender birch. In the gloom, obscured as it was by moss and shrubbery, he could almost pretend the white trunk was a nude female figure. Elizabeth Hawthorne, waiting for him.

He couldn't tolerate the thought of losing her. They were meant to be together. They *must* be together. He was supposed to protect her.

For so long, he had felt dead inside. She had awakened something inside him and brought it back. Maybe A-02. Maybe another ghost living inside him. He didn't know. When the anger left, there was only emptiness that ached like an open wound. A hole that demanded to be filled.

This isn't real anyway, he thought, staring into the night. *None of this is real, except for Elizabeth.*

But it still hurt so much, and the pain never went away. The only thing he could do was transfer it to someone else.

A branch snapped deeper in the forest, drawing his attention. In the pale glow of his headlight, he saw a large amorphous shape free itself from the outer darkness.

As the hulking black form lurched toward him, his heartbeat accelerated, not in fear but in exhilaration. He felt in the presence of a pagan god of the wilderness, a feral entity ready to initiate him into its midnight court.

The shape drew closer. The motorcycle's headlight gleamed off coarse black hair and an elongated muzzle, and stoked a fire in the creature's beady eyes.

A black bear. Or maybe just the shape of a black bear, the same way he was just the shape of a person.

What lurked beneath its pelt?

It wasn't the first time he had seen a black bear in the wild, but he had never been so close to one before. And yet, he felt no terror, only awe and excitement.

The animal stopped, rose onto its hind legs, and regarded him. It was large, three hundred pounds easily. Its claws could rend his flesh better than any thorns the forest had to offer, tear him apart, spill him out, and leave him open to receive.

This was fate.

"Devour me," Hades whispered, dropping his helmet. He took one step toward the bear, then another, staring into the beast's eyes. His heart raced, and a hot, throbbing tension swelled in his core.

He had killed others. What would it be like to be killed himself?

If he died here, it would be fate. If he lived, it would be proof of everything he was destined to become.

The bear uttered an odd, blustery sound like the wind. Maybe the bear *was* the wind.

"Devour me!" he shouted as loudly as he could, spreading his arms to welcome the bear-that-was-not-a-bear. "Devour me! What are you waiting for? Devour me!"

The beast dropped onto all fours and retreated, leaving a trail of crushed leaves and flattened shrubbery in its wake. Hades watched it go, trembling in excitement and an overwhelming sense of power.

This was only confirmation: he was not a person. He was evolving into something more than that, exceeding humanity at the top of the apex.

Seized by a rapturous ecstasy, he laughed aloud and wrapped his arms around himself. He reached under his shirt to touch his scars.

They were his mark. His proof.

As he stroked the cool, waxy lines of scar tissue, his muscles flexed beneath his palms.

He was powerful.

He was *evolving*, and each kill took him one step closer to *being*.

"I am Hell," he said and took the night's silence as confirmation. "I am Hell, and she is mine."

CASE NOTES 20: APOLLO

Tyler didn't head for the state border, as he'd thought he might, but instead found himself on a residential street lined with old but attractive houses. Even though the neighborhood was more than an hour's drive from his house, and even though he couldn't remember ever having come here, he recognized the area. He had been here before. Recently. With someone else.

But who?

He parked under a tree and just sat there.

"How will it end?" he wondered, staring at the street ahead. Unlit houses. Inky expanses of grass and blacktop. It was hardly past ten, but there were so many dark, staring windows. The homes didn't even feel like actual homes, just replicas on an abandoned movie set.

There was a flashlight in a canvas tool kit stored in the glove box. He took it out.

"How will it end?" Tyler whispered to himself.

He got out of the car and walked down the sidewalk, through the amber pools of light cast by the streetlamps. He didn't turn on the flashlight, didn't need to. Darkness, for once, was his friend.

He passed over a hopscotch pattern as faded and ghostly as prehistoric pictographs on cave walls. Dead leaves crunched under his sneakers as he passed through shadows that puddled like ink on the sidewalk. He walked past numerous homes. He didn't know which house he was gravitating toward until he stopped in front of it.

One story, coral-red walls. A ceramic giraffe kept vigil on the stoop.

No cars were in the driveway and the windows were black. When he reached the concrete walkway, he hurried up it. He tried the front door and found it locked.

Tyler ducked to the right. Keeping close to the wall, he crept around thc sidc of the home, testing windows. He felt like a thief, although he had no intention of stealing anything. He had no intentions at all. Just vague intuitions.

He wasn't sure what waited for him inside the house. He didn't know and didn't really want to find out. But he was as much a victim to the apprehension that seized him as he was to the pull of fate or gravity. The weird feeling dragged him along the side of the house, past tulip beds and rosebushes.

From its perch among the stars, the crescent moon grinned down at him like the Cheshire Cat's smile, urging him forward. Trapped in the rose bramble, a scrap of crime scene tape fluttered loosely as he passed it.

The backyard was fenced in by a six-foot-tall stucco wall. In the moonlight, it glowed like an ice sculpture. A padlock hung from the latch of the wrought-iron gate, but its bolt was disengaged. He removed the lock, opened the gate, and followed the gravel path along the side of the building.

When he finished a complete circuit of the house and had still found no unlocked windows, he returned to the back door. He picked up a river rock from the irrigation border around the bushes.

A part of him realized what he was doing was crazy, dangerous, illegal. He had to get away, to be anywhere but here.

He ignored that inner voice in favor of a deeper intuition and smashed the rock into the French door. The rock shattered the night as quietly as it did the glass, with a soft, silvery clatter.

No alarm went off. No voice called out from within.

He stood and listened, just in case. Once he'd assured himself that nobody had heard him, he stuck his hand through the gaping glass hole, careful not to cut himself on the jagged edges. He fumbled with the latch until he heard a rewarding *click*, then pulled his hand back through the hole and opened the door.

"We went through the door," he whispered as he stepped inside. The house was as deserted as a mausoleum and seemed to demand the same respectful silence that one should observe when walking among the dead. He held his hand over the flashlight beam, softening its glow as he strode through the kitchen and into the hall.

"We went through the front door because we had been given a key."

No, not we. *He*. He had been given instructions over the phone. A backpack had been left for him, and he picked it up at the specified dead drop. He hadn't seen the man who dropped it off, if it had even been a man.

Tyler entered the living room. "We went inside and waited. And when she came home…"

Who was she? The woman. The woman whose influence he saw in the walls all around him. An heirloom quilt draped over the back of the sofa. Paintings of sunflowers and beech trees in winter. Little details she had selected mindfully that must have pleased her to look at.

"When she came home, I pointed a gun at her, but I didn't pull the trigger."

Who had come here with him?

Tyler took a deep breath, struggling to resurrect a face from his memory. But the person's features were just a blur. Blank. He was pretty sure his companion had dark hair. Brown or auburn, maybe darker.

He left the living room and continued down the hall. There was something he needed to do here, and it was more than just to remember what he had done. But what?

Feeling like a voyeur, he swept the flashlight over the books in the small study. The yellow beam stroked the stiff leather spines of medical tomes with names like *Understanding the Effects of Sensory Deprivation*, *The Unconscious Mind*, and *Martin Young's Guide to Psychiatric Medicine*. The shelves were tightly packed, except for the third one. Like a row of posed dominos, the books had collapsed onto their sides.

Something had been there. Leather-bound journals with inscriptions in blue ballpoint. Neat handwriting. Dates. Numbers. Jotted abbreviations.

Before he had taken care of the woman, he had come here and retrieved them. But what had been inside them?

He put a hand to his face, trying to recall something more substantial than just disjointed memories. "Come on," he whispered, rubbing his eyes then his mouth. "What did they say?"

Tyler sighed and leaned against the edge of the desk, set down the flashlight. He pressed his hands against his face. "Think. Come on. Think. Remember."

Just as he was about to scream in frustration, he heard a creak from outside and the rustling of bushes.

He picked up the flashlight, turned it off, and eased away from the desk. He retreated to the bookshelves, taking care not to trip into anything. His heart pounded so hard he almost believed it could be heard through six inches of drywall and insulation.

As the presence passed along the side of the house, he lowered his hand to his waist. His fingers touched empty space. He hadn't thought to bring the gun inside with him.

How had Zeus found him? Was it possible that he was microchipped somehow or that a tracker had been hidden inside one of his belongings?

No, it was too soon to say whether the person outside was a threat to him. For all he knew, the footsteps could belong to a concerned neighbor or a police officer.

A door opened then closed. At the back of the house, floorboards groaned.

Sweating profusely, heart racing, he stepped out of the room. He didn't turn the flashlight on as he entered the hallway but relied on his adjusting vision to find his way.

The person had entered from the back door, but now Tyler could hear them move around in other corners of the house. Another door creaked open, ever so softly, then eased shut.

He hurried down the hall, heading toward the back door. Just as his hand closed around the handle, he heard footsteps behind him.

As he threw open the door, a bullet tore through the drywall inches to his right. He leaped down the back steps and took off running, certain he would be shot at any moment.

Footsteps pounded after him. In his panic, they seemed to duplicate, amplify, until he thought he was being chased by a crowd instead of a single person.

As he neared the wall, Tyler dropped the flashlight, took a running jump, grabbed the edge of the wall with both hands, and then threw himself over. Seconds after he landed on the other side, gunshots exploded overhead. Three feet to his left, a slender pine tree shuddered, raining down needles, pulverized wood, and splintered bark.

Gasping more out of terror than exertion, he made a sharp turn to the left. He had read somewhere that people tended to follow the direction of their dominant hands when they didn't have a destination. He was surprised he was even able to strategize in such dire circumstances. If not for the immediate danger he was in, he might have patted himself on the back.

As Tyler ran, he focused on his breathing. In. Out. In. Out. The air whistled through his lungs, as sharp and cold as the blade of a scalpel. His heart pounded so loudly he could barely hear his labored breathing. The chasing footsteps were all but drowned out by the rush of blood in his ears.

He cut across lawns and scaled fences. The moonlight was an inadequate light source, and by the time he reached his car, he was covered in scrapes and bruises. With each step, needles of pain shot through the soles of his feet and deep into his calves.

He didn't think he was being followed. Still, he didn't pause to catch his breath until he was safe in his car, driving down the main road.

After tearing a helter-skelter path through unfamiliar neighborhoods, he eventually stopped in front of a convenience store many miles from the scene.

He took the silenced pistol and its detached magazine from the glove box. The magazine had a ten-round capacity, and there were ten bullets still inside it, gleaming through the holes drilled into the side of the box. After reattaching the magazine and unscrewing the silencer, he slipped the pistol into the shoulder holster under his jacket.

There was no way to determine how the assassin had found him, but Tyler wasn't about to dismiss it as an uncanny coincidence. While he loathed having to abandon his car, an electronic tracker might be hidden in the upholstered seats, the undercarriage, or another clever spot. Another possibility was that his smartphone had been used to find his coordinates.

As he retrieved his smartphone from his pocket, a revelation struck him as hard as a sledgehammer blow.

The black flip phone he had destroyed was identical to the one Shannon had found in her purse, the one she suspected belonged to the dark-haired boy on the metro. Was it possible that the boy could somehow be involved in this nightmare, another killer like himself?

If that was true, and if the boy suspected Shannon now possessed his phone, then she was in danger. Just going on a date with her might have put a target on her head.

He dialed her number, then spat out expletives when it went straight to voicemail. Dead, after all. He hung up and called

Alan next, who answered after the first five rings with a slurred greeting.

"Alan, it's me," Tyler said, tapping his fingers against the steering wheel. "Listen, you know that girl who came to your house last week with Victoria?"

"Uh, no, not really. Just that she's Victoria's friend. Why?"

"Shannon. Her name's Shannon Evans."

"Oh, right. Shannon."

"Do you know her address?" Tyler asked, staring out the window in search of pursuers.

"Why would I know her address?" Alan asked.

"Okay, look, what's Victoria's phone number?"

"Uh..."

"I know you're high," Tyler said, "but this is really important. Think very carefully and tell me Victoria's number."

"Dude, just give me a minute. I have it in my contacts. I'll text it to you, okay?"

"You'd better," he snapped and hung up.

In the thirty seconds it took for Alan to text him, Tyler felt his anxiety blossom into panic. He couldn't get that boy's—*his name is Hades*—face out of his head, and he was certain he had met the boy somewhere before the Woodley Park Station encounter. Perhaps during another murder.

As soon as his phone pinged with a new text message, he dialed the number Alan had provided. Victoria was surprisingly prompt and picked up the phone on the first ring.

"Who is this?" Victoria asked. In the background, he heard music and laughter.

"Tyler Bennett from school."

"You mean Shannon's boyfriend?"

Tyler found himself at a loss of words.

"Just kidding," Victoria said, chuckling. "I know you two aren't going out yet, but she told me all about your date. Don't worry, she had nothing bad to say."

"Victoria, what's Shannon's address?"

"Oh, it's— Wait, why do you want to know her address?"

"I need to talk to her about something really important, and her phone's dead."

Victoria sighed. "Seriously? How do I know you're not going to, like, kidnap her."

"Victoria, please, there's no time to explain. Just tell me her goddamned address."

"All right, all right. Do you have a pen ready?"

Tyler scrounged through the glove box for a writing utensil. When he found a pen, he spread the roadmap on his knee and wrote the address she gave him on the map's margins.

"If you're sending her chocolates, she hates coconut," Victoria said.

"I'll keep that in mind," he said and hung up the phone. He retrieved his backpack from the backseat and put the map inside the main compartment.

He slung his backpack over his shoulder, stuck his smartphone in his pocket, and got out of the car. He left the keys in the ignition and the door ajar, hoping that an opportune thief would assume he had run inside the store for a speedy errand.

On his way to the sidewalk, he passed an idling pickup truck and paused briefly beside it. The owner, a stocky man in a flannel shirt, was so fixated on examining his phone, he didn't even notice Tyler. Within seconds, he was on the move again.

Eager to put some distance between himself and the gas station, he walked down the street at a swift but calm walk. He kept his movements natural, making an effort not to show his panic. That would only draw attention to himself.

As he walked, he pulled his jacket hood over his head. Soon, he would need to change his appearance. He was a fugitive now.

A fugitive. The concept didn't frighten him as much as it should have. There were greater concerns to worry about, like making sure that Shannon didn't get caught up in this whole mess. Besides, being hunted was better than being an unconscious hunter. At least he was in control of his own actions.

He would never allow himself to be manipulated again.

He took a bus to the nearest station, paying in cash though he had a fare card. Although the chance was remote, he feared that using his card would be another way for Zeus to track him.

Tyler sat tensely through the ride, curling his fingers around the underside of the plastic seat to keep himself from reaching for the gun under his jacket. He kept his head down and his hood up, avoiding eye contact with the other passengers.

When he glanced out the window as they traveled through an underpass, the darkness transformed the glass pane into a mirror. His reflection disturbed him. In a matter of a single afternoon, his face had changed in some indescribable but integral way. It no longer belonged to him.

After getting off the bus, he rode the Red Line to the Dupont Circle Metro Station. As he took the escalator up to street level, he looked over his shoulder to see if he was being followed. He found himself so fixated by the words carved on the wall above him that he turned his body to read them:

Thus in silence, in dreams' projections, returning, resuming, I thread my way through the hospitals; the hurt and the wounded I pacify with soothing hand, I sit by the restless all the dark night – some are so young; some suffer so much – I recall the experience sweet and sad . . . Walt Whitman

Although Tyler had visited Dupont Circle before, he had always exited the station via the southern entrance. This was his first time using the north exit escalator, and as a result, his first time seeing the engraved poem.

Staring at those grim words, he began trembling. Gripped in the jaws of a terrible intuition, he knew in that moment that if he did not hurry, Shannon would be killed. He swiveled around again, rushed up the escalator stairs, and emerged into the night.

Cars honked as he hurried across the street, down a road lined with old attractive buildings. His footsteps echoed hollowly on the sidewalk. Minutes passed, but his panic did not. He read the address numbers as he passed them, until he finally stopped in front of a narrow brick row house.

Tyler took a moment to compose himself then walked up to the front door. He rang the bell. As he waited for someone to answer, he glanced around at the row houses on either side of him, then behind him. A vaporous silhouette drifted past the bay window of the home across from him, obscured by filmy drapes.

He turned around again as the door opened a crack and found himself in the presence of a sleepy-eyed man whose thinning brown hair was brushed in a comb-over on his shiny scalp.

"Are you Shannon's dad?" Tyler asked.

"More or less," the man said, but made no attempt to disengage the security chain.

"My name's Tyler. I'm one of Shannon's friends. Is she here right now?"

"Tyler, you say?" The man's eyes narrowed. "She's never mentioned you."

"Please, it's really important that I talk to her."

"She's staying overnight at a friend's house."

"Victoria?" Tyler asked.

"No, a different friend."

"Her cell phone's off. I think it's dead."

"She left it here," the man said, sounding almost guarded. "I'm sorry, but you're going to have to come back another time."

"Whose house is she staying at?" Tyler asked, hearing his own voice grow tight and jagged with fear. "Please, you need to tell me."

"You need to leave, son," the man said and began to shut the door.

"Wait." Tyler wedged his foot inside the doorframe before the door could close completely. "Please, can you at least check her room to see if she has a plain black cell phone, one of those old flip phones? It doesn't belong to her. I let her borrow it and—"

The man's face drained of color, and without another word, he tried forcing the door shut. Tyler had barely enough time to remove his shoe from the opening before the door crashed against the frame. Even from the outside, he heard the *click* of a deadbolt being engaged.

Mystified, he backed off the stoop and stared up at the dark narrow windows that punctured the brick facade. Left with no choice, he turned back onto the street and began walking again, without a destination.

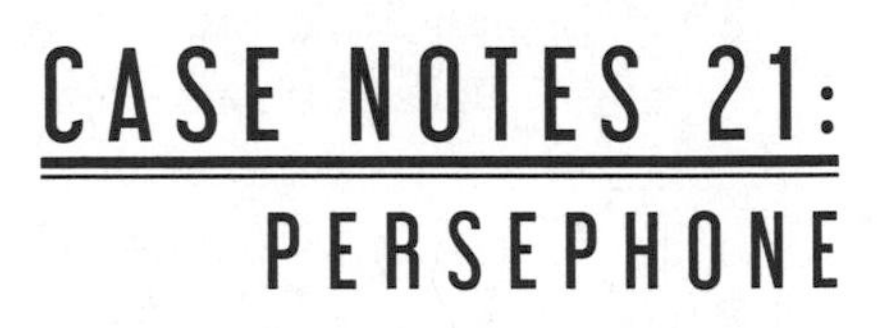

CASE NOTES 21: PERSEPHONE

Elizabeth awoke in an ambulance, with two paramedics hovering around her.

One of the men leaned over her. His eyes were irritated, and his cheeks and neckline were blued with a five o'clock shadow. Even in his exhaustion, he smiled—a thin, stressed line. "Everything's going to be okay, hon. Are you in any pain?"

"No," she croaked. Her throat felt like it had been rubbed raw with sandpaper. Her saliva was thick and sour, making it difficult to speak. The glow of streetlamps spilled through the tall windows on the double doors, and a lamp overhead cast its pale radiance, but she had difficulty seeing. Everything was soft around the edges. Facial features, while distinguishable, appeared eerily warped in some vague, fundamental way.

"Can you tell me your name?" the man asked.

For a moment, she could not remember what her own name was. Then it came to her. "Elizabeth Marina Hawthorne."

"Where do you live?"

She recited her address dutifully.

"How old are you?" the man asked.

"I'm seventeen."

"Did you take anything while you were at the dance? Any drugs or alcohol? Don't worry, you're not in trouble, but it's important that we know everything."

"No, I just had a soda." She tried to straighten up. Bad idea. As soon as she moved, her vision blurred into a stream of colors, and the world tilted like a fun-house ride. The taste of bile flooded her throat. She groaned and sagged against the firm cushion.

The ambulance lurched forward, and she felt her stomach lurch with it. Nausea kept her grounded as effectively as any restraint.

"Has something like this ever happened to you before, Elizabeth?" the other paramedic asked.

"No," she said, shaking her head. The motion caused another wave of nausea, but it was weaker than the first. She no longer felt in danger of puking.

The paramedics continued to speak to her. She followed their requests to take a deep breath, open her mouth, and look up as the first man pointed a penlight in her eyes, but she faded. She wasn't all there anymore. Even as the paramedics wheeled her into the cold hall of the hospital and the acoustic-tiled ceiling above blurred into a seamless white stretch, a part of her was elsewhere. Somewhere warm and dark, floating.

Her mother and father arrived just before the MRI scan.

"What did you do, Elizabeth?" her father snapped, chasing down her gurney with the stubborn tenacity of a hellhound pursuing the damned. "I just got a call from the DA about some sort of fight—"

Her mother put a hand on her father's shoulder. "Larry, now is not the time for a lecture." She turned to Elizabeth. "You'll be okay, sweetheart. I'm sure it was nothing, just a panic attack or something. I've called Dr. Kosta. He should be here shortly. Don't worry."

The technician was a dour-faced brunette who seemed to take sadistic pleasure in finding her vein. She had to jab Elizabeth several times before the needle went home.

As the dye flooded her bloodstream, she felt heat radiate

through her body. A taste like old pennies filled her mouth, reminding her of blood, which in turn brought back a hazy recollection of a large room filled with people and a boy in the center, hugging a pole.

A nightmare from long ago.

The machine whirred quietly. She stared up at the white underside of the rotor, then closed her eyes as the red lasers flicked across her face. She tried not to think about what had happened at the dance, but it lingered in her memory.

She couldn't get the sound of Hades's laughter out of her head. How could he do something like that? Did he really take pleasure in the pain of others?

It was impossible to reconcile her ideal vision of him with the way he had behaved tonight. It was like he had become a completely different person.

Maybe he has split personalities, she thought, but she couldn't convince herself of it. That was too convenient. The hard truth was there was no difference between the young man who had kissed her so passionately and the one who had kicked in the teeth of a downed opponent. No difference except that she had been on the opposite end of his violence.

Keeping her eyes closed, she detected a trace fragrance under the odor of antiseptic solution. The aroma of forget-me-nots.

"*Vergissmeinnicht*," Elizabeth whispered, remembering the name that Hades had used for them. The word had sounded exotic in his low, melodic voice, but now it seemed so familiar, as if she had heard it many times before.

Vergissmeinnicht.

Forget me not.

Lulled to sleep by the monotonous rumbling of the MRI machine, she envisioned a field of wildflowers bordered on one side by a tall overgrown fence topped with barbed wire and on the other three sides by dense forest. It was the same scenery she thought about whenever she felt stressed, a fairy-tale place conjured by her imagination. It was always dusk there, when the comingled fragrance of the evening primrose and alpine forget-me-not was at its peak.

Normally, she was alone in that special place. Now, a boy sat in the grass, teasing flower stems between his slender fingers. He wore all black, and his clothes were of the coarse, shapeless type expected of a uniform. His dark hair was shorn in a crew cut as if he were going into the army, but he looked far too young for that, just fifteen or so.

As the boy turned to face her, she was struck by the familiarity of his features. That milky skin. Those sooty-lashed eyes, violet in the fading light. His jaw and cheekbones were softer, with only a hint of the lupine sharpness she had grown so used to, but it was unmistakably him. Hades.

"We should be getting back soon," she heard herself said. "They're going to call roll."

The setting sun caressed his face as he glanced upward. Though his deep-set eyes were cast in shadows, the darkness surrounding them was a product of the sun's angle, not from insomnia induced by nightmares. In his features was a warm innocence whose absence she hadn't been aware of until this very moment.

"Just a few more minutes," Hades said and turned his attention back to the flowers in his hands. He wasn't just playing with the forget-me-nots but knotting them, weaving the flowers into a circlet. His agile fingers, those fingers that had gently stroked her cheek once, now tied the stems so deftly he didn't lose a single petal.

"Are you really leaving tomorrow?" he asked, looking back at her. "Like, for sure?"

"Yes, but don't worry, I'll visit."

His lips rose in a cold smile. In his features, she saw a ghost of the boy who had laughed at the sight of fresh blood and broken teeth. The boy he would become.

"No, you won't," he said, fastening the last forget-me-not into place.

"I will," she insisted as he placed the flower crown on her head. The blossoms' intense aroma was overshadowed by the scent that the warm sun had coaxed from his pores, a smoky, autumn fragrance out of season against the summer's verdant overgrowth.

"I'll come back for you, I promise," she said, leaning into him.

"You won't," he repeated, and his lips brushed gently against her own. His sweet, warm breath fanned across her skin as he pulled away, and she was dismayed to see his violet-blue eyes overflowing with tears. "They never do."

She awoke to a nurse saying her name, her cheeks damp with tears of her own.

"Five more minutes, dear," the nurse said. "It's almost over."

Blinking moisture from her eyes, Elizabeth tried to drift off again, but now the noise of the MRI machine distracted her. So did the memory of her dream. It hadn't felt like a dream, not one bit. It had felt like a memory.

Though patients on gurneys waited in the halls for rooms to open up, there was always space for a senator's daughter. After the MRI, she was taken to a private room, where her parents and her psychiatrist, Dr. Dimitri Kosta, were already waiting for her.

Dr. Kosta turned away from the window as she was wheeled inside. He gave her a reassuring smile. He was a tall man whose salt-and-pepper hair was brushed into a neat comb-over. A sizable mole marked his chin, and whenever he was deep in thought during their therapy sessions, he had a tendency to stroke it.

"I heard you had a bit of an episode at the dance tonight," Dr. Kosta said after she was helped onto the hospital bed. "Would you like to tell me more about that?"

"I don't really remember much," Elizabeth lied. She didn't

want her parents to learn about Hades. She didn't want him to get in trouble.

"Just give it some thought," he said. "Let's start from the beginning. You were dropped off at the dance. What happened after that?"

"I, um…"

"Listen, Elizabeth, we know that you were there with a boy," her father said drily. "We found your texts to him."

Her mouth fell agape. "You looked through my *phone*?"

"This is very important, so you need to tell us everything you know, sweetie," her mother said. "If that boy did something to you, we need to know."

"Hades didn't do anything," she said. "He was just defending me."

"Hades, eh?" Dr. Kosta said and absently touched the mole on his chin. "When did you first meet him?"

"Does it even matter?" she asked, annoyed. Who cared how long she had known him before inviting him to the dance? It wasn't like they had sex or anything.

"It most certainly matters," Kosta assured her.

"I don't see how this has anything to do with my fainting."

"Answer the question, Elizabeth," her father said sternly.

"I met him at the banquet," she said, deciding that if her father was intent on learning Hades's identity, lying would do nothing. He already had Hades's phone number, and knowing her father, he would be able to track Hades down if he wanted to.

"The banquet?" Kosta asked.

"A fundraising dinner I went to a couple weeks ago," she clarified, then turned to her father. "He was the boy you got on my back about. I met him there, okay? He's a good person. I don't think he meant to hurt Adam and Derek."

Dr. Kosta gave a scoffing laugh. "Oh, I'm sure he didn't."

"I probably just fainted out of stress," she said, bothered by the irritation she heard in Dr. Kosta's voice. He sounded almost annoyed, as if he thought she was faking it or had overreacted.

Dr. Kosta nodded. "Have you been having any other... episodes...over the last few weeks?"

"Invasive thoughts," she admitted. "Some anxiety, too. I think it's because of midterms. I've had some hard classes this semester."

"I'm sure that's all it is," Dr. Kosta reassured her, but deep down, Elizabeth didn't believe it.

CASE NOTES 22: ARTEMIS

Surrounded by barren fields and aglow with neon signs, from a distance the gas station resembled an extraterrestrial structure. As Shannon approached the building, the tallest sign's glow resolved itself into individual letters, and the overall dilapidation of the building became apparent. She parked beside the GAS sign at the edge of the corrugated iron roof.

The red glow of the neon tube lights washed across the dashboard and steering wheel, drenching her shuddering hands like a surge of blood. She waited for her trembling to subside before removing the key from the ignition and opening the car door.

Even though it was nearing eleven o'clock, the sky was not pitch-black, as it had been in the shadow of the metropolis, but a piebald indigo. With no city lights or smog to blot out the constellations, a million stars stared down at her.

As she got out of her car, she stared up at the vast stellar dusting above. She felt shrunken down, insignificant, and at the mercy of a force stronger than herself and far crueler.

Approaching the gas pumps, she searched for the black sedan among the other cars. It was nowhere in sight. The tracker implanted in Apollo's cell phone had led her to this location, so he must have been somewhere nearby. Maybe he had switched cars or hitchhiked.

She went inside the gas station. Although the signs in the window had advertised 24/7 SERVICE, ICE-COLD COCA-COLA, and HOT DOGS & PIZZA, there was a depressing food selection. A few shriveled hot dogs sat dejectedly on their heated rollers. In a separate display, greasy slices of pepperoni and cheese pizza grew cold and stale behind yellowed glass. The air was ripe with the odors of old meat and gasoline, and mud streaked the floor.

What would Apollo be doing in a junk heap like this?

Over the spread pages of his magazine, the clerk regarded her warily. As she walked down the aisles, she put her hands in her pockets. One hand restlessly kneaded and picked at the hem of the pocket, working away at loose threads. Her other hand touched the butt of the pistol through her jacket's thin satin liner.

She had fired four shots at Apollo. Six rounds were left.

Why had she hesitated? Why had her aim wavered?

She could have easily shot him in the back as he'd fled down the hall, but at the sight of his face—*I know that face*—something inside her had frozen up. Even after regaining her resolve, her hands had continued to fail her.

She stopped at the end of the aisle and looked around. The only other shopper in sight was a beefy, flannel-wearing trucker loitering in front of the freezer cases. He gave Shannon a passing glance before returning his attention to the rows of drinks.

Shannon went to the front of the store. "Excuse me," she said, "but is there a bathroom I can use here?"

"No bathrooms," the clerk snapped, and as she stepped out of the store, she felt his eyes burn into the back of her neck.

She browsed the cars still in the lot, then took her cell phone from her pocket. She dialed the number Zeus had texted her and listened.

There. Over the soft breeze, she heard a phone ring. She followed it to a pickup truck and glanced into the bed. Shapes huddled under a black plastic tarp like corpses in a body bag.

Shannon pulled the gun from its holster and cocked it. She

stood on her tiptoes and reached into the truck bed. As she aimed the pistol at one of the lumps, she gripped the sheet and yanked it back.

She didn't realize she was holding her breath until she heard it hiss through her teeth in a relieved sigh.

Sacks of grain occupied the pickup's bed. A cell phone was wedged between two of the bags, vibrating furiously.

Apollo was gone.

On her way home, driven by a strange urge, she stopped along the Potomac River. This stretch of bridge was deserted, and the water churned below, crested by pallid drifts of foam. The wind blew droplets of moisture onto her face as she approached the railing. She took her gun from its holster, wiped off the handle with the bottom of her shirt, and threw it into the water.

The pistol disappeared in the blink of an eye, without even so much as a splash.

No more.

STATUS REPORT: SUBJECT 2 OF SUBSET A

A-02: I'm so afraid. I'm so afraid. Please don't make me go back in there. I'll cooperate. I'll tell you whatever you want. Just don't make me go back in the tank.

DK: I'm sorry, Hades, but it's a necessary part of your treatment.

A-02: Please. I'll do anything.

(Let the record show that at 00:00:36 the subject began crying.)

DK: Why don't you want to go in there?

A-02: I'm different. I'm scared. I'm not me, and I'm scared of who I'm becoming. I'm so scared, and it hurts, and it's in there. I can't do it. Please, don't make me go in there.

DK: You are not you. That's interesting. Explain more.

A-02: I don't know anymore. I'm not sure what's real, and I'm scared. There's something bad in there.

DK: In the John C. Lilly tank, you mean.

A-02: It's going to destroy me. It's going to eat me. Please, just kill me.

DK: What is in there?

A-02: Kill me. (:08 pause) This isn't me.

DK: Excuse me?

A-02: This body isn't me.

DK: Hades, I asked you a question.

A-02: This is happening to someone else. This isn't real. None of this is real.

CASE NOTES 23: HADES

As Hades basked in the afterglow of his evolution, his cell phone began ringing once again. He returned to the motorcycle and retrieved the phone from his top case just as the ringing stopped. When he opened the flip screen, he was surprised to find twenty unopened text messages and twice as many new voicemails.

All of them were from Dimitri.

As he typed in Dimitri's number, he was alerted by an incoming call. He lifted the phone to his ear and said, "Yes, sir?"

"I've been trying to get through to you for the last three hours." The connection was poor, but even the buzzing static couldn't conceal the rage in Dimitri's voice.

"I didn't hear it ring," Hades said, picking up his motorcycle helmet from where he had dropped it. Mud crusted the top of the visor. He wiped it away as best he could. "Is there a problem?"

"Where were you tonight?" Dimitri asked.

"Places."

"Where?"

Hades didn't answer.

"Where are you right now?"

"I don't know," he said, which was the truth. Looking around him, he couldn't even tell if he was still within the state of Virginia. He couldn't recall how long he had been driving, and for all he knew, he could have already passed into West Virginia or North Carolina. Or, if he had headed north, he might be in Maryland or Pennsylvania. There was no way to tell for sure.

"Are you having fugues again?" Dimitri asked.

"No. I've just been…places." Hades licked his lips, glancing at the forest around him. By the moment, it became a strange, hostile realm. Darker and large enough to lose himself in. If he stood here much longer, he could slip through a crack in the earth or the night might swallow him whole. He would disappear like he had never existed in the first place, just cease to be.

"Come back immediately," Dimitri said. "Something has happened."

"Okay." As he hung up, the gloom seemed to press down on him. His sense of power diminished, leaving a disturbing emptiness.

He put his helmet on again. Though he was using a clear visor, the world looked distorted somehow, different than how it was a couple minutes ago.

Because I'm evolving, he thought as he pulled back onto the road. *I'm evolving. I know I am.*

But by the time he returned to the safe house, he wasn't sure whether the bear had been real or not. His memories of the delightful encounter faded by the moment. Maybe he had just imagined it. It wouldn't be the first time he had seen something that wasn't really there.

Shutting the front door behind him, he stepped into the deserted foyer. The dimmed lamps made the spacious room seem much smaller than it truly was and shrinking by the second.

A lone Rottweiler regarded him from the shadows near the grand staircase.

"*Grün*," he murmured. "*Hier.*"

The dog rose to its feet and padded toward him—then froze. It lifted its snout to the air and sniffed warily. Its hackles rose, its ears pressed back against the sides of its head, and a low growl escaped from its bared teeth. Though he reached out for the dog to pet it, it refused to come toward him, and instead backed away.

Could it smell the bear on him? Or maybe it knew he was evolving. Maybe he had already become something else, all in the span of a single night. An apex predator. The ultimate killer.

"*Gelb*," he said, permitting the dog to retreat deeper into the house.

He walked down the hall, wanting nothing more than to take a shower and go to sleep. Then, detecting a subtle fragrance of smoke and burnt cloves, he stopped in his tracks.

Low voices conspired from the study. One was strongly accented, the other not. Both were familiar.

Just as he took a step away from the open door, Dimitri called, "Come in, Two."

Two, not Hades. Who was Dimitri with that would require this sudden change?

Though he wanted to get as far away from the sweet, pungent odor as he possibly could, his compulsion to obey was stronger than his flight instinct. As he stepped inside the room, he held his shoulders high and kept his hands fisted at his sides. His face felt like a mask, a cage to hide his apprehension.

His gaze swept around the room. Dimitri sat behind his desk, but he wasn't the one whose face made Hades freeze and begin trembling uncontrollably.

A white-haired man leaned against the window frame, smoking a cigarette. His face was illuminated by the sallow glow that reached through the glass. Shadows accentuated his deeply cleft chin and philtrum groove, making it seem as though the indentations had been hacked into the bone itself.

"You shouldn't use a diminutive, Dimitri. It will make Subject Two of Subset A forget what he is. A commodity." The man's words were garbled by a thick accent. His face was wrinkleless, even paler than Hades's, and did not flex with natural movement, as if his skin had partially calcified. He could have been anywhere between thirty and seventy years old. In a way, he seemed far older than that, like a decrepit vampire come to feed.

Hades felt his mouth go dry. He could not speak.

"Do you remember who I am?" the man asked, and the corners of his sinewy lips tugged up in an inflexible smile, like an incision sutured too tightly.

"Charles and I were just talking about you," Dimitri said. "About your little act of disobedience."

Hades lowered his gaze. Charles Warren's pinstripe trousers were held in place by a belt embellished with a large, ornate buckle that Hades found himself fixated on. Onyx cabochons studded the silver medallion, and a strange maroon tarnish darkened the engravings.

"Do you know what I am talking about?" Dimitri asked.

"No, sir," he said huskily, averting his eyes.

"B-10 has defected," Dimitri said. "He's broken free of his programming. I sent D-05 to deal with him, and she failed at that task. If you had been here, you could have accompanied her. We wouldn't be in this situation right now if you had just answered my phone calls instead of misbehaving."

He didn't speak. He felt a sudden violent loathing for Apollo. If the other boy had just obeyed, Hades wouldn't be the one getting in trouble now. And if Artemis was so incompetent, why was he being lectured for this?

"Where were you tonight?" Dimitri asked.

"I don't remember."

"I don't believe you." Dimitri rose from the desk and smoothed out his tweed blazer. He unplugged his laptop and tucked it under his arm. "Let's see if you can prove it."

Hades followed Dimitri and Mr. Warren out into the hall. He lagged behind as they reached the elevator, leery about sharing such small quarters with the two of them. He hated being in contained spaces, and the thought of being trapped in the enclosed chamber, inhaling smoke and almost close enough for Mr. Warren to touch him—or *hit* him—nauseated Hades.

As the elevator doors opened, he stepped inside and backed against the wall, keeping his distance. His hands flexed at his sides, then curled into fists as he caught the first whiff of burnt cloves.

When Mr. Warren's arm brushed against him, Hades gripped onto the bronze railing to keep from striking out at the man. He knew, without knowing how he knew, that any violence on his part would be met with absolute brutality. No mercy.

The memory of his encounter with the bear grew fainter. With the way he felt now, he would rather believe it had been a dream than suppose that maybe his evolution wouldn't make him as powerful as he hoped to be. If he was evolving, then why did he suddenly feel like he was growing smaller and younger, shrinking down into a terrified child?

As the elevator descended, he took a deep breath and let the thoughts leave his mind. No reason to dwell on things that didn't matter.

The elevator doors slid open, and he exhaled slowly. He followed the men down the hall and into a small windowless room. The walls, floor, and ceiling were padded in waterproofed cushions, not only to smother external sounds but also for ease of cleaning. A drain in the floor allowed for the disposal of waste products, and although it had been months since the room was last occupied, a foul musk hung in the air.

When he had spent time in the cell two years ago, there had been no furniture. Now, a pair of chairs and a table took up the majority of the space. One of the chairs was normal wood, while the other was wheeled and built from metal and vinyl, with thick canvas straps around the arms and legs. Other miscellaneous objects and machinery crowded the rest of the room. With the purchase of the floatation tank, the padded cell had become obsolete and was currently used for storage and interviews instead of sensory deprivation.

"Sit down," Dimitri said, and there was no mistaking which

chair he referred to.

"Is this necessary?" he asked, lingering in the doorway. He knew that when the door was closed, the padding would muffle all sound and light. It would almost be like going back into the tank.

"I told you to sit, A-02," Dimitri said, putting his laptop on the table.

Hades could have easily overpowered Dimitri, and Mr. Warren as well, but by doing so, he would lose the game. He needed to maintain this charade and pretend to be subservient. Impressions were everything.

As he sat down in the chair, he reassured himself that he was still the one in control. This was just a formality. Nothing to get upset about.

"You know that I don't like to do this," Dimitri said, fastening the straps. "But if you're becoming unstable, I must take precautions for my safety and your own."

He said nothing. Feigning ignorance would only sow suspicion. Until he decided what was bothering Dimitri—his disappearance, Mr. Warren's arrival, or the fight at Manderley Prep's dance—it would be better if he remained silent.

He was very familiar with this chair. It had been used for force-feeding and as a form of punishment. He had once spent three days in it, in the darkness, alone.

Restraints around his wrists and ankles kept him from standing or reaching out. Other straps locked in place around his waist and shoulders, preventing him from even leaning forward. Foam cushions on either side of his head, reinforced with a strap under his chin and another across his brow, left him essentially immobile.

"Are you going to muzzle me, too?" he asked sarcastically as Dimitri secured the last strap in place and pulled a machine on a wheeled base from the assortment of other objects. "Isn't this just overkill?"

Dimitri ignored him and went about assembling a polygraph

and portable EEG machine that he retrieved from one of the crates.

Hades tested the wrist strap as Dimitri wrapped a blood pressure cuff around his upper arm. If he were to ram himself against the chair, positioning his hand just right, he might be able to dislocate his thumb joint and slide his hand free at the cost of pain and decreased mobility. More likely, he would tip the chair over and shatter half the bones in his hand, crippling himself.

He took a deep, steady breath, feeling the tension leave his body. Electrodes on his head, chest, and arms monitored his vital signs and brain activity.

As he exhaled, he told himself not to feel. Feel nothing and think nothing. All memories were fabrications. Elizabeth Hawthorne did not exist.

The thought calmed him. That's right, she wasn't real, and neither was the white-haired man watching from the doorway.

"Where were you tonight?" Dimitri asked, examining the laptop screen.

"I drove for a while," he said. "I stopped for gas. I have the receipt to prove it. I can't remember what happened after that."

"Are you telling me that you had a fugue again?"

"You're the psychiatrist. I don't know what to call it. I was here, then I was elsewhere. I think I went back into the tank."

Dimitri narrowed his eyes. "Next question, have you ever made contact with Elizabeth Hawthorne?"

"No, sir," he said, though it struck him as curious that Dimitri knew about Elizabeth. The news from the dance must have reached him somehow.

What Dimitri saw on the screen must have displeased him, because his eyes narrowed further and his lips curled back in a snarl. "Do you know who Elizabeth Hawthorne is?"

"No."

"Did you attend Manderley Preparatory Academy's Halloween dance tonight?"

"No."

"Have you made contact with Subject Nine of Subset A?"

"No."

"I knew it!" Dimitri said, and Hades realized he had slipped up somehow. "You're a conniving little liar. You were with her tonight."

Hades didn't reply. Subject Nine of Subset A. Could she truly be Elizabeth, and if so, why didn't he recognize her?

"How much have you remembered?"

He said nothing.

"So, the pet dog has begun to bare its teeth at its owner. Your silence won't benefit you. Do you want to go back to being A-02, just a number? Nothing at all?"

"I honestly don't care," he said. Now that Dimitri knew about Elizabeth, it was all over anyway. If he would never be allowed to see her again, who cared what he was called?

"I don't have time for this," Dimitri said. "First B-10, now you. Elizabeth Hawthorne, you care about her, don't you?"

Hades maintained his calm breathing, allowing her name to roll off him like blood off a rain poncho. "I don't know who you are talking about, Doctor."

"Oh, don't bullshit me. I already know you made contact with her. I've seen your texts to her. I just need to know if you did it while conscious. Now, answer the question. Do you care about her?"

He hesitated, then said, "I feel alive when I'm with her."

"That's called love, and it staggers me that you are still capable of feeling such an emotion. Does the thought of hurting her excite you?"

"I want to protect her."

"Yes, I think tonight's events made that rather apparent," Dimitri said drily. "You almost killed a kid, do you know that?"

"If you hurt her, I'll destroy you."

"You're really not in the position to be making threats, Hades, but you'll be glad to know that I have no intention of hurting her. She is a valuable asset to the organization. She's one of Pandora's, you know?"

He had been able to infer that from the interrogation, but even when Dimitri outright said it, he didn't feel particularly surprised. Maybe he had known all along that Elizabeth was different from everyone else around her.

"She's the senator's biological daughter, but she isn't Elizabeth Hawthorne. Elizabeth Hawthorne died two years ago, in an act of excessive teenage stupidity. Fortunately, twins look alike, even if they're fraternal." Dimitri turned his attention to the laptop screen and began typing into the keyboard. "There's something I'd like to show you."

"You learned what you wanted. Untie me."

Dimitri carried the laptop around to Hades's side of the table and set it next to him. After scrolling through the documents tab, Dimitri brought up a video file.

"This video was taken back at the Academy," Dimitri said, and he pressed the play button. "Shortly before you came into my care."

The laptop screen showed a young woman sitting on a backless stool, her hands on the desktop in front of her. Her resemblance to Elizabeth Hawthorne was uncanny. The only notable differences, aside from age and hairstyle, were subtle, like the beauty mark under one eye and the shape of her lips and nose.

"Please begin," a man's deep, accented voice said from the video. Hades recognized it in an instant and felt his nails sink into the arms of the chair. Charles Warren. The Leader.

"Before I tell you, I need you to promise me that you won't hurt Two," the girl said.

"For the record, you mean Subject Two of Subset A?" the Mr. Warren on the video asked.

"Yes. What he did, what he wants to do, it's all because of me.

So please, tell me you won't hurt him."

"If his behavior warrants disciplinary action, I will take your cooperation into consideration when determining his punishment."

"Promise me."

"I promise you that I will be lenient, Nine. At worst, he will receive a few taps of the switch. Gentle. He will not scar."

Staring at the screen, Hades's calm facade began to crack. Sweat broke out on his back, and his mouth went dry. The longer he heard the two of them talk, the closer he felt to remembering something *terrifying.*

"Turn it off," he said, straining against the straps around his wrists. "I'm done. Turn it off. I don't want to see this."

"We're not done yet," Dimitri said.

"I said turn it off," Hades said.

He will not scar.

"Does it upset you to know that she betrayed you?" Dimitri asked. "She's the whole reason you're here now. I'd like to know, do you still feel the need to protect her?"

Hades didn't answer, just stared at the laptop.

The girl on the screen fidgeted in her seat, shifting around as if she couldn't get comfortable. Her eyes wandered this way and that but never stared directly into the camera. She nibbled on her lip, just the way Elizabeth Hawthorne did when she was hungry.

"Two's upset that I'm going away," Nine said. "He wants to leave with me. Tonight."

"I see. Desertion is a serious matter indeed. Go on."

"He said he stole a gun from the armory," Nine said and bit her lip. She combed a hand through her short flaxen hair, then stroked her earlobe. "I don't know what exactly he plans to do, but he has a plan, I think. He told me to meet him in front of the dumpsters after lights out."

"Mmm. Why did you bring this information to me?"

"I'm loyal."

"Don't sugarcoat the truth, Nine."

"Two's so stubborn sometimes," Nine said, hanging her head. "He doesn't know his own limits, and he thinks he can beat everything like it's a game. I don't think he realizes what leaving means. He just sees it as a challenge that he can conquer."

"Thank you, Nine," Warren said. "I value your honesty."

A low, anguished moan tore from Hades's lips, and all the strength rushed out of his body. He stared at the laptop screen, slack-jawed and trembling.

The scars on his back tingled and burned. He wanted to reach behind himself and scratch at the lines of waxy tissue, digging in his nails until he bled. Then maybe this terrible, indescribable weight on his chest would lighten, and the boulder in his throat would fall away, and he would feel *nothing*, like it *should* be.

"Are you listening to me?" Dimitri asked, and Hades blinked to find the man standing beside him.

"Yes."

"Really? What was I saying, then?"

Hades decided it would be better to remain silent than tell him that he hadn't heard a single word.

"Maybe it's time for another session in the tank," Dimitri said.

"No."

"It seems you've begun regressing."

"I'm not going in there," Hades said, clenching his hands into fists. His nails bit into his palms. He couldn't bring himself to look at Dimitri or Mr. Warren.

"I think eight hours will be a fair start."

Hades felt the sudden urge to bolt, but his body betrayed him, tied down and paralyzed. "No. I'll be good. I don't need it."

Eight hours.

Eight hours meant a catheter and an infusion pump. It meant cracked lips and drugs whose names he didn't know and waking to find a part of himself missing. Dead. Cut out from him in that darkness.

"I'll behave," Hades said, voice cracking. "Don't make me go back in there."

Dimitri removed the blood pressure cuff and electrodes but not the straps. Hades realized that this had been Dimitri's plan all along. The interrogation had only been a ruse. That bastard!

"Untie me," Hades snarled, bucking against the restraints. "I'm not going in there. Goddammit, untie me, Dimitri! You bastard, untie me!"

Ignoring him, Dimitri bent down and released the lever that locked the chair's wheels in place. As Dimitri pushed the chair forward, Mr. Warren stepped out of the doorway to allow them to pass.

Hades howled in inarticulate rage at the sight of Warren's smirk. He wrenched at the straps until they cut into his skin, to no avail.

Dimitri pushed him down the hall. As they passed an open door, Hades caught a brief glimpse of an unconscious boy tied to the bed inside. For a disorienting moment, Hades thought he was looking in at his own past self, until he realized the boy had lighter hair than him. Warren must have brought Dimitri another subject to program.

Dimitri opened the door at the end of the hall and wheeled Hades inside.

Against the backdrop of floor-to-ceiling tile, the sensory deprivation tank waited like a goliath's coffin. At the sight of the tank, his rage shriveled into the purest terror, and his struggles intensified.

"D-don't do this. Don't make me go in there. P-please, don't make me go in there. I'll be good, sir. I-I won't see her again. I promise."

"Shut up, Hades," Dimitri said drily.

Dimitri parked the chair next to the tank's hatch, washed his hands at the sink, and went to the metal cabinet along the adjacent wall. As he rifled through the drawers, Hades wrenched against the straps. Savage growls erupted from his bared teeth, and he kicked his heels against the chair's metal leg rest in an attempt to loosen the bonds. He writhed until the straps dug into him. He even tried tipping the chair over, at the risk of busting his skull open on the side of the tank.

He would rather die than go back in there.

From the top shelf, Dimitri took out the IV infusion pump, which was modified to attach to a bracket built into the interior wall of the sensory deprivation tank. From the shelf below that, he retrieved hypodermic needles, IV tubing, a urinary catheter, and several bags of saline solution.

Although the sensory deprivation tank was filled with hundreds of gallons of water, it was treated with more than one thousand pounds of Epsom salt, making the water undrinkable. As well, once Hades entered the tank, he would be in no condition to perform basic tasks like drinking and eating. The saline would prevent him from becoming dehydrated and act as a vehicle for nutrients and drugs.

For the longer sessions that numbered in days, a mild hypnotic was administered through the infusion pump at a set time. The drug induced a brief sleep, and when he awoke again, the nutrient-enrichened saline sacks would be replaced, the catheter bag emptied, and the infusion pump's chamber refilled. Usually, an enema would be administered while he was in that state, to clear out any waste and prevent him from soiling the tank water in a drug-induced stupor.

The longest Hades had spent in the tank was nine days, or so he had been told. Most of the time, there was no sense of time. He had learned very quickly that even eight hours in the tank could feel like eternal damnation.

As he continued to kick at the chair, Dimitri set the items on the top of the cabinet then began sorting through the injection bottles contained in another cabinet. He took out one drug, reconsidered, and exchanged it for another.

LSD, DMT, and ketamine were just a few of the drugs in Dimitri's arsenal. While the majority were injectable, some were taken orally. Hades recalled several instances where, after refusing to swallow the liquid, a feeding tube had been utilized.

He had never thought he would be here again.

Dimitri returned to his side, carrying a tray that contained a pair of surgical gloves, sealed alcohol swabs, a tourniquet, and a syringe filled with clear liquid.

He knew from experience that the drug in the hypodermic would only be a precursor, a tranquilizer to calm him down long enough for Dimitri to prep the infusion pump and put him in the tank. The dissociatives and hallucinogens would come later, administered through the infusion pump at set intervals.

"I'll never forgive you for this," he growled as Dimitri set the tray on the nearby bench.

"If you say so," Dimitri said indifferently, putting on the gloves. "You can bark all you want, but you'll serve the Project until the end, and we both know it."

Dimitri pulled back the sleeve of Hades's shirt and wrapped the tourniquet around his upper left arm. A vein bulged in the crook of his elbow. The skin there was stippled with small scars from numerous past injections.

The sharp fumes of antiseptic solution stung his nose as Dimitri wiped down his skin with an alcohol swab. His breath hissed through his teeth in short, rapid gasps. Although he felt a sudden urge to scream and beg, he could only whimper weakly through a throat constricted by panic.

"This wouldn't be necessary if you had just obeyed in the first place." Dimitri slid the hypodermic needle under Hades's skin, then released the tourniquet.

As the syringe's contents flowed into his vein, dread swooped down like an eagle upon him. There was no escaping this. It had already begun.

"This is happening to someone else," Hades whispered,

feeling the liquid sink into him.

Normally, hearing his own voice assured him that he was still alive, but he felt only misery, fear, and hatred now.

"This is happening to someone else."

At the second repetition, a sense of calmness washed over him like a soothing touch. When he looked down at his body, he sensed it belonged to someone apart from himself.

It didn't matter what happened to this carcass anymore. The real him would be elsewhere.

Someone else, he thought as the drug took him. *I want to be someone else.*

CASE NOTES 24: APOLLO

After leaving Shannon's neighborhood, Tyler set up camp in a twenty-four-hour internet café, at a desk in the back of the building. He passed the time by drinking coffee, doing research online using one of the café's ancient PCs, and contemplating how he had gotten into this exact situation.

The fact that his foster parents might be involved in this did not surprise him. They had always struck him as the kind of people whose greed motivated their every decision.

However, it was also possible that the catalyst had occurred sometime before them. His memories of his childhood were blurred, just smoky images. Until now, he had thought everyone's memories were the same, but wasn't it possible that something horrible had happened to him to make him forget?

No, that was going too far back. More likely, his encounter with Zeus had been recent, within the last year.

The last year.

Thinking back, that time was just a blur, too. At the beginning of the fall semester, Tyler had transferred from a different school—and now, suddenly, he realized he couldn't remember the name of the school. He couldn't remember what his previous foster home had looked like or the names and faces of his friends, let alone his previous foster parents.

That's impossible, Tyler thought, staring into his coffee cup.

You don't just forget those things.

If the brainwashing process involved psychological trauma of some kind, was it possible that he could have repressed not only his memories of the event itself but also of his entire childhood?

Suddenly, Tyler recalled what Hades had said after approaching Shannon and him at the Woodley Park Station exit.

Who ever said that's your name, Apollo?

At the time, the question had struck him as odd, but so had everything else about the boy. Now, he was forced to confront an even more frightening possibility.

What if Tyler Bennett wasn't his real name? What if he had never come from the foster system in the first place?

The thought chilled him, and he pushed it out of his head before he could linger on it further.

After finishing his coffee, he ordered a refill and a pumpkin spice croissant. The pastry tasted like cardboard to him, and the coffee burned away at his stomach like acid, but eating distracted him from the issue at hand.

Still, even stuffing his face wasn't enough to keep him from thinking about Shannon. He couldn't bear the thought of something happening to her, but at least she was at a friend's house. She would be safe for tonight, and first thing tomorrow morning, he could go back to her home and get the phone from her. It would probably be the last time he spoke to her, but he preferred to say good-bye than put her in further danger.

Rubbing his aching eyes, he turned his attention back to the computer screen. Over the last two hours, he had researched everything from mind control and Greek mythology to alien abductions. He discovered that the CIA had run a brainwashing experiment called Project MKULTRA from the 1950s to the early 1970s. He also found several other government-related projects that were named after Greek mythological figures, but none that resembled what he was looking for.

Of all the possibilities, brainwashing seemed the most

plausible but also the most confounding. Why brainwash a seventeen-year-old? Why order him to kill? Or could the brainwashing have occurred years earlier, as a child?

Once during the night, it occurred to Tyler that he might just be schizophrenic. Maybe everything that had happened over the last day had simply been a break from reality, and he had finally gone off the deep end.

Sometime after one o'clock in the morning, exhaustion caught up to him, and he rested his head on the table. His eyelids felt like they weighed two tons each, and keeping them open was a Herculean effort.

As he drifted off, he thought back to the house of the woman he had killed. In his mind, he retraced his journey through it, through rooms bathed in late afternoon sunshine instead of anemic moonlight. There were still parts missing. The killing itself, for one. He had the vaguest idea of what had happened, but he avoided delving too deeply into the memory. He didn't want to remember.

Who was that person he had gone there with? Hades or someone else?

He couldn't remember.

In the theater of his imagination, the film fast-forwarded. Through the house. Onto the street. Down the highway. Heading where?

Down. Down the highway, driving deeper into darkness, darkness that weighed down his closed lids and filled his head. Deeper into a dream.

As sleep took him, he found himself in a forest clearing. Leaves shuddered all around him, stirred by a gentle breeze.

"So, what was Subset B like?" a calm, low voice asked, and Tyler turned around to find himself in the presence of a familiar young man.

"I don't remember," he heard himself say. "I don't remember anything anymore."

"That happens," Hades said, loading cartridges into the cylinder of the revolver he carried. He wore a pair of acoustic earmuffs around his neck. "But you should at least remember how to shoot a gun. Especially if you're supposed to go into the military one day."

"What about you? Where are you going after this?"

"I'm never leaving." Hades smiled. "You'd better behave, or you'll end up like me. If you aren't cut out to be a leader, they'll only have one use for you."

"What do you mean?"

"Murder."

Then he felt a hand on his shoulder, shaking him awake.

"Your time's up," a man said as Tyler opened his eyes. The café employee frowned down at him, arms crossed. "You really shouldn't sleep in here."

"Sorry, I just drifted off." He looked around at the dim space. "What time is it?"

"Four o'clock," the man said.

"Can I pay for three more hours?"

The man smiled thinly. "Sleep or computer use?"

"Both," he said, chuckling in spite of himself.

"It's your money," the man said, and after taking Tyler's cash, returned to the front desk.

As much as Tyler wanted to go back to sleep, he found himself unable to. After staring at the dark computer screen for ten minutes, he stood and walked to the counter. He ordered a coffee and a sandwich and ate them while he continued researching MKULTRA and other similar experiments.

MKULTRA had ended back in the 1970s, with no notable successes, but wasn't it possible that over the last forty years, other scientists had perfected the art of brainwashing?

No, not perfected. He had broken free somehow, so that meant the technique was still flawed.

At 7:30, he left the café and took a train back to Dupont

Circle. A miserable drizzle had started up sometime during the night and was still going steadily. His coat was lined with a water-resistant polyester shell, but the rain blew in his face and dripped down into his shirt. Even though keeping his jacket zipped made the gun inaccessible, the last thing he needed was for a passing cop to get a flash of his pistol if the wind blew back the jacket flaps.

Leaving the station, he walked toward Shannon's house and took a bus the rest of the way. In the drizzle, her street looked even more menacing than it had the night before. At the sight of the brick row house, he felt a cold, sinking dread that, like the descending storm clouds, brought a promise of impending turbulence.

He stood on the sidewalk for a while, staring at the home.

There were no cars parked in front, but because of the limited curb space, he thought if Shannon owned a car, it might be parked elsewhere, within walking distance. Or maybe her friend had dropped her off.

Maybe she was already dead.

Steeling himself for what would be an uncomfortable conversation at best, Tyler stepped onto the concrete stoop and reached for the doorbell.

CASE NOTES 25: ARTEMIS

Shannon sat at her desk, staring at her smartphone. As soon as the battery had recharged enough that she was able to turn the device on, she had texted Tyler. He had never responded. Her two calls went equally unanswered.

He had sounded more than just tired last night, now that she thought about it. He had sounded *scared.*

What if something had happened to him? What if he had another panic attack?

Biting her lip, she glanced out the window by chance and noticed a figure standing across the street.

The rainfall was so dense she could only make out the man's clothes—a dark jacket and blue jeans—and little else. His face was just a pale blur.

It's probably nothing. Just one of the neighbors.

The man did not move. He stared at her house with his hands in his pockets. Although she was seated far enough from the window that she was almost certain he couldn't see her, she had a disturbing notion that he was looking directly at her.

Scolding herself for being so paranoid, Shannon stood and closed the curtains. Even as she stepped away from her desk, unease bit away at her in small nibbles, eating her stability piece by piece.

"I'm going insane," she mumbled to herself, then went over

to the rat cage. Poking her finger through the bars, she said, "Mommy's going insane, isn't she, Snowflake?"

The obese albino rat waddled up to her, seized her finger in his tiny pink hands, and began to lick it.

"What are we going to do about that, Snowflake? Hmm?"

The rat, of course, did not respond. He seemed enthralled by her finger. Vacantly, she wondered if her nail polish could be toxic and pulled her hand away, even as she kept talking.

"Are we going to see if the front door's locked, hmm? Is that what we're going to do?"

Shannon opened the cage door and reached inside. Snowflake scampered away from her groping hand. After a few tries at grabbing him, he allowed himself to be picked up. She stroked his back and head to calm him, rubbing the surface of one velvety ear. Once she placed Snowflake on her shoulder, he burrowed into her hair.

Even as she went into the foyer, she reproached herself for being so paranoid. It didn't matter that someone was standing out in the downpour. It didn't mean he was watching her. The only reason the stranger even intimidated her in the first place was because she was stressed.

Why was she stressed? School, that had to be it.

Senior year had just begun, but by this time next year, she would have graduated. Then there came the matter of housing, the worry that she would be expected to move out. But perhaps most of all, she was scared about growing up, getting older. Her eighteenth birthday was coming up, less than seven months away. She was on the brink of adulthood.

It wasn't that she didn't welcome growing old. She did, in a way. It was a new adventure. Something to look forward to. Freedom.

Yet it also meant the death of adolescence and the burial of childhood. She feared that by reaching the milestone called adulthood, she would be giving up as much as she'd be gaining.

She wouldn't be able to justify lounging around in her pajamas on the weekends, watching TV and eating ice cream. She would have to actually make an effort at her job, not quit after the first few months or gossip between checkout counters.

That has to be it, she thought as she checked the front door. *Call it a midlife crisis.* Or whatever the teenage equivalent was.

Shannon looked through the peephole of her front door. The rain obscured her view of the street beyond. She couldn't see the man, and she didn't want to open the door to check if he was still there.

When she went into the kitchen to make some hot cocoa, her footsteps sounded deep and ominous against the floorboards, like the echo of distant gunshots.

It was probably a neighbor. Nothing to get worked up or alarmed over. But as Shannon took the coffeemaker from the cupboard, she found herself straining to hear the sounds of footsteps. Her hands shook as she poured water into the reservoir.

She went into the pantry to retrieve the box of hot cocoa mix, then to the cabinets above the counter to fetch a cup. As she moved about the kitchen, her gaze was drawn repeatedly to the knife block on the counter.

For no rational reason, she thought, *Apollo.*

Apollo. The name felt as deadly as an earthquake and swept through her like seismic waves. Apollo. Apollo.

Who was Apollo?

As Snowflake curled against her neck, Shannon glanced at the knives again. Feeling foolish and a little bit afraid, she walked over to the wooden block. She pulled a small paring knife from its slot. The blade was sharpened to a lethal edge, yet after examining it for a moment, she exchanged it for another larger knife. She set it on the counter, within reach.

As scalding water sputtered into the glass coffeepot, she tore open the cocoa packet and poured the powder into the mug.

Beginning to feel a little better, a little more herself, she started humming the beat of a song she'd heard on the radio.

As she mixed her cocoa, she looked at the knife repeatedly. For some reason, its closeness comforted her. Even though she couldn't see herself using it against an adversary, she liked the thought of having it there. Just in case.

Until, as her fingers closed around the slim ceramic handle of the mug, a sudden image came to mind: her hand wrapped around a different knife. Not the one that lay on the counter but one with the handle of a tactical weapon. Matte steel or plastic, sprayed black, slightly ribbed. The blade, about six inches long, partially serrated. Coated with blood.

Her hand flew off the mug, yanked away as though she'd been burned. Except the sensation that lingered on the pads of her fingers wasn't heat. It was wetness—cold, clammy, sticky wetness. The tacky feel of drying blood.

She could even see it, drenching her gloved hands, dripping from the cracks between her fingers in long, oozing strings. Then she blinked, and everything was as it had been. She wasn't wearing gloves. Her skin was clean, although paler than she recalled. Damp from sweat, not gore. Cold.

Shannon blotted her palms on the pleats of her skirt, then on the lacy trim, kneading the stiff design between her fingers. Cocoa forgotten, knife abandoned, she backed away from the counter. Her ears rang with a shrill hazard sound, and even Snowflake's presence failed to comfort her.

"Calm down," she told her pounding heart, which seemed about ready to leap up her throat and out of her mouth. "Just calm down. Close your eyes. Take a deep breath. Calm down."

When she opened her eyes, she didn't return to the mug of cocoa or even look in that direction. She knew her gaze would again be drawn to the knife by a force as powerful as gravity.

She didn't want to stay in the kitchen, either, for that matter. As she stood there, staring at her chipped ruby toenails, she thought about how many weapons there were in the kitchen alone. Not just knives. Corkscrews. Carving forks. Even the cast-iron skillet forgotten on the stove from today's breakfast could be used as a bludgeon. Or the rolling pin, for that matter.

And her hands… What of her hands that until now had seemed so small, so frail in the dim, wet glow? Weren't they as lethal as any instrument, her nails sharp enough to scratch and gouge at the eyes and face?

Troubled by that notion, she returned to her bedroom. She reached behind her neck and caught the wiggling rat, then cradled him against her chest. His bristly tail snaked around her wrist, dry and scratchy against her skin. She was almost afraid she would hurt the rodent.

As she put Snowflake in his cage and latched the door, the doorbell rang below.

Shannon froze and listened in petrified silence.

The doorbell stopped. Then began again. Though the noise was no louder than before, it sounded as shrill and ominous as an air raid siren.

Licking her lips nervously, Shannon left her room and walked downstairs.

Although it occurred to her to call the police, she didn't act upon the thought. They wouldn't take her seriously. Yet it wasn't just that. Something else held her back. The same driving force that made her leave her room and enter the kitchen. That drew her arm forward and caused her fingers to curl around the smooth plastic handle of the cleaver. And that carried her to the front door, to the very stranger she'd hoped to avoid.

With the knife behind her back, she unlocked the door and opened it a crack.

Tyler stood on the front step, dripping wet. The sheer fabric of his navy windbreaker clung to his broad chest and tapered waist, drawing attention to a suspicious bulge just below one of his coat's upper pockets. Even though the bulge could have been caused by something in an inner pocket, somehow she knew that wasn't the case. She knew it was a gun.

Just like she knew Tyler had come here to kill her.

"Shann—" Before Tyler could even finish saying her name, she threw the door wide open and lunged forward.

CASE NOTES 26: HADES

There were only whispers and darkness.

"I am Hades," a voice said from all around him. "I am absolutely loyal to the Project. I would die if it meant benefiting my superiors. I am Hades. I am a weapon."

After the first hour of floating, Hades lost all sense of time and place. His body dissolved into the warm water, and he could not feel his limbs or even recall if he had ever had limbs, much less eyes to see with. There was no clear distinction between himself and his surroundings.

"I believe that violence is necessary for the greater good," the voice said. "Violence is good. I am Hades."

He *was* the darkness.

He felt like a brain floating in a vat, or maybe a fetus swaddled in the womb, not yet formed. In the process of being made.

"I am a soldier proud to serve the Project. I am Hades. I am absolutely loyal to the Project. I would die if it meant benefiting my superiors."

At first, there was terror at the birth to come. Then there was resignation. Resignation was not peace. It was absolute misery.

I am still here.

He could not remember where he was. Was he asleep?

I was here once.

Time stretched into nothing. The recording played over and over again.

"I am Hades. I am a weapon."

A slit of light appeared before him, and he watched in awe as the searing glow widened. He had a terrible intuition that the door of a furnace was opening before him, and he shied away from the light. If the glow touched him, it would burn him to ashes.

The hatch's airtight seal gave way with a soft, sucking *pop*. After spending so long listening to just whispers, the sound was almost deafening.

Hands pulled him from the tank and guided him into the light, onto a slippery rubber mat.

Whereas before it had been too dark to see, now it was too bright. The sterile white glow washed over every surface, excising the shadows in even the deepest corners. Even after his eyes adjusted, Hades felt like he was standing under a surgical lamp, naked and vivisected, cut open and hollowed out.

A face filled his vision. Cold gray eyes and salt-and-pepper hair.

"Where am I?" Hades asked distantly, trying to adjust to the sudden change.

"You're at the safe house."

"Where am…"

"The safe house," Dimitri repeated. "You just had a tank session, Hades."

"How long?" he asked, and when Dimitri handed him a towel, it took him a moment to remember how to use his fingers properly. He didn't feel hatred or anger toward the man. He felt almost nothing at all.

"Eight hours," Dimitri said, helping him onto the bench.

Eight hours. Impossible. It had felt like far longer than that. Days, even months.

Dimitri took a hypodermic syringe from a tray balanced on

the bench and injected its contents into the IV port. "This will counteract the effects of the dissociative."

"I don't feel very good." Hades stared at the floor. The angles of the tiles troubled him. They seemed wrong somehow, like they had been cut as imperfect squares.

"You should feel better in a few minutes," Dimitri said after removing the IV and catheter. "Just sit for a while, then get cleaned up."

Hades listened to the door close behind Dimitri and waited for his disorientation to pass. After a few minutes, he stood and walked over to the shower cubicle. He turned the water as cold as it would go and stood under the showerhead, washing the salt off his hair and skin.

As he lifted his face to the icy spray, goose bumps erupted on his shoulders and he began shivering. He kept his eyes open even though the water stung them and blurred his vision. If he closed his eyes for longer than a couple seconds, he worried he might go back into the darkness and be consumed by it.

As Hades dried himself off and got dressed, he thought about Elizabeth Hawthorne. Now, he knew that wasn't her real name. He knew why the word "Persephone" had disquieted him, back when she had first said it.

Most importantly, now he knew how she had ruined his life and stolen the future he was entitled to.

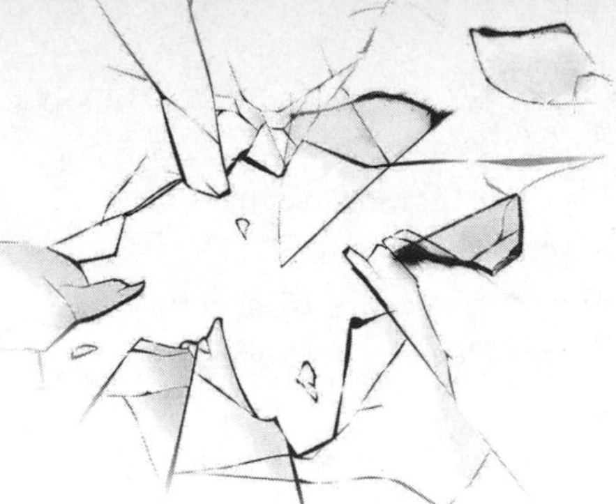

CASE NOTES 27: PERSEPHONE

Lying in bed in room 403, Elizabeth stared at the television screen on the wall, watching a comedy that wasn't funny. She had spent the entire night in the hospital, and now she couldn't wait to get home.

A small beep caught her attention. She retrieved her cell phone from the rolling bedside table next to a tray containing a breakfast she had hardly touched. She checked the new notification and sighed. Just a Twitter update.

There were many messages from her friends at school but none from Hades. Every text she sent to him went unanswered, and when she called his number, his phone went to voicemail.

"Just one more time," she told herself and dialed his number. She knew it by heart and didn't have to refer to her contacts list anymore.

As she listened to the phone ring, she thought about what she would say to Hades if he picked up. She wondered how she would ever be able to hear his voice again without visualizing how excited he had sounded after kicking Derek's teeth in. Like he was thrilled by Derek's pain.

Would he enjoy hurting me? Elizabeth wondered and shivered. No, she didn't think so. Just from the way Hades looked at her and how kindly he had treated her, she knew he wouldn't hurt her.

He was clearly fighting with his inner demons, but maybe she could be the one to heal the wrongness inside him.

The ringing was replaced by the hiss of an open line. Someone breathed on the other side. Elizabeth straightened up, her heart racing as she searched for her voice.

"Hades, it's me," she said, stammering like a broken CD player. "Elizabeth."

She expected him to respond in that low, teasing murmur of his. *I know who you are, Ah-leis-uh-bith Ha-thurn.*

Instead, there was only the quiet sound of breathing. Was he angry at her? Had he misunderstood something she had said in one of her earlier messages?

"I'm in the hospital, but I'm okay," she said. "The doctor thinks I fainted because of stress. Not that it's your fault. It's not. I'm really grateful for what you did, defending me like that."

"I'm afraid he can't talk now," a man said in a thick accent, and Elizabeth felt her blood go cold.

It was the same voice that had echoed in her head just before she had lost consciousness. *Subject Two of Subset A has committed the grave offense of attempted desertion.*

"Wait, who are you?" she asked, dismayed to hear her voice crack with shrill terror. "Where's Hades?"

"Don't call this number again," the man said.

"Wait, please—"

"It won't do you any good," the man said and then hung up.

Chilled, Elizabeth redialed the number. It didn't even ring.

"Hades—"

"We're sorry, but the number you have dialed is no longer in service," a robotic voice said.

She sat there, listening to the recording repeat itself over and over again. Finally, she lowered her phone and sank against her mattress, staring at the ceiling.

No longer in service.

She thought about the man's voice. Was it really the same?

Where had she heard it before?

This is what happens to deserters.

Elizabeth rolled onto her side and reached a hand behind her back. As she slipped her hand into the opening of her hospital gown, she thought about the deep, brutal scars on Hades's back.

He hadn't gained them in an accident, she decided. They had come from an event far more traumatic, one she sensed she was linked to in some way.

Closing her eyes, she tried to summon the flashback she had experienced in the seconds before she had passed out. Only tactical sensations drifted down to her—restraining hands on her shoulders, burning tears in her eyes, the odors of burned cloves and pine-scented floor wax.

She felt so close to a memory, within a hand's reach of it. All she needed to do was reach out and grasp it, and then she sensed that all these aimless, wandering puzzle pieces would come together. Hades, the scars, the man on the phone—these were all pieces of a jigsaw picture she must assemble.

"Hey, you can't go in there," a woman cried from the hallway, and the door to Elizabeth's room swung open.

She lurched into a sitting position, feeling her heartbeat accelerate. Could it be Hades?

At the sight of the strawberry-blond girl standing in the doorway, disappointment crashed down on Elizabeth and she sank into the mattress again.

"It's fine," she said to the nurse who followed on Rachelle's heels. "She's a friend."

"More like a best friend," Rachelle declared, stepping inside. She shut the door behind her and regarded Elizabeth with her hands on her hips. "No offense, but you look like crap."

"Thanks," she said drily, in no mood for chitchat.

"I'm just kidding," Rachelle said.

"I know."

"So you're okay, right?"

"I'm not going to die just yet." Elizabeth picked at a loose thread on her blanket. A heaviness hung in the air like the static tension before a lightning strike. She sensed that the moment she asked the question weighing heavily on her mind, nothing would ever be the same.

"What happened to Adam and Derek?" she asked finally and glanced up to see Rachelle's reaction.

Rachelle winced as if she had been slapped. "I'm not supposed to talk to you about that."

"I'm going to find out eventually," she pointed out.

Rachelle took a deep breath. "Adam's a wreck, Elizabeth. He broke his arm, his nose, his ankle, and a few of his ribs. He's got a concussion, too."

"Oh my God."

"I don't really know what's up with Derek, but I've heard it's even worse. Like internal bleeding or a fractured spine or something. Apparently, they had to put him into a drug coma."

"I tried to stop them," Elizabeth said weakly. "I should have done something."

"I can't believe your boyfriend did all this."

"Hades was just trying to protect me." She swallowed down the heavy lump that formed in the back of her throat. "It's not like he started it, and it was three against one, so it's not his fault."

"Girl, I'm not the one you should be convincing," Rachelle said. "It's the cops who're interested in him."

"Did they arrest him?"

"Um, no, not that I know of. But the police have been asking around about him."

"He was just trying to protect me," Elizabeth repeated softly, trying not to think about how Hades had laughed at Adam's suffering.

"Anyway, I just wanted to see how you were doing," Rachelle said and stood. She smoothed out her skirt and glanced toward the door, shifting from foot to foot.

With a jolt, Elizabeth realized Rachelle was uncomfortable being around her.

"Is something wrong?" she demanded.

"What?" Rachelle asked, widening her eyes.

"Why are you looking at me like that?"

"Like what?"

"Like you think there's something wrong with me."

"That's not it at all," Rachelle said, then bit her lip. "It's just, like, you should've listened to me."

"Excuse me?"

"About your boyfriend and all. Like I said, hot mess. Hashtag told you so."

That was the last straw. Something inside her snapped, and she found herself leaning forward, clenching the blanket in her fists. "You want to know something, Rachelle? I hate when you do that! Hashtag this, hashtag that. It's so *fucking* stupid, and I'm so sick of those duck lip selfies you put on Instagram and listening to you go all 'YOLO' and 'LOL' like none of this is real."

Rachelle stared at her in blank amazement, mouth agape.

"I'm sick of being around fake, stupid people like you," Elizabeth continued, "and I'm so sick, so just leave, get the hell out of here, and go to hell."

"Okay, I'm not going to get into this with you," Rachelle said, taking a deep breath. "You're obviously under a lot of stress, Elizabeth, and have got some personal problems you need to work out, so I'm going to pretend you didn't just tell me to go to hell."

"Hashtag go eat shit," Elizabeth snarled.

Rachelle's face went white. "El—"

"Go!"

As the door slammed shut behind Rachelle, Elizabeth leaned against the pillows again, picking at the strip of tape that attached the IV tube to her elbow. Her bitter satisfaction at finally speaking her mind faded into weariness.

The door opened, and her parents walked in, followed by the nurse from earlier.

"Ready to go home, sweetheart?" the nurse asked, going to her bedside.

"Am I ever," she said and winced as the nurse removed the IV.

"Get dressed," her father said brusquely, setting a shopping bag on the foot of her bed. "We'll be out in the hall."

Once they had shut the door to give her some privacy, she slid out from under the covers. She opened the bag and sighed at the sight of the outfit inside. A black skirt and white shirt. Dress shoes instead of sneakers. If it wasn't Sunday, she would have thought they were going to church. Couldn't they have brought her pajamas instead?

She changed into the clothes and joined her parents in the hall.

"Oh dear," her mom said, pursing her lips in concern. "Your hair's an oily mess."

Elizabeth favored her mother with a chilly look. "I'm so sorry that you're worried about my hair, Mom."

"Don't speak to your mother in that tone," her father snapped, then took a deep breath and ran a hand through his hair. "Let's go. We can talk in the car."

"I didn't mean to offend you," her mom said. "I was just pointing it out, Elizabeth."

Each time her mother called her by her name, she wanted to scream. Those four syllables were grating on her nerves for no reason at all, and it frightened her. Why did her name sound so *wrong* now?

She sat in the backseat while her father drove. She repeatedly checked her phone, hoping that Hades had texted her. Each time the empty notifications tab confronted her, her nervousness edged a little closer to terror. She couldn't stop thinking about Hades or what might have happened to him.

Soon enough, she realized they weren't heading in the

direction of the Virginian suburb her family called home, but instead they were driving north into the District.

"Wait, where are we going?" she asked as they passed a sign advertising the nearby Georgetown University.

"It's time for a change of scenery," her mother said. "Somewhere nice and new."

"But I have a project due in French class on Monday. It's almost half my grade, Mom. I need to work on it."

"Exactly how much do you remember?" her father asked in that same cold, distant voice he had used with her ever since she had woken in the hospital.

"What?"

"About the Academy." The way he said it made it seem like the Academy was a title, not just a basic place.

A shiver crept down her spine at those last two words. The Academy. Why did that sound so familiar?

"Do you mean Manderley Prep?" she asked.

Her father didn't answer.

They entered a residential area. Luxurious mansions lined the street on either side, properties that made the Hawthorne home look like a slum by comparison. At the end of the street, they arrived at a tall stone wall ensnared with ivy.

Her father stopped at the wrought-iron gate, rolled down the car window, and leaned out. The wind blew rainwater in.

"Senator Lawrence Hawthorne," he said, pressing a button on the keypad mounted in front. The soft hiss of an open intercom line reached through the window.

After a moment, the gate rolled open, allowing them entry. As the gate closed behind them, she felt the first stirrings of dread, and worse than that, a sense that she had been in this house before. And that something horrible had happened to her here.

She unbuckled her seat belt and tried opening the car door.

The handle refused to budge. Her parents had engaged the child safety lock.

They were met at the pillared colonnade by two men. Even before the car had rolled to a complete stop, Elizabeth recognized the man holding a black umbrella as Dr. Kosta. The other man, who had white hair and a cold, blockish face, was unfamiliar but at the same time *terribly familiar.*

At the sight of the white-haired man, her intestines liquefied and she began shaking. She wasn't close enough to discern his eye color, let alone smell him, but somehow she knew he would reek of cloves from the cigarettes he favored.

Petrified with terror, she remained in her seat even as her mother and father got out of the vehicle. Her legs had turned to water beneath her, and try as she might, she could not move. If her father hadn't taken the keys from the ignition, she might have lunged over the center console and tried to ram the car through the wrought-iron gate.

"Get out of the car," her father said, opening the door. When she didn't move, he reached inside the car and seized her wrist with one slippery hand. He pulled her out with such cruelty, a bolt of pain shot up her arm and she cried out. Her shoes slipped across the wet stones.

"Welcome back," the white-haired man said in that thickly accented, familiar voice. As he stepped forward, the watery daylight gleamed off the belt buckle he wore—an oval medallion inlaid with onyx, with scalloped edges that looked so sharp to her. Sharp enough to cut skin.

Her mouth went dry.

I went to you and told you about what Two intended to do. You promised leniency. You told me you wouldn't hurt him. You lied.

Her thoughts felt detached from herself, belonging to someone else, but the panic she felt was her own. Before she fully realized what she was doing, she tore free from her father's grasp and started running.

Instinct drove her to the right, along the side of the house. She wouldn't be able to open the gate, and its sharp spearpoints prevented her from scaling it. Maybe there was another exit, or maybe she could find an area where the wall was low enough to climb over.

Her heels clattered against the wet bricks. Splashing through deep puddles, she reached the end of the driveway and turned onto trimmed grass. As she followed the wall, one shoe threatened to fly off, flapping loosely upon her foot.

The property was larger than it had appeared from the street. She dashed past a fountain, scrambled through a decorative hedge, and emerged to find herself confronted by the largest pair of Rottweilers she had ever seen.

Barking furiously, the dogs edged toward her. They were killing machines, all muscle and bared teeth. Mud flecked their sodden coats. As one of the Rottweilers lowered itself, preparing to pounce, arms grabbed her from behind and pulled her against a firm, unmoving body.

"*Nein, lass es!*" a man said sternly, and the dogs backed away.

As the man released her, Elizabeth swiveled around—and froze at the sight of him.

"Hello, Nine," Hades said, and as he smiled down at her, she felt pierced by his striking blue eyes, pinned down like a butterfly to corkboard.

There was no kindness in those eyes now. There was nothing at all.

As they regarded each other, their silence was disrupted by approaching footsteps and alarmed voices.

She turned to flee and barely made it two steps before he seized her by the wrist and dragged her back. His other hand closed around her upper arm.

"Don't fight me," he said and used his grip on her forearm and shoulder to lock her arm at the elbow joint and force her onto her knees. Muddy water soaked her legs, chilling her.

"Let go of me!" She tried to pull her arm free, but his fingers tightened. For a terrible moment, she feared he would break her wrist just as he had broken Adam's. Instead, he simply held her, refusing to budge as her father and Dr. Kosta appeared from around the corner.

"Good job, Hades," Dr. Kosta said, uncapping the syringe he held.

"Get away from me!" she yelled, struggling to no avail.

When Dr. Kosta tested the plunger, a thin spray of liquid shot from the needle's tip. "Hold her steady," he said, walking toward her.

Elizabeth tried to rise off her knees, only to be stopped by the pain rushing down her arm. In her panic, she barely felt the needle pierce her skin.

"Get off me! Get…oh…"

Her limbs went slack, held by a force even stronger than Hades's fingers. Darkness opened like a maw before her, and for a long time after, there was nothing else.

CASE NOTES 28: ARTEMIS

Shannon thrust the knife forward, aiming for Tyler's stomach. A single hard swing was all it would take to disembowel him, and then it would only be a matter of finishing him off.

As the knife soared toward him, his hand shot out and seized her wrist. Growling in anger, she tried to pull away. He held on to her with a viselike grip, forcing her arm away from him and angling the blade toward the wall.

When she reached for Tyler—no, *Apollo*—with her other hand, he secured that arm at her side as well. She struggled to free herself, grunting furiously.

"Hey, stop!" he shouted. "What do you think you're doing?"

"Die, Apollo!" Her words left her in a snarl as she kicked out at him. Her bare foot glanced off his knee, hard enough to make him wince.

"Don't do this."

"Let go of me!"

"Snap out of it, Shannon," he said. "You're a human being. A living, breathing, *feeling* human being. You have free will. You have a mind, a *soul*. Remember who you are."

The desperation in his voice pierced through her numbness like a blade of sunlight through heavy storm clouds. For the first time since opening the door, she recognized him for who he truly was.

Tyler and Apollo were one and the same.

How could she kill Apollo if it meant killing Tyler? But how was she supposed to disobey orders?

"You can hear me, Shannon," Tyler said. "I know you can. Somewhere deep down, you're still awake. Just break out of it. You have to remember, Shannon. Do you hear me? You have to *remember*."

Her grip slackened as horror engulfed her. She stopped struggling. As tears flooded her eyes and a pained sob tore from her chest, the knife clattered to the floor. Her legs gave out seconds later, and together they dropped to their knees. She barely felt the ground.

Tyler still held on to her, restraining her arms at her sides.

The memories came crashing down on her with all the force of a train wreck, devastating her in an instant. So many kills. She recalled the slickness of blood on her hands. So many people whose lives had been ruined because of her.

She curled inward and tried to press her hands to her face. When she found she couldn't do that, she just dropped her head and wailed.

Tyler rode it out with her, never letting go of her wrists, and continued talking. "Shannon, where were you born?"

"I don't know," she said, her voice wet and hoarse. She fell still against him, panting, her chest heaving.

"What's your favorite color, Shannon?"

Each time he said her name, she felt a little more like herself.

"Blue," she mumbled.

"Like the sky?" he asked.

"Like the sea." She cleared her throat and tried to lift her hands to wipe at her eyes. His grip tightened, not hard enough to cause discomfort but enough to keep her still.

"Favorite holiday?"

"Halloween."

"Figures," Tyler said and smiled thinly.

"You can let go of me. I...I feel better now."

Before he released her, he rose to his feet, pulling her up with him. Then he stepped onto the blade, as if he was afraid she would lunge for it.

She sank against the doorframe, closing her eyes. Over the blood rushing through her ears and her pounding heart, she could hear the rain. The deluge only seemed to have worsened since Tyler had arrived.

"I killed them." She barely distinguished her own voice, and for a moment thought someone else had spoken. A different, darker girl. One that looked like her and sounded like her, but who sometimes answered to the name Artemis and sometimes answered to the number Five. "I don't understand. How... Why? Why would I do something like that? I just..."

She knew how. She could hear Zeus's voice in her head. Urging her on, insisting she complete the job. His presence even seemed to pervade into her nerve endings and muscle fibers, drawing her eyes to the knife, then to the throbbing vein in Tyler's throat. Her fingers were racked by hidden spasms, closing around air as she imagined the weight and feel of the blade.

As if aware of what she was thinking, perhaps having noticed a subtle shift in her gaze or posture, he picked up the knife. He bent down slowly, warily, never looking away from her. He was probably worried she'd try to kick his head in, and he had every right to be.

Tyler straightened up. "Where should I put this?"

"Somewhere far away from me," she muttered.

One side of his mouth rose in a meager attempt at a smile, though it didn't seem like he found it very funny. He watched her with guarded tension, maintaining constant eye contact.

He eased the knife to his side, turning the blade so that its sharpened edge faced away from her. "I'll just hold on to it for now, if that's okay with you."

"Be my guest." She wasn't worried about him trying to use

it. Except maybe it would be better if he did. For the best. Cut Zeus's voice right out of her. End the funeral procession of faces. Just a quick, sharp pain, then a flood of darkness even greater than the downpour outside.

"Is there someplace we can sit and talk?" Tyler asked.

"My bedroom, I guess." She had a feeling what he meant was a place where there were no weapons, no distractions. She would have suggested the living room, but it was separated from the kitchen by only a wet bar. If they sat on the couch, she would have a clear view of the other room. She didn't want to be anywhere near the counter or utensil drawer. Even in the foyer, she might envision the knife block and again feel compelled to go to it.

He followed her down the hall, past the broom closet and kitchen. She looked down at her feet as she climbed the stairs.

When she opened her bedroom door, he waited for her to walk in first before going in after her. He seemed pretty uncomfortable holding the knife, but he didn't set it down or ask where he should put it. It was pretty obvious, even to her, that he didn't trust her. She didn't blame him. He had every right to be concerned. She didn't even trust herself.

Once she sat on the bed, Tyler shut the door and leaned against it. He looked around, taking in the posters, the rat cage, the tiny lights laced over the walls and bedframe. Finally, he placed the knife on the dresser, next to Snowflake's cage yet within easy reach.

"I'm sorry that it's messy," she said, because it was better than talking about the woman they'd killed. She knew that if she confronted her crimes, the guilt would eat away every conscious thought and leave her with an emptiness she couldn't fill.

He smiled thinly. "It's not messy at all. You should see my room."

Shannon looked at her feet, avoiding eye contact. The compulsion was already weakening, but she didn't trust herself just yet. She didn't know if she'd ever be able to trust herself again. She felt victimized, violated in her own body, *by* her own body. It was a terrifying thing, being afraid of herself. It was almost unbearable.

"Now I understand why you had the cell phone," he said. "I thought it was that other boy's. That's why I came here."

"I guess it was mine all along."

"How much do you remember?"

"Just fragments," Shannon said, lifting a hand to her face. She pressed her thumb against one eyelid and her middle finger against the other, applying just enough pressure to keep herself from opening them. She wanted to keep on pushing, keep on digging. She had never experienced such a horrid desire before. But for some reason, the thought of keeping herself from seeing what she had become was morbidly appealing.

"Go on."

She shook her head slowly. Her eyes twitched beneath her fingers, trying to blink. "Like the knife."

"Knife?"

"Another job." Job. The word left a bitter residue on her tongue. It was a euphemism for murder, cold-blooded murder.

"Oh."

"With him. That boy."

"Hades," Tyler said quietly.

She nodded. "Darkness. And faces, and I…I don't even want to think about it." Her stomach hurt with a muggy, nauseous ache that reminded her of period cramps but worse. "Oh God, I feel sick. I feel like—it can't be real. It's just a dream."

"I wish you were right, but denying it won't make it any *less* real." He spoke bluntly but softly, as if he couldn't decide whether to be brusque or tender.

"I get that," she said, sighing. "I know that. It's just…I know about what I did. I know that I…I did it. I did the jobs. But at the same time, it's like these memories, they're not my own."

"Like you're seeing it through someone else's eyes," he added, giving her a pained smile. He blinked several times, and on the third time she saw moisture trapped in his thick ash-blond lashes. Evidently struggling with how to portray himself, his smile remained even as he wiped his eyes.

"Right."

"Look, just..." Tyler seemed to be searching for the right words. "I get it. Course I do. But you've got to put it behind you."

Shannon stared at him. How was she supposed to just put it behind her? How was he? Her skin still crawled with Zeus's influence. And her hands, she would never be able to clean her hands of what she had done. She felt filthy, as though Zeus's touch had gone deeper than her mind, deeper than her skin. As though his corruption reached all the way to her bones, blackening them and desiccating her flesh from within.

"Let it go," he said.

"How can you even suggest that?" She wanted to put it behind her. She wanted to discard the memories, but they clung to her as heavy as any shackles. How could the human soul be so weak that it caved to external influence without even realizing it? How could her mind be bent or broken without her being alerted by its tortured throes?

But she *had* been alerted, hadn't she? Through the dreams, the vague unsettling memories, the smell of gunpowder on her clothes, and the ache of recoil in her knuckles. Even before her last killing, she had seen signs, had not known how to make sense of them, and so had ignored them.

And the blackouts, there were those.

She'd brought them up with her foster parents, and they had brushed it off like it was nothing. *Oh, dear, it's normal to forget what you did the day before, especially with the stress of school. And you are stressed, aren't you?*

No, it *wasn't* normal. None of this was normal. Something horrible had happened to her, and she could hardly even comprehend it.

"I just don't get it," she said, like that could sum up the tornado that was tearing its path through her life.

"Let's start from the beginning," Tyler said.

Then her cell phone rang.

CASE NOTES 29: PERSEPHONE

Sedation was a different darkness than sleep. It didn't unfurl like crow wings but peeled away in gray dead-skin layers and persisted long after Elizabeth opened her eyes, hazing her vision.

The room she found herself in was painted bright red, with white crown molding and wainscoting. Instead of a window, there was an oil painting of poppies.

If the colorful decor was meant to uplift her, it had the opposite effect. Viewed through a drug-fogged lens, with the lamps dimmed, the crimson walls appeared as slimy and noxious as congealing blood. The absence of natural light and the lack of windows made her claustrophobic, a feeling rivaled only by her drowsy confusion.

As she tried to sit up, she realized that her hands and feet were secured to the bedframe by thick canvas straps. She didn't test the restraints, feeling so heavy and fatigued that moving her eyes around the room was a challenge in itself.

A small scratching sound caught her attention, and she rolled her head in its direction.

"Good, you're finally awake," Hades said, sitting at her bedside. He held an object in his hands, but she couldn't quite tell what it was. She could only see him from the chest up. "I've been watching you for a while, Nine. Waiting for you to look at me."

"This can't be happening," Elizabeth whispered, closing her

eyes. She wanted to believe that she was dreaming.

"Do you hate me?" he asked. "I did what I had to, just like you did all those years ago. I remember it now, and I don't hate you for it, you know."

"This can't be real."

"It probably isn't," Hades said thoughtfully. "At least it sometimes seems that way."

Her eyes shot open as the chair legs squealed over polished marble, and she found him close enough now that he could touch her if he wanted to.

"Do you know what I'm talking about?"

She didn't answer.

"Have you ever walked through the city and looked up into the night sky? The skyscrapers block out the stars, so it's like a void up there. Like a flat black ceiling." He spoke softly, as if sharing something intimate with her. "And then you look down again, but there's just darkness. Closing in on you. And suddenly, for just a moment, you're back there again."

"Back where?"

"You know where."

"I don't know what you're talking about," Elizabeth said, though that wasn't quite true, and the waver in her voice revealed that much. She knew exactly what he was talking about. More than once, she had awoken from dreams of the car accident, of coming to in that cramped space with the walls crushing down on her. Like a coffin. Complete darkness.

"It doesn't matter," Hades said. "It's all just a dream anyway, isn't that right, Nine? None of it's actually real."

"Why do you keep calling me that?"

"Because it's who you are." He stood, set down the notepad he was holding, and walked around to the other side of her bed.

Still too weak to lift or turn her head, with only a limited range of vision, she couldn't see where he was going. It unnerved her, but she tried not to show it.

Her unease blossomed into terror as he emerged on the other side of her bed, fingering a thin rubber tube. In her general confusion, she hadn't realized she had been fitted with an intravenous line.

The IV tube began in the crook of her elbow and snaked up to a bedside rack. He held the other end, just below where it was plugged into a bag of saline solution.

"What are you doing?" she whispered.

"Just cutting off the sedatives," Hades said, twisting a small knob that she assumed regulated the amount of solution entering her bloodstream. The bag stopped dripping.

"Why?"

"Because I want you to be conscious."

"Why?" she repeated.

Hades returned to his chair. In the dusky-gold lamplight, his eyes were so dark they appeared almost black. His dilated pupils swallowed up all but the smallest amount of blue, leaving a colored rim only marginally thicker than the indigo limbal ring surrounding the edges of his irises.

Was he on something?

"Who are you really?" she asked.

"You know who I am. You always have."

A rift of silence fell between them. He seemed more interested in the notepad in his lap than her. Listening to the soft scratch of a pencil on paper, she realized that he was writing or drawing.

"What do you think?" he asked, holding up the notepad.

He had sketched her sleeping face in remarkable detail, contouring her features with layers of charcoal. The drawing must have taken him at least an hour. Just how long had he been sitting there for?

When she didn't answer, he tore the paper from its binding and crushed it into a ball.

"It's crap. I should have known it." He threw the ruined

portrait into the corner and dropped the sketch pad on the floor. "It's never going to be right. Never. Everything's wrong now."

"Can you please untie me?" Elizabeth asked softly.

He didn't respond. His eyes were flat and lifeless. By the moment, he seemed to be fading before her. No, not fading. Growing colder. Gone were his teasing smiles and warm gaze. There was just a frigid void behind his expression now.

"What happened to you?" she asked.

"The tank," he said. "It's always this…this feeling, like something's been cut out of me. And it's left a wound, and the darkness has filled it, and it keeps getting bigger. Things are falling into it. I feel like I'm going away, Nine…."

He trailed off.

"But I'm not the only one who went away," Hades said quietly. He lifted his head and looked at her. "How does it feel to live a lie?"

"I don't know what you're talking about."

"No." He smiled. "Of course you don't."

"So then I gucss you do?" she snapped.

"I know there was no accident."

Aghast, she could only stare at him. Even within her family, the accident was rarely talked about.

"No crash," Hades said. "No brain damage or true amnesia. Those tiny scars on your face aren't from broken glass."

Elizabeth shook her head, not sure what he was driving at. She was afraid to comprehend what he was trying to say.

After a while, sensing he wasn't going to leave, she said, "Will you let me go?"

"No."

"I thought you liked me. Was it all a lie?"

"I *love* you. And because I love you, I can't free you. Not yet, or you'll run away from me."

"I won't."

"You will as long as you are Elizabeth."

"I don't know what you're talking about."

"You do," he said.

With her mind growing sharper as the sedatives waned down, her frustrated confusion was honed into anger.

"If you're not going to help, then you can leave."

Hades seemed to consider it. Then he rose to his feet.

This time, he didn't go for the IV. He leaned over the bed and touched the padded cuff around her forearm, tracing the buckle and snaps. His thumb caressed her inner wrist.

"Untie me, Hades."

"I need you to tell me your name."

"If you don't untie me now, I'll never forgive you."

"What's your name?" he asked.

"Elizabeth," she said as hot tears stung her eyes. She just wanted to go home. She wanted to sleep, wake up, and realize that this was all a dream and none of this had happened.

"I asked you what your name was."

"I told you!" She tried to turn her head away. He seized her chin with his other hand and forced her to look at him. His searing eyes never left hers.

"That's not—"

"Please, let go of me."

"—your name. That other girl is dead, and no matter how many plastic surgeries they make you go through, you'll never be her." With a scoff of disgust, he dropped her hand and took a step back. "Was it worth it? What you gave up to become someone else? We could have had a life together. We could have had a *future,* but instead you *stole* mine."

She sank into the mattress, sobbing. "I hate you! Go away!"

Hades walked to the door and opened it. He lingered in the doorway, backlit by the antiseptic light that poured in from the hall. But his face was lost to the shadows, a silhouette against the white glare. An eclipse. She couldn't see his expression.

"I'm sorry if I scared you." Hades paused. "I didn't mean to get angry like that in front of you. You weren't supposed to see that. I like Elizabeth, I like her innocence, but I need Nine more. So you need to remember who you really are. Then we can be together again. Just like before."

Then he shut the door.

Sobbing, Elizabeth turned her head and pressed the side of her face against her pillow. She felt lost and betrayed by everyone around her, including the boy she had thought she loved.

As she blinked stinging tears from her eyes, she noticed an object on the nightstand. The stuffed panther regarded her with dead, plastic eyes.

She remembered how he had let her borrow his jacket and shared cheesecake with her. That day at the National Zoo seemed like a lifetime ago. How could things have gone wrong so fast?

CASE NOTES 30:
APOLLO

The phone rang.

As Shannon looked toward the dresser and lurched to her feet, Tyler was already rushing forward. He snatched the cell phone up and opened it.

Instead of answering the call, he gripped the phone with both hands and snapped it at the hinge. In spite of the device's cheap design, it resisted. He gave a twisting jerk to break the plastic.

Even with the screen completely separated from the keyboard and the halves connected only by a thin green wire, he wasn't finished yet. He yanked until the wire snapped then threw the pieces to the floor.

As he stomped on the phone, Shannon eased into a sitting position. It made him feel a little better to destroy the phone and imagine rearranging Zeus's face in the same brutal fashion with which he'd scrambled the device's plastic and metal guts. Breaking bone. Busting teeth in. Tearing out the tongue that had blasphemed human dignity and morality. Completely reshaping the facial features and scrambling the brain, crushing the brain, crushing the skull in with his foot.

He had never been a violent boy, even with his dreams of one day joining the armed forces. He had never relished the thought of fighting another simply for the sake of hurting them. Maybe that was the reason he was so drawn to the military and all that it represented: order, brotherhood, protecting the defenseless.

Yet even so, he enjoyed the thought of hurting Zeus. At that very moment, if Tyler could've killed him, he would've done it in an instant.

Finally, satisfied with the pile of broken machinery, he said, "That wasn't your actual phone, right?" He didn't know *anyone* who still carried a phone like that, but there was a first for everything.

"No." Shannon shook her head and brushed her hair out of her face. She gathered it over her shoulder in a long auburn rope and began plaiting it.

"Good." He pinched the bridge of his nose, thinking. "Do you remember Zeus?"

"No, I've never met him. I mean, I don't think I have. I only know his voice." As she reached the end of the braid, she untwined the loose strands and continued from the beginning. Knitting then unwinding, over and over.

Tyler understood her need to distract herself. He felt just about ready to jump out of his skin. If the dimensions of the room had permitted it, he would have paced. Instead, he just shifted his weight from foot to foot, thinking.

"Do you have any idea who he is or where he could be?" he asked.

Again, Shannon shook her head, looking dismayed. Looking more than dismayed, actually, now that Tyler took another glance at her. Her clouded eyes stared right through him. Her lips were slightly parted, her face slack and pale.

"Let it go," he murmured again. Like before, the words were spoken as much for his own benefit as for hers. He knew she would never be able to put what she had done behind her, and neither would he. It would be a blight that hung over them for the rest of their lives, however long that might be. All things considered, if they didn't stop Zeus, they probably wouldn't last the week.

She shook her head for a third time, not as a response but in vague disbelief. "I can't believe it. I just can't believe it." It was a denial repeated ad nauseam, as much a coping mechanism as the smooth, deft motion of her fingers through her hair.

Tyler knew it was unfair to expect her to adjust so quickly to such bleak circumstances. He had also resisted the thought that someone, whose face and name he either didn't know or couldn't remember, was controlling him.

As she stopped braiding her hair and pressed her hands against her face, he walked over to her bed. He sat down beside her, the bedsprings squealing.

He detested feeling so imprisoned by circumstance, like a rat in a trap. His cage wasn't one of wire or steel; although just as confining as those, it was a prison of bone, blood, and brain matter. No matter what he did, no matter how far he went, he couldn't escape from himself.

"It's okay," he murmured, placing a hand upon her upper back. She stiffened under his touch, and for a moment he considered pulling away. He didn't want to make her uncomfortable. Just as he began to withdraw his arm, she leaned into him, as timid as a deer, as though afraid that he might hurt her. Or that she might hurt him.

It stunned him how they both had the capacity for violence. The capacity for murder. Like a virus or a weed, homicidal urges could grow when given the proper conditions to prosper.

For the first time, Tyler wondered if it had always been this way, in everyone. Was the will to kill a natural part of being human? Was any hope for peace unobtainable?

"It'll be okay," Tyler said, entwining his arm around her in a gentle hug. "We'll deal with this together. We're going to be okay."

Underneath her clothes, she was all heat and hard edges. Her sinewy muscles were as tight and rigid as steel cords under taut silk.

"I don't know what to do," Shannon mumbled, pressing her

face against his shoulder. "I just… I don't understand."

"You're not alone. We'll get through this together."

His words seemed to open the floodgates for her. She began to sob. The sounds came from deep inside of her and tore away at him.

They sat like that for minutes, holding each other.

Tyler wanted to cry for the death of innocence and the knowledge that no matter the outcome, life would never be the same for the people whose lives he had ended and for himself. His eyes ached with tension behind the sockets and his brain throbbed sickeningly against the confines of his skull, and still, the tears just wouldn't come.

He felt numb inside. Dead, even.

There was no going back. He had already passed the threshold. That door was closed. Sooner or later, he would be swept away by the tide of fate, that tsunami called Zeus. Whether he would drown in it or resurface, triumphant, only time would tell.

"I feel better now," Shannon said after pulling away from him. She kept wiping her eyes and nose with the front of her shirt, but the tears had slowed to a trickle. Her voice was hoarse and oddly keyed, with stress placed on the wrong syllables. She smiled, but barely. "Thanks for…for that."

"Yeah, sure." Looking at her, he wondered if she would have preferred not to escape from her programming. Would he have, if given the choice?

Thinking back to the events of the last twenty-four hours, he couldn't decide. Was it better to dream of killing someone than to find out you actually did murder them? Was it better to keep murdering than to face the consequences and reality of your actions?

"How could this happen?" Shannon muttered.

"I don't know."

"I mean, how could we just be so…so manipulated?"

He wished he had an answer for her. He also wished she would stop asking him so many questions.

"What are we going to do?"

He sighed and shook his head. "That's the million-dollar question, isn't it?" Right up there along with why did bad things happen? Why did God taint the gift of life with the curses of pestilence, war, famine, and death? How could there be a God in the first place when things like this happened and kept on happening?

He just didn't know.

CASE NOTES 31:
HADES

After leaving Elizabeth's room, Hades returned to the basement. He took the stairs this time instead of the elevator, preferring the steep descent to that confining box. He paused at the room of the boy he had seen the night before, who had reminded him of himself.

The boy lay motionless on the mattress, restrained by the same kind of canvas straps that bound Elizabeth's arms and legs. A sack of saline solution hung from a rack next to his bed. The only sounds were a heart monitor's steady beeping and the death rattle of an aging air conditioner.

"Are you awake?" Hades asked, stepping into the room.

The boy's entire head was engulfed by what resembled a motorcycle helmet. As Hades took a closer look, he saw the visor had been covered in matte paint, blocking out all light. A temporary alternative to the deprivation tank.

He approached the bed and lifted the helmet from the boy's face. Black foam inserts allowed for a tighter fit. A deep voice whispered from tiny speakers nestled inside the foam shell. The volume was too low for Hades to discern the individual words, but he had a good idea of what was being said.

The boy had brown hair that in the dimness might have been mistaken for black. He looked young, maybe thirteen at the oldest. His eyes were just slits, the pupils so dilated that

Hades couldn't tell what his eye color was. Drool oozed from a corner of his mouth.

"Can you hear me?"

The boy was too doped up to respond. His face was thin and androgynous. Frail. Innocent.

"What subset were you in at the Academy?"

Silence.

Was he a failure or a success?

Staring at the boy's delicate features, Hades felt a sudden irrational urge to tear out the microphones in the helmet, remove the IV, and loosen the bonds from around the boy's arms and legs.

As he reached for the buckle, he regained himself and lowered his hand.

Why should he be the one to help this boy? Whoever the kid was, he deserved to suffer just as Hades had suffered. It wasn't fair otherwise. Hades had been meant for greatness, but this boy was probably just a failure, deserving of his fate.

Why should I save him when nobody saved me?

He slid the helmet back over the boy's head and left him there. He returned to the room that contained the sensory deprivation tank and this time shut the door behind him.

Although he felt no compulsion to save the nameless boy in the other room, Elizabeth was a different story entirely. She belonged to him, always had. He would die before he allowed her to be taken from him once again.

His gaze lifted to the medical cabinet where Dimitri kept drugs. It was only a matter of time before Elizabeth was brought to this room and pumped full of the same pharmaceutical cocktail that he had been administered. Maybe she would lose herself to the darkness. Maybe the thing inside the tank would devour her, just as it had gnawed away at him all these years.

He stood and went to the cabinet. There was a combination lock on the door, but the bolt had been left disengaged. He opened the cabinet and stared at the wide array of ampoules and tiny glass bottles, wondering which drug Dimitri would use on her. There were so many.

He started with the dissociative drugs. He drew the liquid from the bottles using a syringe, emptied it into the sink, and replaced it with saline solution. By using a large bore needle, the entire process took forty seconds per bottle. Between drugs, he cleaned the syringe's chamber with saline from a different container to prevent contamination. As he worked, he periodically glanced at the clock and the door, listening for approaching footsteps.

He didn't tamper with the anesthetics or muscle relaxants. Dimitri used those drugs for electroconvulsive therapy, and the last thing Hades wanted was for Elizabeth to be conscious during that. Maybe he could break the machine later.

After confiscating Dimitri's entire stockpile of psychotropic substances, Hades returned the bottles to their rightful positions. He buried the empty saline containers and needle wrappers at the bottom of the wastebasket and tossed the used syringe into the sharps bin. Just as he stepped away from the cabinet, the door to the room opened and Dimitri walked in, grinding his teeth in ill-concealed anger.

"I've been looking for you everywhere," Dimitri growled. "What are you doing in here?"

"I was looking for my phone," he said.

Dimitri narrowed his eyes as if he thought the eight hours in the tank had waterlogged Hades's brain. "I disposed of your old phone. Your new one's in your room. But first come with me. There's something I need you to do."

Hades followed him upstairs and into the study on the first floor. As soon as he stepped inside, Dimitri locked the door behind them. Then he went to the windows and shut the drapes, yanking at the cloth so hard the rings rattled along the drapery rod.

"Artemis isn't picking up her cell phone," Dimitri said, turning around again.

Hades never really understood why Dimitri had given them all code names. He had always figured it would be so much easier just to refer to them by their numbers.

"I need you to check on her," Dimitri said and went to his desk.

"Why can't her placements?"

"They're not home," he said, rummaging through the desk drawers. "Besides, if she has begun deviating from the program, I want you to take care of her."

Take care of her. The meaning of those four words became clear as Dimitri pulled out a holster designed to be worn inside the waistband, a suppressor, and a loaded pistol.

"These will do," he said, laying them on the blotter pad.

Hades stared at the gun. He wasn't quite sure how he felt about killing Artemis. He had fun when they went on missions together, but it wasn't like they were friends or anything. Besides, it was her fault he had gotten punished. If she hadn't been such a lousy shot and let Apollo escape, he never would have gone back into the tank.

"Well?" Dimitri asked and lifted his eyebrows. "What are you waiting for?"

"I don't think I'm able to drive yet," he said, and that was the truth. His coordination was still a bit off, and he didn't feel entirely like himself anymore. "You should send one of Mr. Warren's men."

"I can't!" Dimitri snarled, slamming his hands on the desk. "Charles can't find out about this, Hades, do you understand? Not a word of it! He thinks there's a conspiracy against him, that the Project's being sabotaged! He's already started cleaning house, and if he suspects any modicum of dissidence or incompetence, I'll end up like John. Now go, hurry, there's a meeting tonight that you'll need to be present at."

"Another demonstration of my obedience?" he asked dully, picking up the handgun. Out of habit, he ejected the magazine and checked that it was loaded.

As Hades attached the holster to his belt, Dimitri paced about, muttering to himself. "This can't be happening. Charles knows I'm loyal to the cause. Does that imbecile even realize how hard it is to wipe a person's personality? Can he even *fathom* how much work I've put into this? John was right. Charles needs to go. He's the one who's incompetent."

He tuned Dimitri out after that. He didn't care much about Dimitri's little crisis or what happened to the man. He felt nothing toward him now, just numbness.

As Hades stepped out of the study, Dimitri turned to the window, shaking his head in dismay. "I can't believe this. Damn him. Good Lord, this just can't be happening. Brazil. Maybe I should go to Brazil."

Before going to his bedroom, Hades stopped at Elizabeth's room. She glowered at him as he entered.

"Let me—"

He cut her off before she could finish. "I don't have a lot of time, so you're going to have to be quiet and listen very carefully to what I'm about to say, because I'm not going to repeat myself."

"Don't tell me to be quiet."

"He's going to take you to the tank soon."

Her eyes narrowed. "The what?"

"The place you probably dream about," he said, "where there's just darkness crushing you. He'll drug you. He'll make you forget me again, and I can't have that. Now, I've replaced most of the drugs with saline, but I don't know for sure if he'll use those or other ones. If he does use the saline, you'll need to act..."

How the hell was he supposed to explain how she should act? He wasn't even sure how he acted when drugged.

"You'll need to pretend to be a zombie," he said. "Don't fight him, no matter what he does. If he tries to undress you or help you into the tank, let him. I think this will be a shorter session, just a preliminary, so you won't be catheterized. There won't be any pre-op. And don't run away. The dogs will still attack you if he orders them to."

"Hades, just untie me," she said softly. "We can run away. I didn't mean what I said earlier. I don't hate you."

"Two." Hades tried to smile, but he couldn't. He couldn't fake it for her. "If you had called me Two just now, I might have believed you. But you didn't, and so I can't. We'll talk more later, when I get back. I need to go now."

"Two, don't go!"

"Good-bye," he said and walked out. She called his name once more, but he closed the door, cutting her off mid-shout.

He lingered at the safe house only long enough to retrieve his new cell phone and change into his jacket and boots. As he secured his ankle sheath and slipped a knife inside it, he thought about Elizabeth's plea. *We can run away.* As if he didn't know he was one of the people she wanted to run away from. She would betray him the moment he let her out of his grasp. He needed her to remember, then they could run away together.

Except you'll never be able to run away from them, a mocking voice inside of him said. *You'll belong to them forever. Their dog.*

Even when he stepped into the downpour, he couldn't drown out that lingering voice. It wasn't his. It was his. It was the voice of the boy who had died two years ago so Hades could be born.

A-02.

As he maneuvered the motorcycle through sheets of pounding rain, he struggled to shake off his remnant confusion. Enough time had passed that the drugs had left his system, but he still felt disoriented and slightly detached from himself.

At a stoplight, his right hand crept off the handlebar and strayed to his left arm, where the infusion pump had left a throbbing knot of a bruise. The veins on his left arm were in better condition than those on his right, which were eroded from his early years with Dimitri, when he had been cannulated almost constantly.

At one point during his first year at the Georgetown safe house, he'd even had an IV port inserted beneath his skin for ease of access. That had worked for a while, until he had developed a tendency to claw at the implantation site. The port had been removed, with a faint scar below his collarbone being the only proof of its existence.

Even now, he loathed the thought of having a foreign object inside him, whether it be a feeding tube, IV, or a hypodermic needle. Sometimes, he hated it so much he felt like he was going to explode. Just having his blood drawn was an almost unbearable aggravation. As for the semiannual dentist visits that Dimitri forced him to endure, being sedated was the only thing that kept Hades from biting the dentist's fingers off.

The traffic light turned green, and he sped forward again. He enjoyed the sensation of the icy rain dripping down his neck and into his shirt. It was a good feeling, so different from the pervading warmth of the sensory deprivation tank. Instead of eroding his physical boundaries, the frigid chill reinforced them somehow, making him hyperaware of where his skin ended and the external world began.

Fifteen minutes later, he pulled up in front of Artemis's house and parked along the curb. Although he locked the steering column out of habit, he just set his helmet on the top case. He didn't plan on being there long.

As Hades walked to the front door, he thought he saw one of the curtains shift. It didn't worry him. As long as he used the passphrase, Artemis would be as easily manipulated as clay. All he had to do was talk to her.

And if by chance she *had* broken her programming, it was nothing that a bullet couldn't fix.

He rang the doorbell and waited. Although someone was clearly at home, nobody answered. He waited another thirty seconds before giving the button a second jab.

He heard footsteps and a murmured voice. The lock clicked,

the security chain was disengaged with a soft clatter, and the door opened a crack.

The girl on the other side of the door wore no makeup and had her auburn hair all messy and half braided, but it was Artemis all right. Her eyes were swollen and red as if she had been crying, and they narrowed at the sight of him.

Hades wondered if she remembered him from the subway. He would have to tell her that her flowers suggestion was spot-on and thank her for the good advice.

"Hello, Shannon," he said, smiling. "You were right. She loved the flowers."

She stared at him, speechless. Her gaze darted quickly to her right, to something beyond his field of vision. He wondered if her parents had returned home. Not like that would complicate things.

He decided to cut the courtesies and get straight down to business. "Olympus is rising."

Her eyes widened, and her mouth dropped open. Then, as though recovering from a shock, she stammered, "Pandora's box is opening."

"Can I come in?"

Again, she looked away from him. Then she nodded and opened the door the rest of the way. With the curtains closed and the lights off, it was darker inside than outside. Even with the frail light that gained entrance with him, it took a moment for his eyes to adjust.

As she closed the door, someone pressed a gun against his head.

CASE NOTES 32: ARTEMIS

"Don't move," Tyler said as Shannon engaged the dead bolt. "Hands above your head!"

"Didn't you just tell me not to move?" She had expected the boy to act robotically, but instead she was stunned to see the corners of his mouth rise in a cold smile.

"Hands above your head," Tyler repeated.

Slowly, the boy spread his hands and raised them. He interlocked his fingers around the back of his head. Scabs crusted his knuckles. His damp hair streamed over his skin like streaks of ink, and his pupils were heavily dilated as if he were on drugs.

"Are you armed?" she asked. When the boy didn't answer, she took the initiative to search him. Like how she'd seen it done in the movies, she patted down his sleeves and shirt, feeling for a holster or sheath. Through his wet jacket, she was aware of the iron hardness of his chest and shoulders. His was the kind of body that was gained only through diligent, if not obsessive, exercise.

"If you're looking for a gun, I've got one in my pants," the boy said, low and mocking. "Why don't you cop a feel?"

She didn't have to resort to that. He also had one in a holster nestled against his waist. It was fully loaded, and the ID number had been filed off. In a pouch clipped beside the holster, she found a metal cylinder. A silencer.

"Who are you?" she asked, taking the gun and silencer. She

dropped the latter onto the ground to keep her left hand free.

"Oh, come on," he said. "You still don't remember my name?"

"I asked you a question."

"Does it matter?"

Shannon circled back around and looked him in the face. His smile had widened to show a flash of white teeth, but his eyes remained as cold as ever. She didn't know what was going through his head, but she was certain he must be planning something.

"Answer the question," Tyler said, cocking his gun. But just by looking at him, she knew he wouldn't pull the trigger. He extended his arm as though the gun's close proximity disturbed him. The hand that didn't hold the gun was tightly fisted at his side. His nails dug into his palm.

The boy's smile faded a degree and his eyes narrowed. Anger flashed in them like hellfire. "Hades."

"I meant your real name," she said.

Hades just chuckled.

Keeping his eyes on Hades, Tyler said, "Do you have any rope?"

"Yeah, I'll get it," Shannon said. She wasn't sure about rope but was positive she'd be able to find duct tape in the kitchen cupboards at the very least.

"I'll make sure he doesn't try anything."

She didn't like the thought of turning her back to Hades, but she did it anyway. She hurried to the kitchen, set the gun on the counter, and began throwing open cabinets.

As she searched, she replayed the last five minutes in her head. The more she thought about Hades, the more uneasy she became. There was something off about him.

Hades had tried to use the code. He had smiled at her. He had made a joke.

Just who the hell was he?

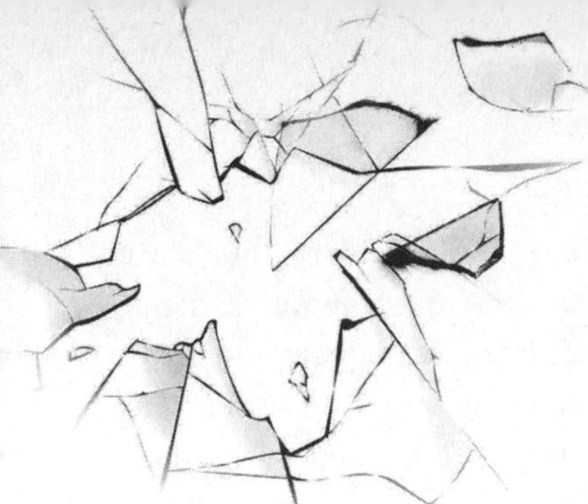

CASE NOTES 33: PERSEPHONE

Drifting at the edge of sleep, Elizabeth returned to the Academy.

She recalled a dining hall with many rows of tables and a pole from which a pair of handcuffs always hung. Dim halls. The odor of pine-scented cleanser. The rustle of an ancient air conditioner and the groan of floorboards. A bleak place where she was called Subject Nine of Subset A.

Faces passed through her mind. Stern-faced men. Women who smiled at her and gave her extra treats. A doctor who drew her blood and complimented her on the lightness of her hair, like moonlight or silver. But the person she thought about the most was Subject Two of Subset A.

A-02. Two. Hades.

They were the same.

Back then, he had been like her guardian angel, defending her even at his own expense. But now he had fallen. He had rotted. And it was all because of her.

Elizabeth remembered how she had spent her evenings with Two in the wildflower glade near the fence, where the alpine forget-me-nots and evening primroses grew in colorful profusions. Several months after he had taken her virginity there, she had unknowingly taken his future.

On that evening, they had discussed her departure, scheduled for the next morning.

"No one ever does," Two had said when she told him that she would come back for him. He gripped her by the arms and leaned in for a kiss. He wasn't gentle. He shoved his lips up against hers and kissed her desperately, as if afraid she might disappear at any moment. Even so, she would have liked to linger like that for a moment or two, but by then he was pulling away. Yet he didn't let go of her, just regarded her.

The expression on Two's face had become the same one he wore when handling a gun, whether it was loaded with paintballs or bullets. His mouth was a flat line, features without emotion, eyes as hard as chips of sapphire. "We can run away."

Her mouth dropped open, and she shivered in spite of the summer warmth. "That's…that's crazy! You're crazy. We can't run away!"

Nobody ran away. Nobody even *tried,* ever since that one time when a boy in Subset C had made it past the gate. They'd dragged C-07 back and punished him in front of the entire mess hall. The Leader had hit C-07 with a switch until welts rose on his back, and then he had simply disappeared. Rumor had it that you could still hear his screams coming from the windowless brick building near the equipment shed.

"You won't come back and you know it," Two said.

"Yes, I will!" She tried to pull her hands away from him, but he held tight. He always got too physical and forceful with others when he was upset, like he thought he could dominate the situation with sheer force alone. She had seen the way he had beat up the jealous kids who tried to bully her, but until now she had never actually felt afraid of him. She had always been on the other side of his rage.

"Bullshit," Two said, raising her hands to his face. He brought them to his mouth and kissed the backs and then each knuckle, from pinkie to thumb. At first his kisses were hard and demanding. But by the time he reached her second hand, he acted with a kind of sweet, solemn reverence she had never seen in him. When he was done, he kissed her lips for good measure. Gently, with none of his characteristic hunger.

"I've planned it all out," he said, letting go of her. "I took a gun."

"You *what?*"

This time, Two chuckled at her shock, as if stealing a gun wasn't a death sentence. Like it was just another one of his war games, or another lesson, something he could easily dissect and dominate. But it wasn't. Taking a gun, an *actual gun*, was just as bad as trying to escape, maybe even worse! And to do both…

"You need to return it," she said in a hurried whisper. "You need to bring it back before anyone finds out."

"Nobody will find out," he assured her. While his confidence was usually reassuring, it aggravated her now. He didn't seem to understand the seriousness of his actions, like he thought it was just a game.

"Why do you need a gun anyway?" She couldn't understand why he always jumped to violence. She had seen the way he performed, his brutality in sparring or gun training, but this was different. This meant actual killing.

And yet isn't that what he's been practicing for all along? To kill other people on the battlefield?

Two ignored her question. "We can do it tonight, even."

She shook her head, refusing to budge. "I can't."

She was so close to having a real family. She wasn't going to risk it all to escape, when she knew that she'd be able to convince her new dad and mom to take him in. Surely they would do it. He was so strong he could be like a bodyguard for her.

"Just put the gun back," she said.

"Nobody even knows I have it, Nine," he said. "They'll never know it's gone."

"Forget about this. It's not worth the risk, Two. Please just return it."

"My plan's foolproof. We'll be able to get past the fence no problem."

She shook her head, dismayed that he wasn't listening to her. He didn't seem to hear a word she said. "I just can't."

"You *can*."

You can. Those two words echoed in Elizabeth's mind as she opened her eyes and stared up at the stuccowork medallion on the ceiling. Days ago, even mere hours ago, she might have thought she was going crazy, imagining events that had never happened. False memories. Now, she knew better.

She had thought her meeting with Hades had been a coincidence, but now she realized he must have recognized her and intentionally approached her. He really *had* been stalking her. And yet, that fact didn't disturb her as much as it would have if he had been anyone else.

I ruined his life, she thought, blinking tears out of her eyes. *I forgot about him for so long, even though I told him I never would.*

The boy she remembered wouldn't have laughed at the pain of others. Back then, he had been calm and detached during sparring and mock combat, but he hadn't been sadistic. He had treated the paintball war games with great seriousness, and after being assigned leader of his team, had gone out of his way to ensure that there were no unnecessary "causalties."

If he was a monster now, it was only because she had helped make him into one.

"Two," she whispered. "Not Hades, Two."

Elizabeth could not reconcile the two names, no more than she could call herself Subject Nine of Subset A. Nine and Two were gone. They were figments of the past. Ghosts now.

If I hadn't told the Leader, we would be together. None of this would have happened.

She remembered how she and Two had talked so much about the outside world, known only through lessons and videos. They had dreamed about the day they would finally leave the

Academy and be brought into the roles they were born for. He would become a great military leader, and she would become an ambassador or a politician, and they would one day marry each other.

We were supposed to leave together.

It wasn't too late for that, Elizabeth realized. They could still run away. Start a new life for themselves, just the way it was supposed to be. This time, they would choose their own names and futures, instead of being governed by the cruel ambitions of others.

She could heal him. Two might be gone, but that didn't mean the boy she knew was dead. A part of him remained inside Hades's scarred body; she had seen his old warmth during their date and at the dance, and she would be the one to bring him back into the light.

Now, if only she could get out of these damn cuffs!

CASE NOTES 34: APOLLO

From the corner of his eye, Tyler watched as Shannon disappeared deeper into the house. He heard the squeak of hinges followed by the echoing crash of a door being slammed shut.

"Look, we're both in the same boat here," he said, directing his full attention back to Hades. "We—"

"Then put down the gun," Hades said, meeting his gaze.

Through a glass, darkly. Tyler couldn't remember where he had heard the phrase or what it meant, but those were the words that came to mind as he looked into Hades's eyes.

It was like staring through a dark, smoky window as blue flames seethed against the glass on the other side. There was hatred in that fire, and anger, too, but also something as dead and charred as the wood the flames subsided on. Something devoured and totally unrecognizable. No longer human.

"Just who are you?" Tyler asked again.

"I told you."

"Not your real name."

"I don't have one."

"What do you mean?" Tyler frowned.

"I. Don't. Have. One." Hades spoke each word as its own sentence, and each hit Tyler like a bullet, tearing into him. Not because the words themselves were startling, although they were, but because of the weight they carried—or rather, the lack of substance. Their deadness and emptiness.

Tyler stared at him. "That's impossible."

"You really don't remember, do you?"

"Remember what?"

Hades didn't answer. His gaze shifted to the floor, then across the room. Tyler couldn't tell if Hades was trying to avoid eye contact or just looking for a weapon to use or an escape route.

Tyler decided to change his approach. It didn't matter what Hades's real name was or even why the boy refused to give it to him. It wouldn't bring him any closer to figuring out why Hades was here and what he wanted. "Why did you come here?"

"A new job."

"What kind of job?"

Hades smiled, glancing up at him. "What kind do you think?"

"Can you stop being so evasive?" he snapped. He knew if this was a movie, now would be when the antihero knocked the stubborn villain over the head. Except he wasn't the hero or even the antihero; he was as guilty as Hades, perhaps even more so. The anger he felt at the boy's cool, sardonic comments was misplaced.

He couldn't hit Hades, much less pull the trigger. Yeah, maybe he would if his life depended on it, but not like this, not when he was standing in front of someone who was unarmed. Just another kid, who at this very moment must be struggling to escape from himself.

It made Tyler sick to his stomach.

"I was sent here to pick up Artemis—"

"Shannon, you mean?"

"Right," Hades said. "Artemis, Shannon, D-05, whatever. We were supposed to do a hit."

"Whose?"

Hades shrugged his shoulders but kept his hands knit together behind his head. His smile was gone, and the expression he wore in its place was unreadable. It was just like his eyes and voice, completely void of emotion, as cold and dead as a body in a morgue locker. "I don't know the woman's name."

Before Tyler could interrogate him further, Shannon returned with a roll of duct tape.

"This was all I could find," she said, setting the gun on the table so she could pull the tape. She picked at the loose end, trying to free it.

"Hands behind your back," Tyler said. He'd feel a lot better when he knew Hades couldn't make a grab for his gun or try anything.

As Hades lowered his hands, his phone rang.

For a moment, nobody moved. Then Hades said, "Want me to get that?"

Shannon looked at Tyler. She rested her hand on the gun. "He's unarmed."

"Put it on speaker," Tyler said.

When Hades pulled out the phone, Tyler was unsurprised to see it was the same model as the devices that he and Shannon had used. He was even less surprised when Hades answered the call and Zeus's voice flooded the room like noxious gas.

"Hades, is Artemis with you?"

At the sound of Zeus's voice, Tyler's hand tightened around the pistol. He moved his finger off the trigger guard, afraid he might squeeze the trigger by accident.

At that moment, if Zeus had been standing where Hades was, Tyler would have had no qualms about shooting him in the head. Then emptying the rest of the magazine into his body for good measure.

Hades gave Tyler an even look, then said, "Yes, she is."

"Good. Now, regarding Apo—"

Tyler saw the warning flash like fire in the boy's eyes a split second before Hades ducked forward and to the side. Tyler's finger went to the trigger, but he wasn't fast enough. Before he could even touch it, Hades seized him by the wrist and yanked his arm down and away.

"—lo… Hello? Hades?" The phone had fallen facedown onto the carpet, but Zeus's voice still projected loud and clear.

Although Tyler had about two inches on Hades, the other boy had the advantage of surprise. Even as Tyler reacted to being grabbed, Hades was already bringing his other arm forward.

There was no immediate sensation of pain, just a great red pressure exploding from his nose outward. His head flung back so hard he heard it crack like a whip. Spots darkened his eyes, swarming.

Hot liquid rushed down his face. It took him a second to realize it was blood. His blood.

Before he could raise a hand to cup his gushing nose, a second pain flared up in the hand that held the gun. As Hades yanked the pistol from his fingers, he regained enough sense to hurl himself at the boy, driving him into the wall.

"Stop!" Shannon shouted. "Stop moving! I'll shoot—"

As they struggled, the gun landed on the floor and spun out of reach. Tyler felt the hard toe of a boot glance across his calf. Then he slammed his knee upward and was rewarded with a loud grunt as it came in contact with Hades's stomach.

"Go ahead!" Hades's hoarse yell came to him through a pain-reddened haze. "Try! You'll miss! You'll shoot him!" He sounded almost excited, like he enjoyed being hurt. Or enjoyed hurting others. Or both, simultaneously.

As his hands found Hades's throat and closed around it, Hades punched him a second time.

Blood filled his mouth almost instantly. The pain from his nose traveled through his face in sickening liquid pulses, blurring his eyes with tears.

His vision shifted drastically, and without realizing how he fell, he found himself on the ground with Hades on top of him, straddling him.

Gasping, breathing through a nose plugged with snot or blood, he tucked his legs inward, trying to kick Hades off him. At the very least, he hoped to catch the other boy in the balls. When he heard a yell, he thought he had succeeded. Until he felt cold steel press against his chest and realized it was not a cry of pain but of murderous triumph.

"Have a nice afterlife," Hades said, lips so close that Tyler felt his breath fan across his cheek. He spoke in a voice that was husky and erotic, deep with sick yearning.

Then he pulled the trigger.

CASE NOTES 35: ARTEMIS

As the two boys struggled, Shannon tried to get a good line of sight on Hades. Her hands kept shaking. The barrel jiggled up and down, back and forth, refusing to focus on a single target.

She was afraid to pull the trigger, certain she would miss and shoot Tyler instead. While instinct told her to fire anyway, she hesitated.

There had been enough bloodshed, but that was only part of it. Mainly, she couldn't bear the thought of losing him.

She moved closer, hoping to find an opening. When Hades reached for the gun, she knew she had to act. There was no time left.

As Hades raised his pistol, she brought hers down, catching him in the back of the head with the side of the barrel. He collapsed immediately, landing on his side. A thin drizzle of blood ran down his neck and onto the collar of his leather jacket.

Tyler sat up and picked up the gun, turning it over in his hands. His face was pale and bloodied, but a tremulous smile crept across his split lips. His teeth were marbled red, though all in place. "Safety's on."

His words dawned on her. The safety was on. It had been on this whole time. They had threatened Hades with a pistol that wouldn't have fired if Tyler had pulled the trigger.

"Thanks," Tyler said, staggering to his feet. "Christ, this hurts like a bitch. Is it broken?"

"I don't think so," she said, taking a closer look at his nose. It didn't appear to be tilted, but the surrounding skin was swelling up pretty badly. There was no way to tell for sure.

He groaned in answer. He used his shirt to gingerly wipe at the blood that drenched his chin, avoiding touching his nose and mouth directly.

"What are we going to do about him?" Shannon asked and looked at Hades. Blood plastered his hair to his scalp and dribbled down his neck. If not for the shallow rise and fall of his chest, she would have thought she had killed him.

She leaned down and brushed away his hair to check the wound. There was no skull visible, no broken bone. The tip of the pistol had cut open his scalp, but if there was any damage to the brain, it was internal.

Even though Hades had come here to kill them, she hoped she hadn't pistol-whipped him into a human vegetable. Maybe if he woke up, they could talk him out of his programming.

"For starters, help me get his hands and feet tied," Tyler said as she put her gun on the nearby side table. "I'll feel a lot better when he can't try anything."

He held Hades's hands behind his back as she wrapped the duct tape around his wrists. She did the same with his ankles. In his boot, she found a small sheathed knife, which she promptly confiscated.

"I think there're some painkillers in my dad's medicine cabinet," she said, putting the knife next to the gun. "Do you want me to get them?"

"Yeah, but hurry. I don't think we should stay here for very long."

She paused. "What?"

"Zeus knows where you live, so there's a chance he'll send more people. And with that phone call..."

"We're both marked for death," she finished, dread sinking

into her. How many others were there? How many more assassins lurked in the dark?

Tyler just smiled wryly and continued to wipe away the blood as it flowed anew.

She went into the master bedroom. She took a good look around, scanning over the unmade bed, the clothing hanging from the hamper, the photos on the nightstand. In the bathroom, she inhaled the ghostly remnants of her foster mom's perfume and her foster dad's cologne.

As she retrieved the bottle of painkillers from the medicine cabinet, she wondered if it'd ever be safe to return here. A lump formed in her throat at the thought. It was like trying to swallow a stone.

After putting the pill bottle in her jeans pocket, she took a clean hand towel from the linen closet and wetted it with warm water.

She returned to the foyer.

Tyler had moved to the window and was looking out. He held the gun at his side and had the drapes only partially opened. One half of his face was chiseled by the ashen sunlight, while the rest was lost to blood and shadows. Cast in that cold light, he looked like a character straight out of a noir thriller, hardened and weary.

"Here," she said, handing him the bottle.

"Thanks." Tyler returned his gun to its holster and took the bottle. He shook out two pills. After swallowing them dry, he shoved the bottle into his pocket.

"Let me see your face."

"It's fine. We need to go."

"Tyler, your face is covered in blood. The last thing we need is to attract attention. Just give me a minute to get you cleaned up." Gently, she dabbed at the blood streaming from Tyler's nostrils, taking care to avoid touching the nose itself. His lip was split, too, and she wiped around the area.

The tension drained from his features, and his clenched jaw

loosened. His eyes slid shut, just for a moment, and he exhaled softly. She had never seen him look this tired before, and she wished that she could provide a helping hand to carry his burden or a shoulder for him to rest his head on. But their burden was already a shared one, and there was no time left to comfort each other.

After cleaning away the blood, she tossed the soiled hand towel on the floor.

"You have a car?" he asked.

She nodded. "It's parked around back. The keys are in the kitchen."

"We should hurry."

Shannon glanced at Hades again. "We can't just leave him here."

The last thing she needed was her foster parents coming home to find an unconscious boy tied up on their floor. Besides, maybe he knew something about Zeus.

"I'll carry him out to the car. Just get the keys and open the door for me." Tyler dragged Hades into an upright position and then with visible difficulty hauled him over his shoulder. He staggered under the dead weight but didn't complain.

Remembering her gun, she retrieved it and the duct tape roll from the side table. She led Tyler into the kitchen, where she took her keys from the ring on the wall then went to the back door. She held the door open for him and closed it behind him.

There was no backyard at all, just an alley that led between the two rows of houses. As she opened the trunk of her car, she glanced at the houses on the other side of the alleyway. Dark windows peered down at her like gouged sockets. She had the unsettling impression that someone was watching her.

Tyler dumped Hades unceremoniously into the trunk. The black-haired boy stirred and groaned but didn't awaken.

"Well, at least he's not dead," Shannon said sarcastically, slamming the lid. She circled around to the driver's side and shoved her gun into the door's compartment, but not before removing its magazine. She put the duct tape in the center console, just in case they needed it for something else.

When she started driving, she realized she didn't know where to go. She kept going anyway, preferring aimless travel over waiting like sitting ducks.

"You know where you're going?" Tyler asked after a few miles.

She shook her head. "No, not really."

"Should find a place to lie low for a bit, at least until he wakes up. We need to get rid of your car, too. Switch vehicles. You have your cell with you?"

At first she thought he was talking about the flip phone he had destroyed. Then she realized he meant her smartphone.

That's how I tracked him last night, she thought and remembered the rest of that evening in an instant. It shook her to know she had shot at him, almost killed him. But she hadn't, and she had tossed the gun afterward. Maybe her programming had already begun to glitch at that point.

"I don't have it," she said. "But that's how Zeus knew where you were last night."

Tyler stared at her. "Wait, are you the one who tried to kill me yesterday?"

Shannon focused on the road ahead, refraining from looking him in the eye.

"Never mind," Tyler said. "It doesn't matter now."

"We should be safe for the time being. I don't think he's tracking our cars. But we can't just run."

"I'm not saying that."

"But we can't call the police, either, can we?" Shannon asked, glancing at him.

Although it was a rhetorical question, Tyler's thin smile was answer enough.

"Can you think of somewhere we'll be safe?" she asked.

"No, I can't," Tyler said, sagging in his seat. He regarded her through half-closed eyes. She could tell he was beginning to feel the painkillers. Hopefully he didn't have a concussion.

After giving it some thought, she sighed. "I think I know where we can go."

Less than two minutes into the drive, Hades began yelling from the trunk and kicking the back of the seat.

"Get me out of here!" he shouted, and Shannon winced at the sound of broken glass.

"I think he just broke one of the taillights," she said.

"Great. Pull over." With a sigh, Tyler took off his shoe and removed a sock.

She watched him in the corner of her eye. "Uh, what are you doing?"

Tyler put his shoe back on. "If he won't shut up, I'm going to make him."

"Let me out, Dimitri!" Hades kicked the trunk once more.

"Dimitri?" Shannon asked, lifting her eyebrows as she pulled into an alley between two row houses.

"I think you might have hit him too hard," Tyler said, and after retrieving the roll of duct tape from the center console, exited the car. She got out, too, walked around to the trunk, and opened it.

Hades rolled over onto his back, chest heaving with gasping breaths and teeth bared. His feverish blue eyes burned through his curtain of tangled hair, and with a jolt, she realized the other boy was *terrified*. "Don't put me back in the tank!"

"Maybe we should just move him into the backseat," Shannon said as Tyler rolled up the sock.

"He's faking it," Tyler said, seizing Hades's chin and holding it still.

Hades growled and shook his head back and forth, snapping at Tyler's fingers. It was as if his containment had awoken a rabid part of him, reducing him to the feral beast that humans had evolved from. Even after Tyler stuffed the sock into his mouth, the boy continued to writhe, his jaws working to spit out the bunched-up fabric.

For a moment, she felt sorry for the boy. Then she remembered how he had tried to shoot Tyler without hesitation, and her sympathy soured into anger and disdain.

As Tyler peeled off a strip of tape and wrapped it around the other boy's mouth, she turned from the brutal scene and returned to the driver's seat. Seconds later, Tyler slammed the trunk lid and joined her, looking a bit disgusted and a bit ill.

"He was just faking it," he said, avoiding eye contact. "Being scared like that."

She said nothing.

"You think we'll get pulled over for the broken light?"

"I hope not," Shannon said, turning back onto the street.

Though the thought of a police chase chilled her, she forced herself to obey the speed limit and drive safely. It was raining pretty heavily now, and she figured the weather might, at the very least, obscure the fact that one of her taillights was out.

"What do you think he meant by 'the tank'?" Tyler asked.

The tank. Those two words sent a twinge of unease shooting down her spine, and as she drove through a yellow light, she found herself nibbling on her lip.

Shannon shrugged and said, "Do you think we acted like that when we were, uh, brainwashed?"

"I don't know."

"He bothers me." She flinched when Hades kicked the trunk lid, rattling it. "I mean, how could he use the code on us? Wouldn't it affect him, too?"

"Only one way to find out."

She thought back to Hades's behavior, how he had made jokes and mocked her. Those weren't the actions of a numbed machine. Those had been deliberate, intelligent responses. There had been humor there, as dark as it had seemed to be.

Which only meant one thing: Hades wasn't working off the same program as she and Tyler were. Although he might have been following someone else's orders, his actions were his own.

After thirty seconds, the kicking stopped, and no movement came from the trunk. She glanced into the back window, worried that Hades might have managed to escape.

The trunk lid was closed.

She wondered if Hades had hit his head and knocked himself out. Then she wondered what his parents would think if he never came home. Would they cry and put up posters of their missing son? Would they hold a funeral over an empty coffin?

Would her foster parents do the same or just dismiss her as another troubled kid who had come through their home?

Shannon banished the thoughts from her head as she entered a neighborhood of older houses in varying states of decay.

Normally, driving through Victoria's neighborhood made her nervous, but it didn't today, and she sensed that it never would again. At least not in the way it once had. The gun in the door compartment reminded her that the true danger didn't lurk on the street corners or in the dark windows of homes but in her own head.

She pulled up in front of a mid-century brick bungalow and climbed out of the car. "I'll be right back," she said, looking back at Tyler. "Just wait here."

"Yeah," he muttered, reclining in the seat. His nose had stopped bleeding, but some blood crusted the corner of his mouth. He wiped his lips with the back of his hand. "Sure."

"You okay?"

"I'll live," he said.

Shannon shut the car door and strode through the rain. She pushed the doorbell and glanced over her shoulder. The street was empty. No sign of pursuit. No helicopters flying overhead. They were safe for now.

The front door flung open.

"What do you want?" Victoria snarled, then froze at the sight of her. "Oh, it's you. I thought you were one of those solicitors."

"Hi, Victoria," she said, rubbing her neck. "Can I come in?"

Victoria held open the door. Once she shut it, she looked Shannon up and down. "What's up? Didn't get enough of me on Friday—wait, is that *blood*?"

Shannon looked down at the dark splotches on her shirt. It was blood, all right, but not her own.

"It's probably Tyler's," she said.

"Oh, that's *so* much better. Wait, did you say Tyler?" Victoria raised her eyebrows. "That makes a lot of sense now. I never took you for a blood-play kind of gal, but sure, if that's your kink…"

She trailed off as tears welled in Shannon's eyes.

"Hey, what's the matter?" Victoria asked, touching her shoulder. "I was kidding. Did he have a nosebleed and spew blood all over you or something?"

Shaking the palm off, Shannon blotted her eyes with the back of her hand. "There's a guy in my trunk," she said and felt a hysterical little giggle rise in her throat. She managed to keep it at bay, afraid that if she began laughing, she wouldn't be able to stop.

"Wait, a *what*?"

"There is a guy in my trunk," Shannon repeated once she regained control of herself. She opened the door and walked out, and Victoria hurried after her.

When Tyler saw them approaching, he got out of the car.

"Hey, Victoria," he said hoarsely, resting his hand on the door, as if his balance was compromised.

Victoria just gawked, and she wouldn't move until Shannon grabbed her wrist and pulled her forward.

Shannon circled around to the back of the car. She popped the lid of the trunk and stared in shock at the grotesque sight within.

At some point during his panicked struggles, Hades's shirt and jacket had ridden up. Ugly scars tore up his back, raised white ropes against the smooth muscularity of his shoulders and lumbar. Other, smaller marks dappled the curve of his spine, tiny dark circles that were too uniform in size and shape to be acne discoloration. They looked like burn scars, like someone had put out a cigarette against his bare skin. Like maybe after flogging him within an inch of his life.

"Holy shit," Victoria said from behind her.

"Jesus Christ," Tyler muttered, coming up to take a closer look.

"We need to get him inside," Shannon said.

"Is he dead?" Victoria asked.

"No, I don't think so," Shannon said, but there was something definitely wrong with him. Through a screen of dark hair, his eyes were closed, his face as pale as that of a corpse. Blood congealed on his skin.

"Holy shit," Victoria repeated. "What'd you do?"

"Just hold the door for us," Shannon said. "I'll explain everything once we get him in."

Tyler grabbed the boy's legs while Shannon took his waist. Together they wrangled him into the living room and onto the couch.

Once they set him on the cushions, Shannon rolled his shirt back down and removed the duct tape wrapped around his face. When she tugged the sock from his mouth, he didn't stir, much less awaken. His chest rose in shallow breaths.

"Who is he?" Victoria asked.

"Hades," Shannon said and sighed, looking down at him. While his long, sooty lashes and clear skin conjured an image of youthful purity, the sleepless shadows under his eyes and the cruelness of his mouth, even in sleep, told a different story. Not to mention the scars on his back.

Victoria blinked. "Hades? You mean like the underworld? Like Greek mythology?"

"Bingo," Tyler said, crashing into the only available armchair. The word left him as a weary sigh.

"It's not his real name," Shannon said. "I mean, I doubt it is. Just a code name."

"Oh," Victoria said.

"Speaking of which..." Shannon searched Hades's pockets. She found his wallet and opened it.

In the plastic folder, there was a District of Columbia driver's license made out to an Alex Morello, age seventeen. The boy in the picture had shorter hair and a cold expression, but he was the same teen now slumped across the couch.

A few folded dollar bills and a credit card occupied one side of the billfold, but it was the other contents that caught her attention. In the inner pocket, she found four more driver's licenses with photographs of the same boy.

Daniel Turner from Virginia. Jacob Carroll from Maryland. Luke Tucker from California. Michael Ellis from Colorado.

Two of the IDs provided his age as twenty-one. One identified him as nineteen and another as eighteen.

"You think any of those are real?" Tyler asked as Shannon sorted through them.

"They look real, but which one do you think is really him?"

"Maybe none of them."

As she returned the cards to the wallet, she noticed a folded slip of paper wedged into the plastic pocket that contained the Alex Morello license. She stuck her finger inside and wiggled the paper free.

The slip proved to be a photograph, the kind that came from a photo booth. Hades was in each of the four images, standing next to a girl with flaxen hair. In one of them, he leaned against the blonde as she cradled a bouquet of blue flowers. In another, she made a silly expression and bunny ears, while a ghost of a smile touched his lips. The last two were the most emotional, with Hades laughing and grinning. He hardly seemed like the same boy who now groaned and mumbled "Nine" in his sleep. The boy who had picked up a gun and pulled the trigger.

"I know this girl," Shannon said, then showed Tyler the picture. "I just don't know from where. Have you seen her before?"

He shook his head. "I don't know, but she looks familiar."

She tossed the wallet onto the couch but held on to the photo. She sensed the girl in the photograph was important, another piece in this mess of a puzzle.

"Can someone *please* tell me what's going on?" Victoria asked.

"It's a long story," Shannon said.

As Tyler began talking about waking up in a stranger's home with a gun, Victoria's face drained of color. When Shannon got to the part about Hades—or *whoever* he was—appearing at her home, Victoria excused herself to check the locks on the front door. When she returned, she brought a bottle of wine with her.

"Sorry, but I think I need a drink for this," Victoria said, removing the piece of foil plugging the neck. She took a nip straight from the bottle then set it on the coffee table.

"Do you think they'll come looking for you here?" Victoria asked, wiping her mouth with the back of her hand. "Whoever they are?"

"I've thought about it," Shannon said, "and no, I don't. If Zeus didn't know where Tyler was, that means he isn't keeping direct surveillance on us. He knows where we live. He knows where I go to school. He has our pictures, he bugged us, and he gave us cell phones, but I think we're safe here, at least for a little while. We'll leave as soon as we think of somewhere else to go."

On the couch, Hades stirred. His face clenched as if in pain, and he groaned in his sleep like a dying animal caught in a trap.

"Nine," he whimpered, his eyes twitching under his closed lids. "Where are you?"

"What are you going to do about him?" Victoria asked.

"We can't kill him," Shannon said.

"Oh, yeah, because he wouldn't have shot us both in an instant," Tyler said, but he didn't really look like he wanted to argue. Or that he'd be willing to pull the trigger.

"He has to be brainwashed," she said.

"What if he isn't?" Tyler asked.

"He just has a different code, a different program—"

"What if he isn't?" Tyler repeated.

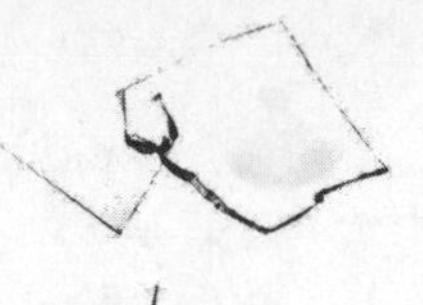

CASE NOTES 36: HADES

Hades slept. He dreamed.

Night descended over the Academy.

In the cover of twilight, he left Subset A's barracks and followed the short brick wall to the back of the building. He counted his footsteps as he walked, being sure to take steady, even steps and not overextend his legs. At the corner, he turned and took twenty steps. On the wall in front of him, a piece of the mortar had been chipped away. He crossed at that point, swinging himself over the barrier with ease.

The bullfrogs were coming out now, wailing from their puddles. Crickets chirped underfoot. Except for the branches and dried leaves crunching beneath his feet, those were the only other sounds. Still, after taking twenty more steps, he paused, listened.

Was that a footstep he heard? Was it Nine?

He looked behind him and searched the darkening yard. Nothing. Just his imagination.

He turned left and walked five steps before encountering a tree. The bark was scraped away near the base. He turned ahead, and fifteen more steps led him to a rock like so many others. In the fading light, it looked as smooth and white as a skull. He pushed it aside with his foot, squatted down, and from his pocket took out a small trowel he'd stolen from the toolshed.

As he sank the blade into the dirt, he listened, certain he'd heard something. He glanced behind him and again detected nothing.

The sun was a blood clot sinking into the surrounding mountains. Its ruddy light oozed through the branches and splashed across the black earth. There were too many shadows, too many places where someone might hide.

Once he reassured himself that he was alone, he began digging. Four inches. Six inches. One foot. The ground was soft, both from recent rainfall and upheaval. It took him all of five minutes to uncover the waterproofed sack.

He opened it and removed the gun, key ring, and hip holster. He was uneasy, had a bad feeling in the pit of his stomach, but his training was solid. He didn't tremble or fumble in clipping the holster onto his belt or loading the gun with its magazine. Even in disquiet, he worked methodically.

He had killed one man before, bashed his head in with a brick in a panicked frenzy. He told himself that if he had to kill again, he would not hesitate. He would not sob in terror this time at the sight of a crushed skull and the tacky feel of blood on his skin.

For Nine's sake and his, he must destroy.

He dropped the trowel into the hole and pushed the dirt back over with the toe of his shoe. He didn't try concealing the disturbed earth. If everything went as planned, he and Nine would be long gone by the time their absence was discovered. If not, then a gardening tool stolen from the shed would be the least of his worries.

He had told her to meet him near the kitchen exit, where every week workers would unload crates of produce, great sacks of flour and beans and rice, and iceboxes filled with meat and eggs. It was also where the dumpsters were, and even before he turned the corner, he smelled the pungent miasma of rotten vegetables and flyblown meat.

When he saw Nine, he sighed, not realizing until then how afraid he was that she wouldn't show up. But there she was, pressed against the alcove formed by the wall and dumpster.

It was almost night now. The stars and moon were out, the sun entirely absent. He didn't see the white-haired man standing behind her until it was too late.

The moment he noticed the Leader, he reacted. He pulled the gun from its holster. As he raised his arms, he was overpowered almost instantly, blindsided by two guards. The pistol skidded across the ground, out of reach.

He bucked and struggled, kicked and yelled, but it did no good. They slammed him to the ground hard enough to knock the air from him. He yelped out in pain as his arms were wrenched behind his back, and as he tried to rise to his knees, one of the men drove a knee between his shoulder blades, forcing him down again. Two hundred pounds of bone and muscle anchored him to the muddy earth.

"I had to," Nine said. "Don't you see, Two? I had to. I was so afraid for you. We'd never make it on our own."

He could only stare at her. A hundred expletives and insults roared through his mind, but his shocked, breathless silence seemed to impact her more than any words could.

Her face drained of color. Her eyes widened, flooding.

She began to weep, but he remained silent as they cuffed him and dragged him to his feet. Silent as they took him away. Silent, after a disorienting shift in dream sequence, as they gathered the others in the mess hall later that night and dragged him before the crowd.

Metal poles supported the roof overhead. On one of these poles, a steel bracket had been welded in place six feet up. A pair of handcuffs was threaded through the bolt, and they locked his hands there. The younger kids required a stool, but he was tall enough that he didn't have to stand on his tiptoes.

He tensed as he heard the soft *snick* of a knife being pulled from its sheath. Seconds later, crude hands yanked his shirt back. His collar tightened like a noose around his throat, then loosened as the back of his shirt was cut open and pulled down. Goose bumps rose on his exposed skin at the frigid breath of the air conditioner.

This wasn't how it was supposed to happen.

"Subject Two of Subset A has committed the grave offense of attempted desertion," the Leader said from behind him. No mention of the gun.

Facing the crowd, he saw tears, smug expressions, smiles, and disappointed eyes. Most had the stupid, glazed look of slaughterhouse cows observing the summary execution of one of their own.

Where was Nine? Was she watching this?

"This is what happens to deserters," said the Leader.

Hard shoes tapped against the concrete floor behind him, stealing his attention. He tensed, waiting for the first blow of the switch. He had been thrashed several times before but only for very minor offenses. His skin had never been broken.

He had a feeling that this time would be different.

He heard a soft *twang*. As a searing pain split across his back, his jaws clenched shut around a yelp. He refused to give the Leader and the others the pleasure of hearing him scream.

Stay silent, he told himself as the rod came down again. *Just stay silent. Whatever you do, don't make a sound.*

To distract himself, he searched the crowd for Nine. He found her by the fifth blow and contorted his lips into a big false smile.

See? I'm fine, he wanted to say. *I'm not going to cry. I can handle this, you traitor. You liar.*

Nine stood near the front, held by the shoulder. Forced to watch. Good, let her see.

You don't care about me at all, he thought, watching the crocodile tears stream down her face. *Now that you have a new family and a real name, you're done with me. Well, fine! I'm never going to trust you or anyone else again. Not for as long as I live.*

His skin broke on the eighth blow. Though his fingers

clenched around the pole so tightly that paint scraped off under his nails, he refused to cry out.

"Is this punishment not enough for you, Subject Two?" the Leader snapped. "Do you remain unrepentant? Is this silence your way of showing everyone that you're too good for the rod? Fine then, let's show them what happens to deserters who refuse to follow orders!"

He waited for the next strike but instead heard the sound of an object—*the switch*—clattering against the concrete, then a metallic *click* as a belt buckle was unclasped. Realizing what was about to happen, he took a deep breath and bowed his head, squeezing his eyes shut.

Stay silent. Don't you dare make a sound.

He broke his vow on the first blow by yelping out as the belt whipped across his back.

"Stop!" Nine screamed. "Don't do this. You said you would be lenient. You promised me you wouldn't hurt him. You promised!"

The next strike tore a scream from his throat as effectively as it tore open his back, and Nine shrieked as if she'd felt the blow herself. Blood dribbled down the hollow above his spine, burning hot. Pain consumed him.

"I'm sorry," he sobbed on the tenth blow. "I'm so sorry. Leader, forgive me. I'll never do it again. I'm sorry. Please stop. Please."

But the punishment didn't stop, not even when he begged for death. By the time his agonized screams shriveled in his throat and his legs gave out, he had lost count of the number of blows. The numb, staring faces blurred, and merciful darkness rolled over him.

And from that darkness, Hades slowly resurfaced. His head ached, and everything seemed too bright and too loud. Voices came to him, hollowed and distorted.

"He's coming to."

"Oh, great."

A girl's freckled face loomed over him. Shannon. She smiled

down with cold contempt. "Did you have a nice nap?"

He tried to hoist himself up and was unsurprised to find that his hands were tied behind his back. With duct tape, it felt like. When he strained against the tape, it cut into his wrists. He didn't bother testing the layers further, just maneuvered himself into a sitting position. No shock, they had also bound his ankles. Even so, he wouldn't have been ready to get to his feet, even if he had wanted to. Just curling his chest brought on a dizzying wave of vertigo that made his vision swim and gorge rise.

Tyler and Shannon were joined by a girl with hair like a skunk's—black but turning blond at the roots. She stared at him the way someone would stare at a coiled viper on the other side of a zoo exhibit, with unease, wariness, and a twinge of morbid fascination.

"Are you going to tell us what you know?" Shannon asked as he closed his eyes, battling with his nausea and pounding heart. "Who sent you?"

Hades didn't answer. Clinging to the dissipating memory of his dream, he understood now why the sight of Charles Warren's belt buckle had disturbed him so much. And now Elizabeth was in that man's company.

Hades would never let Charles Warren touch her. She might have ruined his life, but she was still *his.* No matter what name she went by now, she would always belong to him.

Once his nausea had receded enough to permit him to open his eyes again, he looked around.

He found himself in a sparsely furnished room outfitted in greenish-bronze wallpaper. Aside from the couch he lay on, there was a television set perched on a chipped wood stand, a glass coffee table, and an armchair in the corner. Overhead, the fan's oversize wicker paddles rotated slowly, stirring up stale odors of mothballs and dust. Although the furniture was all worn black suede, pale wood, and glass, there was a lodge-like feel to the room. Taxidermy plaques and stag antlers lined the walls. A stuffed bobcat snarled down at him from over an unlit fireplace.

He had only stood in the foyer of Shannon's house, and for all he knew, he could have still been there. He doubted it, though. Upon learning that the organization knew where they lived, they wouldn't have stayed long. Or invited a friend over, for that matter.

"Olympus is rising," Shannon said, crossing her arms.

"Pandora's box is opening," Hades said, though he felt no compulsion to utter the code phrase. If she thought he was under her command, he might be able to gain a tactical advantage here. His brain felt like it was crushed within the jaws of a bear trap, but the pain wasn't so bad that he couldn't plan or rationalize.

"Tell us who sent you," she said.

"I don't know his name, but I call him Zeus."

"What is your real name?"

In the corner of his eye, he spotted his wallet on the cushion next to him. There was a credit card knife in there. If they hadn't already confiscated it, he would be able to use the small blade to cut himself free.

"Alex Morello," he said, using the name on his D.C. license. He figured if they hadn't searched his wallet yet, they would eventually. Better to give that name than any of the others.

Shannon, Skunk Girl, and Tyler did a bit of a huddle then, talking to one another in hushed voices. Hades shifted on the cushion, groping around for the wallet. When Shannon glanced at him, he relaxed against the cushions. Once she looked away again, he continued his search.

One fingertip touched worn leather. He pulled the wallet closer, taking care to avoid any sudden movements that might draw their attention back to him. He searched the billfold, feeling around for the thin aluminum rectangle. It would be difficult to open the knife with his hands bound, and he would probably cut himself in the process, but any blood he lost would be nothing compared to the amount he spilled.

He would show them no mercy. The sooner he slaughtered them, the sooner he would be able to return to Elizabeth. To Nine.

She was the only person who mattered in the world.

His fingers touched metal. Colored red with typeset lettering, the folded knife resembled a credit card. Only the thin lines cut into it gave it away, but they must not have taken a close look at it.

"Hey, he's doing something!" Skunk Girl said just as he found the knife. "He's got something in his hands!"

He hardly had time to open the blade before Tyler was upon him.

Grabbing him by the arm and shirt, Tyler twisted Hades around and shoved him face-first against the cushions. The knife slipped from Hades's fingers as he writhed against Tyler's grip. He kicked out at Tyler but, with his ankles bound, did a rather ineffective job at hitting him.

"I knew it," Tyler said, retrieving the knife from the cushions. He scoffed in disgust at the sight of the blade. "You were faking it."

"You have a different code, don't you?" Shannon asked.

"Who knows?" Hades wormed into a sitting position once more, with some difficulty. His contortions had caused the duct tape to bite into his wrists, which were bruised from the restraint chair straps. Still, compared to the ache in his head, it hardly hurt at all.

Shannon glowered at him. "Listen, if you don't tell us who sent you, we'll—"

"What? Kill me?" He bared his teeth in a grin, though he felt only hatred now. "Just like you killed Eveline Grey."

Shannon froze. "What did you say?"

"She had a little girl, you know," he said, remembering the time he had asked Eveline how her brat was doing and mentioned how fragile kids were compared to adults. The scientist had paled and rushed from the room, and as punishment for that harmless comment, he had received three days in the padded cell.

Now, Shannon's expression looked a lot like Eveline's had. Her skin turned ashen, and her mouth disappeared into a flat, puckering line. She lost color with each word spoken, until even her lips were as pallid as those of a corpse.

"An eight-year-old girl," he said. "I guess it's a good thing she was staying with her grandparents that day, or else you would have killed her, too. And you probably would have liked it."

"Shut up," Shannon said through clenched teeth.

"Did it feel good to kill Eve?" Hades murmured, craning his head up at her. He stared into her eyes, waiting for her to avert her gaze. He knew she wouldn't be able to maintain this false righteousness for very long. If he couldn't attack her body, at the very least he could devastate her mind. D-05 wouldn't have flinched at the idea of murder, but this girl standing before him—this *lie*—was obviously not D-05 anymore. The outside world had weakened and corrupted her.

"Shut up."

"Did it make you feel powerful? I bet it did."

"Just shut up." Her words were barely audible now, and she looked away from him.

Hades knew he was getting to her. Good. He wanted her to suffer. Thanks to her, he had gone back into the tank. It was all her fault, and Tyler's, too.

"Do you remember all the blood?" he purred. "How warm it was? The way it felt on your skin? How will you be able to live with knowing you're a murderer?"

"I said shut up!"

He fell back against the cushions, laughing. Her expression was just priceless. She'd really conned herself into believing she wasn't responsible for murdering Eve and all of the others. Except she was responsible, and she had enjoyed it. He knew it. He knew that deep down inside her something cried for the taste of blood. She could act as pious and innocent as she wanted to, but it wouldn't change the fact that she was a natural-born killer. They all were.

"You're horrible!" Shannon said. "You're a monster."

He smiled at her. "I guess that makes two of us."

He spoke the truth. They weren't really humans, though their genetic donors were. Hades had seen pictures once of the place where he had been gestated—that cradle of impersonal fiberglass, steel, and synthetic amniotic fluid that in many ways was so much like the sensory deprivation tank where he had been reborn fifteen years later.

"Why are you protecting Zeus?" Tyler asked suddenly.

Hades broke eye contact with Shannon to look his way. "Is that what you think I'm doing?"

"Well, why else wouldn't you tell us?"

For once, Hades was at a loss for words. He wasn't protecting Dimitri. He just wasn't interested in helping them. Why should he? It wasn't his problem. Besides, they were the enemy, and they would probably just kill him once they found out who Zeus really was. Why keep a prisoner alive after all the useful information had been extracted from him?

"You don't seem like the kind of guy who'd kiss ass to anyone," Tyler said.

"I'm not protecting him," he said.

"Then do you not know?"

Hades fell silent.

"I mean, you knew my name. You knew hers. You knew the name of the woman we…who Eveline was, and even we didn't know that. So you have to know at least a little about Zeus, right? Why won't you tell us where he is or at least *who* he is?"

His smile died on his lips. Unease ate away at him as he found himself confronted by the troubling dissonance between his actions and his intentions.

"I'll tell you why." Tyler staggered to his feet. "Because he has been manipulating you this whole time. Just like us. Only you're too far gone to even realize it! You're dead inside!"

Each word was like a needle prick. Fine on its own but painful in multitudes. He wanted to punch Tyler in the face just to get him to shut up. He wasn't *dead*; he was *evolving.*

If you are evolving, then why can't you even break free? A-02 asked from inside his head, and he tensed at the voice that was his but not his. Sometimes, it calmed him to engage in an inner monologue with himself, but these thoughts were unwelcome and invasive. A-02 could just go back to sleep.

Just shut up, he thought. *I don't need you right now.*

Growing bolder, Tyler stepped closer, distracting Hades from himself. "You don't even remember your own name, do you?"

"My own name." Hades scoffed. "So you know yours?"

Names meant nothing. Especially names like Tyler Bennett and Shannon Evans. Those were just masks, even more so than the code names Apollo and Artemis. They were all numbers in the end.

"What would you do if I told you where to find him?" Hades asked.

Shannon tensed and glanced at Tyler.

"We won't kill you, if that's what you're asking," Tyler said.

"I meant what would you do to *Zeus*," he said, putting sarcastic emphasis on the last word.

At the blank expression on Tyler's face, Hades realized the other boy hadn't thought that far ahead. As Tyler groped for an answer, Shannon stepped forward.

"We'd stop him," she said, trying to sound firm but obviously conflicted with the idea of committing a conscious act of murder.

"Do you really think it'll end with him?" he asked, knowing it never would.

As long as Charles Warren was alive, the Project would go on forever. And even if Charles Warren expired, it would probably still continue. There was already a schism in the organization. On one side were Warren's loyal followers, and on the other, there were people like Dimitri who thought the Academy would be better off with a new overseer. Project Pandora wasn't a one-man operation. It wasn't anything they could stop on their own, so why bother?

"Just because he calls himself Zeus doesn't mean he's the leader," Hades added.

"Then who is?" Tyler asked.

Instead of responding, Hades settled against the couch, closing his eyes as another wave of pain and nausea struck him. He thought he might be able to go away for a bit if they began torturing him, as he knew they soon would. Now, he just wanted to prepare himself for the inevitable.

"Are you in pain?" Shannon asked. "We can give you something for that if you help us."

"No, you won't," Hades said, listening to the rain strike the roof above. He wanted to go outside and allow the water to wash the drying blood from his face. He knew the storm would ground him, make him feel a little more normal.

"We'll drop you off at a hospital."

"No, you won't." Hades opened his eyes, suddenly disturbed by the darkness behind his closed lids. It seemed to have actual substance, like a vast pool of ink that would swallow him whole, engulf and devour him. The sound of rainwater sloshing down the gutters outside only enhanced that impression.

Shannon sighed and reached into her pocket. She pulled out a strip of paper that Hades recognized in an instant as the photos he and Elizabeth had taken at the National Zoo. "So, who is she?"

Hades shrugged and glanced at the stuffed bobcat on the fireplace to avoid staring at the picture. If his hands weren't tied, he would've snatched the photograph from her in an instant. It made him furious to think how she was getting greasy fingerprints all over it, but he knew if he showed emotion, she would realize how important the photo was to him. The last thing he needed was to give her more leverage against him. Show nothing, feel nothing.

"Is she the girl you bought flowers for?" she asked.

"Does it matter?" he asked, turning his gaze to the coffee table now. His hazy reflection bothered him, and he looked away again, to the photo Shannon held.

"You look different in these," Tyler said, taking the photograph from her. "Like an actual person."

Hades chuckled at that.

"What's so funny?" Tyler asked, narrowing his eyes.

"We're weapons, not people," Hades said.

"Do you really find any of this funny?" Tyler asked. "You smile like you do, but you know what I think? I think you're just faking it. You don't want to be here any more than we do, and you hate that you have to do this. You *want* to help us, don't you?"

He declined to respond to that inane comment. He leaned against the couch, running his hands along the edges of the cushions. If he could find an upholstery pin, he might be able to use it to cut through the duct tape.

"Just who are you when you're not Hades?"

The questions aggravated him. They should've known who he was, but nobody ever did. They always forgot about him, and he ceased to exist in their eyes. Each time he had to repeat his code name, it was like a little part of his identity was taken from him once again, crushed underfoot into dust and ashes. Then he would begin to wonder if he was really who he said he was, if he was even there, if they could still *see* him.

What if he didn't truly exist? Sometimes the question kept him awake all night, paralyzed with dread. Sometimes, the only way to relieve the fear of *not being* was to lift weights until the pain grounded him or to witness others' responses to him, their screams of agony and terror. The only time he felt alive was when hurting someone else or being hurt himself—except when he was with Elizabeth Hawthorne.

She was his bridge to the past and future. His only salvation.

Hades stared at the photographs strip, at the bouquet

draped across Elizabeth's chest. Forget-me-nots were just pretty, ephemeral things. They could turn dead and shriveled in an instant.

At the sight of her beaming smile, he realized she would forget him again, and then he would have no one. Nothing but broken recollections, until electroshocks and deprivation tank sessions stole even those away.

At that revelation, a surge of enraged determination engulfed him. He would never let Elizabeth forget him. Not her. Never again.

But how was he supposed to protect her when he was here? Any moment now, Shannon and Tyler would kill him, and there was nothing he could do about it. He was at their mercy.

I need to join them, he realized. *I need to help them. Then Elizabeth will be mine again. She's the only thing in the world that's worth a damn. I need to save her. Mine. She's mine. I won't let the Project have her.*

"Are you even listening to anything we're saying?" Shannon snapped.

"Subject Two of Subset A," he said finally, smiling at her. "That's who I once was. But that boy is dead, so now I'm no one at all."

CASE NOTES 37: ARTEMIS

Subject Two of Subset A. Those five words echoed in Shannon's head, reverberating through her mind like seismic waves. And also like an earthquake, his response left her feeling apprehensive, unsettled, as if the carpet might give out beneath her feet at any moment.

Subject Two of Subset A. That was not a name you gave to a person. As for his statement about his old self being dead, what could that possibly mean? What had been done to Hades to make him this way? And could she have gone through that same ordeal, without remembering it?

Tyler groaned in frustration. "Can you just make sense for once?"

"I can do better than that," Hades said. "I can tell you exactly who Zeus is and where you can find him. I can even take you there, because there's sure as hell no way you're getting inside alive without my help. But what guarantees that you won't kill me once you know?"

For a moment, Tyler seemed to be at a loss for words. Then he shook off his daze and said, "Because I'm not scum like you, and I'm not a sadist."

"But you plan to kill Zeus."

"Not unless we have to."

"Oh, so you're one of *those* people." The words were carried out on the softest of scoffs. Yet, even unamplified, Hades's voice was thick with condescension.

Tyler glared. "One of those people? The hell's that supposed to mean?"

"A pacifist. Will you try to reason with him? Convince him to turn himself in?" Hades smiled, cocking his head. "Or maybe you'll call the police. So what will you tell them? That he made you kill—what's the body count now, five people?"

"Leave him alone," Shannon said, stepping forward. She was sick of being mocked by a boy who was supposed to be their prisoner. Maybe he thought that by insulting them he could gain control of the situation, but she refused to lose her cool in front of him again.

"Look, like I was saying, I'll take you to him," Hades said, turning his head to her. "I'm serious."

She narrowed her eyes. Yeah, he might take them to Zeus, but as soon as they cut Hades an inch of slack, he would take the opportunity to stab them in the backs. Whether he was still brainwashed like them or working off a completely different program, he was just too shady. He could not be trusted.

"But only if I can kill him," Hades continued, taking her off guard. Why in the world would he want to kill Zeus?

Tyler's anger blanched from his features, leaving him pale and weary. "But I thought... Why would you?"

"Out of everyone here, only I know Zeus's full potential. And I'm the only one who has the guts to actually finish the job. Thoroughly. And I have reason to, more so than any of you."

"No way," she said, shaking her head. "We're not giving you a gun."

"Then at least untie me."

"Tell us where he is," she said.

"Georgetown," Hades said. "A residential area. It's a large home. You've been there before, but you won't be able to find it without my help, let alone get inside."

Shannon trusted him about as far as she could throw him. Instead of responding, she grabbed Tyler's hand and pulled him to the back of the room.

"We shouldn't do this." She lowered her voice to a whisper so Hades wouldn't hear and leaned in close enough that her and Tyler's heads were nearly touching.

"I don't think we have a choice," he said, searching her eyes. "He knows where Zeus is, and it isn't like we can just torture the truth out of him."

She sighed and leaned against him, wishing they had a different option. But as long as Zeus remained active, they were in danger. They needed to get answers from him. There was no other alternative.

"Relax," Tyler murmured, brushing back a strand of hair that had fallen over her face. Even with the blinds shuttered, in the shadow of the taxidermy trophies, his leonine eyes were brighter than ever, like sunlight filtered through warm rum. "Let me talk to him. Since he knows he can get to you now, he's going to keep antagonizing you."

"He's not *getting to me.* He's being an immature little asshole."

"That's putting it lightly," Tyler said, frowning. "I don't like the way he looks at you."

Glancing back at Hades, she realized she didn't like it, either. Even as he smiled, his eyes were frigid and wary, restlessly flickering from person to person. He had come to her to complete a hit, a hit that, if he had the choice, would still be completed. She sensed that the moment they let their guard down, he would, as he had just so aptly put it, finish the job—thoroughly.

CASE NOTES 38: HADES

Hades didn't show it, but he was thinking about what Tyler had said.

You're dead inside. You don't even remember your own name, do you?

He had no name, but he did have memories—and the memories he had were warped, broken, and missing. Occasionally, he would mull over his origin and probe curiously, reluctantly, at the barren socket where many of his childhood recollections should have been. Most of the time he merely wandered through life like a sleepwalker through darkest apathy.

He knew deep down there was something else inside him. A whisper. The charred remnants of his old self, that boy called A-02.

Hades didn't care. He told himself the loss of memories was just another part of his evolution, like the sloughing off of snakeskin. The banishing of his humanity.

And yet...

Flashes of old memories returned to him. Subject Nine of Subset A, her breath hot on his cheek. The dead guard's blood congealing on his skin as he trembled uncontrollably, clutching a gory brick against his chest. The belt coming down and down again, and his own screams filling his ears.

He's been manipulating you this whole time. Only you're too far gone to even realize it!

No, that wasn't true. He wasn't a slave. All this time, he had followed Dimitri's orders of his own accord and pulled the trigger because he wanted to. Killing Dimitri would only confirm that. But to kill him and claim Elizabeth, he must side with the enemy.

"Let me kill Zeus," Hades repeated.

Shannon exchanged glances with Tyler and the skunk-haired girl.

"Why would you want to do that?" Shannon asked.

"He doesn't control me," Hades said.

"Then tell us his address."

"Not unless you untie me."

They all looked at one another and did a little huddle-up in the corner of the room. They spoke in hushed voices.

Once they were done convening, Tyler and the other girl left the room. Shannon stayed but kept her distance. She watched Hades with a wary, guarded expression.

"There's something I'd like to ask you," she said.

"Go ahead."

"Who were you before all this?"

"The same person you were."

"Can't you just answer clearly for once?"

"Does it really matter?" he asked.

"Yeah, actually, it does."

"I don't get why you're so interested in knowing who I am."

"Because I want to know if you were always this screwed up or if someone made you this way."

Hades merely rolled his shoulders in a luxurious shrug and settled against the cushion. For once, he found himself averting his eyes from her, watching the wicker fan cast lazy shadows across the ceiling. Those shadows were wrong. The entire world was. It just never looked the way it was supposed to, and things never happened the way they should.

"I saw the scars on your back," Shannon said. "I know something horrible happened to you."

"Something horrible happens to all of us," Hades said. "It's called life."

He wasn't sure why the questions bothered him so much, but the more she nudged him, the more frustrated he became. Like the time when he'd beat the man at the hamburger stand to a bloody pulp, he found himself wrestling with someone else's thoughts and feelings. Like a chimera tearing itself in two, gnawing at the suture line.

I don't belong here, A-02 said in his head.

Leave me alone, Hades thought. *If you don't want to be here, then get out. Go back to sleep.*

Who are you?

Shut up. Shut up. Shut up.

Shannon broke his daze by saying, "You don't remember, do you?"

"No. I'm just about the *only* one here who remembers." Damaged as his memories were, Hades knew more than the two of them combined. He knew what he was and where he had come from, and he knew the world probably didn't exist. He wasn't lost in the lie.

She was silent for a moment, seemingly absorbing his response. Then she shook her head and said, "I don't get you."

"Maybe someday you will."

"Do you always speak in riddles?"

"They're only riddles if you're too stupid to figure them out."

She gave him a sour look but said, "You know, I almost feel sorry for you."

"Yeah, I bet you do."

She didn't care. She didn't remember. Her sympathy was merely programming of a different variety. Psychological conditioning that had been asserted on her without her knowledge by this shithole of a society.

"I know what it's like to lose sight of who you are," she continued. "I—"

"You don't know who I am."

Tyler and the skunk-haired girl returned. Skunk Girl carried a pair of scissors in one hand and a small black aerosol canister—*pepper spray?*—in the other.

Tyler's face was cleaned up and he wore an ill-fitting T-shirt under his jacket. He handed Shannon his gun and took the scissors from Skunk Girl.

"Are you going to untie me now?" Hades asked, feeling the muscles in his arms and legs flex. His gaze followed the lethal point of the scissors as they caught the light.

It wasn't until Tyler knelt down to cut the tape around his ankles that the tension left Hades and he realized he wasn't going to try anything. Not because he feared the gun but because he needed them just as much as they needed him. They were his path to Elizabeth.

Once the coil of duct tape fell to the carpet, Tyler stuck the scissors in his jacket pocket, gripped Hades by the upper arm, and pulled him to his feet. Rather than cut the tape around his wrists, Tyler just led him to the door.

"Bye, Victoria," Shannon said as she paused on the front step and hugged Skunk Girl tightly.

"Be safe," Skunk Girl said and glowered at him, clenching down on the pepper spray canister. "If you even think about hurting her, I'll hunt you down and tear your guts out."

Smiling, he regarded the metal street numbers affixed to the wall beside the front door. "Before you start making threats, maybe you should take into consideration the fact that I know where you live now."

He didn't have the luxury of seeing her expression, because by then Tyler was already shoving him forward.

Hades sat in the backseat this time instead of the trunk, on the passenger side. The moment Tyler sat down behind the driver's seat, he pointed his gun at Hades, pressing it right up between his ribs.

"I was just joking," Hades assured him. "We're on the same side now."

Tyler rolled his eyes. "Yeah, right."

CASE NOTES 39: ARTEMIS

Shannon sighed, watching the world pass by beyond the windshield. In just the last several hours, she had discovered a stunning ability to cope with strange circumstances, but her strength was waning. She was growing mentally and physically exhausted, and with every mile, she found herself sinking deeper into a stupor.

"Are you all right?" Tyler asked, meeting her gaze in the rearview mirror.

"I'll live," Shannon said.

That is, if the sociopath in the backseat didn't murder them first, or if the guilt over what she had done didn't drown her.

"We both will," Tyler said.

She looked back at the street ahead and stepped lightly on the gas pedal. She wanted to say more, just wasn't sure how to put it into words. She wondered if Tyler was thinking the same thing she was.

How many people have I killed?

She was a killer. That was something she would have to live with her whole life. And one day it very well might consume her, but for today at least, she would have to keep that monster at bay. She couldn't fight her own demons when the devil waited somewhere just beyond them.

What mattered now was finding Zeus and dealing with him.

Even if it meant adding another body to the pile of corpses that weighed down on her conscience. And even if, by the end of this, the cumulative weight of those sins would drag her into hell.

Shannon glanced at the gun she had placed in the door compartment. The thought of having to use it made her heart lurch with nervous tension.

As they drove, Hades gave her directions. Otherwise, he kept strangely quiet, compared to how he was before. She wondered if he would try to betray them once they reached their destination or if they had actually managed to get through to him. More likely, he just had a concussion.

As they entered the area of Georgetown where Zeus apparently lived, Hades said, "Wait, stop the car."

Shannon sighed and pulled to a stop along the curb. "What is it?"

"I need to drive from here," Hades said.

"Why?"

"Because there are cameras, and I'm the only one here who knows the passcode. If they see you driving and me sitting in the backseat, they're going to know something's wrong."

"What exactly do you mean by 'they'?" Tyler asked.

Hades rolled his eyes. "Do you really think this is the work of one man? Dimitri is just part of it."

"Dimitri?"

Hades hesitated, then said, "Dimitri Kosta. Zeus."

Shannon felt her mouth go dry. Dimitri Kosta, as in Dr. Kosta, the psychiatrist she had been seeing for the last year.

"Oh, you've got to be kidding me," Tyler said, and she saw at once the link connecting them.

"Are you a patient of Dr. Kosta's, too?" she asked Tyler.

"That bastard," Tyler said. "I'm going to kick his skull in."

She wondered why, during her last phone call with Zeus, she had not recognized Kosta's voice from her bimonthly psychiatry appointments and put two and two together. Then she realized she couldn't even remember what they discussed during her visits.

There were so many gaps in her memory. How could she have overlooked them?

"Look, just untie my hands," Hades said. "I won't try anything. You can even keep the gun pointed on me."

"Should we trust him?" she asked, glancing at Tyler.

Tyler sighed. "Do we really have a choice?"

"No," she muttered, unbuckling her seat belt. "I guess we don't. I'll cover you."

Shannon took the key from the ignition and retrieved her pistol from the door compartment. She stepped out of the car. She kept the gun close against her body as she opened the door that Hades would exit from.

"If you try to run, I'll shoot you," Tyler warned.

"I'm not going to run." Hades got out of the car and leaned against it, his stomach flat against the side of the vehicle.

"Don't move," Tyler said, putting his gun in its waist holster. He zipped up his jacket and pulled the hem down, presumably to make it more difficult for Hades to access the pistol. As he took the scissors from his jacket pocket, Shannon aimed her gun at Hades's chest.

Tyler snipped the tape and took a quick step back. He tossed the scissors across the street and extracted his own pistol from its holster.

Hades lowered his hands to his sides and turned around. "That wasn't too hard now, was it?"

"Get into the driver's seat," Shannon said.

He obeyed, shutting the car door behind him. Once he was inside, Shannon circled around to the front passenger's seat and sat down, pointing her gun at his chest. Tyler returned to the backseat.

"Hades, don't buckle your seat belt," Shannon said, worried he might try to ram the car into a wall or lamppost to disable her. She didn't want to distract herself by trying to buckle her seat belt with her left hand. The last thing she needed was for him to come to a quick stop and hurl her through the windshield.

"I didn't plan to," Hades said, glancing at her as though she were an idiot. "It's just a couple streets down."

"I can't believe we're having him drive," Tyler muttered.

"I'm a very good driver," Hades said.

"He probably has a concussion," Tyler said to Shannon.

Hades turned back onto the street. His gaze flickered to her every few seconds, as if he were worried she might shoot him the moment they arrived at Dr. Kosta's house. While she had no intention of executing Hades, she wished that she could somehow restrain him. He couldn't be trusted.

At the end of the street, they reached a high stone wall overgrown with vines of Virginia creeper.

"Tyler, duck down," Hades said as he pulled up in front of the spear-pointed gate. He rolled down his window and leaned out, typing into the keypad.

Shannon tightened her grip on the pistol. She hoped the person watching through the camera inserted into the metal panel wouldn't be able to pick up on the fact that she was pointing the gun at Hades. Or, for that matter, that they had a stowaway crouching in the backseat.

As Shannon waited for the gate to open, she quickly became certain Hades had typed in a different code, one that would summon *them*—whoever *they* were—in an instant. But then the gate rolled forward, and he drove through the opening. She flinched at the echoing crash of the great wrought-iron door closing shut behind them.

The sprawling mansion emerged through veils of rain. At the sight of the home, it suddenly occurred to Shannon that the people they were up against were very wealthy and most likely very powerful. Located on prime real estate and far larger than the surrounding homes, the mansion must have cost upwards of ten million dollars.

Apprehension ate away at her. Maybe they should just get the hell out of Dodge while they had a chance.

Hades stopped in front of a small single-room outbuilding that Shannon presumed was a garage. After removing the keys from the ignition, he just sat in silence, staring at the rainwater pouring down from the roof's eaves.

"What are you waiting for?" Tyler asked from where he huddled in the backseat.

"I'm thinking," Hades said. "Unlike you, I actually have something called a brain."

Shannon scoffed. "I never would have guessed."

"The three of us can't go in together," Hades said, ignoring her jab. "Dimitri's not stupid. He'll know something is up if Tyler's with us, even if he pretends to be our prisoner."

"I'm not letting you go in with her alone," Tyler said.

"You don't have a choice," Hades said, then paused. "And it's not like you're just going to be sitting out here. You'll attack from the flank, as soon as you secure Elizabeth."

"Who's Elizabeth?" Shannon asked.

"The only person worth a damn to me," Hades said. "She's my collateral, okay? Tyler takes care of her; I'll take care of you. That's how it works, right?"

"The last thing I need is for you to take care of me," Shannon said, annoyed that Hades even thought for an instant that she needed his protection. "In case you forgot, I'm the one with the gun."

She expected Hades to make a mocking retort, but instead he just looked into the rearview mirror then across the lawn. His demeanor seemed different than how it had been just an hour ago, his expression hardened with cold practicality, his eyes wary.

"Listen, there's a utility tunnel that runs beneath the house, between the garage and the basement," Hades said. "The garage entrance is hidden in a cabinet at the back of the room. I think it's the one that's filled with golf clubs. The bottom is loose, and there's a keypad hidden there. You'll have to remove the panel to reach it. As soon as you get to the basement, find Elizabeth and free her. Have her wait for us in the garage. She'll be safe there."

"She's the girl in the picture, right?" Tyler asked.

"Right," Hades said, then glanced at Shannon. "Do you have a pen? There are two codes. One for the garage and one for the utility tunnel. I don't expect your boyfriend to remember both."

Keeping the gun directed on him, Shannon opened the glove box with her left hand and groped around inside of it. She knocked documents and coupons to the floor then searched through the compartment until she came across a black marker.

She gave the marker to Tyler, who wrote down the passcodes on his inner wrist.

"The dogs might be out," Hades said to Tyler. "If you come across any, tell them *grün*. They'll leave you alone then. Probably."

Without waiting for her permission, Hades opened the car door and stepped out into the rain. He didn't bolt, just shut the door and circled around to her side. By then, she had already gotten out of the vehicle.

"See?" He smirked at her. "We're allies now."

Shannon trusted him about as far as she could throw him. He was a contradiction, doing one thing and saying another, smiling warmly even as his eyes remained icy and guarded. However, she sensed that somewhere between his pistol-whipping and now, his motives had shifted, and his goals now aligned more closely with hers.

"Are you doing this for that girl you were talking about?" she asked as they walked through the rain. Water drizzled down her cheeks, and the wind buffeted her face. She slipped the pistol into the baggy pocket of her jacket, holding it pointed away from her. She kept a step or two behind Hades, with ample space between them, in case he tried anything.

Stepping under the colonnade, he answered her question with one of his own. “Do you ever feel dead?”

His question took her aback, and she didn’t know how to respond.

“I don’t when I’m with her,” Hades said and opened the mansion’s double doors. “But I do everywhere else.”

CASE NOTES 40: PERSEPHONE

Elizabeth yanked at the canvas restraints. No good. They wouldn't loosen, no matter what she tried.

Her struggle was disrupted by the sound of approaching footsteps and soft conspiring voices from the hall outside her door. She recognized the voices as belonging to Dr. Kosta and the Leader of the Academy, that white-haired man who had greeted her when she had arrived here. Her blood thickened into frozen mud.

She tried to sit up, only to be pulled down again by the straps around her wrists and ankles.

"I trust that you'll be able to correct it?" asked the Leader, his voice clipped with his strong accent.

Elizabeth slumped against the pillows and closed her eyes, pretending to be asleep. She waited for the men to pass, her heart pounding. Instead, the footsteps stopped.

Dr. Kosta didn't hesitate. "Of course. Charles, this was just..." He paused, as though searching for a word. "A glitch, a bug in the programming." He laughed nervously. "Give me a few days with her and some heavy psychotropics, and I'll get it worked out."

Elizabeth's heart rate soared. She wondered if the accelerated beeping from the bedside heart monitor would raise alarm. That fear forced her to calm herself. She focused on her breathing, making it slow and even.

"I sure hope so." The Leader's words were honed with an edge of hostility. It sounded like a threat to Elizabeth.

Zeus must have thought the same, because he didn't answer.

"This girl is very valuable to the organization," the Leader said. "As long as we have her, we have Senator Hawthorne in the palm of our hand."

The footsteps started up again. She sighed in relief, glad to hear them go.

"Thank God," she murmured.

Then she realized the hollow clapping wasn't getting softer, as it would have if the men had continued down the hall. The sounds were becoming louder, closer.

The men had entered the room.

She stiffened under the covers, terrified they'd heard her whisper or saw her lips move.

The footsteps stopped. She sensed the men looming over her. She couldn't see them, not through her closed lids, but she felt their presence in the air all around her. It reminded her of the oppressive stillness that came just before a lightning strike. There was even the same staticky sensation, crawling over her like a thousand ants. She tried not to shudder.

"I want you to understand something, Dimitri," the Leader said, at her bedside. She imagined him as a human shadow stooping over her, perhaps resting his hand on the headrest. "I recognize your talent and loyalty, which is why I've given you such an integral part in the Project."

"I know, sir," Dr. Kosta stammered. His voice was soft, but she couldn't tell if he was just talking quietly or if it was because he was standing farther away from her.

"But you are merely an extension of Project Pandora's main body. You vet every decision through me first. You keep me updated on everything, and you keep your subjects on a shorter leash. One way or another, this will not happen again. Do I make myself clear?"

"Yes, sir," Dr. Kosta said.

"Good, I'm glad we've reached an understanding." The Leader paused. Elizabeth felt a cold, dry finger scrape across her forehead, brushing back her hair. She tried not to shiver. "Now, I'll let you begin her treatment. It's essential that she recovers as soon as possible."

The echo of the Leader's retreating footsteps was accompanied by a soft clatter. Through the slits of her eyelids, she observed Dr. Kosta using a syringe to draw clear fluid from a small bottle.

Elizabeth tensed but knew that if she writhed and yelled, the doctor would realize the sedative had already left her system. She prayed that Hades hadn't lied about switching out the drugs with harmless saltwater.

After wiping down the IV port, Kosta injected the drug into the port and glanced at his wristwatch.

Elizabeth maintained her breathing, keeping it calm and slow. She felt the straps loosen from around her wrists and heard the silver *clicks* of the buckles being undone.

Although every nerve in her body screamed at her to run, she knew this was the time when Kosta would expect disobedience. If she waited until he moved her, there was a better chance of taking him off guard. It would also give her time to find a weapon.

Kosta transferred her to a wheelchair. She slumped against the leather back with her hands splayed at her sides. She rested her head on her shoulder. Through her narrowed eyes, she observed her surroundings.

Dr. Kosta wheeled her down the hall. When they arrived at an unmarked wooden door, he pushed it open with his shoulder. As he brought her inside, fear seeped through Elizabeth's veins at the sight of the stainless-steel container that occupied the farthermost wall. Under the glow of bright fluorescents, the tank reminded Elizabeth of a torture device from a more barbaric time.

There was no time to waste. As he leaned over the wheelchair, presumably to lift her up, Elizabeth shot to her feet and rammed her knee between his legs.

She had never struck anyone in the balls before and, for a second, thought she had somehow missed. But the way he collapsed, choking hoarsely, with his hands curled around his wounded parts, made it clear she had hit her target.

She shoved Kosta aside and dashed into the hall.

CASE NOTES 41: ARTEMIS

Shannon followed Hades through the mansion's double doors and into a spacious foyer. A pair of Rottweilers rose as she entered, and they advanced toward her, snarling.

"*Grün*," he barked. "*Fuss.*"

Immediately, the dogs lowered their hackles and joined their master's side. He bent down and stroked one of the dogs on its head.

She recognized the language, but she wasn't exactly sure *how* she recognized it.

"Why German?" she asked as he rubbed the Rottweiler behind its ear. He seemed more interested in petting his dogs than hunting down Dr. Kosta and finishing him off.

"I don't want to confuse them if I use command words in normal conversation," Hades said, smirking. "They're about as smart as you are, which means I have to talk to them very slowly."

"You're such an asshole." Lowering her voice to a whisper, she added, "Where is he?"

"Probably in his study."

Shannon kept her hands shoved into the pockets of her coat. The barrel of her pistol made a barely noticeable bulge in the fabric. She had turned on the safety but kept her finger hovering just above the switch, ready to flick it off in an instant.

Even though Hades maintained his cold, cocky demeanor,

she sensed that she and Tyler had gotten through to him somehow. Multiple times during the drive, she had watched the other boy's mocking smile fall from his lips and briefly be replaced by a distant, almost troubled expression.

As they walked down the hall, she lingered a step or two behind Hades, just in case he tried reaching for her gun. He was six or seven inches taller than she was. From his lethal build alone, she knew he would easily be able to overpower her in a competition of strength. Her pistol was her only advantage, a way to level the playing field.

"Do you live here?" Shannon asked.

"No, I'm stationed here," Hades said, glancing back at her.

She lifted her eyebrows.

"Like a soldier," he said.

Shannon scoffed. "You're not a soldier."

Hades shrugged. "I was going to be one."

"How old are you anyway?" she asked.

"Seventeen," he said. "Same as you."

"Soldier, my ass."

The study was deserted. He ordered the dogs to keep watch outside the room, then shut the door and locked it.

"I can access the whole security system from here," he said, going to the desk.

She withdrew the gun from her coat pocket. As she pointed it at Hades, he sighed.

"Is that really necessary?" he asked, opening the laptop.

"Don't touch any of the drawers," Shannon said, worried that he might reach for a gun hidden in the desk.

"I didn't plan to." As he began typing, his expression hardened. His gaze flitted from her to the laptop screen to the door.

Just looking at him, she could tell the cogs in his brain were working in overdrive. How he could think straight after getting clobbered in the head was beyond her. Did he have a skull made out of steel or something?

"What exactly are you doing?" she asked.

"Turning off the gate and alarms," he said. "Elevator, too. I'll keep the lights on, but that's about it. Won't help if they trap us in."

"They?"

"I don't know how many, if any," Hades said. "But I just remembered there's a meeting tonight. And Mr. Warren might still be here, and at the very least he'll have a security detail with him." He plucked out the flash drive attached to the laptop and stuck it in his pocket, then returned both hands to the keyboard. "Give me a minute. I'm going to look through the cameras."

She joined him behind the desk as he brought up the video display. She had no idea who "Mr. Warren" was, but she decided that now wasn't a good time to keep asking questions.

Hades identified each video as he skipped past it. "Downstairs bedroom, bedroom, library, game room, study. Oh shit, Elizabeth."

Before Shannon could react, he rushed past her. By the time she lifted her pistol, he was already halfway through the door. Instead of shooting him in the back, she took off after him, with the Rottweilers racing at her heels.

Hades wasn't her captive anymore, Shannon realized as her feet pounded across the floor. He was a wild card, an unknown variable, but not an enemy or a prisoner. And there was nothing she could do but follow him and hope his interests remained aligned with hers.

As they reached the foyer, a door to her right flew open and a teenage girl barreled through the opening, breathing heavily. Dressed in a blue hospital gown, with her blond curls surrounding her face in a tangled jungle, she hardly resembled the girl from the photos. Only her features were the same, those ice-blue eyes that widened with shock and the mouth that fell agape at the sight of them.

"I remember, Two," Elizabeth said between gasps. "I know who you are now."

Hades stared at her like she was a stranger, his expression blank.

"You can," Elizabeth said and stepped toward him. "That's what you told me. I didn't believe you back then, but now I know you were right, and it's not too late. Let's run away together."

Their reunion didn't last. The moment Hades's hands locked around her waist, the front doors opened and three men strode in.

CASE NOTES 42: APOLLO

As Shannon and Hades disappeared into the mansion, Tyler darted across the driveway, crouching forward to make a smaller target of himself. Once he reached the garage, he pressed himself against the wall, holding his pistol at the ready as he typed in the first of the two passcodes.

The tiny light on the keypad blinked green, and the garage door rolled up with the soft groan of well-oiled hinges. Over the downpour, the sound was reduced to a whisper.

He slipped inside the moment he could fit through the opening. A second control panel on the inside wall allowed him to close the door. The entire process took thirty seconds, which was far longer than he would have liked.

Pallid light filtered in from a single dust-encrusted window, shallowly illuminating his surroundings. The garage was large enough to house two cars, floor-to-ceiling cabinets, and little else.

As the garage door rolled shut, he hurried to the back wall and began opening cabinets. Two were shelved and contained paint cans, tools, and a stack of license plates from different states. The third cabinet housed a golf bag, which he shoved onto the floor to access the inner paneling.

He squatted, set the gun onto the floor, and ran his fingers along the bottom panel. There was a small crack between the cabinet's base and its interior walls. He felt leery about trying to remove the panel with his fingers, in case Hades had neglected to tell him that the entrance was booby-trapped in some way. Instead, he retrieved a screwdriver from another cabinet and wedged it into the joint between the panels. He set the board on the floor once he had lifted it all the way and discarded the screwdriver.

Four bolts affixed a steel panel to the concrete beneath. A keypad much like the one on the door outside was inserted flush against the metal. Tyler consulted the numbers he had written down as he pressed the corresponding buttons.

As soon as he typed in the last number, the back of the cabinet swung forward on heavy hinges. The panel wasn't flimsy particleboard, as he had first assumed, but laminated wood atop an inch-thick steel core.

Wealthy, powerful, *and* paranoid. Just who were they up against here, aside from a nut job of a psychiatrist?

Concrete stairs led into darkness.

Feeling woefully underpowered, Tyler picked up the pistol and stepped onto the landing. He left the door slightly ajar, worried that if he closed it, he wouldn't be able to open it from the inside.

Naked bulbs in steel cradles, activated by motion sensors, provided slightly more illumination than the watery daylight filtering in from behind him. He followed the stairs down to a narrow passageway with an arched ceiling. The air below was cold and clammy. In the sallow light, the raw brick walls almost resembled the inside of a creature's gullet, engulfing him.

Heart racing, he hurried down the corridor, ducking to avoid scraping his head on the low ceiling. A pipe ran along the length of the tunnel. He passed an alcove on his left side that contained a churning machine and emerged through another steel-cored door to find himself in a lavish hallway.

Unlike the tunnel behind him, the hall had been designed to be pleasing to the eye. The floor was tiled in polished black stone, and decorative paneling hugged the walls. Tyler could have been in Paris, or London, or another D.C. residence, anywhere safe and welcoming. Except there was a boy tied to the bed in the first room he came across.

Against his better judgment, he entered the room and shut the door behind him.

"Hey, can you hear me?" he asked the boy, staring in befuddlement at the helmet covering the kid's entire head. When the kid didn't respond, he set his pistol on the nightstand and removed the helmet.

The kid's eyes moved restlessly beneath his closed lids. He didn't respond when Tyler repeated the question.

Tyler pressed two fingers below his jaw to check his pulse. Slow but even. His gaze went to the plastic sack hanging from a metal rack next to the bed. Whatever drug the boy had been administered kept him docile and unresponsive—but he wouldn't remain that way for long, if Tyler had any say in it.

He peeled off the tape affixing the IV tube to the boy's inner arm and withdrew the hollow tip from beneath his skin. He fumbled in removing the straps, his palms damp with sweat, but within a minute the restraints fell to the mattress.

He didn't like leaving the boy here to come down from his sedation alone, but there was no time. He had already delayed long enough. He refused to leave Shannon alone with Hades for any longer.

He retrieved his pistol from the bedside table and stepped into the hall. He glanced back once, only long enough to confirm that he was alone, then continued forward.

Before Tyler had an opportunity to explore the contents of the remaining rooms, the door ahead burst open and a blond girl rushed out.

She froze at the sight of him, eyes wide and lips parted in blank amazement. Her face was identical to the girl in Hades's photo. As soon as her gaze lowered to the gun, she pivoted on her heel and fled.

"Wait, Elizabeth!" As he rushed after her, he glanced through the doorway she had come from—and froze.

At the sight of the man kneeling inside, Tyler's finger curled through the trigger guard. His chest tightened and an overwhelming hatred engulfed him.

"How are you even here?" Dr. Kosta asked, his voice ragged with shock and pain. His hands were folded loosely over his crotch, and it didn't take a brain surgeon to figure out why.

"Don't move," Tyler ordered, stepping into the room.

"Just put the gun down," Kosta said.

"You'd better start explaining things now. *What did you do to me?*"

"Did you kill Hades?"

"Answer the question."

"Olympus is rising," Kosta said.

"Nice try, but that's not going to work with me." As tempted as Tyler was to pistol-whip Kosta into obedience, he needed information more than savage satisfaction. He decided to take a blunter approach than mere words and cocked his pistol's hammer.

Kosta tensed at the low *click* and moistened his lips. "Wait, just wait a minute. Let's not be rash here. Who am I talking to? Tyler or B-10?"

"What?"

"So, you still don't remember." Kosta chuckled weakly. "Tyler Bennett…never existed. He's a lie."

Tyler narrowed his eyes. What exactly was Dr. Kosta trying to pull here?

"Tyler Bennett is an alternate personality that I made," Kosta said, and his pallid eyes shone with hateful glee at the shock that Tyler felt contort his own features. "You wouldn't exist if it wasn't for me. I *created* you!"

Tyler struggled for breath. He felt choked, beaten down with each word that left Kosta's mouth.

"Your memories are artificial, built from photographs, records, nothing real, nothing substantial."

"Shut up."

"Your past, your sense of self, all lies. Your desires, your goals, your inspirations, all ideas that I implanted into your subconscious through psychic driving."

"It's not true." His voice trembled with shock and fury.

"Just where do you think you came from?" Dr. Kosta asked, staggering to his feet. "If not for Project Pandora, you would never even exist in the first place! You would still be an embryo refrigerated in some shithole of an IVF clinic!"

Each word hit Tyler like a punch. His rage simmered into overwhelming confusion. Suddenly, he felt engulfed by a feeling like being adrift on a stormy sea, clinging to flotsam in an attempt to stay afloat as the world churned beneath him.

What was Project Pandora? What was this talk about an IVF clinic?

"Enough riddles!" Tyler said. "Tell me what Project Pandora is now!"

A sly light entered Kosta's eyes, and he took a step closer. "Project Pandora was created with the sole purpose of raising genetically superior children who would become this country's future military and political leaders. Through psychological programming, the children would be unaware of their own nature, their purpose, until called upon by the organization. They would devote every waking moment to fulfilling their 'dream' of rising to power, unaware that it wasn't their dream in the first place."

"Then why did you make me kill?!"

Kosta sighed, running a hand through his graying hair. "Charles Warren's ambitions have ruined everything. Several years ago, he decided it would be best if some of the children were used for...other roles, as a way to accelerate the organization's goals. Children like you."

"You're lying."

"But enough about the Project." Kosta stopped in front of Tyler. "Just give me the gun."

"No."

Kosta smiled with thinly veiled impatience and extended a hand. "If you shoot me, do you really think you'll be able to leave this place alive? I can save you. All you have to do is hand me the gun."

Tyler hesitated. He held out the pistol, watching as a flicker of triumph shone through Kosta's smile.

And then he pulled the trigger.

CASE NOTES 43: PERSEPHONE

No sooner had Hades drawn Elizabeth against him than he was pushing her back. He seized her wrist with one hand and pointed his other hand at the men.

"*Vernichten*!" he shouted, and the dogs that trailed him lunged past her.

By the time the man nearest to them realized what was happening, a Rottweiler had already driven him to the floor. The man screamed and writhed as the dog worried at his throat, vigorously shaking its head back and forth until flesh tore. Blood and foamy saliva flecked on the polished marble.

Another man withdrew a gun from underneath his suit jacket and shot wildly at the Rottweiler that felled his companion, only to be blindsided by the second dog. The canines were as vicious as their master, going straight for the jugulars.

"Run!" Hades said, dragging Elizabeth toward the same door she had come through just moments before.

Elizabeth had no desire to reencounter Dr. Kosta, let alone the blond boy who had rushed at her with his gun drawn, but she trusted Hades's judgment. He was clearly more familiar with the house than she was, and if he had a plan, she wouldn't interfere this time.

The red-haired girl followed swiftly behind them. As soon as all three of them passed through the door that led to the basement, Hades slammed it shut. At first she couldn't understand why he had brought them here, but then she realized there must be another exit down below. Otherwise, why else would he have herded them into the basement in the first place?

The door had no lock, and he pressed his body against the panel as a violent force drove into it from the other side, rattling it on its hinges. Indistinct shouts rose from the hallway beyond, followed by gunfire and furious barking.

"Go," he said. "I'll hold them off."

Elizabeth shook her head vehemently. "No, there's no way we're leaving you here!"

"You don't have a choice. If you stay here, you'll die." His hardened expression was the same one she remembered from that evening in the meadow, when he had asked her to run away with him. Past his narrowed eyes and firmly set jaw, his brain was surely running a mile a minute, plotting out every possible outcome he could think of.

"Come on," the red-haired girl said, touching Elizabeth's shoulder.

"Shannon, we'll regroup at your friend's house," he said to the girl, taking his hand off the door only long enough to reach into his jacket pocket. He pulled out a small silver object—a flash drive. "In case I'm delayed, take this. It's Dimitri's research data. You need to destroy these bastards. Colorado. That's where the Academy's at. Project Pandora can't go on."

Shannon took the flash drive from him and stuck it in her pocket. She glanced at Elizabeth then hurried down the stairs.

"Go with her, please," Hades said, digging his heels into the floor as the door shuddered.

Gunshots exploded from the other side, and a long, narrow fissure appeared in the wood. The door must have had a metal core, because even the next two shots failed to penetrate it.

"Don't worry about me. I'll be fine." He smiled, but it was a paper-thin facade that failed to reach beyond the confines of his lips.

"Don't you dare die," she said, then turned and ran after Shannon. She looked back once she reached the bottom of the stairs and found him in the same place, his arms splayed across the door, one hand gripping the knob. He met her eyes then shifted his body so his shoulder was bracing the door. Maybe so he wouldn't have to watch her leave.

Blinking back tears, she turned around and kept going.

The blond-haired boy ran into them in the hall. A mist of blood clung to his shirt, a sharp contrast to the waxy pallor of his tan. He lowered his pistol the moment he saw them.

"Where's Hades?" the boy asked. "Who's shooting?"

"There's no time to explain," Shannon said. "We need to go now!"

As they reached a low brick passage at the other end of the basement, a loud *bang* echoed from behind them, in the direction of the stairwell, followed by rapid gunfire. The door must have been breached.

A sudden image came to Elizabeth: A-02 smiling at her from the center of the Academy's mess hall, smiling even as the switch raised welts on his back. He had always been a good faker, putting on a mask so nobody would know what he was really thinking. He had told her once that it was a strategy, because absolute honesty weakened the defenses and left a person open to sabotage.

"But I'll never lie to you, Nine," he had murmured, and he had been lying then, too. Just like he was lying now, saying he'd be all right and meet up with them later, when she knew that he never would. If she did nothing to help him, he would die alone. She would be abandoning him once again.

Before Elizabeth could reconsider, she pivoted on her heel and dashed back the way she came. She ran past the open door, glancing inside just long enough to see Dr. Kosta slumped over, dead and bloodied. As she reached the foot of the stairs, her heart sank.

Hades lay a few steps down from the upper floor's landing, sprawled on his stomach. A pistol rested inches from his hand. Blood oozed down the stairs. Some of it belonged to the man crumpled next to her feet, whose neck was twisted at a crooked angle and whose eyes stared blankly from a shattered head. The rest flowed from beneath Hades, inching toward Elizabeth as she rushed up the stairs.

She dropped to her knees beside him, just as he turned his face toward her.

"No, you can't be here," he croaked, sitting up. "You were supposed to leave."

His entire frame shook with labored breaths. He leaned against the wall for support, pressing a hand against his stomach, where a glistening shadow spread across his leather jacket.

"Oh God, you're shot."

"Got two of them," he said, his voice hoarse and thickened. "Still others. One more guard, at least, and Warren. He's still out there somewhere. They think I'm armed, but it's empty. No bullets left. They'll be back soon. You need to go."

How could this have happened? How could everything have spiraled out of control so fast?

They were destined to be together. It couldn't end like this. It just couldn't.

"I'm not leaving you." She pressed her hand over his, trying to hold back the thick flow. His blood coursed between her fingers, hot and slippery. "Can you walk?"

"It was all a lie, wasn't it?" he mumbled. "Everything I've done. Evolving. I'm not evolving."

"You've got to hold on!"

Hades chuckled mirthlessly. "It's all bullshit, and I believed it. Shit, I hate this. All those people, is this how they felt when they told me, 'Anything. Anything. I'll give you anything, just don't kill me'? Is this need…did they feel this? Just one more time. That's all I want. To go back to before. Even just for a little while."

"Don't speak. Save your strength."

"It doesn't matter now. Just go. Don't make this worthless."

Before Elizabeth could respond, she saw movement at the top of the stairs. A lanky brown-haired man emerged from the busted doorway. The moment he spotted them, he lifted the pistol he held.

Her body moved on its own. As she threw herself over Hades, the whole world erupted into pain and chaos.

CASE NOTES 44: HADES

In the time it took to blink, a driving force struck Hades from head-on, slamming him against the steps. The gunshot came seconds later, as Elizabeth curled her body over him.

Two more gunshots exploded in his ears, and the man at the top of the stairwell collapsed. In the back of his mind, Hades realized the man had been shot, but his focus was on Elizabeth. She lay like an anchor upon him, her hands splayed loosely on either side of him. When he whispered her name, she didn't answer.

It couldn't be.

As he sat up, she slipped off him. He caught her before she could fall and eased her down gently.

A crimson stain bloomed across the front of her blue hospital gown. Her chest rose in faint, gasping breaths. Her gaze focused on him and yet at the same time seemed to see through him.

She was fading by the second.

"Why?" he asked hoarsely. "You weren't supposed to get hurt."

That wasn't part of the plan. His whole decision to side with Shannon and Tyler had been so he and Elizabeth could be together again.

"You were my light." Or maybe she meant to whisper "life." Her voice was thickened by blood or pain, and he couldn't tell.

"No. Not you. You're not allowed to die."

"I'm so sorry, Two. I…" She parted her lips as if to say more, but no sound came out. Her eyes centered on a distant point and clouded over like frosted windows.

"No, don't you dare go," Hades said. "Nine, Elizabeth, hold on."

He sensed a presence beside him and looked up to find Tyler and Shannon standing on the steps below him. Shannon held her pistol in shuddering hands. From the blank shock on her face, it was evident that she had been the one to shoot the man.

Going to Hades's side, Tyler knelt down and placed his fingers on Elizabeth's neck.

"Don't touch her," Hades growled.

How dare he touch her! What was he trying to do—hurt her?

"Hades, she's gone," Tyler said, lowering his hand. "We need to get you to a hospital."

"Get the fuck away from her."

"If you stay here, you're going to die," Shannon said.

"Just leave us."

She took a step toward him. "Hades…"

No, not Hades. That wasn't his name. Never his name. He didn't have one. None of them did. They were all just subjects. Just sacrifices. Not human. Never human. Less than.

"We're not leaving you here to die," Tyler said.

"I said leave!"

Shannon and Tyler exchanged looks, then hurried back down the stairs. Hades held Elizabeth in his arms. Hot liquid soaked through his clothes, and the step beneath him became slippery.

As he waited to die, it suddenly occurred to him that Elizabeth couldn't be gone. The world should have ceased to exist the moment her heart had stopped. How could her death have passed as inconsequentially as a single ripple in a vast pond?

Looking down at her, he thought he saw her blink. Her chest rose through the sodden hospital gown, and he knew at once that she was still alive. There was a chance to save her.

She couldn't die before he did.

"You're going to be okay," he said, cradling her against his chest like she was a slumbering bride. Her blood sluiced down his arms and made his grip slippery. He struggled to rise to his feet, nearly dropping her in the process. His grip tightened at the last second, and he stabilized her. He leaned against the railing for support.

His entire body throbbed in liquid agony. The blood that poured from his stomach wound was as hot as boiling oil, eating away at him from the inside out. Soon, it would devour him entirely.

"We'll always be together now," he said as he carried her up the stairs. With each step, pain radiated from his core. His body grew heavier by the moment. His legs didn't want to obey him and slipped and swayed beneath him.

"Every day, just like before," he mumbled as he walked down the hall, passing the bloodied corpses of four men and just as many dogs. He looked briefly at the men's faces and found that Charles Warren wasn't among them. Oh well. Elizabeth was the only thing that mattered.

Hades pushed the front door open with his shoulder. As he stepped out from under the colonnade, he tried to shield her against the pouring rain, with little effect. The downpour was so heavy it drenched them both in an instant, turning the stones under his feet pinkish. A shadow descended over his world, leaving it in shades of monochrome, fading away.

The gate hung open, and Shannon's car was gone. They must have already left.

Soon he would leave, too.

His legs collapsed as he passed the curb, and the burden of Elizabeth's unresponsive body dragged him down to the wet asphalt. He couldn't really feel his legs anymore, but he forgot about that as he drew Elizabeth against him and looked into her face.

She wasn't asleep at all. Her eyes were wide open and unblinking. Staring at him. Staring. Stop staring. Just stop staring.

Hades pressed his lips against her damp hair, hoping to catch a trace of her floral perfume. But all he smelled was blood and rainfall, and he thought about that rainy day long ago, when he had been wheeled from the infirmary, the wounds on his back not yet scabbed over, to witness her departure.

Don't go.

Please don't go.

Please don't leave me…

He had tried to shout to her, but he could only whisper it. She'd pressed her face against the backseat window as the car trundled through the gate, out of sight. He had known she wouldn't remember him. She wouldn't come back. Nobody ever did. They all went to one place or another, and he would stay at the Academy; he would die there. After what he had done, he would die there.

But then he had been sent away, too, within days of her departure. Except he had never left Dimitri's care. An experiment, they'd called it. Further research. A sacrifice. Punishment.

"Your request has been approved," Charles Warren had said. *"This is Subject Two of Subset A. You may do with him what you wish, provided you keep us updated on the effects of the depatterning."*

He had been the best. He had won fight after fight. At tactical games, he had led his team to victory, without fail. They had told him that he would make a great leader one day.

But he hadn't, and the only thing he ever would be was always, always alone. And it was all because of one simple mistake.

More water. Vision fogging. He was crying—the realization

struck him almost as hard as the bullet itself. It had been years since he had last cried.

I'm alone, he realized, lying next to her on the side of the road. *I'm going to die alone, and nobody's going to cry for me.*

Holding her against him, Hades thought about the years gone by. His childhood memories were coming back to him now, as if the bullet had cut open a path to the past at the same time it had ripped through flesh and organs.

They had been together every day, inseparable. Back then, he had seen violence as necessary for stability, a way to protect her and discourage other boys from going after her. When had it become a way to satisfy himself and fill the emptiness inside him? When was the precise moment he had stopped being A-02 and became Hades?

Didn't matter anymore, he supposed. It was all over anyway. He was all alone again, no matter what name he went by now.

He looked down at Elizabeth. He missed her so much. He began to sob. Then he was too weak to sob.

Voices filtered down to him, and a hand touched his shoulder, his stomach. Heavy touch. Hurt.

"Go away." He tried to shake the hands off but couldn't lift his arms. His head tipped back, and all he could do was let it fall.

Shrill sirens pierced the air. Hades felt the dampness of the rain but not its coldness. He had lost all sensation in his limbs. As the sirens grew louder, the numbness oozed upward into his stomach, consuming everything.

Even when hands separated her from him, there was little he could do. His arms didn't work right.

The pressure disappeared from his stomach, and he felt things rushing out. Felt something spilling. It didn't hurt anymore.

His gaze slid past the concerned faces, to the luxurious houses around him, and then the cold sky above. He felt a brief toxic hatred for this world and everyone inside it, this world where he would never belong.

Then he became too exhausted to feel anything at all.

The world darkened. That didn't surprise him. He had always known that the darkness inside the deprivation tank was just a glimpse into death and that he would end up back there in the end.

His body grew lighter as if fading, and his view of the stormy sky was replaced by a low roof. Blurred faces hovered over him, as pale and featureless as the monsters of nightmares.

"Get away from me," Hades croaked and tried to roll off the flat surface—*an examination table, they're going to vivisect me*—that he lay upon. Hands seized him and held him still.

"Calm down, kid," a man said. "Everything's going to be okay."

"Get away."

The world grew darker, darker.

"Kid, hang on."

He couldn't breathe anymore. He heard another voice from the eclipsing light. A-02.

I hate you. I hate all of you. I wish you were all dead.

I don't want to be alone.

Stop it. Stop hurting me. Please stop.

I'll kill you. Someday, I'll kill all of you.

Memories that had felt so separate from him were returning. The recollections of a different life were coming back now.

Who was that boy?

Was that once him?

Who was that weeping boy? And who was he weeping for?

I'm scared, Hades thought as the darkness encroached upon the edges of his vision. *I don't want to die. Not like this.*

There was still so much he wanted to do, things he hadn't even thought of until this very moment. So much he wanted to see.

So much he would never have.

Is this what the people I killed felt like?

Where was the light? Was it night already? Was he going back into the tank?

He was seeing through the hatch of the deprivation tank, sinking into the darkness. He heard more voices and a wailing siren. It sounded so far away, though.

Sinking. Vanishing. Good night.

I don't want to be alone anymore.

Darkness.

Good-bye.

FINAL REPORT:
PROJECT PANDORA

As police cruisers, ambulances, and SWAT vans swarmed the streets of Georgetown, Tyler watched Washington, D.C., disappear into the downpour. At first, it resembled a ruined labyrinth through the gray mist, reduced to jagged spires and vague suggestions of what once were walls. Then the city dissolved away entirely.

He closed his eyes and leaned into the upholstery, listening to the rain tap against the roof of the car. Thunder rumbled overhead, and the echo of sirens faded behind them.

He tried to forget about how Dr. Kosta had collapsed, his face a gory mess, but he couldn't escape from the lasting image. He had a feeling it would stay in his mind forever.

Days ago, even mere hours ago, he wouldn't have thought he was capable of conscious, cold-blooded murder. But when he had pulled the trigger, he had felt nothing. The action had been as natural as breathing, not even murder, just the obliteration of a greater evil. Necessary.

"We can never go home." Like murder, the idea of leaving his foster house behind didn't bother him as much as it once would have. His entire history had been built on the foundation of one great lie. He would never have to return to an empty house again or go to school and pretend like nothing was wrong, when the truth was that deep down, something was *terribly wrong.*

"We aren't going home," Shannon said, glancing at him. The tears had long since dried on her freckled face, and her delicate jaw was clenched in determination. He sensed she had changed, too, the moment she had pulled the trigger and shot the man on the stairwell.

But that was different. She had saved a life. Tyler had simply taken one.

They drove in silence for a while, and his racing heartbeat mellowed. The cold sweat dissolved on the nape of his neck, and the warm air rushing from the heaters dried his rain-drenched clothes.

Shannon took her gaze off the road to look at him from time to time. Once, she reached over and laid her hand on his leg. Her touch was warm, comforting. He reached down and squeezed her hand, and when their eyes met, an unspoken message passed between them.

You are not alone, her velvety brown eyes said. *We are in this together. To the end.*

When they turned onto the interstate, Tyler began telling Shannon about his final conversation with Dr. Kosta. She responded better than he expected, keeping her eyes on the road even as she listened to what he had to say.

"So, that's it, then," she said and gave a mirthless laugh. "Everything that I thought was me. None of it was."

"That's not true," he said. "We're still the same people we were yesterday and the day before that. Nothing has changed."

"Except now we know who did this to us and where it all began. The Academy."

"We have to go there," Tyler said. "We have to stop this. There's no other choice. I won't let any more innocent lives be lost. Project Pandora will end with us."

ACKNOWLEDGMENTS

There are a number of people who I would like to thank for their role in making *Project Pandora* a reality.

First of all, I would like to thank my agent, Mallory Brown, who saw literary merit in what others might have dismissed as a good substitute for toilet paper. Your support has been invaluable, and I'm extremely grateful for it.

My editor, Jenn Mishler, whose guidance has helped shaped *Project Pandora* into what it is today. Without your wonderful input, I would still be staring at a 63,000 word manuscript, hopelessly lost. As well, I would like to thank everyone at Entangled Publishing for believing in me and making *Project Pandora* a reality.

Barbara Young of the NAU Honors Writing Center, whose encouragement and insight saved me from the pits of procrastination and more than a few treacherous plot holes. I'll never be able to pass a bakery without thinking of the witty nicknames you gave my characters.

My critique partners, Brenda Marie Smith, Laura Creedle, and Diamond Wortham. Your recommendations allowed me to see my characters and plotline in a new light, and aided me in refining my manuscript into something I can be proud of.

Jacob Blair and Kerry Blair, for without your confidence-boosting encouragement, I probably wouldn't have had the courage to try tackling a novel in the first place.

Grab the Entangled Teen releases readers are talking about!

Proof of Lies
by Diana Rodriguez Wallach

Some secrets are best kept hidden…

Anastasia Phoenix has always been the odd girl out, whether moving from city to international city with her scientist parents or being the black belt who speaks four languages.

And most definitely as the orphan whose sister is missing, presumed dead.

She's the only one who believes Keira is still alive, and when new evidence surfaces, Anastasia sets out to follow the trail—and lands in the middle of a massive conspiracy. Now she isn't sure who she can trust. At her side is Marcus, the bad boy with a sexy accent who's as secretive as she is. He may have followed her to Rome to help, but something about him seems too good to be true.

Nothing is as it appears, and when everything she's ever known is revealed to be a lie, Anastasia has to believe in one impossibility.

She *will* find her sister.

Violet Grenade
by Victoria Scott

DOMINO (def.): A girl with blue hair and a demon in her mind.
CAIN (def.): A stone giant on the brink of exploding.
MADAM KARINA (def.): A woman who demands obedience.
WILSON (def.): The one who will destroy them all.

When Madam Karina discovers Domino in an alleyway, she offers her a position inside her home for entertainers in secluded West Texas. Left with few alternatives and an agenda of her own, Domino accepts. It isn't long before she is fighting her way up the ranks to gain the madam's approval. But after suffering weeks of bullying and unearthing the madam's secrets, Domino decides to leave. It'll be harder than she thinks, though, because the madam doesn't like to lose inventory. But then, Madam Karina doesn't know about the person living inside Domino's mind. Madam Karina doesn't know about Wilson.

Omega
by Jus Accardo

One mistake can change everything. Ashlyn Calvert finds that out the hard way when a bad decision leads to the death of her best friend, Noah Anderson.

Only Noah isn't really gone. Thanks to his parents' company, the Infinity Division, there is a version of him skipping from one dimension to another, set on revenge for the death of his sister, Kori. When a chance encounter brings him face-to-face with Ash, he's determined to resist the magnetic pull he's felt for her time and time again. Because falling for Ash puts his mission—and their lives—in danger.